Time Famine

a novel

Lance Olsen

Permeable Press • San Francisco
1996

A Permeable Press Book

Excerpts from this book appeared previously, in slightly different form, in *Compact Bone, Kiosk, Streetmag* and *Sugar Mule.*

ISBN 1-882633-15-6

Permeable Press
47 Noe Street #4
San Francisco CA 94114-1017
Internet: bcclark@igc.apc.org
World Wide Web: http://www.armory.com/~jay/permeable.html

Cover illustration by Andi Olsen
Cover & book design by Brian Clark

Time Famine

a novel

Lance Olsen

Also by Lance Olsen

NOVELS
Live from Earth
Tonguing the Zeitgeist (Permeable Press)
Burnt

SHORT STORIES
My Dates with Franz
Scherzi, I Believe

POETRY
Natural Selections
(With Jeff Worley)

NONFICTION
Ellipse of Uncertainty
Circus of the Mind in Motion
William Gibson
Surfing Tomorrow (Editor)
Lolita: A Janus Text
In Memoriam to Postmodernism: Essays on the Avant-Pop (Co-Editor)

To Andi, for feeding every minute...

"I've seen the future, baby:
it is murder."
—Leonard Cohen

ONE

1

BelsenLand: Live Sex: Mr. Death Himself

The last thirteen minutes of Izzy Slakker's life were really pleasant.

Mostly this was because they began when Teresa Ptomaine, drastic tour guide with the crank triple-sixes branded upside her fuzzy cream-green head, led him into the storeroom down the concrete corridor from the reactor in the power station at BelsenLand, Klub Med's latest concentration camp theme park (raised atop the post-Shudder UCLA campus a hubcap's throw from the San Diego Freeway to the west, silver gleam of the Beverly Hills guard towers and razor fences to the northeast, and vast HDTV screens broadcasting commercials twenty-four hours a day from each copper face of the new Diacomm Labs pyramid to the south), and sunk her warm fingers down the front of his baggy string-tied polyester pants.

It'd been hot for 10:00 in the morning. Temp was already slinking toward 40 degrees C, and the September sky had taken on that brownish-amber blush associated with the semi-transparent wings of certain semi-solid insects that crawl out of your drain the moment you start up the chlorine pump.

The air was so moist, so dense, so gritty, Izzy, even beneath his lilac filtration mask, had the distinct impression he was pressing through vaporous apricot light that'd actually begun precipitating out of the atmosphere like rain.

On top of which he'd been late again. No matter how hard he tried to convince himself otherwise, truth was the rapid-transit bus commute from the condemned mall on the perimeter road of LAX where he crypted never took the two hours he estimated. More like two and a half, if he was lucky. Today three. A truth that his boss, Mi-Lai Rodriguez, this tremendous dweeb of a Mexiental hausfrau who could not for the life of her wipe her mouth after eating (thereby letting all these little whitish curds of Izzy dared not think what rice her chin), frowned upon, if that's what she was in fact trying to do, shark cartilage injections in her rigid purplescent lips causing no end of trouble on Izzy's part in pinning down her facial semiotics.

He was in this big skorry...had three public johns to disinfect, basement corridors in the power station to mop, one-fifth of Öfen Straße to tidy, spiking up discarded styrofoam cups, paper plates, used diapers, balled Kleenexes, slimy rubbers, toothless combs, torn tickets, crumpled maps, half-smoked muggles, half-deflated balloons, the odd hypodermic, gelatinous blue Elsie popsicle sticks, broken plastic scalpels and forceps that once served as dining implements at the local franchises, and any other cultural detritus he might happen on along the way. All before his twenty-minute lunch break at 11:30.

And here it was 10:10.

And he was only just now finishing sloshing this bright chartreuse goo called Trash Flash down the last toilet in the second restroom, watching it fizz, fumes scintillating his raw sinuses, the surface of his pinkish eyeballs, counting to ten, trying not to think what kind of dance this junk might be doing with his DNA, whether he was wearing those latex gloves or not, which, skorry being so monstrous sometimes, his disinterest in his job so great, he didn't.

He flipped up his filtration mask, tore off a gob of toilet paper, and blew his nose. All manner of clearish gunk laced with blood came out.

Some toxman he was, hustling through the automatic tinted-glass doors and past the pearl-blond pretty-boy security guard dressed as an SS officer except for that really online Ralph Lauren lipstick he was wearing, metallic indigo smudge-proof cream that matched his Cover Guy mascara.

Izzy stepped onto Giftgas Gaße, busy ashen packed-dirt street shimmering in poisonous light, and aimed toward Anne Frank's

FestiLand for Tots.

He began sweating freely. His large green plastic Honda trashcart-drone hummed along beside him, carefully avoiding the tourists teeming around it like smoke around a car model in a wind tunnel. Izzy tugged an already crusty handkerchief from his hip pocket and dabbed his face with it, doing what he could not to mess up his sunscreen...high quality stuff, SPF 75, Jordache's Doll-Rubber Caucasian. He honked his nose and shoved the handkerchief back, thinking: "Can't even do the max minimal without skrimming up. So what's the fugging deal here? What. Is. The. Fugging. *Deal*?"

Nine to five, four a week, then as much time off for good behavior as any diligent governcorper should in his right mind expect. Visit some VR parlors around the airport. Play a little Jet Crash or Suzy Simulacrum. Drop into the local mesto on Friday night to check out the latest plasma-wrench band. Maybe even shoot a joybang or two if it's pay day. Nothing really freaky or anything. Small intense happy azure high.

He hurried by the Lampshade One-Stop. Near its entrance three bony construction workers dressed as bony prisoners (highest-paid employees in BelsenLand, needing as they did to maintain that emaciated look week after week, month after month, their existences adding up to a bland string of illegally obtained lettuce leaves, Christian Dior bottled water, and what seemed like meter-long lines of cocaine) pickaxed the lane, breaking ground for a new holographic info-display pedestal while feigning the tribulations of hard concentration-camp labor for the guests.

They were clearly overdoing the torture bit, grunting and huffing, while Mongo Koyote from the north gate tower, costumed as a soldier, kept a vaguely bored watch over them.

"What," Izzy said, "a fucking flatliner."

Meaning, not Mongo, but himself seen through Mongo's eyes, who probably was thinking at that very moment: "What a fucking flatliner, that doofus over there with the samurai topknot and goofy headlong gait. Hey, isn't that Izzy? Izzy Slakker? What a fucking waste."

Thing was, he didn't mind the embarrassingly low credit or frontal-lobe-numbing routine. After all, that was the *point*, wasn't it? Labor as little as you could, think even less, trouble yourself not a smidgen with anything even remotely complex or challenging. Thus would life swerve leisurely into a comfortable Brownian motion, one day hemorrhaging into the next, one week into three months. Stuff would take care of itself. There'd be plenty of time to drink, sex up, sleep the way only the truly unmotivated can: deep, dreamless, utterly satisfied.

Izzy could imagine a whole lot worse to do, even if time *did* have this habit of sneaking up behind you, tapping you on the shoulder, making you look one direction when you should be looking another, overtaking you and leaving you in the existential dust...standing on the side of the highway with your thumb up and this shit-faced plaque-crammed grin spreading across your face while you wondered *now where the fuck did THAT year go?*

Plus it was never as easy as it seemed in theory, was it?

He checked his watch, nice Sanyo deal that actually *told* time. Thumb its shiny black face and it spoke.

"Ten twenty-two," it said. "UV rays twice acceptable limits."

Izzy inhaled a lungful of oily air and quickened his pace, picturing the ominous red light pulsing beside his credit rating next time he called it up on his computer screen. One more bungle this quarter and his total would start creeping *down*, shrinking like the midriffs of those skeletal coked-up prisoners, mainframes at Klub Med compensating for his poor performance, lost time, bad fricking attitude toward this fricking awful job.

Increasing numbers of all-American families emerged cautiously around him like humanoid groundhogs.

They'd ventured to DisCal in the wake of the all-clear signal sounded during the final stages of the post-Shudder cleanup underway now for more than a decade. Beaches were finally free of slicks, if no longer quite their natural width and whiteness. Most of the freeways, burbs, strips, refineries, airports, and skyscrapers had either been leveled and rebuilt, or (like the mall Izzy inhabited on the LAX perimeter road) condemned and abandoned. One of the President-and-CEOs had appeared on national television six months ago to promise the radiation business was hardly worth thinking about these days, steady rise in cancer rates just a statistical fluke having nothing at all to do with those toxins released from ruptured nuclear reactors, burning oil platforms, and fire-engulfed city blocks constructed *way* too close to the San Andreas Fault when it decided to flinch and throw everyone off for a while.

Tourists were jittery, literally sniffing the sour breeze for signs of menace, trying to enjoy their one-week-a-year governcorp-paid vacation in peace and quiet without bringing back some hideous malady to Davenport, Raytheon Iowa, or State Hospital, Teledesic Arkansas...dad, small-shouldered, wide-hipped, white-faced, black Fuji camcorder helmet meticulously logging each important event that'd seem so much more real to everybody when they finally congregated on the living-room futon back home to watch...mom, gray bobbed hair, beflowered Patagonia UV-resistant leisure suit, Lee's press-on serial-number tattoos across her lotioned bare flabby arms...kids, completely into BelsenLand's Full Victim Experience ("History," the commercials said, "is what *you* make it!"), duded up in their baggy grayish green polyester concentration camp uniforms by Gap, McQuik King roachburgers in hand, all agoggle at the low windowless concrete buildings housing the gas-showers, faithfully rendered fetid stench tanging the stagnant morning, pausing at a holographic info-display pedestal to learn about how when the British liberated the camp near Hamburg on April 15, 1945, they found (and here the old documentary-footage began to float before them in the muggy, soiled, glittering atmosphere) ten thousand unburied dead and forty thousand starving, sick, and dying lost ones.

Izzy happened to raise his head just as the throng before him parted to reveal Teresa Ptomaine...Terri...Izzy's new girlfriend, standing with a group of twenty-five or so Japanese tourists (a razor's lip below the governcorp's limit for lawful assembly) at the exit to the Himmler Barracks across from the entrance to Anne Frank's FestiLand for Tots, drastic Elan Blanc Herr Nazi Doktor tourist-guide uniform with epaulets and nearly knee-high instapump Reebok ersatz-leather boots so shiny mom could read her tattoos in them if she'd wanted to, medical bag in hand.

He touched his palm to his wine-and-shamrock-striped samurai topknot, parked his trashcart-drone next to the walkway leading up to an Aunt Eichmann's Golden Fillings Pie Shop, and ambled over.

"Und don't forget, bitte," she was saying in her best contrived accent, spine straight as a plumb line, boot heels tight together as two stones in a Mayan ruin, "today our lunchtime spezial at the Offizers' Club on Buchenwald Straße consists of bread, farm-shrimp zoupa, und Christian Dior wasser, all for yust seventeen touzand credits."

Behind her, fake living prisoners were hoisting fake dead prisoners into what looked like a large wooden medieval wheelbarrow for transportation to the fake ovens. Their fake fires, whose thick fatty smoke drifted into Izzy's consciousness as he crossed the street, were kept burning around the clock for effect…with the EPA's blessings, National Security Profit Margins Amendment engaged.

Loud speakers atop five-meter-tall synthetic wooden poles looped the stately, meticulous, sorrowful strains of Bach's *Goldberg Variations*, interspersed with frequent announcements for blue-light bargains at the hypermart on Opfer Weg, folksy sing-alongs in Goebbels Welt, and the attempted escape scheduled at the westgate guard tower for 10:45.

"In closing, meine Damen und Herren," Terri said, "I vud like to tank you vunce again for choosing BelsenLand, und hope you enjoy the rest of your fisit mit uns."

Japanese tourists, each wearing a miniature Minolta respirator, bowed and Terri clasped her hands before her and bowed back. When she straightened, the tourists, promptly blank-eyed and slack-faced, wandered off in search of something more interesting.

Izzy flipped up his filtration mask and kissed her on the cheek, let his tongue linger on the scarred rills of her brands. She squirmed away, laughing, officer's cap askew. Her mirrored Ray-Ban contacts flashed in the hazy sunlight.

"What's drastic, Ms. Braun?"

"Not much, sweetmeat. Just spendin' mosta my mornin' thinkin' bout them pants of yours."

"Them pants of mine?"

"How good they look off you, honey." She patted him on the

butt. Beyond the entrance to Anne Frank's FestiLand for Tots went up shrieks of pain. Another round of Interrogation Hour, emceed this week by that new talkshow host from ChaseMan York, S. T. Lauder. "Got ten for Terri?"

"Oh, man, I don't got like one for Izzy. Gotta clean half this fuggin' park in the next…let me see here" (shamming a listen to his watch) "five minutes or so."

"Don't wanna stand a lady up, now, do you?"

Izzy looked over Terri's left shoulder for help, only there wasn't any, just this oil-burner in a concentration camp uniform leaning on his shovel in the shade of a gray cement wall, smoking a Marlboro muggle and watching the crowd hubbub past. Mustn't've handled his tools very well at some point in his life, big toe having been grafted on to where his right thumb should've been.

"Mommy, mommy!" a six- or seven-year-old boy with spiked strawberry hair yelled close by. "I wanna go on the BoxCar Ride again!"

His progen, angular black woman in her mid-twenties with a bronze lip plate, said: "You already been on dat ting tree times."

"Shee-it," Izzy said, lingering on her. "Damn straight I don't. But, well, what's a poor boy to do?"

"Ain't polite one bit," said Terri.

"I hear you."

"Do you? Maybe you don't. Maybe I just ain't talkin' *loud* enough for you."

"You talkin' plenty loud for me, only—"

And then her fingertips were down the back of his pants.

Izzy and Terri studied each other briefly, gauging the parameters of this maneuver.

Then her whole hand was submerged, trouting around, so deft and practiced that no one except the most observant about such matters could've noticed.

The ground beneath them rumbled, enormous BoxCar Ride cannonading past on the other side of the barbed-wire fence.

And that hand was out again.

Somewhere machine guns commenced popping, 10:45 escape attempt underway at the west gate.

Izzy clucked.

"You gonna get me busted, girl, you know that?"

Two minutes later they stood among the packed shelves of the cavernous storeroom down the corridor from the reactor in the power station. Bio-light strips hung in rows across the ceiling in meter intervals, photons a bluish vapor. Canisters of cleaning agents banked beside pressurized tanks of paint, cartons of batteries, crates spewing bullwhips, pandybats, fluorescent orange flashlights, cotton-candy insulation, spare parts for trashcart-drones beneath and around which were stacked gray rectangular signs printed with white warnings and arrows, most having to do with small noxious spills and minor radiation leaks at the park, some with crowd control, no-smoking ordinances, sniper alerts.

A lightweight aluminum pillory sat in one corner, beside it a matching whipping post imprinted with the Clinique logo. On a low metal pedestal bulked a Mercedes-Lancôme Iron Maiden of Nuremberg, hour-glassed dull gray-black coffin ajar revealing a core teethed with six-inch spikes like a lamprey's oral cavity.

Which is where Terri proceeded, opening her medical bag and extracting a Shure Beta liquid crystal HDTV with a seven-centimeter display and a Minolta micro-camcorder, both of which she perched on the contraption's base.

She plugged the micro-cam into the television and jabbed a red button. A tiny image interlaced on the screen, luxuriant jungle surrounding a wisteria-blue crow-shaped pond, NutraSweet-white shores, Trix-colored beach umbrellas, thonged women and bikinied men lounging on oversized pastel towels, flesh tanned in crazy-quilts of shades like extravagant daydreams by Braque, or sauntering hand-in-hand toward the swarming nanodrug mesto built beneath a wide high-impact plastic half-bubble under a waterfall.

"Visit the past in the future," a pleasingly genteel British voice said. "Erewhon One. The moon's first full-destination orbital resort. More affordable than you think. More necessary than you know."

Terri poked another button, green, and Izzy's image gathered. He was naked from the waist down and held a bullwhip in his right hand. The real Izzy looked at the simulated Izzy, then at the real Terri, then at the simulated Izzy, who had just looked at the real Terri, who was suddenly stripped from the waist up, divulging the top half of her black corset trimmed in scarlet lace, and was in the process of stepping out of her instapump Reebok boots and Elan Blanc trousers.

Izzy pointed at his simulation. His simulation pointed back.

"Is that live?" they both asked at the same time.

"Every inch, sweetmeat."

She dogged over to the Minolta to make a few last-minute adjustments, then back to Izzy, who tossed his shirt onto an antique gray-shelled computer with a smashed-in screen.

Izzy's Jordache Doll-Rubber Caucasian sunscreen ended abruptly at his neckline, accenting the wormish whiteness of the rest of his body, especially his gaunt legs, around which Terri, still on her knees, wrapped her arms.

Her moist tongue licked the soft hairless skin on his inner thighs.

Izzy peeled off his lilac filtration mask and inserted a nine-volt battery he'd removed from one of the nearby cartons into his mouth. Focusing on the HDTV screen, he started to suck.

They'd been into recording their illegal acts on the Minolta from the get-go, Terri producing her micro-cam at the conclusion of their second date back at Izzy's crypt.

Izzy tickled the whip's wasp-stinger tip across the brands laddering down Terri's vertebrae in russet rungs.

"Mmmmmm," she moaned. "Mmmmmmmm. Do it, sweetmeat. Do it."

She craned her neck and her eyes met Izzy's. Her mirrored contacts caught the metallic light off the television screen and rolled up inside her head. She leaned forward and took him into her mouth, letting her teeth drag along his glans, sliding him back across her soft palate toward her uvula.

Izzy massaged the top of her head, into the coarse stubble against his palm, and sucked harder on the nine-volt. His tongue fizzled with electrical static. He angled to get a good profile of this action for posterity, sure not to disturb Terri, who was into these seconds in a profound way, sloppy sounds purling through her moans as she swallowed him, warm damp cloud of numbness around his hips.

He brought down the whip, snake-skin clone beaming in the bluish illumination of the storeroom, weightlessly at first, on her spine, and, raising his arm again, whip's beak pausing a meter below the bio-light strips on the ceiling, with a bright snap on the backs of her legs beneath the taut curves of her buttocks, rosy pink welts budding even before that whip had a chance to lift once more, Terri's breath catching, modulating into a groan as she cupped her right hand between his pale legs and palmed his testicles.

The storeroom wrenched and shuddered.

In some minor fold of his mind, Izzy assumed it was the BoxCar Ride drumming in the distance. Only it couldn't be. It was too far away, walls around the reactor too thick.

Another jolt struck and a queasiness surged up to replace Izzy's excitation.

Terri was no longer between his legs. She was scrambling to her feet, or trying to, only the planet wasn't letting her. A tremendous shiver shook the storeroom, and then the concrete beneath their feet became liquid.

Chunks from the ceiling dropped, cracking like gunfire. Shelves rattled. A pressurized paint can exploded. The air swelled with the smell of ammonia and pine oil.

Seasick, Izzy lurched to his knees.

His wristwatch began talking, reading out various times at random.

Even though he had the faint impression he was still walking, he found himself lying on his side.

A shelf flexed and disintegrated. Terri screamed. Izzy looked up and saw the Iron Maiden slam across her legs. Her upper torso thrashed, arms flapping like hooked eels.

He crawled toward her.

The noise was astonishing, a fighter jet revving its engines, prepping for takeoff.

Fissures netted the wall near the door a split second before it ruptured. Concrete and iron mesh spewed into the hall. The air fogged with gray-white dust.

Izzy coughed, grit membraning his tongue. His teeth couldn't stop vibrating. Another set of shelves crashed down.

And then he saw her pinned there, on her back, Iron Maiden crushing her knees. Her neck was cocked awkwardly so she could get a good view of him. She wasn't shouting, just staring, mirrored contacts dusty. Izzy tried to stand but his legs buckled. He lay still listening to the end of the world, studying his lover study him.

The ceiling torqued. Huge slabs of concrete spun down.

Izzy wanted it so bad to be love...he'd have done about anything to've made it true, just for this moment, these few heartbeats.

Except he knew as Terri reached for the Minolta lying nearby it couldn't be. No, not at all...this was blond, blue-eyed Mister Death himself, tall, thin, and hunchbacked, drool filamenting off his whiskered chin, chapped lips spread in a wide and insincere grin, sticking out his scrawny arm for one firm dry final handshake.

2

Ulysses Sysop-of-the-Plains Stray

Elektra Geestring's bust, kil wide by nearly two tall, hovered several hundred meters above the cluster of fastfood franchises and fuel enclaves surrounding Donner Lake a short distance on the NorCal, Inc. side of the NorCal, Inc./IBM Nevada border.

Yellow-brown skin. Blue blue Optikon eyes. Braided black hair looped atop her wide-jawed skull like a dozing cobra. She wore that sexy signature grin of hers, part Buddha, part Himmler, part your mom on ludes, and her patented Robomatrix simucort exoskeleton. Through its carbon braces and nylon-and-velcro straps you could make out a white scar where her left breast used to be, huge swollen bulge of her superimplanted right, tops of her finger-thin arms eaten away by the osteal liquefaction she'd contracted from mosquitoes as a child in New Delhi.

The Gynorad queen of the obscene opened her mouth and a plump fuzzy tarantula and its babies scurried out. They darted over her features and disappeared into the coils of her hair. She grinned again, parted her lips, and a swirling waterfall of plaids and paisleys flowed between them.

Over the undulating 3-D graphics scrolled an advertisement for her posthumous box-set of holoporn vids, including the best seller *Elektra's Complex*:

SHE MAY BE DEAD–
BUT SHE STILL GIVES DRASTIC HEAD...
SO ORDER NOW!

VISA & MASTERCARD ACCEPTED.
OPERATORS STANDING BY–
"BRING IT HOME TO MOMMA PAIN..."

Ulysses Sysop-of-the-Plains Stray, kneeling on a granite pine-sprinkled ledge overlooking the Tahoe National Forest, continued pressurizing his JanSport camping stove, trying to remember how she'd final-dined. Wasn't pretty, that much he got. Backseat of a car, east coast, something to do with choking on her own reproductive organs. It all came down to some heavy-duty gangbang thing, ConservoFem extraction business.

Uly flipped channels in his head, reached into his backpack and found the box of Diamond strike-anywhere matches. Removed one, dragged it across a five-centimeter stretch of rock, fired up the stove.

An orange-white flame sputtered and hissed from the circular burner. He adjusted the small aluminum lever on the side till the orange-white darkened to azulene, then poured a deciliter of Christian Dior water from his plastic canteen into the top of his mess kit and set it on the fire. The water jiggled, currents of heat churning.

He reached into his backpack again and took out a pink and green packet of NorthFace freeze-dried farm-shrimp chili, tore it open, removed the clear plastic pouch half-full of brown-red crystals.

He looked up and Elektra's gigantic bust was gone, replaced by the governcorp Surgeon General's warning about not drinking from the local streams, no matter how untainted they might appear, accompanied by shots of newborns with the telltale spina bifida tumors on their lower backs.

When the water came to a boil, Uly poured it into the clear plastic pouch and folded over the top rim. Steam collected and zagged down the insides. He shook it and set it on the ground to steep.

Leaning back against a boulder, he enjoyed the extravagant sunset, rich with sulfur dioxide and petroleum distillates, endosulfan and chlorine compounds. It turned the sky into one of those technicolor velvet paintings in the art section of a Binge&Purge truck stop.

Carhoods and bullet-proof plate-glass franchise windows glittered across extensive stretches of parking lot far below. Chrome-red sparks erupted off bomb-proof metal exteriors of fuel enclaves, electrical hookups in the RV parks, silver stumps stubbed across clear-cut mountainside after clear-cut mountainside. Rush-hour traffic on fourteen-lane Highway 89 flittered under a layer of golden particulate matter.

It was beautiful, beautiful stuff, Uly thought, opening his food pouch and starting to eat. The very stuff he'd come all the way from Moston in Turner Columbia to witness. Though by now he was pretty tired, neck and shoulder muscles slow-burning with fatigue. He'd spent most of yesterday driving down from his burbrise, most of today ascending the mountain, parking at the McQuik King at the base last night, sleeping in his Thai Khon Kaen urban light assault vehicle, first thing in the morning riding the switch-back escalators to the Long John Sliver's at the one-thousand-meter level, footing it from there.

Presently he was close enough to the summit to pick up some of that evergreen scent, sample the prickling ultraviolet rays penetrating his sunscreen. What remained of the pine forests dotted the landscape below in small balding clusters mazed with cement drainage ditches. The view permeated his chest with a warm juice of satisfaction. He hadn't been able to escape into this kind of peace for months…maybe longer, if he bothered to figure it, which he didn't, not wanting to deject himself on his full-throttle hurtle toward his thirty-third birthday at exactly 12:21 tomorrow morning.

Uly was poised to encounter that incandescent instant far from his job at Merging Angels Satellite Shop as possible. Every day, every day, every day, he woke with the embryonic dabs of dawn, slouched toward his Thai Khon Kaen, handful of Vivarin pelleting from his mouth onto the asphalt as he shuffled across the underground parking garage of his Russian-fabricated burbrise, White Bird Six, part state, part corporation, part its own country, serving those who mostly served those living in the high-walled safe-zone compounds on the outskirts of the city, drove twelve kils in a glassy daze through the local labyrinths of concrete barriers designed to confound looters and shooters, and picked up his partner, Tammy Lee Numbers, sweet purple-haired bulimic with a propensity for very tight leatherette black jeans accenting her wide hips and lacy off-white halters accenting her maraschino-cherry breasts, who lived on Lapwai Road on the rez with her mother and five siblings in a cinderblock shack furnished with seven army cots and an assortment of large green plastic garbage pails that doubled as tables, dressers, a washing machine, a bath, and sometimes chairs.

Together, they'd spend the next eight or twelve hours crisscrossing several thousand square kils of more cinderblock shacks, governcorp projects, burbrises, and overpopulated arid desert hills, installing satellite dish after satellite dish, many as five a day when business was good.

Besides all the legal aboveground labor, they'd also on the sly load some illicit non-traceable hardware and software into dishes for Vacants, marginalized hackers who'd for one reason or another (and you never, ever, wanted to ask why) had erased their own NorAm ID numbers from the matrix, helping them receive (among other things) all the same channels registered NorAms did, not to mention a few extra pirated bonuses, and earning Uly some healthy credit, not to mention continual bags under his eyes (one blue for his father, one brown for his mother) and a genial gluey feeling he was at least doing his share to keep things bouncing.

The sun flared and the fog that'd begun fingering over the jagged western horizon suffused with life-jacket-orange light.

Uly slipped on his Nautica solar-powered wind-breaker. It blushed from cool methyl green to comfy hazel brown. He rigged his Sanyo digital sound soother on a log, hit PLAY, and random noises washed into the evening...distant owls, doves, loons, and wolves against the background of a mountain stream.

Above the lake, the huge hologram of a harried Japanese businessman in a black suit, pressed white shirt, and white beekeeper's veil stepped into a GTE oxygen booth on a jammed side-street in Mexico City. He inserted his credit slab into a slot beneath a small olive computer screen and punched up some classical music and lemon scent. Palming his veil back over his head, he leaned against one of the gray-foamed walls, closed his eyes, and smiled to himself. A phrase whirled in midair, stabilized, strobed in various colors:

GTE
COME BREATHE WITH US.

≋

Uly's need to get away to a place like this had infiltrated his cells over the past few weeks...in the middle of calibrating a dish behind someone's rust-splotched Airstream trailer, skinny retriever busy sniffing Uly's Keds...strolling through the graffitied halls of his burbrise after a day in the field, every third bare yellow lightbulb on the ceiling whacked out.

These mountains held a resonant aura for him, a sense of accord and relatedness. He couldn't explain why, just that his mother, Donna Reed-in-the-UNIVAC Stray, programmer from the Nez Perce tribe, had always persuaded his father, Boris Kharkov, ex-Ukrainian lab technician, to camp here during their governcorp vacations.

Told him holidays were times to look inside instead of out, nature a vast AT&T switchboard designed to patch you into the world's real data flow.

Uly's progens met late in life, Boris middle-aged, in his early thirties, Donna older, by chance ending up at Mainline Pharmaceuticals, a subsidiary of Diacomm, in Portland, joining the pearlstring of possibilities revealed by the Northern Migration after the Shudder. Donna asked Boris for a muggle (still illegal off the reservations back then) at a party celebrating their company's leveraged buy-out of NASA, hurting financially ever since funds'd been allocated away from its Mars and smart-probes programs toward the post-Shudder cleanup project. Six months later they moved into a tidy white tube-room on the one-hundred-and-eleventh floor of one of the company towers on Lombard.

For young Uly, those trips into the mountains represented a wide belt of freedom. Growing up in the Diacomm childcare complex, he got to see his progens only five or six times a month, but on vacations he was with them all week long. Even as the National Security Profit Margins Amendment took effect, and heavy machinery grumbled onto the scene, franchises and fuel enclaves sprouting and knotting, these mountains embodied a region where Uly could always feel like he belonged to something larger than himself, where he networked with his own history, made the clock that never moved backward at least stop ticking...the Big Television analog for the *there,* the interconnectedness of his forefathers, he encountered in cyberspace, a domain he spent an admittedly unwholesome amount of time frequenting, his earliest recollection his mother sitting beside him in the glow of her Compaq.

Thirteen, Uly saved enough to purchase his first wireless modem, allowing him to jack into the matrix via satellite from anywhere, or at least ninety-five percent of anywhere, on the planet, and these days, rocking beside Tammy Lee in the Thai Khon Kaen on long between-mission hauls, he'd excuse himself, open his Aiwa 3500, and surf for hours on end, always haunted by the fear he was missing something really interesting in there, that somewhere, on some newsgroup or in some virtual mesto, something amazing was going on *right now,* some discussion or bit of bytes that'd change his life completely, and if he missed it this time, he'd miss it forever, doomed eternally to the lamentable land of the techno-damned, and so was one of those people who needed that near-hourly hit of interlinkage, worldwide consciousness, no matter what, no matter how inconvenient it might be, except, in all fairness, his addiction wasn't exactly as bad as some of his acquaintances', emailing him as they did extended and daily messages about their computer-induced complications, Jerry Seinfeld-Dermatage and his headaches, Magdalene O'Pizza-Hut and her wrist-joint pangs, Xylene Huang and her frequent spontaneous ocular bleeding, pow, right out the tear ducts.

So now, as he finished eating, set down the empty pouch, it was reflex that made him burrow into his backpack and extract his Aiwa 3500, full look and texture of a leather-bound hardback novel, right down to his name embossed in imitation gold script across the raw umber cover, cross his legs, and hunch forward into hacker posture.

Light around him was gray, and the fog had arrived, wisping through the branches of the dwarfed pines, obscuring the parking lots and fuel enclaves below, traffic on Highway 89 and the prodigious holograms over Donner Lake gradually evaporating. Uly felt his wind-breaker generate more warmth to compensate for the moist chill.

Inside each cover of the Aiwa was a backlit flicker-free display. Uly punched up the clock by touching the options box on the screen with his forefinger. It was already 9:31. He reached into his back pocket, tugged out a reading slab, and inserted it into the slot on the side of the computer. Both screens illuminated, taking on the appearance of cream-colored pages from the latest Ford McCarver, Inc. novel, *Pretty Hate Machines*, part of that computer-generated Zero Series of clone-texts that'd struck the perfect balance between romance, triple-X, religious longing, and a general mood of cultural malaise.

Uly tapped the upper righthand corner of the display and the copyright material dissolved into the first two pages of story. Each novel in the series evinced slightly different details, but the flat staccato style and narrative cores felt comfortably similar. A hard-drinking, substance-abusing, strikingly handsome and/or beautiful (in an androgynous sort of way) twentysomething blue-collar worker with a name like Boo, Swish, or Lepp realized s/he was doing a lot worse than her/his parents. Her/his existential discontent was manifested through her/his voracious, indiscriminate, and highly imaginative sexual appetite. S/he longed for her/his innocent days of childhood while sexing up with anyone exhibiting anything even remotely resembling opposable thumbs. Though s/he thus undertook a necklace of corrupt and hollow misadventures, the reader came to understand those misadventures weren't really the protagonist's fault so much as a symptom of a larger, if difficult to articulate, social ennui. On the last three pages of each story, said protagonist attained a subtle metaphysical epiphany, often involving some near-death experience, that hinted at a profound (though quite possibly dull, at least from a narratological point of view) rebirth set to begin in the chapter immediately after the one concluding the novel in hand.

Uly found himself alternately embarrassed by these simple-minded plots and deeply dependent on them. Just like those sacred places around him, like cyberspace itself, they let him occupy the past, present, and future, the here and there, simultaneously.

Except as he began this one about the exploits of Stash, computer artist amassing credit as a deckhand on a floating island in the South Pacific, he started feeling funny.

Seemed like his wind-breaker had malfed, so he stood and wrapped himself in his Army-surplus foil sleeping bag he kept folded in a neat handkerchiefed square in his belt. Only when he sat down again and tried to reenter the novel's world, the chill didn't go away.

Plus he was starting to have a hard time concentrating. The plot, originally simple as a flatworm's thought-processes, began forking in directions Uly couldn't foresee, dividing, propagating, tentacling down weird alleys and subterranean passageways, and the sentences...they began gunking up with too many subordinate clauses, adverbs, adjectives, too much linguistic cellulite grown too swiftly on the narrative bone to make much sense.

Uly thumbed his eyes, closed his machine, and stood.

Nausea cuffed him.

He sat down again and put his head between his knees and took deep breaths, trying to flip channels in his brain, only that sick feeling intensified, and a blue taste from his father's lab, metallic, oily, seeped around his tongue.

The back of his skull ached like an aug there was misfiring, and a red light drilled up his optic nerve.

He raised his hand to rub his head and a stunning white light flared in the middle of his consciousness. For a second he thought the sun had blown itself apart, and then everything, absolutely everything, changed.

3
Golden States

He sat in a hospital room, his fifty-two-year-old mother dying of cancer before him.

The unruffled sheet was tugged up to her armpits and her arms, stained with purple blotches where the needles went in, lay on top of it. Her expressionless face was swollen with cortisone and her eyes, once moist chocolate, were dry and pale.

The building that housed Mainline Pharmaceuticals had been constructed in the eighties. It contained few windows and those that did exist couldn't be opened, so the air in the sealed interior was recirculated mechanically, exposing employees to cadmium compounds, diazomethane, aluminum dust, vinyl chloride and sodium cyanide. When Uly's father turned thirty-five, he developed a deep spongy cough and within months he started bringing up blood. Two years after his death, during a routine governcorp mammogram, the Uncle Meats found a tumor in Uly's mother's right breast. Company surgeons performed the radical mastectomy and followed with chemotherapy and radiation. She lost weight and vigor, her dark brown hair turned white, but after half a year the Uncle Meats gave her a clean bill of health and sent her home. Next spring the cancer resurfaced, this time in her lungs and stomach.

Now Uly sat in a stainless-steel-and-leatherette chair by her bedside and watched her watch him. The nightstand was crowded with empty juice glasses, vat-grown pulp filming the sides, a box of Kleenex, a phone. The catheter ran from under the sheet to a plastic bag half-filled with reddish-orange liquid hanging off the end of the bed frame.

"What's it like?" he asked.

Unable to focus, his mother's eyes slid toward the ceiling. Her breath smelled like infection and malignancy. She tried clearing the mucus from her throat and hacked.

Uly slipped one hand behind her damp head and the other beneath her shoulderblades. He eased her up, this movement taking immense strength because she couldn't help him, and rearranged her pillows wet with perspiration and the faint whiff of ammonia. What was left of her thin white hair was matted to the back of her skull.

When he shifted her she moaned reflexively, pain as much a part of her as her chromosomes. It took her a while to find her breath.

"When you're healthy, you can't remember being sick," she said. "When you're sick, you can't remember being healthy."

"It's all right."

"My old handwriting looks like someone else's. 'Who wrote that?' I say. They say, 'You did.' I'm so…" She hacked again, but with less conviction. It sounded like jelly clogging her throat. "Embarrassed."

"Embarrassed?"

"No one's home."

Uly listened to his mother trying to breathe.

"Want me to get Uncle Meat?"

She closed her eyes.

Uly remembered getting the call from the Mainline Pharmaceutical people just past dawn. He was opening the door, on his way to pick up Tammy Lee Numbers. His hand reaching for the phone seemed more real to him than anything he'd ever seen.

Donna waited so long to speak he thought maybe she'd skidded into one of those pseudo-sleeps brought on by the morphine derms attached across her bloated stomach.

She never awoke even remotely refreshed anymore. She was never fully conscious. It was like she'd begun shedding her personality the same way you shed tiny flakes of dead cells every day, becoming a little less yourself with each motion you make.

Her fingernails were yellowish blue. In six months she'd aged twenty years. She'd become his grandmother. Her skin didn't look like skin—just some flimsy, baggy, rubbery membrane nature used to cover a clump of miscarrying organs. Time had made her somebody else. Uly could feel it grating on, fierce as a pair of tectonic plates.

"Because you don't experience death once," she said.

He looked at her.

"You don't just experience death once. You experience it over and over. It keeps showing up all around you in different forms. Like H_2O."

Uly walked to the miniature refrigerator in the corner by the sink. He took out the ice tray and ground up four cubes in a blender, tapped the mush into a plastic cup, returned.

She parted her lips. He spooned in a little. She worked it around inside her mouth and began coughing again, meaty, soggy, from far down in her lungs.

Uly tried propping her up farther, massaged her back between her shoulder blades and some watery green bile bubbled on her lips.

She was breathing rapidly, scared, like a hummingbird.

He wiped off her mouth, waited, offered her another half-spoonful of crushed ice.

"If you could have one wish," he asked, "what would it be?"

She sucked, swallowed carefully, stared past the ceiling.

"I want to go back," she said.

"What?"

"I want to go back...I want to go back...I want to go back."

4

Amerika Eats His Young

"Show us your refrigerator," Polymox Epoxi said, winking one of those Bausch & Lomb full-eye ebony contacts at the camera, "and we'll show you your soul."

Her cosmetically toothless smile splayed behind her diamond-studded face cage.

Norton Amerika, exploring the plaque encrusting his left rear incisor, slumped so far back in his beanbag chair in the middle of his cabin in the middle of the night in the middle of Black Rock Desert in the middle (more or less) of IBM Nevada that his body weight rested on the thoracic region of his spine. He half-lidded his screen, old Nip model dating from the turn of the century, and thought about exerting the energy necessary to finger the remote on his wristwatch, maybe check out one of those courses on the Interactive University channel.

Except he just couldn't get enough of that elective harelip, startling pinkish-orange Plughead tassel, eyes all black, shiny, rich as fresh-poured tar.

And her show?

Her show was nothing less than a cathode-ray church, amassing a team of anthropologists, psychologists, sociologists, cultural semioticians, and criminologists, five new faces a week to pay these ostensibly unannounced visits to crypts of the grotesquely wealthy and disgustingly famous, raiding their refrigerators to analyze the contents on global television between ads for Frigidaires, south-of-the-border cosmetic mouth surgery, and Poly's Morphous Fashun Line.

Tabloid vids said (maybe predictably) those visits weren't un-announced at all...that behind-the-scenes bidding wars could whip-lash your neck with the massive figures being hurled back and forth. Allegations even circulated of a extraction plot, taking out the com-petition (Sali Schismatrix's *Pornstyles of the Demopublicans* among them) with a fiery corporate car wreck off Highway 1 just north of San Francisco, everything very Hollywood, or breaking into a rock'n'roller's crypt after hours and doing some serious nerve-dam-age to the hired help who happened to be in the right place at the wrong time, only that conspiracy thing was kinda hard to believe, given the crap that'd sometimes show up behind those stainless steel doors. Take, for instance, that well-preserved human arm, sans a chunk of neat sandwich slices of muscle, on the parsley-garnished platter in that Global Space Administration CEO's cooler. The guy turned out to be a member in good standing with the serial-killer pack, Cannibalists, based in Mitsubishi Wyoming...led right onto *Crime Deterrent Digest,* increasing Billy Yahweh's ex-ecution talkshow ratings to the max the night they noosed *that* radical omophagist.

Or what turned out to be a liter jug of sacred Thai monkey blood in what's-her-name's crypt, Italian, last week indicted on charges of running a voodoo ring out of Zurich into stealing relics from Asian sanctuaries and selling them on the blackmarket to the highest bidder, which, CNN revealed, usually shook down to the Vatican itself. Vanessa Dispepsia. Yeah, that was her. Like she saw them coming. Unless, come to think of it, the whole business was nothing less than this brazen PR ploy during sweeps week, a dis-tinct if daunting supposition, given the stellar rise in Dispepsia's Fame Index Rating within twenty-four hours of the incident.

Nort adjusted his antique wire-rimmed spectacles.

He'd been working outside all day, sealed in his white solar-protection outfit, sweating like a Christian on his first and last visit to the coliseum, busy raising his liebchens, genetically enhanced cockroaches, by the millions, *billions,* as nutrition supplements, suckers stuffing glass cage after glass cage in his greenhouses, flat-tened slippery yellow-brown bodies roiling over each other so crazily seemed the tanks themselves were organic entities, antennae twittering, bristly legs seething, not a damn thing to accomplish in the whole of creation except eat, excrete, and reproduce, high in protein, high in fiber, shot through with many of your basic daily governcorp-recommended vitamins.

Only thing Nort needed to do was keep the dampness in those tanks up, the garbage coming in. Food scraps, old clothing, rotten bookbindings, discarded furniture, whatever. Those bugs, man, they'd eat the nails right out of a coffin, nature's ultimate recyclers, in a single year one well-fed female producing more than four-hundred-fifty-thousand offspring.

Which fact, admit it, you just *had* to admire.

They knew how to use space, knew how to survive...first thing to rise after Demolition Day would be one of their robotic heads from a drainpipe, scouting to see if the coast was clear.

Didn't need any tech to do it, either, which amounted to a real bonus, philosophically speaking, since Nort was a hardcore Techno-Hickster, had been for nearly three decades, and for a Techno-Hickster there was only one thing worse in the world than a lot of technology, and that was even a little technology.

He was still a teenager living with his Gearhead progens in the Exxon Jersey rustbelt when one day at school a friend of his passed him a smuggled print copy of Philament Pheedbäk's underground classic, *Luddite Cookbook*, named after those English workers who from 1811 to 1816 attempted preventing the introduction of labor-saving machinery into their country by burning the factories housing it.

Scales fell from Nort's eyes.

Look around you, Pheedbäk said. Take a peek at what's left of this sorry-assed planet. And ask yourself why it's as sorry-assed as it is.

Shee-it. Rain takes paint off carhoods. Air in NorCal, Inc.'s like inhaling three packs of unfiltered Camels a day. And people? Oh, man. *People.* They're just a little less people-like each time you look at them with all those gadgets hanging in and off them, hearing aids and pace-makers, plastic hearts and collagen shots, tekked muscles and brain augs. Take that guy, what's-his-name, lead singer from My Friend Noo and the Biohazards. Jaysus.

Universe'd wanted us to be vacuum cleaners, would've given us rubber hoses for dicks.

Tech added up to a big fat case of the Great Enlightenment Fakeout. Supposed to eliminate disease, only all it'd really done was create a host of nastier, more committed strains. Supposed to make your life easier, only'd made it faster, more disorienting, crammed with data, deadlines, demands.

And those semi-automatics, bazookas, nuclear devices, slam guns, rail guns, claymores, incendiaries, bio-grenades, fusion bombs, chemical warheads, stealth tanks, anti-radar subs, invisible fighters, and CO_2-cartridge-propelled ballistic batons it'd brought about?

Well, you tell *me* about the joys of technology, the pleasures of progress, the ecstatic gains at the metallic hands of mechanical invention.

Listen, Pheedbäk said, just stand still and *listen* for just a fucking second, and what you'll probably hear is the planet trying to shake you the hell off, earthquake by earthquake, flood by flood, eruption by eruption, tornado by tornado, fire by fire, tsunami by tsunami.

You fuckers had your chance, she was saying. Now get the fuck away from me. Get outta here. Beat it. Date's over.

Which is just what Nort Amerika did, in a manner of speaking. He left Exxon Jersey, aimed for the territories, migrated away from industry, population concentrations, over-fucking-achievers, worked a year on a Hickster commune northwest of Dodge City till he'd amassed a little credit and then headed west, found himself one spring day on the side of Route 447 in the IBM Nevada desert, standing next to the rusted-out hull of his 2007 Geo Electrix, hitchhiked to the nearest real estate agent, bought a scrappy cabin, worm-infested tin cistern on the roof, couple of rocky acres of dead land on a rugged rise: no electricity, no heat, no nothing except a generator to power that Nip tube (gotta make allowances, man, gotta understand the limits of the paradigm...), and he called it home, settled down, dropped out, burrowed in, holed up, prepped to leave the smallest imprint on the earth he could...

≋

Poly and the Epoxi Mob had coptered under radar and over the electric fences surrounding FundGrounds, Everglades estate of Tyrone O'Kult, major stockholder in the Lazarus Project, deal which allegedly sent extraction groups into underdeveloped areas of the globe to kidnap newborns dying of famine and sell their otherwise-soon-to-be-useless organs to wealthy NorAms for some hefty markups.

Compound reminded Nort of computer-generated footage televangelist Joey Taboo'd once shown of what Eden was supposed to've looked like...clusters of orange and lemon trees, chinaberry and papaya, forsythia bursting among oleander and honeysuckle and jasmine, birds fricking *every*where, toucans in the branches, fat polychromatic beaks cracked open, scarlet ibises poised in clumps of eelgrass, colored-glass-shards-and-cement path leading back along a meandering stream to an imitation Roman temple size of a gazebo on a small mound overlooking a blue lagoon in whose shallows a small flock of flamingos balanced on single legs not twenty meters away from floating logs that weren't really floating logs at all, you realized, once you made out those ten-centimeter teeth punctuating those gnarly cartoon gator grins.

Three Mexiental guards in camouflage gear and greased faces (cayenne-pepper-filled aerosol spray cans raised, threats humming in the afternoon of burning skin, swollen tongues, leaky eyes clamped shut for forty-minutes at a stretch) stepped from the undergrowth and blocked the Epoxi Mob's way, patrol's expressions so flat you had to think somato-enhancement, one restraining a muzzled pitbull on a leash whose head yanked side to side, snarling, gagging, trying to break free and charge.

"You go back," she said with a Mexiental accent.

Her hair was clotted and blackened with shoe polish, cut long in front and short in back, skin blotchy from prolonged unprotected exposure to the sun.

"I'm Polymox Epoxi," Poly said, proud as a caped crusader. "Channel 163. On behalf of the Gameshow Network, I demand to exercise my team's Thirty-eighth Amendment rights and broadcast from Mr. Tyrone O'Kult's kitchen."

"You go back now," the guard said, yanking the choker collar to force the razzed pitbull to heel, foam frothing between muzzled lips, its incessant guttural growling stirring up a chatter of wildlife in the trees.

"Our viewers have a right to see Mr. O'Kult's refrigerator," Poly said. Her toothless smile had thinned to the width of a fiber-optic strand. Her ornery-looking elective harelip twitched behind her face cage. "Unless, of course, he has something to hide."

"These is private proportee. You leave now."

The dog leapt in place, strangling itself. The other two guards remained patiently behind the first, faces empty as puppets', one of them lowering his spray can to scratch his stomach through his uniform.

"Let me speak to Mr. O'Kult," Poly said, narked quality in her voice announcing the patented slide toward trance. "Data wants to flow. Spirit wants to open."

"You have three minute to vacate these proportee."

"We speak many languages, my parallel processors, but zeros and ones divide them all equally. Embrace the motherboard. Plug your heads into the electronic beyond. Let me hear your modem sing, kissed by the angels of the digital matrix..."

The cameraman was obviously growing agitated as the exchange heated up. The image on the screen'd gotten jerky, catching glimpses of Polymox Epoxi beginning to speak in cybernetic tongues, other members of the gang trading edgy glances, colored-glass-shards-and-cement cupolas and minarets of O'Kult's simulated mosque joggling over the lush treeline.

Only that wasn't what'd snagged Nort's attention. It was something else, something more profoundly unsettling.

He concentrated, clearing his mind of superfluous stimuli. Yeah...there it was...certain sound behind the television and generator, or, more precisely, *absence* of a certain sound...

He sat up, unexpectedly alert, poked the remote on his wristwatch, and the picture on the tube remained but the chaotic noise snapped off.

The generator's rumble jumped to the fore of his consciousness. He listened, doing the calculus, then stood, picked up the orange flashlight he kept on a hook by the front door, hoisted his shotgun from the wall, released the safety catch, and stepped outside.

≋

The sky was black as a crow's wing, atmosphere crystalline and thin, the Milky Way misting a huge swath through space, a satellite gliding above him like a tiny white spark.

He stared at it, eyes adjusting to the darkness, traipsed around back and shut off the generator. A high sharp whine crowded his skull, clamor of nerves aligning themselves with silence. He paused, waiting for his temporal lobe to calm down, pushed up his spectacles on his nose, and crossed the expanse separating his cabin from the greenhouses, navigating around clumps of sagebrush illuminated by a fingernail moon.

Pebbly sand crunched beneath his beat-up unlaced Army-surplus boots. Through a solitary stand of organ-pipe cactus, he made out the valley to the southwest tinseling with thousands of windmills in opal light, one of the Reno-Diacomm power plants stretching through desert and over mountains most of the way to the NorCal, Inc. border.

But he wasn't paying much attention to it. What he was trying to do was *hear*, block out his vision and *hear* because something wasn't right.

Nort passed the rickety outhouse painted cinnabar maybe forty or fifty years back by some rabid misanthrope who, his realtor'd told him, had shot himself up with AIDS-infected blood just so people'd leave him alone.

What *was* that thing he wasn't hearing...the thing that wasn't there but should be...the piece missing from that thousand-unit pizza-with-everything-on-it jigsaw puzzle? He halted at the toolshed, unlocked it, stuck his head in. A small animal skittered clear. Place smelled like old wood and oil. He flipped on the flashlight and swept the beam across his rack of roach-tending equipment, work table, stack of five-gallon plastic gas tanks, wood ladder leaning in the corner, flipped off the flashlight and locked up, put it down gently on the ground beside him, leaned the twelve-gauge on the shed, tucked his shabby undershirt saying GUN CONTROL IS A STEADY HAND into his beltless kneeless jeans.

The desert breeze'd picked up, bringing in the pure cool evening air. Half hour after sunset you could always feel that wind stir, temperature dropping, probably already 25 or 30 degrees C, and on such clear autumn nights it'd go down another five or ten before morning, easy, good sleeping weather, snuggling up in that seedy Army-surplus sleeping bag, tuning out the firmament, dreaming those great wild technicolor fresh-air dreams...

There were three greenhouses, slabs of yellowed high-impact plastic over aluminum skeletons, each twenty meters long by five wide, roofs peaked to allow in maximum light.

Rows of long gray wooden benches lined with ten-gallon roach tanks ran the length of the structures. Near the entrances were food bins overflowing with slimy chicken bones, rags, dead cacti, farm-shrimp goo, rotten planks, bubbling roadkills, old boots, porno zines, strips from cardboard cartons, snapped shoelaces, half-smoked cigarettes, wads of hair, sticky dustballs, dented cereal boxes, pink fliers, turn-of-the-century Yellow Pages, spoiled canned vegetables, dingy shredded underwear, maybe even a wad or two of body waste if you wanted to look hard enough, which you didn't, ever, because the reek in those edifices was like journeying up the hot boiling intestines of an eighteen-year-old hyena who's just fed on a cankerous warthog dead three weeks in the Serengeti, licking all the way.

Nort set down his shotgun and flashlight again and took his filtration mask off the hook inside the door.

Before he'd snapped it into place, though, reality reordered.

He stood next to the food bin and listened, astounded...what he hadn't heard was the low continuous frenetic activity of his babies, his sweeties, his lambkins, a sound so much a part of his being that he *sensed* instead of heard it, *felt* it among the abdominal vat of his juicy organs.

The greenhouse was quiet as the desert at night, still as Nort Amerika's hope.

He bent down and picked up his flashlight. When he hit the switch, he saw row upon row of inanimate roach tanks.

He went over to one, removed the wire screen on top and furrowed his hand through the garbage.

Corpses.

Everywhere he looked, immobile leathery shells. Bunches of them. Piles of them. Lilliputian yellow-brown snowdrifts.

His heart muscle collapsed. His throat filled with smooth stones. Nort Amerika wanted to cry.

He scooped up a palmful, examined them closely in his light beam, let them rain down. He tweezed a single carcass, bit it in half between his incisors, let it mix with saliva on his tongue, washed it in his mouth, filtered the semi-crunchy remains through his teeth.

He couldn't figure it, just couldn't figure it. He stood there, pondering, sifting, waiting for revelation to strike.

"What the fuck?" he said aloud, then swallowed.

5

Feedback Loop

"I think we have a little problem here, sir," Stanley Zircon announced early the next morning at the daily briefing on the Klub
Med floating-island yacht off the coast of what till less than a decade before had been Vancouver Island, British Columbia, and was
now DisCouver Island, Gates Washington.

"Little problem?" Telly-Savalas Dahmer asked.

Stanley looked at his hands. They were whitish-pink and pudgy,
like the rest of him, and when his boss spoke in that stern voice of
his, all menace and metal and moodiness, wrath of a pissed-off
prophet pullulating through each vowel, those hands curled into
themselves on the cold synthetic fool's-gold conference table like
two sea anemones in a rough tide.

His colleagues around the long oval table shifted uneasily. Three
counterfeit stone chairs to the left, Kobalt Run-for-the-Bucks Blieu,
Coeur D'Alene tribe from way back, now market analyst and PR
manager, reached for the Oxybuster canister in her purse and took
a hit. Fourteen chairs to the right, Ron Trinidad, big hairless mushroom of a damage-control coordinator from Chicago with a passionate fear of meeting other people's eyes and wicked ability to
transform underachievement into an art form, stared intently at
the ceiling above him. Across from them Oona Hombre, tech con-
sultant based in San Diego, pressed in the face of her personal brass-
plated compu-translator hooked to the lapel of her beige business
suit, inserted the wireless earphone into her ear, and began to fin-

ger the platinum ring hanging from her left eyebrow. Oona'd been on that new and improved Treblinka Diet for almost two months now, had had her tongue and hence taste-buds cauterized ("EAT TO LIVE," the promo said, "DON'T LIVE TO EAT!"), lost something like twelve kilograms, and was presently excitable as one of those lab mice inhabiting a cage with an electric floor.

Stanley hated this part of his job as advisor to the VP of Klub Med, division of the Global Drug Administration, Ltd., subsidiary of Diacomm...Klub Med being short for Klub Medellin, as in Medellin Cartel, an economic entity that diversified after most previously illicit drugs were legalized over the course of the first two decades of the century, market became regulated, and the bottom dropped out of the MC's formerly lucrative enterprise.

Execs conducted interest-analyses on the general population and found, much to their palm-rubbing delight, that people experienced just as much joy getting off on violence as drugs, so first Klub Med bought up a few cable channels and a satellite or three, and began broadcasting syndicated shows featuring huge explosions, demolition derbies, South American war-vet nightmares. From there they eased into the nebulous terrain of pseudo-torture shows featuring victims, who weren't really victims, undergoing, or seeming to undergo, various bone-breakings and electrical proddings performed with state-of-the-art special effects equipment. From there it was a short step to execution talkshows, in which studio audiences got to interview and bet on the responses of real-life convicted killers, a bevy of prizes waiting in the wings...and *then* the stunning stroke of genius: theme parks based on the most violent events in world history...Roman atrocities, the Spanish Inquisition, African tribal massacres, Russian gulags, Viking assaults, Cambodian killing fields...

With carefully orchestrated special travel packages, visits to those parks were cheap, educational, and fun for the whole family, and the public snarfed them up the same way aardvarks did slurpy nests of termites with their long sticky tongues, always famished for more, always clawing the next clump of dirt.

Hated didn't do this emotion justice. Stanley'd rather chew on a mouthful of tinfoil with two jawfuls of cheap fillings for a week on end while being pecked in the flabby butt with whitehot fecal-tipped pins by the complete cast of *Lord of the Flies* while forced to count backwards from a million by threes than do what he was about to do.

He closed his eyes and saw his resumé pass before him.

"Um, well, uh, er, yes, sir," he said. "It seems—"

"Seems?"

This interruption so soon in the course of his explanation took Stanley by surprise. He paused and peeked at his colleagues, who were all too busy doing something else to return his beseeching look, so he snuck a glimpse at his boss, who was standing before the plate-glass wall, hands clasped behind the back of his dandelion-yellow simulated silk Shock suit.

"'Seems,' sir?" he asked, befuddled.

Stillness inflated through the room like light through the universe during the first billionth second after the Big Bang.

Telly-Savalas Dahmer was short. He was mostly square. He possessed only a vestigial neck. And he loved Napoleon I in the dribblingly enthusiastic manner only short, mostly square, and vestigially-necked people can.

He was paying virtually no attention to his employee. This was nothing out of the ordinary. In fact, Stanley was to Telly-Savalas's consciousness as the broken leg of a solitary mite on the back of a napping elephant is to the consciousness of that elephant.

Telly-Savalas was watching other floating islands cruise the Strait of Rockefeller, each at least a kil wide, some almost three, varying dramatically in appearance and function, yet embodying a massive subaqueous power, and it was this (and not, alas, poor Stanley) that interested Stanley's boss's brain.

On the sulfurous horizon, just off the San Mickeys, amid hovercrafts, rafts, speedboats, and the twenty-story burbrises beneath the surface, you had one of the utilitarian models designed by Norwegian Cruise Lines for the homeless from Bellingham and environs, large as two Shea stadiums, low to the mucky café-au-lait water: mainly sand, nondescript cement boulders for windbreaks, and a miniature mountain range of tents among which threaded smoke plumes from garbage-fueled campfires. Several commune islands barged near the entrance to Saanich & Goofy Inlet. There were condo islands and prison islands, islands housing mobile safe zones and modest factories, resorts and prep schools, pseudo-paradises and military depots, submarine-tour bases and shrimp farms.

But the floating island Telly-Savalas Dahmer enjoyed contemplating most was the one on which he stood, Elba, *his* island-yacht, built by Switzer-Craft Inc. just after southwestern Canada, collapsing beneath the weight of economic depression and the television-tax revolts, fell to the NorAm governcorp.

Klub Med had flown him up from Phoenix to manage their interests in what overnight had become DisCouver Island off Gates Washington, a semi-state that connected old Washington to Exxon Alaska along the coast and swept inland to include everything west of the Continental Divide and south of Shelagyote Peak. Kil across, two long, Elba was replete with its own airstrip, indoor and outdoor swimming pools, tennis courts, meadows, humble pine forest, beach, lake, hills, streams, solar power station and, at the bow, Khufu, scale-model bronze-tinted plate-glass smart-house pyramid designed by the illustrious Japanese architect, Saki Modo, nearly a football-field large at the base, in imitation of the blueprints of the pharaoh's original, circa 2500 BC.

This morning's briefing was being conducted in the King's Chamber, about halfway up the structure, from a vantage point with a great view of the craggy mountains on DisCouver, deep green plugs of the San Mickeys bunching out of the dying strait, and approximations of arabesque late-eighteenth-century rollercoasters (or what late-eighteenth-century rollercoasters would have looked like had they existed) and amusement park towers marking the skyline of VictoriaLand, the recently opened Reign-of-Terror franchise...and Telly-Savalas had been only distantly attending to the morning's affairs (standard stock reports, growth projections), happy instead to be daydreaming about the immense brawn beneath his feet and huge diamond ring in the shape of Elba luminescing on his pinkie, which ring he was in the process of thumbing sexily as though it could have been the nipple of a twelve-year-old toyboy he'd just hired for the day...when that asshole, Stanley Zircon, sat up and took a big steaming dump right on his reverie.

Telly-Savalas let the tension around him tighten a couple of notches for effect. Then he repeated himself.

"Yeah," he said. "'*Seems.*' As in 'appears.'"

Stanley sat slackjawed at the immense sparsely-populated table. He concentrated on his boss's ring, which'd caught some buttery photons and flashed, a kind of splashy period on the clipped sentence declaiming just how small he, Stanley, was.

"Um, I don't understand," he said.

Telly-Savalas, hands still clasped behind his back, turned toward the conference table. On the fake fool's-gold wall above it hung a large abstract L. Dopa liquid-crystal painting that changed color and texture according to the prominent pheromones in the air at a given time, signed with ink infused with DNA extracted from the artist's saliva, and hence uncounterfeitable. Today it was primarily carmine and black and mighty broom-sized brushstrokes.

A compact rainforest of plants with large droopy spade-shaped leaves asphyxiated a distant corner of the hall. Meandering through the middle of the floor trickled a pristine brook leading to a small fish pond stocked with orange-and-white carp and bordered by a stone-substitute mesto.

God, he loved this dominance stuff. Made him feel like he'd *earned* his floating island-yacht, lock, stock, and perimeter machinegun nests.

"Is the 'little problem' you're about to tell me about a 'seeming' little problem or a 'real' little problem?"

"Real, sir," Stanley said.

"How real?"

"Very real, sir."

"Fine. Now we're getting somewhere. English is a great language, Zircon. Let's try and use it once in a while."

"Certainly, sir." Stanley looked at his hands again. They were vying for lowest profile. The left was winning. "Okay. Well. Um. As you know, yesterday, just past noon, LA experienced a major seismic event circumstance."

"How major?"

"Um, well, let me check my notes here." He opened his Mac pocket computer and punched up some numbers. "That would be six-point-one on the Richter scale."

Telly-Savalas examined him, trying to make him go away.

"Who cares about a six-point-one on the Richter scale? Buildings down there are reinforced, cushioned, built on bedrock and shit. Right?"

"Absolutely, sir. Only, well, the thing is? The epicenter? Well, the epicenter turns out to've been unusually near one of our fiscally significant recreational interests."

Something big and bleak began swimming just outside Telly-Savalas's comprehension.

"*BelsenLand?*"

Stanley raised his head. His weak hazel eyes met Telly-Savalas's severe penitentiary-cement-gray ones. He lowered his head and his hands scrambled off the table.

"That would appear to be the case, sir. Yes."

"*How* unusually near?"

Stanley's hands were in his lap now, and he was leaning forward, speaking directly to his pocket computer.

"Within the, um, impairment expectation arena."

"*And?*"

"And, well, the thing is? Within the impairment expectation arena? It turns out there exists—"

Kobalt coughed diffidently.

"Existed," she corrected, fondling her Oxybuster canister.

"*What?*" Telly-Savalas snapped.

The big bleak thing circled closer and closer.

"Existed," Kobalt repeated, studying the contents label.

"Exactly," Stanley said. "Thank you, Ms. Blieu. And, well, within the impairment expectation arena *existed* a...consequential fuel reservoir."

"*Existed?*" Telly-Savalas said.

Blood squirted into his cerebrum under rapidly increasing pressure like a bicycle tire connected to a 250 psi pump.

"A meaningfully prominent energy initiator," Kobalt clarified.

"Exactly," Stanley said. "Of an autoluminescent category. Yes. And, well, not to put too fine a point on it, it sort of, well—"

"Ruptured," Kobalt said.

Telly-Savalas studied them for a few seconds, then the epiphany came walloping down on him, great white on an unsuspecting surfer. His arms dropped and he leaned back from the waist.

"You mean the fucking nuclear *reactor*?"

"Well, yes." Stanley said. "That appears to be the case. At the present time. Yes, sir."

Telly-Savalas was shot. He was stabbed. He was beaten and left for dogfood in a grungy alley.

Exhausted, defeated, he shuffled over to the table and crumpled into an empty chair. The square hand sporting his pinkie ring fluttered about his head, then perched atop his thinning greased-back wine-purple hair.

"I'm fucked in the ass by a Trident submarine," he said.

He sat statue still. He had no idea what was going to happen next. He looked at Kobalt. Kobalt looked at Oona. Oona looked at Ron. Ron continued inspecting the ceiling.

"Ms. Blieu," Stanley said, "would you be so kind as to get Mr. Dahmer a, um, drink or something?"

Kobalt, grim, shook her head yes-yes-yes, put down her Oxybuster canister and padded over to the mesto.

"And, well, to speak frankly, sir," Stanley continued while she was gone, "that's not exactly all."

Telly-Savalas didn't respond. He just stared past Stanley with those glazed penitentiary-cement-gray eyes. L. Dopa's painting gradually turned the color of the ocean floor twelve-thousand meters into the Challenger Deep, southwest of Guam.

Stanley cleared his throat.

"There's, um, this other matter that needs tending to. The thing is this. The reactor? Well, we've had this kind of...a sort of...the thing is..."

Oona, diddling with her eyebrow ring, said something in Spanish.

Khufu, the smart-house, was listening, heard the foreign language uttered, and translated it into English in a rough approximation of Oona's voice over the loudspeakers built into the walls at ten-meter intervals around the chamber.

"A situation," Khufu-Oona said.

"Gracias," the real Oona added, pressing in the face of her personal brass-plated compu-translator again but not taking the earphone out of her ear.

"A really big situation," Stanley agreed.

Kobalt returned with a Xanax dissolved in a bourbon-on-the-rocks and set it down on the table in front of Telly-Savalas. But he wasn't interested. He was busy watching a film behind his eyes of Elba being dismantled by corporate executives in black business suits divot by astro-turf divot. There went the tennis courts. There went his favorite swimming pools. And, soon, there he was, naked and shivering, sitting in the last chair on the island in the middle of a vast pile of tekked plastic and steel.

When he opened his mouth again, two syllables issued forth: "Uh-oh."

"Exactly, sir," Stanley said. "You see, Mr. Dahmer, we have this...Our people have detected the presence of this *thing*."

"Thing..."

"A cloud-like eventuality, sir."

Telly-Savalas tried to focus on Stanley. This proving too difficult for him, he gave Kobalt, who'd just taken her seat again, a go. She smiled nurturingly and moved her mouth. Telly-Savalas could make out the words *formidable distribution grid*. He reached for his drink and didn't stop gulping till it was gone.

Oona then spoke in Spanish and an instant later Khufu-Oona said: "We have located a spacious anti-hygienic horizon, Mr. Dahmer, and it appears to be moving north-northeast."

"Which means," Kobalt said, "if we bottom-line the monetary environment in the present context, we have a potential marketing issue on our hands."

"Something, in any case, to keep an eye on," Khufu-Oona appended.

"Exactly," Stanley said, pushing back from the table and standing. "Here's the thing. Khufu? Holographic display, please."

"Yes, Mr. Zircon," said Khufu.

"If I may—"

A colorful holographic weather map of the western semi-states bloomed out the center of the conference table. The topographics were shades of green and beige, the clouds grays. But from LA almost directly north through Barstow and the desert, up along the eastern side of the Sierra Nevada, across Lake Tahoe, over into Reno, then northeast well into IBM Nevada, churned a radiant red 3-D plume glittering with a thousand crystals of light.

Stanley patted the pockets of his Nike flight suit, found what he was searching for, and pulled out his laser pointer. He touched a button on its side and a white meter-long straw bulleted out.

"Okay. Well. Here's our anti-hygienic eventuality. And here's NorCal, Inc. And here's IBM Nevada. And here's this weird weather pattern. Jetstream just sucked this baby right up. Look at it go. In a little over nineteen hours it's covered, oh, roughly—how much has it covered, Ms. Hombre?"

"Six hundred kilometers."

"As the crow flies. Right. That's really something." He coughed. "Anyway, that's sort of the bad news." He scratched his head. "The good news, though, is, way our people see it, the worst is pretty much behind us."

"The event horizon is shrinking," Khufu-Oona said.

"Exactly. And, well, so now all we've got to worry about is this marketing situation business."

"We were burning a plutonium-uranium mix," Khufu-Oona said, "which we bought from the Russians, military-surplus."

"Real powerful stuff," Stanley said.

Kobalt took another hit from her oxygen canister.

"And, well, the truth is, our reactor's, um, sort of been partially chernobylized," Stanley said.

Telly-Savalas stared at him.

"I'm a pile of cat shit," he said.

Stanley, startled, looked at his boss.

"The quake, um, ruptured one of the, um, cores."

"I'm rat vomit."

Stanley looked at him again. Then back at the map. Then he turned off his pointer and slipped it into his pocket and sat down.

"One of the cores and the, um, the housing."

"I'm fucking rat vomit."

Telly-Savalas slumped there letting this revelation sink in. Everyone went quiet as a bank's safe at three in the morning. His eyes rolled into focus.

"Okay, well fuck," he said. "So. What's the on-site personnel penalty?"

"Media-version or actuality-version?" Stanley asked.

"Both."

"Right. Well. Let's see. The media-version is none, sir. We're employing the National Security Profit Margins Amendment in that department. White House gave us the go-ahead to issue a report saying minimal compromise to the structure. Minor injuries. No personnel penalty. BelsenLand, report'll state, will be shut down for a couple of weeks for repairs. Month tops."

"Actuality-version?"

"Actuality-version is slightly less promising."

"Meaning?"

"Meaning we don't, uh, exactly know."

"Don't *know*?"

"Well, in all fairness it's really hard to find out. There're all these fires and radiation? We can't get a team in there to run an inspection of the premises. Maybe in forty-eight, seventy-two hours."

"A week, tops," Khufu-Oona said.

"And the cloud?"

"That?" Stanley asked. "Well, that's a really strange thing, too. See, honestly? Well, it's kind of hard to say."

"Oh Jesus."

"The wind was really strong and high? So we don't really know where the stuff'll come down? Or how much? And, well, everybody responds differently to radiation? And so, the thing is? We don't exactly have that clarified to our liking, sir. But, well…"

"Excuse me," Khufu said.

"*What*?" Telly-Savalas shouted.

"You've just received an important vox message, Mr. Dahmer."

"Shit. Tell 'em to call back later."

"I'm afraid I can't do that, Mr. Dahmer."

Telly-Savalas glared at one of the speakers in the wall, never certain where to look when Khufu spoke to him.

"Why the fuck *not*?"

Khufu's voice didn't fluctuate. It remained pleasingly calm and feminine.

"It's from the company headquarters computer," it said. "Message states: 'Return immediately. Repeat: return immediately.' Your plane has been programmed. It's standing by on the runway, sir."

A whimper rose to Stanley's right.

It was Ron Trinidad. Without taking his eyes off the ceiling, he'd begun crying, almost mutely, like a proud three-year-old in a crowded shopping mall who's just realized his mother's presence, her density and concomitant sense of hope, is no longer beside him.

6
Spasm

The fact snuck up on Uly Sysop-of-the-Plains Stray that he was lying on the ground in a fetal curl.

Sunlight neon-pinked the screen behind his eyelids and on the other side of that screen he heard his Sanyo digital sound soother mimicking distant owls, doves, loons, and wolves against the backdrop of an electronic mountain stream.

He also became aware, from another angle, it was his thirty-third birthday. He was a year older. He'd become someone else while sleeping.

He opened his eyes, lay there waiting, gingerly eased onto his elbows and took stock of his campsite.

The sky was a lemonish yellow that said 40 degrees C was going to seem downright cool by the time *this* day was done. His stove tilted near a rock half a meter away. Red, white, and blue box of Diamond strike-anywhere matches. Crinkled pouch of NorthFace freeze-dried farm-shrimp chili.

Above the fastfood franchises and fuel enclaves around the lake, Elektra's holographic bust, kil wide by nearly two tall, opened its mouth and the same plump fuzzy tarantula and progeny scurried out that'd scurried out yesterday, darting over her features, disappearing into the coils of her hair. She grinned, parted her enormous lips, and the identical swirling waterfall of plaids and paisleys reflowed between them.

Far below, morning rush-hour traffic busied itself on Highway

89 under a layer of chestnut atmosphere so rich with poison it twinkled as if shot through with diamond powder.

Uly tentatively stood and found his balance. His thigh and calf muscles burned like he'd been doing sprints.

He gimped over to the sound soother and shut it off, looked around for his Aiwa 3500 and found it beneath his foil sleeping bag, sat again, opened the manufactured leather covers, extracted and pocketed the reading slab with *Pretty Hate Machines* on it, then punched up the time. It was already nearly 9:00...except it felt like he'd been asleep maybe fifteen minutes.

He raised his head, eyeing the drainage ditches labyrinthing below, reached over and called up the medical program, fingered the question-mark icon triggering the diagnostic protocol. The screens darkened and directions pitched into view.

<<<PLEASE EXHALE INTO MICROPHONE CASING>>>

Uly leaned forward and did. The icon of a small clock appeared. Its hands rotated quickly. He remembered the phenomenal white flash, the granite leaping up to meet him, the hospital room.

<<<RESPIRATORY SYSTEM: WITHIN NORMAL LIMITS>>>

<<<CIRCULATORY SYSTEM: WITHIN NORMAL LIMITS>>>

<<<SKELETAL-MUSCULAR SYSTEM: WITHIN NORMAL LIMITS>>>

<<<DIGESTIVE SYSTEM: WITHIN NORMAL LIMITS>>>

<<<REPRODUCTIVE SYSTEM: WITHIN NORMAL LIMITS>>>

<<<URINARY SYSTEM: WITHIN NORMAL LIMITS>>>

NERVOUS SYSTEM...
NERVOUS SYSTEM...
NERVOUS SYSTEM...

The computer harmonized.

<<<PERIPHERAL NERVOUS SYSTEM: WITHIN NORMAL LIMITS>>>

<<<CENTRAL NERVOUS SYSTEM: IMPAIRED>>>

Uly stared at the screen. He tried to incorporate this information into his understanding of the world.

He shut down the computer and restarted it, punched up the medical program, touched the question-mark icon, activated the diagnostic protocol, exhaled into the microphone casing. The machine cerebrated and announced all Uly's systems were within normal limits except the last. Uly ran his forefinger over the words CENTRAL NERVOUS SYSTEM: IMPAIRED, highlighting it, and tapped the burrow icon.

<<<INJURY TO RETICULAR FORMATION>>>

Uly called up the keyboard, typed in the command DIAGNOSE INJURY, and hit RETURN.

<<<INSUFFICIENT DATA FOR ACCURATE DIAGNOSIS>>>

LIST DIAGNOSTIC OPTIONS, he typed.

<<<INSUFFICIENT DATA FOR OPTIONS LIST>>>

DETAIL INJURY, he attempted.

<<<OUTSIDE PROGRAM DESIGN>>>

He sat there several seconds, looking at the screen, punched the shut-down icon, closed his Aiwa 3500, and began to pack up.

7

God's Logon

Krystal Silikon, who'd been a philosophy major almost nine months once when she was eighteen, liked to keep things simple.

Ockham's Razor all the way, is how she viewed it. Principle of parsimony. *What can be done with fewer is done in vain with more,* read the tatt on the shaved half of her gray-haired head.

Silikon's Directive the First: own your own car. A car was essential, getting you any place you needed to go, becoming your home away from home when you were unemployed, a state Krystal not infrequently sampled, having dabbled over the last year, give or take (the concept of time having become slippery in Krystal's cosmos of late...as in she often couldn't precisely discriminate between such ideas as *today* and *yesterday, last week* and *tomorrow*), in stuffing envelopes for a mail-order company, operating a copying machine for a franchise, gofering for a dating service, waitressing, bartending, laboring as a part-time mechanic, a bicycle repairer, and, most recently, a receptionist at a Klub Med Travel Agency near Winnemucca, IBM Nevada, which booked dull schlumps vacations at those new catastrophe theme parks springing up around (and sometimes off) the planet.

Directive the Second: forget credit, and credit will no doubt forget you. Sooner you understand you will never, *ever* make one-tenth as much as your progens (in Krystal's case the worst of both worlds, a plastic surgeon and psychologist, first generation NorAms from a tiny village right down the superhighway from Hiroshima, currently of Las Vegas), the better.

Directive the Third: glom on to those more fortunate than you, preferably those richer, younger, and more gullible, desirably in their late teens, who think it's crank to be poor and live out of your own car...kind, in other words, who've never lived out of a car who feel they're surfing the edge, experiencing Real Life when they hang out with you, getting you food, television, beer, admiration, a shower, and the odd place to crash when it starts feeling just a little like you're sleeping in a fish bowl on wheels.

Directive the Fourth: assume all things will always, somehow, work out in the end since it'll make you feel a heck of a lot better on the day-to-day and, well, if it transpires things *do* in fact work out in the end, you'll feel simply great and spend the remainder of your satisfied life able to wax nostalgic about the lean years, and, well, if they *don't,* then you can always convince yourself that they *will,* just not yet, if you'll only give them a little more time, a little more effort.

And Directives the Fifth and Sixth? Less said about these two the better because they were causing Krystal some major grief these days.

Number Five emphasized the need to make and keep lots of friends to always have heat in winter and air conditioning in summer, even when they're not your friends especially.

And number Six (to a certain extent no more than a corollary to number Five) spurred you to go along with any individual that happened to wash into your path, so long as said individual didn't rant, possess open sores, or stare at you through incredibly scary eyes, for, again, such a being would almost always lead you to shelter and sustenance, unless, that is, he or she was a psycho-killer or, worse, a practico-inert like yourself, in which case you're basically skrimmed, which was certainly what occurred in the person of Johnny-Carson Flamewars, that gray-skinned, greasy-haired, bad-breathed, runny-eyed, stoop-shouldered, emaciated guy Krystal met while trying to mind her own business, more or less, in front of her copying machine, running off these neon-lime posters for a high-strung beaver in a wool cap.

Johnny-Carson drifted in from the summer street and paused inside the front doors under the lazily rotating ceiling fan with his hands in his pockets, checking things out. Then, as though his sonar'd just engaged, he loped over to Krystal, who was being about as busy as possible not seeing him, despite the fact her black body dress, combat boots, lilac-with-yellow-stripes contacts, half-shaved gray-haired head (the other half being divided into halves, the back one spiked, the front hanging in a single meter-long dreadlock), and virtual metallurgy class of pins, studs, nose-rings, and eyebrow-hoops clinking on and around her face worked as a homing beacon.

He didn't so much strike up a conversation with her as a mono-logue about the new breed of kids in the city who'd taken to visit-ing cemeteries, digging up graves for sport, and leaving decom-posed bits of the disinterred hanging around trees and weather vanes in safe zones for unsuspecting suburbanites to discover on their morning strolls down the sidewalk to pick up their plastic-wrapped newspapers.

Krystal should have known better, except, well, there was some-thing kind of *vulnerable* about this guy talking fast as a sparrow on speed, something that needed tending to, plus somehow he ex-uded this sense of confidence, safety, secreted pheromones announc-ing *I may look like a flatliner, sure, but truth is I live in one of the nicest crypts you ever saw*, which, okay, was a big lie, but a lie Krystal, savvy though she was, had somehow bought, finding her-self without much warning bedding down with a Vacant who was in a *lot* worse shape than herself.

Johnny-Carson, it soon came to light, was jobless, homeless, and carless, friendless, hopeless, and lacking a NorAm ID num-ber...and, jeez, pretty happy that way.

He was real content eating Gerber's babyfood in the claustro-phobic frontseat of Krystal's burned-out husk of a Pod People Spe-cial two times a day, content leaving it to her to find the next slice of credit, the next sip of bottled water, the next shard of entertain-ment...content, pretty much, to just sit there and stare at his Keds or an interesting streetcorner for hours on end, immobile, open-mouthed, dull-eyed, conversationless, having apparently exhausted all his energy during the first fifteen minutes of their acquaintance.

That's who Johnny-Carson Flamewars was, the guy who might evaporate into the intricacies of downtown Winnemucca for hours on end, only to reappear at mealtime, and again just before sleep, empty-handed, nothing in his pockets, nothing up his sleeves...except for that grin, that perversely angelic grin which'd melt your resolve, slow-fry your heart, make you feel all gushy inside like you just reached the pinnacle of the highest roller coaster you ever rode in the course of your life, upside down, in the dark, in the midst of a lightning storm, knowing *something* was broken but not knowing what, all in about two seconds, which, damn it, led Krystal to the doorstep of her present situation...namely, leaning back in a wicker chair at a shady table in a little thatched-roofed café called Mocha Jivin' on a simulated stone ledge within a damp forest of leafy trees and chlorinated brooks in the Biosphere 4000 sanctuary, cappuccino in hand, nice little muzak rendition of Nietzsche's Pussies's "Rabies in Boyland" on the sound system, beach and amusement park in the distance, then tundra and specialty shops and exotic restaurants, alpine meadow and picnic area, waiting for nothing less than to break up with Johnny-Carson Flamewars when he showed, *if* he showed, the guy already something like two cups of coffee late for his own funeral, which was nothing if not completely, teeth-gnashingly, foot-stompingly typical.

She had this really sick tendency to hook up with males of her own ilk, like attracting like, a propensity which more than once sucked her into a psychological wormhole of affliction and spat her into an alternate universe constituted of lassitude, underachieving stupor, unhealthy codependency, and parasitic toadyism with guys like Vlad the Inhaler, rapture fiend from way back who could shoot more of that stuff into his nasal cartilage than most could dream about over the course of an average lifetime, and who stayed unfaithfully by Krystal's side, mooching and sponging, sponging and mooching, till Sigmund Feud, body by Adonis, mind by Mattel, showed up and began nuzzling vacuous Vlad out of the apathetic picture, and Sigmund Feud, alas, begat Kristofer Columboid, unwashed percussionist for Voids Where Prohibited, and Kristofer Columboid begat Larry-Li Kimbambu, mental-in-extremis, retrobeat, post-agonistic, hyper-euphoriential, supra-subterranean, rock'n'roll reality pilot, and Larry-Li Kimbambu begat Jolli Llama, paranoid disciple of the Church of the Inside Traders who'd lost all his credit in one afternoon by backing the Army's ill-fated program of voluntary hysterectomies for its FemmeTroopers, what was left of the military's elite core of women warriors, and Jolli Llama begat a year of celibacy and oodles of visits to the spill stalls in the greater Winnemucca area, till, that is, that certain summer day.

Krystal took the last sip of her cappuccino and set down the porcelain cup.

Nietzsche's Pussies's "Rabies in Boyland" deteriorated into Blasted Poindexter's "Bitch Vibes." People chattered noisily around her, silverware tinkling, so it was difficult to pick out the particular primal screams and rhythmically sampled jack hammers, jet engines, and music boxes comprising the present song.

She sighed and slid lower in her chair, tapped the face of her Julia Roberts crammed with tiny useless Victorian gears and springs, held it up to her ear.

"Two," it said in an approximation of the dead actress's voice, "fifteen."

Johnny-Carson Flamewars was over an hour late, meaning he'd forgotten, actually *forgotten*, his own dumping.

Krystal studied the brook dyed electric blue trickling around pygmy boulders in the carefully fashioned forest below, raised her line of sight to include the top of the Hellevator at 666-Land cresting the treeline, ride duplicating the wailing dive of an elevator whose cables'd just snapped, dropping over five-hundred feet, freefall, in the space of a couple of astonished palpitations, leaving people's livers, lungs, and digestive tracts cleaving to the ceiling before the air-cushion kicked in, slowing the contraption to a lotus-petal-soft landing.

She fingered her dreadlock, part of that hip old-age look, huffed, and pushed away from the table.

And the ghost descended on her. Overran her head. Drove out the noise of Biosphere 4000.

She tipped back in her chair, dazed.

The ghost, voice neither male nor female, faint, staticky, had been with her weeks, longer, swooping into her brainstem deep in the night, murmuring amid half-dreams, moonlight, broken columns...she'd wake to it speaking...or, sometimes, from nowhere at all, strolling down a side street in Winnemucca between ancient powerlines, minding her own business, musing about the elsewhere beyond the last star where time would never reach or the crushed paper cup on the pavement in front of her or nothing whatsoever.

Begin over with a dead heart. Start again from nowhere. Nothing else but that, fingers of ice...

Krystal, frightened, had tried to force it out at first, but concentration folded when it was present. Plus, over time, she came to understand something else: the voice was simply there, one day it called upon her, she was where she was supposed to've been, and so it entered.

She didn't struggle anymore.

Death, I don't understand how you can be a doctor. You're the one who's in my thoughts.

She couldn't direct or alter the course of its words. Couldn't block them. Sometimes, though, and for no reason, she could continue to think her own thoughts as it continued to murmur its, soft, warped, exist in a universe paralleling its in her psyche, both hear its language, contemplate what it was saying, and follow her own mind's motion.

Occasionally the ghost made sense. Often it didn't. Just rambled, stream of half-truths, enigmas, nonsense, a child mumbling to itself surrounded by its toys in an attic room...particularly at the outset, when the visitations began, nebulous sounds bobbing and sinking in gray sonic vapor, gradually clarifying, taking on recognizable aural shapes, yet she always imagined this instance would be her last, this visitation conclude them all, whatever'd happened, it'd never happen again...

And each time she was wrong.

Standing with your lover, imagining the miraculous kiss in the white splendor, the violent cloud, brightness as in the instant lightning blasts you, chorus of white noise, remembering the strange bed, the skin instructions, remembering what it is we must remember, the whirlwind, the coordinates, the blueprints, one-hundred-fifty frames per second...

Remembering, not the heat, but the cold. The shock of absolute zero. Frost on the heart. Snow-crystals. The frigid starkness of ice floes. Thinking, no one leaves here. No one gets out of life alive. But you can be happy falling into the years.

With great effort, Krystal eased herself forward, rested her head upon the table.

Everything is ice, hunger, my heart pumping frozen water...

She heard her porcelain cup fall and smash.

Proxima Centauri, four light-years away, its light-cone flying through space, hurtling toward you, here, the metal music doctor, a little closer every second...

Without opening her eyes she saw an old woman, skinny arms spotted with purple blotches, blank face swollen with medication and death, lying in a hospital bed in a white room.

The aura, what is left of the aura, hurtling through space...

The old woman O'ed her mouth to scream. A large black rose unfurled, fat as a fist, from between her lips.

"Pack your ermines, Mary..."

The riot noises, the shabby dressing room, moving so fast through the cold blue silence of interstellar emptiness, smelling Hiroshima, smelling the word. The most beautiful thing, a Rolex.

Time to become someone else.

Time to become somewhere else.

Time to become something else.

Time to be space, eternity's unbroken arc.

Time to experience the center of gravity failing.

The black rose mutated into a glistening hunchbacked beetle. The beetle's head was human. It wore the old woman's face. She O'ed her mouth to scream and a large black rose unfurled from between her lips.

The geodesic.

The shelter inside your mind.

Elaborate theater to fool you, cold to freeze you, because you must hold every word, because you must begin over with a dead heart, remember a final story and then end it and move on again. Nothing else but that, the commands, the sentences, the verbs, the predicates, the connections they always hoped you would miss.

Earth is an airport, Krystal. It's time to catch your flight.

Here, now, the invisible gift. The whisper. The sum curled in the nose-cone of the incoming missile. The dots...dashes...shattering light...

The single mechanical arm...

The future arriving...

8
Blink

Uly was five, scared, crying.

People surged around him, shoving. He fought to keep his balance. Somehow he'd slipped out of his mother's grasp in the commotion and now she was gone.

Everyone was running. Legs. Shouts. Shots cracking in the distance, abrupt and fast, closing in.

He didn't know whether to run with the others or wait for his mother to find him here.

Someone's knuckles snapped him on the back of the head. He flinched, peered up, and, through the glaze of tears, flicker of silhouettes like insects, he saw the sky dark brown, churning with tar-smoke.

The city, he realized, was on fire.

Four hours earlier, Donna had taken him to the park down by the river to hear people talk about the collapse of the Social Security System.

The cost of overseeing it and its assorted mutant descendants had become incrementally prohibitive, unwieldy, doddering since the nineties, and, strained even further by the fat-trimming forays into the national budget to come up with credit to pay for post-Shudder cleanup and other public programs, not to mention the increase in the percentage of elderly in the country (obese demographic bubble of baby boomers and busters having ascended to the top of the population profile), as well as the massive jurisdiction problems arising from the increasingly amorphous delineation of geographical boundaries comprising the country in the first place, the whole brittle structure had creaked, swayed, and caved in beneath its own hippopotamine weight.

Huge demonstrations sparked across the nation. Winona Ryder, one of the vintage President-and-CEOs, face shiny with cosmetic carvings, always playing sweet to the senior vote, took to the airwaves, begging for calm and measured response by police and populace alike.

Therma Payne, first black Asian-Iranian Demopublican urban leader in Portland, appeared on the tube the day of the local protest and, just short of breaking down on the screen and bawling like a frightened choirgirl with Charlie Manson on psilocybin holding a knife to her throat, urged that nothing get really out of hand, while reminding everyone in her own inimitably polite and ominous way that she'd hired one thousand security personnel from Brinks Force to help indigenous law enforcement do its job...along with a good number of Jeep Wrangler urban tanks, forty Chevy assault copters, ten Sasson VTOLs, scads of mortars, droves of tear-gas canisters, and squadrons of rubber and real bullets, *plus* enough flypaper bombs to hold a whole megalopolis's feet fast to the pavement with glue-foam if need be.

It didn't look much like any of that rent-a-riot-control merchandise would see action, though. By 1:00 nearly fifty thousand disgruntled governcorpers had amassed. It was a muggy spring afternoon, haze of humidity and chemicals danking the air, filming the skin. Booths sold cold drinks, weak drugs, junk food. Skeletons strayed through the assembly, hawking their wares, acrid scent of muggles enriching the mood. Retro-bands, simpatico with these people's alienation, mounted the hastily constructed stage one after another and performed. A grizzled Kim Deal, last of the Breeders, cheeks sunken, spine stooped and reduced with osteoporosis, came out of retirement to fly in from her floating island off the coast of Astoria and bang out one more reprise of "Cannonball." A gaggle of disaffected politicians replaced her, ranting about the

failure of universal health coverage, dizzying costs of life-exten-
sion programs, the ageist exclusion of seniors from certain public
housing projects, privileging the young in decisions about aug in-
sertions.

Morphina Dyslexia, Egyptian-American folksinger, next
launched into her classic resistance tune, "You Can't Have My Organs When I'm Dead," a doleful minor-key number played acoustic, and the audience rocked in place, clapping time, singing along,
getting into their dissatisfaction, angst, anger, deep-seated suspi-
cion the world was far down the road, waving back at them, no
matter how fast they sprinted to catch up.

Just past 3:00, a jumbo Brinks Force buffalo in a black turtle-
neck, jeans, and cowboy boots clumped up to the mike, the kind of
hairy, heavily flabby guy who'd give a Hell's Angel the DTs, and
announced the party was over, festivities done, the rally was to
disperse, disperse now, by order of the Portland Police Department
because a group of pro-Social-Security terrorists had just taken over
the top two floors of one of the Diacomm towers on Lombard and,
unless their demands were met within the next hour, and Social
Security debates reopened on the floor of the Senate, they planned
to set off a bomb, a big bomb, a nuclear bomb, in fact.

The consequence was one vast extemporaneous discharge of
emotion, a communal lamentation that within twenty-four hours
would come to be known by the media as The Rage. Some demonstrators, sensing what lay ahead, did what the guy said and dis-
banded. Others, the greatest number, fanned out through the me-
tropolis, incensed, flooding south on Front Avenue, then up Yamhill
into the city proper.

Assault copters lifted off from their base on Hayden Island.
VTOLs, tear-gas launchers mounted under their bellies, fully armored mercs manning live-ammo machine-guns in their hatches,
swooped in from Ross Island and took positions over City Hall,
the Court House, the Federal Building, the city's three major hospitals, airport, key spans over the Willamette. Tanks rolled from
the east. Police and hired security formed a fleshy wall along
Burnside to the north, Market to the south, Highway 405 to the
west, and the banks of the river to the east...and then they began
to constrict the perimeter.

People weren't just mad because Social Security was sinking. They weren't just scared and resentful that the terrorists had taken their city and themselves hostage—on behalf of a cause they actually believed in. It was *way* bigger than that. They were mad because they'd been marginalized by a society they'd helped forge. Because daily they were losing more and more economic and political power. Because younger people, the little short-sighted, arrogant, undereducated, apathetic shits, looked right through them on the street, made fun of them on television and in vids, on albums and in hypertexts. Because something was chasing them and they couldn't see what it was. All they could do was feel it nipping at their ankles, gnawing at the tensile strength in their leg muscles, the resilience of their immune systems, their ability to respond quickly and fluidly to the changes boiling around them.

They were mad at who they were, who they weren't, everything blipverts told them they ought to be and couldn't be and should've been.

Thus the flashpoint, The Rage, that group of contentious old underfed professors, six or seven of them, jobless since the advent of televersities more than a decade before, who psyched themselves at the intersection of Fourth and Alder, on the curb right in front of the blackened windows marking the Ace of Base SinSim Parlor, and next found themselves, surprised by their deed even as they executed it, in the act of overturning a dented yellow Yota which, they believed (incorrectly), belonged to a flatliner who'd with his buddies been taunting them lately. Bluish gasahol pooling beneath the crippled car's hood, the flicking match, and *kaaaaaabooooooooom*, the blast seen by the Brinks Force commander, General Dien-Bien Konichiwa, who masticated on a pulverized stick of Wriggley's endorphin gum five more seconds before giving his troops the order to fire.

Security personnel, itching for a good scrap, gushed forward like water down a flushed toilet, electric batons, rifles, and high-impact plastic body-shields raised, visors lowered, fifty thousand volts of disputatiousness apiece. Tank turrets swiveled and emitted a barrage of sonic-stun shells. Copters dove, launching volleys of tear-gas. Gunners in the VTOLs pivoted, sighted, grinned, and let fly a plague of bullets, *live* bullets, ostensibly over the protesters' heads, and the SWAT team, waiting for the diversions to commence, yodeled a heart-clenching yowl and rushed the terrorists' stronghold, spewing lead and magnesium bombs as they went, some kind of fomenting, slobbering, howling human dust-devil, taking down the perps before the two gaping NorAms and a wayward Brazilian in the process of ducking had even a chance to say *oops*.

And *bam*, that SWAT team was done, mission accomplished, bomb squad tiptoeing around a sinister-looking briefcase in the bedroom while everyone else hung out in the smoky living room, Sangean Zero Sums restrapped over shoulders, tapping Marlboros into their palms and disinterestedly examining the bodies.

Donna Reed-in-the-UNIVAC Stray was still in the park, trying to make her way south through the melee, away from the rally, when she heard the bang, the first shots, that mighty whoop rise.

And then she began to run, towing her son beside her, knowing something collective had snapped, some aggregate sanity just let go.

She wanted to reach Market Street. From there she could swing west, then north, around the mayhem. Only she'd gotten caught up in the tug of the mob, and it carried her inexorably across the grassy field, overturned collapsible chairs, torn-up flower beds, broken bottles, abandoned blankets, with a stubborn forward momentum, relentless, into the erupting megalopolitan streets, so she tightened her grip on Uly's hand, bent her head as in a heavy wind, and pushed forward.

She noticed a number of protesters had acquired impromptu weapons—sticks, bats, trash-can lids, canes, crowbars—and, as she tried to take this in, a frail guy in front of her, sixty or sixty-five, tip of his pointy nose almost kissing the tip of his pointy chin, nonchalantly bent down, scooped up a brown Rainier beer bottle from the sidewalk, and lobbed it through an espresso shop window. Almost as if it were part of the same gesture, a woman about three people to his left, fake melanoma over her upper lip, paused by a parked tuk-tuk, lifted a metal chair leg she must've picked out of some dumpster, and brought it down, first on the gas headlamps, then on the passenger seat.

And then the spectacle was behind her, Uly and she had passed, borne on by the crowd till, twenty meters farther, she came across people circling a jumble of junk where demonstrators'd been piling garbage into a barricade. Donna just had time to register this vision, pull it into focus, when she caught sight of the burning broom. Near-invisible flames spat to life under the orange sun and smoke billowed into the darkening beige sky, the hot steamy air swamped with chemical fumes, burning plastic and tire rubber, garlicky sweat, diesel exhaust, dog carcass, plywood boards, plaster, wooden boxes, old paint cans, turpentine, sheets of asbestos, jugs of pesticide, juicy fecal rot of spoiled fruit and vegetable substitutes.

People were yelling orders. A Molotov cocktail skimmed over their heads and splattered fire against a concert-postered cinder-block wall. Across the street, bricks blew out a storefront and fire jetted from the gap. Another explosion went off in a cluster of overgrown lots where the Yamhill Marketplace had once stood.

The roiling tip of the phalanx rounded the next corner...and plowed headlong into the first reinforced security line which opened up on them with short controlled bursts from their rapid-fire Zero Sums while a VTOL lifted behind the troops, gruesome mechanical shark with its dorsal fin lowered for attack, and dropped toward the demonstrators, strafing.

The mob surged back in one shocked reflex, attempting to reverse its course. Red-hot tear-gas canisters thunked down, clacketing across the pavement. Bullets ricocheted off concrete.

And, in the distance, the thunder came...

Next thing, Uly was alone, mixed-up, turned around, his mother gone.

He felt himself flounder, lose balance, stubby legs rubbery and boneless, powerful impetus tripping him forward.

He was on the pavement.

Feet scuffled and chafed around him...Army boots...the shouts of the teen, close by, flailing above the mob, shirtless, emaciated, full-color tatt of Dali's *Persistence of Memory* across his chest, hallucinatory clarity of melting watches in the arid airless landscape, cosmetically broken teeth catching sunlight through smokewaves, as the mob shouldered him back toward the burning pile of garbage.

He was shrieking for his friends, for the security force, for anyone who'd listen, which nobody did, because rioters had begun turning on the young, clubbing them in the knees, kicking them, bringing them down, leaving them for the mercs to deal with, out of some reptilian-complex need for divine retribution before the fact of receding hairlines, the intensely sad awareness *I'm twenty-three...I'm fifty-seven...I'm seventy-two...*just like that.

Uly heard, and would never forget, that guy pleading and struggling, his high-pitched voice slicing through the din while other voices, lower, more resonant, urged the mob on, shouting *do it do it do it,* and some clouted him with broomsticks, jabbed him with metal rods, drew blood from his legs, arms, unexpectedly bruised face, matte-black assault copter hovering ten meters over the scene, observing, and then the squeal, long, loud, inhuman, flesh finding flames...and his eyes, blue as chlorinated pool water, clear as liquid polyurethane, spacious with disbelief...

Uly was standing again, firm hand gripping his arm.

Donna hauled him up, her expression taut, defiant, grim, a face that spoke less to Uly of love than of their indomitable future together, their relocation with Boris Kharkov within half a year to the rez in Moston, where the spreading riots would prove less disastrous, if not wholly absent, where the crime-rate would prove a little lower and the quality of life a little higher than Portland's, and where tech jobs associated with the flourishing safe-zone compounds would prove more abundant, even as the governcorp proved more recalcitrant, beginning to crack down on the general populace, establishing the Lawful Assembly Decree, whereby NorAm citizens were forbidden by Constitutional Amendment to gather in groups of more than thirty, while arresting key participants in The Rage weeks, sometimes months, after the event, security forces screening their vids and the media's of the disturbance, creating a still of each participant, tracking each down, shipping the worst of them off without fanfare or fuss to the NorAm prison farms up in the Yukon.

But that was tomorrow, next month, next year.

Right now Uly and Donna were running.

9
Uncle Meat

"Well, fuck," Saul-Revere Outryder said to himself when his doorbell at the missile silo buzzed.

He'd been busy with his Sharper Image Relaxation System, kicking back naked on the rose-quartz pink penis-shaped watercouch in his office between patients at the McDomino's Medikal Klinik, open twenty-four hours a day, seven days a week, three hundred and sixty-five days a year, you break it, we mend it, this supposed to be that placid lull Saul-Revere adored so much between sprained-ankled, chafed-kneed, appendix-popped, sun-poisoned, killer-bee-bitten kids that began around 10:00 in the morning and ran till around 4:00 in the afternoon, and the first adult dinner-chokers and artery-busters of the early evening.

Carnations, marigolds, and orchids gently overlapped behind his wide-band VR mirrorshades. Superimposed over these floated a shiny red frog with large golden eyes. In the center where the pupilate slits should have been were aerial views of the torsos of two nude boys, both painted a metallic bronze, both with black bowl-cuts, Indian-fashion. They were lying side by side, one on the left clearly dead, one on the right propped on his elbow, exploring the other's beautiful cadaver. He inserted the forefinger and thumb of his free hand between his friend's blue lips and extracted a long pearl necklace, cause of the deceased boy's demise, each bead a baby's eyeball. He plucked one off and slipped it into his mouth like a grape, bit down. Blood collected unhurriedly along his lower lip.

Meanwhile through Saul-Revere's hearing-aide earphones glided Pluto Prozac's reptile-languid trance music, a liquid blend of oceanic white noise, distant buoy bells in a foggy New England bay, pipe organ's tremulous base note held forever, dreamy monkish chants that rise in the center of your deepest paralytic REM visions, and five-to-fifteen-second segments of absolute silence, the sort of pauses during which you can actually hear your own brain tingle and birr.

It was during one of these worldfreezing hushes that that goddamn buzzer repeated itself, all rattle and blare, pithing Saul-Revere all the way down his spinal cord.

"Fuck," he repeated, this time with more conviction.

He rose grudgingly, tugging out the earphones, tossing them beside him on the couch, and, hesitating another few blissful moments before removing the VR mirrorshades, moments enough to savor the raspberry blood drool from the bronze boy's chin in a salivary flutter; the boy burst into luxurious flames; the flames strobe into a green dragon with a large equine erection, an industrial robot with a woman's eyes, William Burroughs with a metal respirator implanted in his neck, crimson alphanumerics flickering over a white cube…a polychromatic cube…a cube sprouting arms, a web of pumping blood vessels, dwarfish vestigial legs like those you see on genetically engineered eyeless food dogs in the specialty delis, an orange heart throbbing in its chest, growing, stretching, bloating, size of a pear, a basketball, a small car; and then the explosion, a slo-mo blood cloud, black as oil, thick as hurricane rain.

Crap with a twenty-four-hour clinic, major franchise or not, Saul-Revere Outryder realized, exhaling a morose lungful of air, touching his palm to the spiked top of his canary-yellow-tipped-with-black mohawk checking to see if its distinguished plumage was still firm (it was), reaching over and slipping on his lab jacket, and shuffling toward the phone, was that it had to be open twenty-four hours.

Which really sucked, all things being equal, when you were

Saul-Revere Outryder, because you were living by the proverbial economic filament. Couldn't afford even a nurse, let alone a team of something reminiscent of colleagues. Had to set up shop in a place that made the middle of nowhere look like a Tokyo love hotel on a particularly passionate Saturday night...Devil's Hole, pop. 125, just over the NorCal, Inc./IBM Nevada desert border, homesteaded in the teens in and around one of the governcorp's abandoned missile silos as part of the post-Cold War Down-Trending programs, or DTs, enterprise that often attracted the lowest, measliest, roughest, and most excessive riffraff from the sprawls you could ever want to avoid, down-and-outers, ex-cons, religious zealots, political extremists, Gynorads, Catholems, serious bomb-crazed anarcho-hackers, psychotic loners, and even, well, Saul-Revere himself.

The guy, in other words, who hitched down from ChaseMan York, scraped his way through med school in the remnants of Brazil after the war, and would've just eked by had he not on graduation night sampled one of the offerings at the local juvenile meater establishment a little too vigorously, sans condom, sexing up with and unintentionally impregnating a local girl, this incredibly erotic paraplegic named for purposes of their encounter Ariana Orinoco, who happened to be somewhere between eight and twenty-one (with all that makeup and those breast grafts it was hard to tell in the sauna-moist room lit only by votive candles) and who should have known better. But after that mandatory no-frills abortion it was Saul-Revere who was deported back north, only to discover the governcorp up there frowned upon such sexual deviations almost as much as the SoAm governcorp, both spooked by the possibility of increasing their populations, and hence the strain on their food, medical, land, water, and other resources, even by a small handful.

Saul-Revere was thus, per usual, given the choice, without trial, between sterilization and a queer modus vivendi.

And, per usual in such cases, he opted for the latter, within the week finding himself assigned to one of the least desirable McDomino's Medikal Klinik franchises in the west, this sad pustule on the desiccated ass of rocky wasteland which consisted of exactly one Sinclair fuel enclave, one Taco Bell, one crack-riddled parking lot rigged to absorb the sun's heat and store it in below-ground batteries for the town's energy needs, three weathered ply-wood shanties without air-conditioning or fans, some useless fencing that kept nothing in or out, fourteen cartoon cacti, a fluctuating quantity of sage brush, lizards, a broiling heat that turned the air into rippling waves, and a once-abandoned ICBM missile silo replete with tremendous freight elevator, generous number of naturally cool concrete corridors, self-contained (if often malfed) air-filtration and water systems, a single communal toilet and shower, and ninety-eight people inhabiting various nooks and crannies, some in fridge boxes in the halls, some behind Mexican rugs or blankets thrown over ropes in corners, some in US Army-surplus foil sleeping bags in storage closets or beneath welded-down desks, some on rickety homemade bridges and wooden platforms joined by rotting rope ladders.

And Saul-Revere himself, whose cluttered clinic, messy office, and filthy bedroom (all taking up barely five meters by five meters) encompassed much of the base level, level ten, where US soldiers once sat in front of their computers (now purloined by the feds for cyber-scrap or ripped out and used to build makeshift partitions in the silo along with flat empty roachmeat cans, TV sets, plastic jugs, bald tires, car doors, tar paper, dressing dummies, and sections of sewer pipe) figuring out whether this time they were listening to one more dull drill or the chest-wrenching Real Thing that would in less than twenty-five minutes end the earth as they knew it, end everything.

Saul-Revere ground his back teeth as he centered his fluorescent canary-yellow contacts and flicked on the phone. Kids in the area'd been video-streaking him lately, and it turned his stomach to see one more little girl's sensuous virgin alabaster bum compressed against his screen as some kind of perversely innocent joke.

Nor would it thrill his parole officer, female albino with a surgically split black tongue christened inaccurately by her diverse detractors Slow White, whose computer monitored all of Saul-Revere's in-coming and out-going messages, patient records, merchandise bought and sold, around-the-clock surveillance cameras in his abode, and aug implanted below his scrotum that read a partner's gender in a microsecond by analyzing said partner's pheromones.

Except a little girl's bum was not what he saw when the pixels stabilized into a sparkling picture. What he saw was this dazed middle-aged guy who looked like he'd caught the bad gift. He was standing by the elevator doors topside. Hadn't shaved for days, patchy brownish-red beard almost as long in places as the bleached-white hair grooved with crop-circle patterns atop his closely sheared pate, features gaunt, like he was sucking in his cheeks, scratches beneath cheap smudged Pepto-Bismol pink sunscreen, swollen purplish smears under mismatched eyes, one blue, one brown, both, evidently, natural.

"Talk to me," Saul-Revere said, tapping keys to zoom over the guy's shoulder, take a peek around.

In the parking lot, herds of Mexiental women workers were jostling off two flat-jade, rust-chewed, diesel-belching, dent-dimpled, reprocessed school busses in the afternoon heat, probably well over 55 degrees C by now, back to the silo from the dayshift at the Dupont chemical plants in Reno, arms and faces spotted with nicotine-yellow vapor burns.

Near the second bus was one of those vintage Thai Khon Kaen urban light assault vehicles, only other rig there, flat black, rusted metal refitting plates in various places, huge gripping steel-reinforced tires, parallel battering rams instead of bumpers, bullet-proof mesh over the squarish front end and rectangular side viewing slits, hefty roll-bar arcing above those dual insect-eye high-impact plastic bubble windshields…some kind of weird fusion of mutant cicada, big-wheels jeep, and tank. You could still make out the machine-gun and grenade-launcher mounts. What you call them? Armadillos? Yeah. Circa 2009. Originally built by the NYPD for the outbreak of the 09-10 winter food riots, part of Saul-Revere's childhood, sturdy as army-issue, so pared down, ruggedly assembled, it was a good bet they'd see the turn of the next century.

"Was on this camping trip over near Donner Lake and ran into some trouble," the guy was saying. "S'hoping you could take a look."

Saul-Revere refocused the camera on the license plate. Blew it up on the screen. Pecked some more keys to snap a photo while running a search for name, address, and NorAm ID number.

"What kind of trouble?"

"Slipped. Banged up my knees pretty bad."

Computer, Acura-Datsun back-alley special, wheezed, hard drive spinning with difficulty. Saul-Revere slapped it with the flat of his hand. An electrical shiver passed through the machine.

"Knees, huh?"

"Think you can check 'em out?"

"What about those non-cosmetic facial jobbers there?"

"Fell forward. Asphalt."

"And?" Saul-Revere prompted, squinting at him, fingering his own left ear, the one hooped, studded, clipped, glued, bronzed, rhinestoned, ironed, wired, enameled, and pinned with a cluster of earrings. He'd had his lobe pierced and stretched back in Brazil, too, part of a tribal flash trend that swept through his fellow NorAm students, and still fooled with the dangling loop of flesh when he was really intent on something.

Which he really was now. Intent on just about everyone who summoned him from above. Never knew who or what exactly you were inviting down the well.

He'd been skrimmed before, like that time he buzzed in the brawny biker who said he'd been shot in the shoulder at the Taco Bell. All Saul-Revere could see was some fast credit. Only when the elevator door opened, out came this wounded Yeti with an attitude and a flechette pistol...plus maybe ten of his friends, all armed, and the guy was no biker, and his friends were no friends, and everyone was in a rotten mood, and the next thing Saul-Revere knew he was owing the governcorp health care plan another three years of his life to pay back for all the damage the Winnemucca gang'd done to his clinic, office, bedroom, and twenty-five or thirty homesteaders before the grouchy ex-merc on level three came down for a tête-à-tête with his pet flamethrower.

Nor did Saul-Revere like the look of *this* guy one bit. Too...what? Cautious. Yeah. That's it.

God, he hated people.

They behaved just like...people. Geared to be manipulative, pushy, solitary, narrow, out for credit, food, the easiest way through.

He hated people and he hated the governcorp and he hated Devil's Hole and he hated the silo and he hated the desert and he hated his clinic and he hated Brazil and he hated ChaseMan York and he hated IBM Nevada and he hated his phone and he pretty much hated everything else about his existence, too.

"And?" the guy echoed.

"Yeah, exactly. *And...*"

He looked puzzled.

"And nothing. That's it."

"Bullshit. You wouldn't be goin' out of your way to drop in on Uncle Meat for some fucking scab on your knee. Dick with me, you might as well just turn around and fuck off into the sunset."

The guy ciphered a while longer, really bad at the cover-up stuff, transparent as a hologram.

Meantime, results on the license plate appeared in a window in the upper righthand corner of the screen:

CLASS D DRIVER'S LICENSE
NAME: STRAY, ULYSSES SYSOP-OF-THE-PLAINS
ID#: 3.11.59.36
LIFE PHONE#: 1846472030

SEX: MALE	HEIGHT: 172 CM	WEIGHT: 60 KG
HAIR: BR	EYES: R: BL, L: BR	BIRTH: 09-14-97
RESTRIC: NONE	DONOR: YES	

HOME: WHITE BIRD SIX, #1956F   WK: MERGING ANGELS SAT SHP
MOSTON, T-COL 83843-5748   205097 COYOTE GRADE
                                                        MOSTON, T-COL 83843-0043

DOUBLE-CLICK FOR FURTHER INFORMATION:
MED HIST I EDU I CRED STAT I FAM BKGRD
WORK HIST I PHOTO ID I OTHER

Bingo.

"Okay," Stray said. "Okay. Well. Look. I was up there camping and had this, I don't know what, seizure or something. I pass out. Wake up this morning. Start down. Happens again."

"Seizure?"

"Yeah, well. That's the thing. I don't exactly know. I run this computer scan, you know, come up with damage to the central nervous system. Reticular formation. Burrow. Thing tells me it's dumbed down, doesn't have a clue."

"Not your day, huh?"

"'Outside program design,' it says."

"...?"

"Never happened before. I feel sick. Dizzy. Then, wham, I'm gone."

"So you start heading down in the morning."

"Only, like I say, same thing happens again. I'm there. I'm not there. And, well, there're all these, I don't know..."

"Yeah?"

"These really vivid dreams. Hallucinations, more like. Except all the things in them? They really happened to me. I mean, *exactly*. Memories, only more real than memories. Events, like. I *experienced* them. Like I was there again, watching myself on a home vid."

Saul-Revere stuck his finger through his ear-loop and tugged, marked the time readout on the screen, called up Stray's credit status, saw things looked wholesome enough, then his medical history off his bar-coded DNA biometric signature and everything checked out...must've come from a pretty well-off set of progens with company connections...kept up regular Epidemics bloodtests, received a Governcorp Vaccination Booster-Shot Series every six months, no signs of significant illnesses since he was eleven when he caught AIDS Strain 247-Y and received vat-grown bone marrow, a fresh liver, and a kidneys flush, compliments of the Diacomm Governcorp Employee Health Care Plan.

"Okay," Saul-Revere said, "step closer to the camera. Lean forward slightly. Okay. More. Yeah, like that. Hold it."

He fired up the retinal scan. Hard drive spluttered. He smacked it. Unsympathetically. Data spritzed down the line.

It matched what he'd gotten off the license plate...no criminal record, not even a parking ticket, and blood pressure, pulse rate, galvanic reflexes, and breathing pattern suggested nothing but some understandable edginess.

So Saul-Revere switched to the medicals. Took a look around Stray's skull for him. Sony CAT-scan peeled away layer after layer of tissue in fluorescent blues, oranges, yellows. And...sure enough...just like the computer'd told him this morning: right in the core of the brain stem above the spinal cord, the tangled mass of nuclei and fibers comprising the reticular formation and environs were all wrong. You had to look real close to see it, be searching for it.

Appeared at first as some sort of swelling, maybe something that could've been sustained from that fall, but Stray hadn't mentioned anything about hitting his head, and the more Saul-Revere examined it, the more he could see that wasn't it anyway, more like some sort of...what...substantial cellular anomaly...permutation...like things in there had decided to start their own sideshow.

Wasn't a tumor, exactly...much more subtle than that...soft transformation in which cells both remained almost themselves and yet not quite themselves, coloring infinitesimally off, size almost intangibly irregular.

"You still there?" Stray asked.

"Yeah, yeah, I'm still here."

"And?"

"And here's the thing," he said, starting up a file. "Checkup'll cost you double DGE Health Care Plan, it being past five o'clock. Any prescriptions extra. Followup too. Take it or leave it." He pressed ENTER. "Except let me tell you something. You leave it, you got yourself another two hours minimum before you see another clinic on this road. Which, I should point out, may or may not be as accommodating as this one."

Stray looked left, probably at those Mexiental women stripping and hosing off the chemicals at the one-time car wash outside the fuel enclave, then back at the camera.

"Okay, yeah, fine," he said.

"Your choice. So. Okay. Step back. More. Okay. Turn your pockets inside out. I wanna see every speck of dust in there. Hold on. What's that?" He zoomed in on the *Pretty Hate Machines* reading slab, pair of car keys, ebony credit slab with silver bar code. "Got it. Okay. Pat yourself down nice and slow. Let me see those hands travel. Okay...okay...okay. Right. Now run, don't walk, when you hear the buzzer at the elevator door. It'll come up once. You got three seconds to get on." He consulted the time again. "Haul ass, man."

Saul-Revere reached over and hit the up switch. Hydraulics screamed.

"Oh," he added, an afterthought, "and thanks for doing business the McDomino's way."

He slipped off his lab jacket, pulled on his black Akoi drawstring pants and black-mesh t-shirt, shrugged on his lab jacket again, and stepped into his black Birkenstock clogs.

On his way over to the elevator, he voice-activated the Hitachi sound system, speakers and player resembling three purple-black Rothko paintings mounted to the concrete wall above his Acura-Datsun.

Tranquil muzak sorghumed through the rooms smelling of disinfectants, homesteaders' oniony body odor, and jasmine-incense air freshener from Saul-Revere's electric wall unit. He hated those tunes just like he hated everything else about his life, knew them by heart, reshuffled numbers off that defunct band Viva Bonni Suicide's old album, "Hysterically Blue," "Dissolution Planet," all synthesized strings, flutes, and pianos, but, according to the franchise manual, they created that dox office ambience, familiar, cozy, reminiscent of all the good times from your past you experienced when listening to them, and he figured he might as well use them since they were part of the patient-tested startup-kit supplied by McDomino's, as was that huge, dense, plastic Venus flytrap potted beside the elevator doors he now stuck his hand into, withdrawing an easy-loading, rapid-fire, ceramic Viper 200 pistol, packed with twelve exploding shells, which only his trigger finger (or one whose prints matched his at twelve key points) could pull.

Releasing the safety catch, he rocked back and forth thinking about those pathologies...awesome business, first exciting thing he'd seen down here in a year of infectious yaws, since, maybe, that Arab corporal from Armstrong City, first moon colony, who breathed through that scar-pink hole in her throat, exposed to one too many doses of cosmic radiation, came visiting last winter carrying her formaldehyded miscarriages with her in a genuine polished mahogany box with brass fittings and delicate crystal display window.

Hydraulics clunked to a stop.

Red light illumined above the elevator doors.

Saul-Revere raised his Viper 200 and smiled cordially.

"Welcome to the Devil's Hole McDomino's Medikal Klinik," he recited. "In the interest of security, please step forward, turn around, spread your legs, and place your hands on the wall."

"You sure run a tight ship down here," Stray said, doing what he was told.

"Never tight enough, man." Saul-Revere reached over and picked up a portable Lockheed metal detector from his desk, began running it up and down Stray's body. "Should see some of the assholes we get. Cheapo lepers looking for an excuse to get out of the sun. Wannabe homesteaders trying to sweet-talk their way in. Last week this late-stage syphilitic trying to use my office as an Epidemics Hostel. No shit." He chucked the instrument back on his desk and tucked his gun in his draw-string pants. "Makes you wonder where all the decent people went to."

They leadfooted over to the examination bench, Russian-surplus dentist's chair, navigating around an ancient heart-lung machine, two corroded pale green oxygen tanks, a small organ refrigerator (now barren), and several aluminum floor-to-ceiling shelves stacked with mostly empty boxes, piles of useless data readouts, a small selection of vials, a rusty pair of forceps, vaccination equipment, couple scalpels and stained tongue depressors on a gray paper towel, jug of bleach, pus basin, biohazard canisters aslosh with brownish-red liquid, miniature X-ray device, half-full plastic liter-bottles of Coke, heat lamp, stethoscope, music-chip collection, porcelain Fred Flintstone doll, and pair of yellow K-Mart dish-washing gloves, the last of which Saul-Revere nabbed and began to yank on as they passed.

"Thing is," he said, helping Stray into the chair, toeing a button on the floor, easing him back into an almost supine position, "your computer got it wrong."

". . . ?"

"Ran a medical retinal while we were talking. You check out just fine."

"Yeah, but—"

"Programming error, most likely. Oh, no doubt a couple of scratches. Bruises here and there." He pulled a penlight from his lab jacket, thumbed up Stray's eyelids, examined, let them down. "But that's all."

"That's all?"

"That's all."

"What about the seizure thing?"

"Open your mouth. Wider. There you go. Okay." Something scuttled in the corner among the guts of a hashed Daihatsu opened for repairs years ago and never put back together. Stray shifted. "Not to worry," Saul-Revere said. "Rats. Big suckers. Chihuahuas, really. You leave them alone, they leave you alone. Mainly. Except at night, of course."

He felt around Stray's neck, base of the skull, looked in his ears. Picked up the stethoscope off the shelf and listened to his heart, breathing.

"Cough. Okay. Again. Fine." He exchanged the stethoscope for a pressurized syringe, sorted through vials. "One kid on level three had two fingers eaten off. Infant. Two months old. But, hey, Uncle Meat was just down the hall, you know?" He chuckled. "Progen had a NorAm ID. Otherwise things could've gotten real interesting." He selected an orange one and loaded the syringe.

"But *something* happened up there."

"Yeah, well," fiddling, "I'm not saying it didn't. Just that there's no trace. Vitals are excellent. CAT-scan's perfect." He tucked the syringe into his belt next to the gun, tore off a corner of the gray paper towel beneath the scalpels and tongue depressors, opened the jug of bleach, tilted it to wet the shred. "Would that every middle-aged guy could say the same. Sure Lonny Wolf'd agree."

"Lonny Wolf?"

"Baseball player. Pitcher. Exxon Jersey Yankees. You didn't hear?"

"Hear what?"

"Assassinated last night. On the mound. Rail rifle. Gave away one hit he shouldn't've, seems like. Should've seen him. One big blob of jello after another scattered all over the infield." He disinfected Stray's upper right arm. "You eat or drink something before all this went down?"

"Pouch of freeze-dried chili. Bottled water."

"You never know, you know?" He slid out the syringe. "I'm thinking maybe you had some sort of reaction. Bad biologics. Airborne virus could do it, too. This won't hurt." He pressed the syringe against Stray's arm, snicked the trigger. "Anyway," disinfecting again, "important thing is you're doing okay now."

"I guess."

"This'll settle you down. Tomorrow whole business'll seem like less than nothing."

Stray reclined there in the boneless posture of a crash-test dummy, looking up at the bluish bio-light strips crossing the concrete ceiling. He hesitated before gathering himself together and beginning to stand.

"So," he said. "You mean that's it?"

Saul-Revere hovered over him, fluorescent canary-yellow contacts glowing, canary-yellow-tipped-with-black mohawk flaring like a psychedelic crest atop a psychopathic Woody the Woodpecker.

"Trust me," he said.

Minute later Saul-Revere was on the phone again, this time to Slow White, his albino parole officer, and this time using an encrypted video program.

"Thpeak," she said when the screen lit, her split black tongue giving her a mean lisp. "And make it quick. I'm bithy."

She was wearing a loose-fitting white kimono patterned with copper-colored intestines, black shag wig that accented her chalky semi-translucent skin.

Saul-Revere could make out a tube crypt behind her: HDTV, sound system, mini-fan, computer built into a scuffed epoxy wall curving above a foam mat on which lay a virtually naked flat-nosed African with an impressive erection, tribal scars on his cheeks and chest, unhealthy lavender myoelectric prosthetic vibrator in place of a right arm. The vibrator was shaped to resemble a gothic

Madonna and Child. His metallic red condom matched his platform high-heels.

"Got another one," Saul-Revere reported.

"No shit?"

"No shit. Left a minute ago."

He scratched his face, wondering if it was time for another waxing.

"Got the data?"

"Running it up to you even as we talk."

Her tongue flitted out, licked a mouthcorner that'd also been tattooed black. Slow White could control each half of the muscle independently. Electrical implants.

"You wanna know thomething, Outryder?"

"Yeah, sure."

She widened her eyes, revealing their perpetually conjunctive look.

"Thometimes you're not the dumbshit you theem." She punched some keys. "Credit'th in your account. Jutht think. Couple more decades of thith, you'll nearly own your own practicth. Have a nithe evening."

The screen went blank.

"Yeah, well, you too," Saul-Revere said, after the fact, to the AT&T symbol and call-cost readout staring back at him.

10

Binge&Purge

Krystal pulled through the razor fences and beneath the guard towers into the Binge&Purge truck stop, bullet-proof island extending across the desert eleven kils to the east of Lovelock on Interstate 80, just like the ghost'd told her, at sunset, the sky embarrassing itself again.

Everything burned with a grainy mandarin orange tinged with fuschia...low craggy horizon, kil after kil of car, jeep, bus, van, motorcycle, moped, dune buggy, armored freighter, pickup, private tank, velocipede, camper, wind-sled, fifty-four-wheelers, forty diesel and twenty gasohol pumps thorning the tarmac, electrical recharging posts spiking every third parking slot, medivacs, governcorp security choppers, joy-riders tethered to bullseyes here and there, a small forest of steel-and-glass oxygen booths and phone cells bunching around the entrance, enormous concrete rattlesnake mouth flanked by ten-meter-tall stick shifts.

Porno glams coupled, knife-wrestlers sparred, country singers mouthed songs in Arabic and Kickapoo on the full-wall HDTVs, beautiful moving murals, built into the sides of the extensive pseudo-adobe windowless edifice.

Kil-wide-by-nearly-two-tall holographic commercials cycled twenty-four hours a day above the red-tiled roof. You could see them far away as Fernley to the west and Oreana to the east...Brooke Shields Estrus perfume, Avia steel-tipped athletic shoes, the Binge&Purge itself, everything, everything you could imagine.

In the late light, the world existed inside a planet-sized orange balloon...more like vids of the wind-blown melony Martian surface than any earth Krystal'd ever conceived.

She nuzzled into a narrow space next to a paintless Chaika, imported Russian limo from the last century, half a kil away from the B&P, cut the engine, set the emergency brake, took off her reflective ruby aviator shades, and sat collecting herself, feeling the baking heat radiating around her in her Geo Elf, nicknamed by the faithful Pod People Specials, three-wheeler bubble-topped electric one-seaters which, if the breeze was with you, could max out at around eighty kph.

She leaned over and checked her contacts in the rearview mirror and caught sight of a tanker truck tagged with octagonal biohazard and inflammable signs maneuvering between two rows of rigs. The driver, grape-hair, lip ulcers, rolled down his window, met Krystal's eyes, bared his teeth, and heaved a large black-green plastic bag of assorted trash—water bottles, paper towels, fast-food wrappers, soda cans, amphetamine containers—onto the tarmac.

Krystal sucked in her breath and thought about how the present was almost all audience now, one big twenty-four-hour film to watch, without a single actor to perform, to get things done, no one wired to do anything but languidly look and listen.

Whispering to herself Directive the Fourth (*Assume all things will always, somehow, work out in the end...*), she slung up the wingdoor, crawled out, plugged her Elf in to the recharger stake, and began the long march across the parking lot, heatwaves undulating like special effects around her, sorbet sunlight blinding, first traces of sand specks stinging out of the west with the evening wind, practicing her I-can-bring-you-to-your-knees-with-a-sideways-glance walk in her black body dress and glossy will-weakening combat boots.

A cool current of recirculated air flavored with formaldehyde resin used in treating permanent-press clothes wafted over her as she stepped through the automatic glass doors.

She stood in a large holding area fashioned to look like the Hollywood version of the desert outside, virgin white sand, femininely rounded beef's-blood brown rocks, plastic four-meter-tall saguaro sprouting from clusters of white-flowered fishhook cacti, stuffed roadrunner, gila monster, kangaroo rats inhabiting the artificial landscape under radiant white fluorescent lights.

Krystal took her place in line with around thirty other travelers and filed by one of the five genetically enhanced, muscle-grafted, identical Navaho giants who frisked her for weapons. Guard next to her extracted a farmer's glove with steak knives duct taped to each of the fingers from the backpack of a dimple-thighed woman in black acrylic microshorts and black double-D-cup lace bra. Expressionless, he tossed the weapon into a cardboard box full of them and waved the woman through.

The ghost began speaking to Krystal. She followed the bearings she heard in her head, piloting near copious checkout lines, through the clothes department featuring both polyester and paper, junk-food ministore, floor-to-ceiling aisles highlighting velvet paintings, cheap futons and rubber sleep mats, exorbitantly priced hydroponic fruits and vegetables, automotive supplies, music-chips, sporting goods, holoporn vids, cigarettes, booze, drugs, cosmetics, and toiletries, moving deeper and deeper into the luminous complex, aqua-colored Panasonic clerks, plastic bowling balls on wheels, zigzagging around her feet, waiting for her to ask directions or help in purchasing sales items, but she knew where she was going, felt it in her spinal cord like a salmon feels its way upstream.

In the Join&Jet wedding chapel, a blitz marriage was underway. Two Malist truckers stood side by side. One wore a white knee-long dress-jacket supplied by the management that almost hid his shredded jeans and Air Abdul hiking boots. His partner wore a frilly white veil and sari that almost hid his Thorburn-Harding MaleBond Center pregnancy, fertilized egg nourished by a series of hormone injections, attached via placenta to the wall of his abdomen. A Justice of the Peace, duded up like the paunchy, rhinestoned, side-burned, tranquilized, near-death Elvis, stood at the pulpit reading a service collaged from the King's songs while music from Gallo commercials, sitcoms, and Disney movies wove in the background.

Caught up in the kitsch along with several dozen other stragglers, Krystal stood observing till the plastic decoder rings were exchanged, at which point she moved on, cutting through the automated check-in lobby of the Mutsuhito Motel, black consoles looking like ATMs inset into the far fake-adobe wall (slide up a plastic panel, slip in your credit slab, and your room card and receipt clacked out into a plastic dish), through a waterfall of glass beads in a low wide doorway, and into the shadowy crowded Voodoo Lounge where she meandered over to an empty thatched-roof bamboo booth in a corner and took a seat.

Motif was Haitian. Tall leafy synthetic banana plants, bundles of flower buds and yellow fruits at the ends of thick curved stems, and coffee shrubs with white blossoms and glossy evergreen leaves flourished everywhere in the burgundy blush. Simulated wooden dishes, trays, and utensils, glassy with polish, adorned each of the tables. The floor was centimeter-deep in sawdust, the walls decorated with dried blowfish, black-and-white photos of the ruins of the Citadel in Haiti after the third NorAm invasion in the teens, machetes, spears, hoodoo dolls.

A minor-keyed part-African, part-Spanish tune by the Immaculate Contraption, ferment of acoustic guitar, mandolin, panpipes, ankle-shells, water gourds, and a wicked kettledrum resonated on the sound system.

One of the waiters, paid primo no doubt to keep that bloated-stomached bony-chested developing-world look, uniformed in a brilliantly colored Mardi Gras costume with mountainous gold, begemmed, and red-feathered headgear, yellow and green authentic wooden necklace, silky blouse and pantaloons, approached Krystal and, speaking in a bad bogus Caribbean accent, took her order, café au lait seasoned with an 800-milligram attack dose of piracetam.

She sat back and absentmindedly watched a handful of meaters displaying for clients on a pillowy maroon couch beneath a governcorp public health warning about epidemics and sexually transmitted diseases. Most were naked, or almost naked, in order to show off their operations, one fitted with both vagina and penis between his/her breasts, nothing between the legs except a GI Joe mound of smooth hairless flesh; another with shaved beard, pulled teeth, and minor surgery to make his mouth look like horizontal labia; a third having transformed her vagina into an anus surrounded by a bioluminescent tatt of the timeworn Rolling Stones logo: red lips, white teeth, extended tongue. All flaunted thin gold and silver necklaces, body glitter and body chains, black high-heeled thigh-boots...and all made Krystal vaguely horny and restless.

The waiter returned with her bowl of coffee which, upon trial sip, tasted of chlorine from the powerful purification procedure used out here to eradicate some of the tenacious biologics.

Krystal felt sorry for herself. Angry. She just wasn't thinking, wasn't learning what experience had to teach her.

Easy and obvious observation, after another lesson had gone down, gone sour, everything making perfect sense during the fiftieth replay. If she wasn't careful, though, if she didn't master the art of seeing those replays coming, she knew this was what her life held in store for her, this was what the coming attractions amounted to.

"You want some news, child?"

She opened her eyes to discover a corpulent black woman with sunflower-yellow hair and a fungoid infection bleaching out the left side of her face looking down at her with compassionate bloodshot eyes. She wore plastic sandwich bags rubberbanded to her hands and feet, a long jean skirt, and a t-shirt that asked in big black block letters: YUB SO F*CKEN SIC? A wire from a small flat liquid crystal TV attached like a pin to the chest of her olive-green t-shirt squiggled up her neck and disappeared into the skin behind her ear.

CNNer. Pronounced *sinner*. News addict. From Temple of the Manic Broadcasters, ousted faction of Joey Taboo's Cult of Aloneness.

"Looks like you could use some news," she said.

"Thanks. But trust me. Last thing I need right now is more information."

"Little news never hurt no one. Cheer you up. Get you back in touch with the Network."

"I'm not so sure."

"Who is?"

"What's with the baggies?"

"Rhinovirus, streptococcus, spirillum. Age of Latex. Age of the Non-Biodegradable Protective."

"Thanks. I think I'll just nurse this coffee here…"

"Who, what, when, where, how. That's what's what. What's when. Who, what, when, where, how. Gotta open yourself to the scoop, child. I'm tellin' you, you need a headline bad. Can see it in your eyes, sniff it on your breath…Tune in with me. Let's do a little reportin'." She lowered her head, closed her eyes, waiting for the Word. "Last night six eco-terrorists stormed the corporate headquarters of the Roulette Organ-Gambling Club in Bismarck, North McKota. Took fourteen hostages. Security killed the lights, sent in seven Brinks Force robotectors. Used infrared sightin' to locate the perps. Smoked 'em with lasers. Misjudged two hostages in the process. Buildin' was liberated as of five this morning. Relatives of the deceased filed claims by seven." She opened her eyes, studied Krystal, arms crossed, baggies crinkling. "How you doing?"

"So-so. Maybe it'd be better if I just…"

"Ride with me, honey. Let yourself go. Around the worlds in thirty seconds…Fires in the Northwest continue to burn out of control. Drought conditions. Heavy winds. Two million acres destroyed this week. Over seven-hundred-and-fifty homes. No end in sight."

Krystal was walking down a red dirt road in the country. Fenced pastures on both sides, wheat. A car, flashback VW Bug, materialized ten meters above her head. It jerked forward a centimeter. Then another. Then crashed down into the tall grass five or six meters to her left. A second car appeared, same make. A third. A fifth. A twelfth. All began dropping out of the sky around her. She just stood and watched, unsure which way to run.

"Polymox Epoxi, famous gameshow host, was reported missin' yesterday by her producer, Jean Poole. No ransom demands made at this time. Poole and the FBI are quote 'cautiously optimistic' unquote. Klub Med announced plans this mornin' to buy Turner Oregon in a governcorp-sponsored takeover…"

The CNNer winced as though tickled by a stungun.

The bartender, bulging beetle contacts and lilac sunscreen, stopped picking the sores on his forehead and looked over from the mesto.

"You okay?" Krystal asked the CNNer.

"I...wait."

Another tremor passed through her. Her back straightened. She touched her television in a special way, religious sign. "I'm pickin' somethin' up..." her voice loud now, carrying. "News flash...Fresh-breakin' story...Here it comes...here it comes..." People around the mesto quieted down a little. She quavered. Stopped. Calm washed over her. "This just in." She listened and spoke, listened and spoke, translator at the UN. "A youthful-lookin' President-and-CEO Rob Loew...back from a recent series of fetal-tissue injections in Switzerland...went on the air minutes ago to confirm that...only minor structural damage was sustained yesterday by the BelsenLand nuclear reactor durin' the quake in southern DisCal...measurin' six-point-one on the Richter scale...Over a thousand aftershocks reported so far...Allayin' fears generated by the tabloid vid magazines...President-and-CEO Loew assured the media that...a quote 'negligible' unquote release of radiation had in fact taken place...Cleanup efforts are underway...BelsenLand will be open for business again by the end of the week...Soozanne Sakamoto reportin'."

She swayed back and forth, idling, a human receiver drunk on the power of data.

People began chattering again.

Krystal parted her lips to thank her but something caught her attention...there he was, walking through the beaded doorway, right on time, just like the ghost'd said, pausing, surveying the mesto for an empty booth.

Didn't look that different, either, from how she remembered him when they'd first met maybe a year ago...somewhere between Sigmund Feud and Kristofer Columboid, during one of her visits up north, on a meandering trek toward Banff, which she'd heard was magnificent, and which, it turned out, was not, the meteor-wrecked GSA space station Yuri Gagarin III having done some catastrophic burn-damage when it went down in the Canadian Rockies two years before.

Both had happened to stroll out the door of the Datacloud VR Parlor on Main Street in Moston, where Krystal'd pulled in for the night, the same time. She'd been playing three continuous hours of Nanofector, sweet little global genetic warfare game, he two of Splendid Chaos, a cybersport whose goal it was to deactivate as many incoming insidious computer viruses as possible before they got the best of your system (and they always, *always*, got the best of your system)...and, fifteen minutes later, over a slice of pizza at the local Master Race, they were friends. Kept in touch, too, on and off over the months on The Other Side.

She refocused her attention, retargeted her consciousness, raised an arm, waving, catching Uly's attention, a wide smile brightening his face at the velocity of recognition.

"Online tatt," he said, stepping up.

"Made sense at the time. Hey, it's really great to see you."

"You too. Okay if I, um..."

He indicated the bench blocked by the CNNer, and the CNNer, disappointed, looked from Krystal to Uly, and shuffled off.

"I'll broadcast for you, child," she said.

"Thanks," said Krystal. She raised her hands in a what-you-gonna-do gesture. "So. Tell me. What's drastic?"

"Turned thirty-three today," he said. He slid in across from her. "Went up into the mountains. Camping. All of a sudden feels like everything's being shot through a wide-angle lens."

"Moving through dream-time."

The underfed waiter with the defective accent returned and Uly ordered a hydergine daiquiri.

Metrophage's heavy-weather "No One Moves, No One Gets Hurt" replaced French Lesion's speed-riff "Chancroid." A skinny teenage girl in tight jeans, mirrored cowboy boots, and cosmetic stitches tick-tack-toed across her bald head got up and started dancing by herself near the mesto. She was missing all but the pinkie on her right hand, and even that was stubbed off at the second knuckle. Meaters on the couch studied her, figuring if she amounted to competition.

"Time's definitely been pulling some weird shit lately," Uly said.

"When I was a little girl? Every day lasted a month. It was amazing. Now every month lasts a second. And all the days...you don't even know they're going by, they're going by so fast."

"Quick: is this today or yesterday?"

"You know how you sometimes turn on your tube to figure out how to feel? You want to celebrate Christmas, so you turn on a Christmas movie? It's the same with me and time. I turn on the TV to experience a sense of communal duration."

"You hear about Church of the Rotes?"

The waiter returned with Uly's drink in a pseudo-mahogany bowl. Meater with the labia-mouth was being led away by a pot-bellied trucker with a ragged gray ponytail and construction boots bound with unraveling gray duct tape.

"Group over in Saturn Tennessee. Chronic retros. Got together and picked this time and place in history, mid-nineteenth-century England, whole Victorian deal, and now live it down to the smallest details. Talk, walk, dress. Oil lamps, coal heat, buggies, proto-germ-theory, letters, everything."

"How come?"

"Stabilize themselves in time. They know what to expect tomorrow, what they did yesterday."

"Where do I sign up?"

"Me too." He leaned forward, looked into his daiquiri and then at Krystal. "Stanley Kubrick did it. It's his fault. Ridley Scott. All those great Japanese B-films from the fifties and sixties, too. It's destined to be a century that always seems like underachieved science fiction."

"Age manufactured by Industrial Light and Magic."

The piracetam kicked on. Krystal felt extremely alert, her mind spotless and amplified. She listened to the junk-noise around her, everyone talking at once, deep into their own conversations, and, behind this general commotion, more specific sound-bites, CNNer reporting, dancing cowgirl yipping, a legless Iranian in a wheelchair at the mesto loudly cursing Rwandans, and, behind this, a grungabilly song by the Quantum Mechanics on the stereo and the tinny chittering of various other tunes on various other personal boom boxes, miniature televisions, cranked-up walkmans, and, behind this, feet scuffing, a blender whirring, wooden bowls clacking, chair legs scraping, sodas fizzing, a cash register beeping, a restroom door smacking open.

"We're consuming time just like we're consuming everything else on the planet," she said.

Uly looked over her shoulder, past the CNNer two booths down, seeing something not in the room.

"When I was up there camping last night?"

"Yeah?"

"I had these really...I don't know...*intense* dreams. Only they weren't *dreams*, exactly."

"How so?"

"More like *events* from my life...*real* events. Things I'd actually lived through before. Like I wasn't just *remembering* them. Maybe all this time-shortage stuff is getting to me."

"Maybe your mind's trying to work some things out behind your back."

"Yeah, well, too late now. Gotta be in Moston first thing tomorrow morning." He looked at his Rolex, thin black square, and pressed its face. Red alphanumerics lit up, retro-eighties. "Speaking of which...I got some serious driving ahead of me tonight. Modemed in, lined up this job for seven. Dish installation."

"Small world." She drank. "I start work in Moston next week."

"You're kidding."

"Just got relocated. Gotta skorry up there and find a place to crash. Shit. Hardly got enough credit to cover the ride."

A guy in a Diacomm tartan, calves siliconed to three times their normal size, dropped his cup of beer at the mesto. It bounced across the counter. He reached out to pick it up and missed, fingers gripping air, telltale hand-eye uncoordination result of too much VR use.

"Not to worry," Uly said. "I got this extra sleep mat. Has your name on it."

"No, really."

"You're welcome to it till you find something else."

Krystal leaned back in the booth, studying him a while, playing with a napkin. Uly became self-conscious.

"What?"

"You know something?"

"What?"

"You're just really sweet," she said. "*Really* sweet. A regular white-winged angel."

11

The Sacrifice Zone

The paranoid silence nightmares are made of, funerals give birth to, and astronauts hear when their oxygen cuts off without warning in mid-spacewalk sluiced through the situation room at Klub Med corporate headquarters several thousand meters beneath the mountain that once housed the SAC command center near Cheyenne, Mitsubishi Wyoming.

Klub Med bought the fraying colossus in the teens from a collapsing US military as part of its economic restructuring plan, and within three years had converted what was supposed to've been pretty much the last stand of democracy in time of war into a rose-scented below-ground company resort ornamented with elegant Thai and Somalian restaurants, imitation Roman baths, Swiss aging clinics, NorAm exercise chambers, an olympic-sized swimming pool tricked out in Portuguese luxuriance, Japanese gardens, Russian bordellos, astroturf tennis courts, a nine-hole golf course floating in the midst of a manmade lake, multiplexes, Cambodian knife-fighting arenas, Swedish sex shows, Turkish mestos, and assorted conference rooms...all connected by an efficient system of air-cushioned monorails and chauffeur-driven electric BMW golf carts.

Telly-Savalas Dahmer, surrounded by all this tongue-flopping success, the very subterranean ether shot through with the sweet fragrance of prestige and indulgence, felt like a highly polished Oxford leather loafer just dipped into a pile of steaming pumpkin-chunked cat shit.

All that bluster, bravado, bulldozing through the King's Chamber in Khufu off the coast of DisCouver Island earlier this morning? It'd shrunken into a withered beef jerky of its former phallic self. Telly-Savalas was no longer a pissed-off prophet commanding awe and devotion from his sycophants. He was a spineless roundworm trying to stand at attention. His dandelion-yellow simulated silk Shock suit had wrinkled and bunched during the flight. He'd lost three centimeters of height. His vestigial neck had vanished altogether. And his penitentiary-cement-gray eyes had gone into hiding under his brushy brows.

Telly-Savalas Dahmer had forgotten who Napoleon was, and he'd made his gofer, Stanley Zircon, guy with those idiot-anxious pudgy pink hands, look like a cross between Steve McQueen and Zyklon B. Baffo.

When Telly-Savalas wasn't thumbing his diamond Elba-shaped ring on his pinkie, envisioning the company boys in business suits dismantling his dream, he was swilling cup after cup of saké and torpidly picking through the platter in front of him decorated with some kind of bland breaded whitish meat-sticks and red spicy smart-drug dip on a bed of hydroponic lettuce and carrot-colored shreds of tissue culture that tasted a little like sucking on a multiple vitamin. But he wasn't paying attention to what was going on around him, which was a mistake, given the fact that the White House's EPA Advisor was asking him a question for the third time from one of the three large HDTVs at the end of the very long, very crowded table at which he slumped.

"God*damn* it!" the advisor said, "will somebody kick that guy over there or something? We're trying to hold a fucking *emergency session* here."

Stanley Zircon, who sat next to his boss, attempting extremely hard to look like he was taking diligent notes on his pocket computer, obliged.

Saké sloshed over the side of one of Telly-Savalas's many eggshell cups foresting the table in front of him.

"Um, sir," said Stanley in a low voice, sampling one of those breaded whitish meat sticks between words, "Mr. Converse has a question for you?"

A waiter appeared, Japanese man in black face and white tux, dabbed up the spilt drink, removed the empties, and set down a fresh cup. Telly-Savalas polished it off immediately. The waiter picked it up and set down another. Something dim and sputtering illumined the far reaches of Telly-Savalas's mind.

As if from a great distance, the idea of where he was and why beckoned to him.

He raised his head and turtled it forward, then side to side, pulling his surroundings into focus. The walls, floor, long narrow conference table, and bulky chairs were Neo-Shriek. Glass shards, broken plates, space shuttle shingles, ancient fuses, voltage regulators, photoelectric eyes, keypads, car-radio speakers, and fifteen-centimeter-long gray-blue shark fetuses soaking in formaldehyde-filled vials were set deep into a pebbly base and sanded to a smooth mosaic finish. Every chair was occupied by a Klub Med VP or gofer, all of whom were looking at Telly-Savalas. On the first HDTV inserted flush into the wall was Sabrina Triode, President-and-CEOs' Press Secretary. She wore tiger-eye contacts and a yellow bowl-cut. Back in the twenties she'd chemically dyed her skin a rich, silky, anti-melanomatic basalt. Before that, rumor had it, she'd been albino. On the second screen was Vladimir Al-Faruk, SuperFund Coordinator. Although Egyptian by birth, he wore tribal scars slivered into his cheeks and a split right nostril. He was a hero from the South American war where he'd flown laser-armed ultralights on sniper missions for the Special Forces.

The third screen displayed the guy shouting at Telly-Savalas...Neiman-Marcus Converse. Neiman-Marcus was in his early forties now. In his early twenties, already a good old boy out of Saturn Tennessee, he'd spent a fair amount of his inheritance (his parents co-founded Air Pyrate Muzzik) on monthly shots of Blue Prime, an anti-aging drug developed by a subsidiary of Mainline Pharmaceuticals at one of its health-spa research facilities in St. Petersburg. The stuff worked great, keeping the taker's skin moist and supple, crow's feet invisible, hair full-bodied and lustrous, eyes bright, metabolism fast and spunky as any long-distant runner's...till, that is, the greenhouse effect started seriously working its black magic on earth's atmosphere, at which point Blue Prime within the cells' nuclei started interacting with the mounting UV rays, sauteing their basic genetic information in a mean radioactive broth, and, by 2013, those rich beautiful people who'd bought into the Blue Prime mystique had undergone all manner of protoplasmic misfires while their sterile bodies acquired an abiding biochemical addiction to the increasingly expensive (Mainline Pharmaceuticals having got wind of the situation) wonder drug.

For Neiman-Marcus this boded poorly. By the time he was thirty, his skin had tinted a jaundiced yellow and erupted into a glistening topographical model of tumorous ridges, valleys, and hills. By the time he was thirty-five, he'd gone blind in his left eye, cartilage in both ears had crumpled and died, he'd lost handfuls of hair from his ulcerous scalp, and a good portion of his nose had dropped off, leaving two pink commas in the middle of his face with the consistency of the underside of a mushroom.

For obvious political reasons, Neiman-Marcus was a boon to the current administration. He was the embodiment of an environment gone rotten in the teeth, more metaphor than man. The public listened to Neiman-Marcus Converse, believed what he had to say, because how could such a man, struck down by atmospheric calamity, lie? He was a full-service media package.

For less obvious political reasons, Neiman-Marcus was an even bigger asset to the current administration. He was a drug addict who needed regular fixes of his favorite elixir to survive, and, having spent almost all his inheritance on his hunger, and having recently sold Air Pyrate Muzzik to Marco Polydor and his wife for desperate chickenfeed, he tightroped above the squalid abyss of bankruptcy. He was the kind of guy, in other words, who would sell both his grandmother's kidneys for his next hit without exhibiting a moral semi-quaver. He was the kind of guy who *had* sold both his grandmother's kidneys for his next hit.

And now he was in a very, very, very bad mood. He'd been awakened at 6:00 p.m. EST, already two hours immersed in his nightly drug-induced REM, yanked out of his iron lung, plugged into his portable life-support system, and wheelchaired up from the subbasement to his office in the White House, only to be told by the President-and-CEO on duty, Fujiwara Muzaffar al-Din, that the environmental shit had just hit the administrative fan, the Security Profit Margins Amendment had already been secretly invoked, and some major media damage-control was in the cards…and here he was, staring down at this table full of rejects, twenty or twenty-five of them, one blanker and more backward than the next, trying to get an approximation of an estimation of something remotely like the truth, a task more difficult than trying to hold a pissing contest with a steroidal skunk.

"Am I fucking *boring* you or something?" he asked Telly-Savalas. "Cuz if I'm fucking *boring* you, boy, well, then, I guess I'm just gonna have to apologize. Cuz I sure as hell don't fucking want to *bore* you, or anything, on the eve of the biggest fucking scandal to hit this administration in the last fucking *six months.*"

Telly-Savalas, feeling like the water in the Hudson River looked, mumbled something to his crotch.

Neiman-Marcus leaned up real close to the camera. He had no lips, just layers of semi-transparent scars. His dead eye was leaking something the color and consistency of peach yogurt.

"*What?*" he shouted. "*What?*"

"I, um…no, sir."

"No *what?*"

"No, sir, you're not boring me."

Neiman-Marcus leaned back. A whitish foam began oozing from the tumors comprising his left cheek.

"Well that's real good to know, now. I sure as fucking hell don't want to *bore* someone as important as you, you little shit." A latexed hand, probably belonging to his nurse, reached across his face and wiped the foam off with a handkerchief. "So tell me, boys and girls…what the fuck just happened? What the fuck just shat on LA?"

Stanley Zircon, his mouth full of breaded meat sticks and red dip, passed Telly-Savalas his pocket computer with his notes on it.

"Okay," he said "Well. The facts, as we currently understand them, shake out like this. At, uh, 12:07 Pacific Standard Time, an earthquake measuring six-point-one on the Richter scale hit the LA area. And, well…" he coughed demurely "…the epicenter occurred really near one of our concerns."

"BelsenLand."

"Right."

"*How* really near?"

He punched up some numbers.

"Oh, um, about ten meters away from the north entrance."

"*And?*"

"And, well, our nuclear reactor functioned perfectly, given its design parameters."

Neiman-Marcus looked befuddled. A dried pea-sized tumor fell off his forehead.

"So," he said. "What's the fucking problem?"

Telly-Savalas looked at a shark fetus curled into a small gray squash.

"Well, that's the thing, sir. The quake exceeded the design parameters by a, uh, statistically significant margin."

Neiman-Marcus glared at Telly-Savalas with his good eye, which was mostly the color of custard, though there were some awfully mean-looking red veins fissuring around in there too.

"What?"

"A statistically very significant margin."

"Oh," Neiman-Marcus said, "fuck."

"A margin that, well, sir, *reeks* of statistical significance, if I may be utterly frank."

Telly-Savalas was feeling the saké beginning to tiptoe around in his brain. Neiman-Marcus scowled at the camera for what seemed five hundred years. Stanley Zircon popped another breaded meat stick into his mouth and signaled the waiter to bring more. He'd never tasted anything so good.

"That's *great*," Neiman-Marcus said at last. "That's just fucking *great*. This administration's facing a shit-squall, and I'm playing twenty questions with a fucking retard...Okay. So dumb this down for me. By how fucking *much* did the quake exceed the fucking design parameters?"

Telly-Savalas reviewed his notes.

"Well it sort of, uh, blew up."

"Blew *up?*"

"Melted down," clarified Tokyo Sin, dwarf VP from DisCal sitting on a pile of maroon pillows across the table from Telly-Savalas. She wore a sexy cosmetic harelip, one of those Calvin Klein jobs, and a tattooed purple birthmark blobbing like a long drippy continent from her left temple down below the Nehru collar of her lilac silk kimono patterned with silver erect penises and carving knives. She had that toyboyish look which, on another day, in different circumstances, would've hooked Telly-Savalas's attention just like that.

"Like a candle on a hot afternoon, sir," Telly-Savalas said.

"One of the cores and the housing ruptured," explained José Ziff from Turner Oregon. José had replaced all his teeth with gold caps. They matched his gold mirrorshades.

"Two cores, tops," Modesta LaMode from Gates Washington said. Modesta LaMode, who used to be Monroe LaMode, and before that Manny Modus, had slept with every man, and every other woman, at the table. "Plutonium-uranium mix."

"Maybe three," said Tokyo.

"Okay," Modesta said. "Three. Right. Certainly no more than four."

Neiman-Marcus's cheek began foaming again.

Vladimir Al-Faruk, SuperFund Coordinator, shocked, said from the next screen over: "You mean you don't *know*? You actually don't *know* what the extent of the malf *is*?"

"Jesus," said Sabrina Triode, the Press Secretary, from the third screen, more to herself than anyone else.

Telly-Savalas cleared his throat.

"The thing is this. You know all those fires and aftershocks and radioactive clouds and stuff? Well, they're preventing us from getting an inspection team in there. Best we can do are copter flyovers."

"We sent in a squad of robotectors this morning," Tokyo said.

"*And?*" Neiman-Marcus asked.

"They melted."

"It's really, really messy," Telly-Savalas said.

"All going well," said Modesta, "we're thinking a week and a half."

"Two, max," said Tokyo.

Stanley Zircon, cheeks ballooned, lips glistening, flecks of whitish meat and reddish-brown bread crumbs on his chin, looked from one VP to the next like he was watching a ricocheting bullet. He was having a great time. He signaled for some more saké to go with the hors d'oeuvres. Worst-case scenario, he got promoted to VP with a telephone-number-large raise. And if things worked out for his boss, that was fine, too: Stanley got to hold the job he already had for a while longer, biding time till Dahmer dropped the grenade again.

"But from the size and dispersal rate of the leak…" Telly-Savalas continued.

"Leak?" Neiman-Marcus said.

"Well, yes, sir," Telly-Savalas said, surprised. "Leak, sir. The structural compromise and all?"

"Holy shit," Neiman-Marcus said.

"The fallout event has been moving north by northeast," José said.

"Last traces crossed into Brigham-Young Idaho a couple hours ago," said Telly-Savalas.

"The dispersal curve has just about been realized," said Tokyo.

"We're seeing a rapid decline in the negative inorganic output potential," Modesta said.

"Unfavorable environmental impact eventualities are falling, too," said José.

Neiman-Marcus let out a long sibilant breath. The nurse inserted oxygen tubes into his mushroomy commas. He sat there inhaling and exhaling.

Telly-Savalas chugged another saké.

Modesta surreptitiously crossed herself.

"Okay," Neiman-Marcus began again, estimating. "Okay. So. At least we're safe there."

Nobody in the room said anything for a long time. Stanley made gooey wet sounds with his mouth. Telly-Savalas kicked him in the shin. Stanley stopped momentarily, then started chewing again.

"Well," Modesta piped up. "That's correct, sir. To a…a certain degree. Right."

"You're telling me we're *not* safe?"

"No, no," Telly-Savalas said. "Nothing like that. Absolutely not. No. We're, um, safe…there."

"From now on," Tokyo said.

"From here on out," said José.

Sabrina uttered a petite peep that sounded like a field mouse that'd just had a brick dropped on it.

"From now *on?*" echoed Vladimir Al-Faruk.

"Exactly," Telly-Savalas said. "Yes, sir."

"But not *before* now?"

"Well, no, sir. That would be correct."

"Meaning precisely...*what?*"

"The fallout event? It seems to be having a few minor adverse demographically-centered effects."

Neiman-Marcus gurgled. He was bringing up some colorful goop, mostly blues and greens, into a bed pan held at chin level.

"From what we can tell..." Telly-Savalas began.

"At the present time..." Tokyo added.

"At the present time...is, uh...medical personnel? Along the distribution path? Well, they're reporting these cases of...they're not exactly sure what. Some sort of...the word they use is *disorientation.*"

"In a statistically significant portion of their patients," Modesta said.

"Within the last twenty-four hours," said José.

The nurse patted Neiman-Marcus's mouth clean. He spat out a small chip of dried tongue. It stuck to his power tie, blue background studded with maize-yellow nuclear blasts. The nurse picked it off with tweezers and added it to the contents already in the bed pan.

"Well who the fuck cares about some dizzy patients in the middle of fucking nowhere?" he asked. "They probably don't even fucking vote."

"*Time* disorientation," Tokyo said.

"Kind of a syndrome deal," said Telly-Savalas. "People are experiencing these seizure-like things, hallucinations, and a sense of intense *memory.*"

"*Memory?*"

"Yes, sir."

"As in *recollections?*"

"Yes, sir."

"Radiation poisoning?" he asked.

"The wind? It was really strong and high. So it's pretty hard to know when or where or how much of the fallout-event actually came down. We're running tests on that right now. And, uh, everyone responds differently to radiation? In one person a small dose can have huge effects. In another a huge dose can have no effects whatsoever. And the effects? Well, they manifest themselves really differently in different people? One person with a couple of extra rads suddenly breaks out in this humongous gross malignancy. Another gets a little sick to his stomach. So, well, *maybe* this all has to do with the reactor situation."

"...And, then again, maybe it doesn't," took up the Press Secretary.

"Right," Telly-Savalas said. "Exactly."

"And maybe it's all just some new bug that's shown up all of a sudden," posed the SuperFund Coordinator.

"Fresh strain of encephalitis," Tokyo proposed.

"Toxic psychosis," suggested José.

"Altogether new virus, as yet unnamed and undefined," proffered Modesta.

"So maybe..." Neiman-Marcus said, "just *maybe*...the fucking frog-and-beaver crowd can't prove a fucking thing. Maybe they don't fucking have a case that's worth a fucking damn. And *maybe* we can just deny our way right out of this political rattlesnake nest..."

Everyone contemplated this happily.

"So, people," Sabrina Triode asked, tiger-eye contacts wide and searching, "what's our operative sound-bite going to be going into this thing?"

"White House, as you know, okayed our use of the National Security Profit Margins Amendment," Vladimir Al-Faruk said. "We have full actuality-constraint potential here."

"And Mr. Loew went on TV this afternoon, assuring the public that the reactor's structure is secure," Sabrina said. "BelsenLand, according to our press releases, will be up and running within the week."

"Nothing outside the expectational parameters has occurred," Modesta said.

"Perhaps we should recall the tracking teams," said José. "No data, no incident."

"Lose the records," Tokyo said.

"They'll be lost by midnight," Vladimir said.

"We're discussing something that didn't happen, then," said Telly-Savalas.

"We're discussing a non-event event here," said Sabrina.

"Vacationers already booked will be redirected," Vladimir said. "No new reservations will be accepted by the company computers."

"Couple minor injuries sustained, it goes without saying," Modesta added.

"Minor damage to rides," said Tokyo.

"Enough loss to make the public feel like the news coverage was worth it, like they experienced something worth experiencing," said Modesta.

"We don't want to hurt the ratings capacity," said Sabrina. "Cleanup activities underway. Engineers already on the scene. What you would assume from a six-point-one seismic condition."

"I'll hit the airwaves first thing tomorrow morning and turn on the credibility template," Neiman-Marcus said.

"What about the reality scenario?" Vladimir asked.

"The what?" asked Neiman-Marcus.

"The reality scenario. The, uh, truth?"

"Oh," he said.

"I think I can help you there," said Telly-Savalas, consulting Stanley's pocket computer. "Estimations run around eighty to a hundred personnel terminational situations on site. Perhaps another twenty or thirty in the surrounding area, especially downwind."

"So we're really talking full Sacrifice Zone Enhancement here?" Sabrina asked.

"Right," said Modesta.

"Our people are on their way even as we speak," Vladimir said.

"Good," said Neiman-Marcus. "Excellent. Fucking wonderful. Okay. So. This thing didn't happen."

"Absolutely not," Vladimir confirmed.

"What thing?" asked Modesta.

Everyone chortled.

"By noon tomorrow the DT program will be in place," Telly-

Savalas said, confidence returning.

"Governcorp subsidies to the compulsory relocationers within a ten-kilometer evacuation-wellness arena," Vladimir said, thinking out loud.

"Understated media-redefinition campaign," Sabrina added.

"News refocusing enterprise," suggested Vladimir.

"ChaseMan York food riots are always nice about this time of year," Tokyo offered. "Pan-African epidemics."

"Everyone loves a good scene of mass starvation," said José.

"Maybe a little incident on the moon?" proposed Telly-Savalas. "Small terrorist attack? Cult suicides?"

"Former President Redford as well," said Sabrina. "We can ask him to do a little retrospective on his favorite wars."

"I'm getting a readout from our AIs here," Vladimir said. "They're telling us the mean NorAm blip-with-lifestyle's concern will drop exponentially within the next forty-eight hours. Given our current trajectories, polls conducted next week will fail to register a statistically significant reaction to the BelsenLand *contretemps*." He looked up, smiling. His tribal scars flashed. "I think we're in the clear, ladies and gentlemen."

"Halle-fucking-lujah," Neiman-Marcus said. "*Now* we're getting somewhere."

A psychic dam burst, flood of goodwill pouring through the situation room. Everyone began to clap.

Telly-Savalas, feeling a reprieve wash over him as water from a Baptismal font, smacked his palms together like a three-year-old at the head of his own birthday party. Everything was going to be okay. He was going to get through this. He sat jovially among his colleagues, letting this sweet information in.

Eventually Stanley Zircon spoke up. His mouth was still bloated, his chin dappled with sheen and grit. He was delighted by all the festive spirit.

"Say," he said, beaming. "What kind of meat is this, anyway? It's just, um…" He popped another breaded stick between his greasy lips and chomped. "Really *delicious*."

"Succulent, huh?" Modesta said, laughing.

"Juicy," said Tokyo.

"Tender," said José.

"A veritable delicacy," said Sabrina from the screen.

Neiman-Marcus pumped his shoulders up and down, guffawing without a sound.

Stanley looked from one to the other.

"What?" he asked.

"Well," Neiman-Marcus explained, "you're eating...uh...*left-overs* there, boy...And I *gotta* tell you: I've never seen *anyone* take to 'em like you. Regular fox in a henhouse."

"Maybe that's because our young friend here doesn't quite realize just how...environmentally *conscientious* he's being," said Vladimir.

"A veritable recycling machine," said Modesta.

"Whole resource management team in one body," said José.

"Waste not, want not," said Tokyo.

"You ever...you ever hear of Tyrone O'Kult?" Neiman-Marcus asked.

Stanley thought a minute.

"Sure," he said. "Major stockholder in..."

Then it snuck up on him. He stopped chewing. His smile retracted. He suffered a language crash.

"That's right, boy," Neiman-Marcus said. "Lazarus Project. Great enterprise. Major undertaking. Happening all over the globe. What you think? That our Mr. O'Kult'd just go and *waste* all that good unused meat once it's been gutted and all those over-priced organs removed? *Hell* no. We're talking four-star businessman here...fucking world-class entrepreneur..."

Stanley spoke through his food, which seemed to multiply in his mouth.

"You mean this stuff is..."

"Pass the Gerber's," said Modesta from across the table.

TWO

12

Interactive Autism

Uly and Krystal caravaned up to Moston that night, unaware they were cruising toward anything new, and settled into Uly's crypt at White Bird Six.

He was up with the next embryonic dawn, slouching toward his Thai Khon Kaen, handful of Vivarin pelleting from his mouth onto the asphalt as he shuffled across the underground parking garage, driving the twelve kils in a glassy daze to pick up his partner, Tammy Lee Numbers, for that 7:00 a.m. dish installation while Krystal enjoyed some major bottom-feeding on the tube, alternately lounging around and riding the chintzy elevator up and down untold floors in order to move her Geo Elf every two hours or face a mean ticket and wheel clamp, and then, early Monday, wiggled into her black body dress, tugged on her combat boots, frittered around with her complex coif, and walked to the Klub Med Travel Agency which, it turned out, was less than three blocks away, to begin work.

Uly's crypt, #1956, warmed Krystal's heart as the weeks commenced sliding by, it being, after all, the very embodiment of old Ockham's principle of parsimony: a cinderblock square, two meters by two meters by two meters, walls bare and gray, sans closets, an uncovered yellow bulb (almost always lit because the light from the porthole on the far wall was almost always bad) hanging in the middle of the ceiling, beside it a vent the size of your heel which riffled intermittently, exuding a clammy heat that passed for airconditioning. A miniature Kirsanov refrigerator occupied one corner, usually empty, permanently defrosting. On top of it sat a battered Smolensk microwave and, on top of that, two dingy once-white plastic plates, two plastic cups, two forks with bent tines, one butter knife, roll of brown recycled paper towels, and micro-wave cooking bowl. A green plastic bucket sudsing with mucky water squatted beside a small pile of clothes, some clean, most not, mixed with a half-full box of Ritz crackers, nearly clean-scraped tub of Peter Pan roachbutter, plastic bottle of Christian Dior water, and full bag of Kagoshima corn chips. The chemical toilet, shower tube, sink with chlorine pump, and spill stall were down the hall lit by other uncovered yellow bulbs, these at three-meter intervals.

Two rattan sleep mats lay in the middle of the floor, on each a blue foam camping pillow and dingy white towel, cherubim-with-satellites-for-eyes Merging Angels logo across the front, that doubled as a sheet. A messy cascade of computer slabs and music-chips surrounded Uly's Aiwa 3500, pseudo-leather-bound covers opened now in Uly's crossed-legged lap.

Shirtless, in nothing but torn underpants, sweating generously, he was hunched forward like a crow, face illuminated with the double-screens' opalescent shimmer. It was 4:00 in the afternoon, Saturday, Krystal's busiest time at the travel agency, clients lusting for a catastrophic vacation after the sour week they'd just endured, and Uly'd been working at the keyboard since 9:00 that morning, data scrolling up before him through a distracting leaden haze of headache. His eyeballs felt bruised, base of his skull a swollen sponge, so he tried some Anaderms, then escalated to codeine, which made him feel like he was trying to run a marathon with his feet spiked to the ground, and, finally, he gave up on medication all together, gophered to Soundgarden, paid via encrypted credit num-ber, and downloaded onto a blank music-chip Beaver Head and the Chicken Pips' new trad-trank album, *Ethnik Klenzing*, musical mélange of Buddhist chants and Irish folk melodies, Thai pop, ravel-edge, Newfoundlander hiphop, and South-Pacific-style instrumen-tal mood music salted with birdcalls, frog croaks, and other jungle-esque effects that possessed all the depth of a very pretty travel brochure, which was just what Uly, who inserted the chip into his Aiwa and began channeling, needed.

Sometimes, too, the very presence of information soothed him, his mind more comfortable in mosaic than linear mode, surrounded by superfluous shards of inconclusiveness, and so he'd spent a good while in Amphibian, a multi-media virtual space replete with photo-, film-, aural-, voice- and print-capability, dropping in randomly on the NorAm Weather Center (three thousand thunderstorms currently in progress around the globe, up from two thousand at the turn of the century), GSA News Service (lengthy lawsuit spawned two years ago by the Yuri Gagarin III's burn-damage to the Canadian Rockies—more than five million acres, twenty thousand houses, and seven hundred lives—still kindled white-hot debate between eco-terrorists, who tried to take responsibility for the disaster, a dubious claim at best, and yupmen, who shrugged, thinking, hell, what was the use of all those trees anyway...they were just *standing* there), and Paranoids Anonymous Chatsubo, where the truly demented, down-and-out, frightened, suspicious fringe sailors altered their genders, races, and ages before launching into burning electronic bush after burning electronic bush of deranged soliloquies, true confessions, governcorp conspiracy theories, and contemptuous, wry, single-eyebrow-raised one-liners.

Only the muddling pain remained, grew and shrank, bugged up and down the back of his brain, so Uly surfed on, finding himself navigating the online version of the Library of Congress, immense hypertextual Chinese puzzle box of data, info cloistered within info, tangle a novemdecillion more involved and perplexing than the network of tunnels, old phone cords, sewers, drainage conduits, fiber-optic lines, electrical cables, and gas mains crisscrossing beneath the streets of LA, something starting to nudge against his awareness lately, a vague possibility spreading through his cortex, along his spine, like black dye...

He began running across little chunks of related facts suspended in the gray radiance, inconspicuous consistencies and harmonies, almost inconsequential...almost, but not quite...definition of radiation beside a discussion of wave/particle duality beneath an explanation of space-time...an article about the spontaneous breakdown of one type of atomic nucleus into another next to one about the roentgen, measurement named for the German physicist who won the first Nobel prize in 1901, and about how only one hundred roentgens over the entire body in a single exposure can cause massive cellular damage, ionization, mutation, death, certain cells, notably those in bone marrow, lining of the stomach and intestines, skin, sex glands more easily injured than others...

On a whim he highlighted the word *skin* and clicked twice and tumbled into a history of ozone depletion, how since the beginnings of the industrial revolution various pollutants wafted their way into the stratosphere, ten to fifty kils above the earth's surface, breaking down and releasing atoms that ate ozone (one atom of freed chlorine knocking off one-hundred-thousand molecules of the stuff), allowing more ultraviolet radiation to penetrate the atmosphere and hence promoting skin cancers, cataracts, various unfriendly genetic disorders while depressing the human immune system, reducing crop yields, fish populations, ultimately even affecting the weather in myriad sick ways, chlorofluorocarbons being responsible for twenty to thirty percent of the greenhouse effect, joining forces with methane (another twenty to thirty percent), nitrous oxide (ten), and carbon dioxide (a full fifty), the last which people pumped nearly ten billion tons of a year into the air, despite the advent of alternate fuels that were counterbalanced by the tumorous growth of population and each individual's single-minded hankering for fat fast transportation at any cost, lead-acid batteries in electric cars great environmental jokes, contrary to expectations turning out to be six to sixty percent more polluting than gas.

And then a parallel universe of nuclear weaponry, film clips and voice-overs of the Manhattan Project, gothic architecture at the University of Chicago, bland bunker-like research facilities at Los Alamos, the rubble, burn-shadows, surreal solitary buildings left standing after the evaporation of upwards of seventy-thousand people in less than a second in an eight-kil area on August 6, 1945, when Little Boy flashed to life six hundred and sixteen meters above ground zero with the force of twenty thousand tons of TNT, or awesome mushroom of the first nuke exploded by the Soviets in 1949, exponential escalation of Mutual Assured Destruction, weapons now packing sixty megatons of force (equivalent of sixty *million* tons of TNT, three thousand times more powerful than that first rich roar), and more...open-air testing, radioactive iodine throughout the planet's milk supply, whole islands and swaths of desert forever unusable...collapse of an irrelevant, inbred, and progressively ludicrous communism, global nuclear dissemination, rise of dirty-bomb terrorism, first with that blast in Beirut, next the poisoned water supply in New York, then the strike by one of the drug cartels down in Bogota...with thirty, thirty-five, forty nations building or buying, Iran, Iraq, North Korea, China, Finland, Brazil, Mexico, Spain, Switzerland, Hungary, and United States of Africa among them...and with the Ukraine, nearly two thousand warheads leftover from its days as a piece of the Evil Empire, discreetly becoming the world's most powerful nuclear state—not to mention arms dealer—for half a decade.

And, then, then, *then,* the stunning aftermath of the nuclear industry, more than two thousand test explosions worldwide in less than fifty years...almost three metric tons of plutonium left over at Los Alamos, thirteen at Rocky Flats, eleven at Richland (so many different toxic wastes dumped at the Hanford plant in those notorious storage tanks nobody knew exactly *what* was in them any more), another seven scattered here and there across NorAm alone...this with the numbing understanding that only half a kilogram spread evenly throughout the planet's atmosphere was enough to spark lung cancer in every man, woman, and child on earth...or those shocking discoveries of sinking sperm counts (by fifty percent in as many years), plummeting testosterone levels, rocketing cases of endometriosis (from twenty-one reported cases in the world in 1900 to nearly six million in NorAm in 2000), gender-bending results of half a century's delusions of grandeur, enhanced by the proliferation of estrogen mimics like DDE, DDT, PCBs, PBBs, endosulfan, atrazine...even the polycarbonate plastic in many baby bottles and water jugs, the chlorine compounds used to bleach paper...and the bottom dropping out of this data field, Alice passing through the looking glass, swimming through a parcel of untitled governcorp files from the previous century, no idea what it took to reach this address but, curious, skimming some sort of report from the Atomic Energy Commission, predecessor of the Department of Energy, talk of acceptable radiation doses, penitentiary inmates, Oregon, Washington, release forms, hospital patients, plutonium injections, and restricted info flow...and, from another reality, two hands fastening on his shoulders, familiar voice behind him, Krystal asking: "Hey, what's drastic?" and knowing the answer was everything.

She was massaging his cramped shoulders, wearing only a black bikini bottom, breath smelling of Kick, peppermint-and-piracetam chewing gum...scent, too, of Brooke Shields Estrus, all jasmine, spice, and pheromones, Bintang beer...

"Man," he said, bowing his head. "You scared the shit out of me."

"Sorry, babe," kneading, raising her right hand to the base of his skull. "You just seemed really rapt. Didn't want to disturb you, only it looked like you were *never* coming out of there."

"So...oooh, that's *nice*...send lots of folks to hell and back?"

"You have no idea. Listen, smile, reserve. Great road to go eight ways crazy. Be sitting there, talking to someone, thinking: now did I just say that two seconds ago, or did I say that to the guy who came in here yesterday?" She stopped massaging, leaned forward, and, resting her chin on his shoulder, studied his computer screen, took a swig of warm beer. "Hey, what *is* that junk?"

"All manner of lysergic. Somehow I got myself looped into some pretty interesting governcorp stuff." Krystal passed him the bottle. He took a long swig and passed it back. "Except for this goddamn headache."

"Again?"

"Still. Won't leave me alone for like three minutes."

She reached down and spread her free hand on his chest, circled it lower to his firm stomach.

"I got an idea."

Uly leaned his head back into her.

"Oh?"

"Oh."

Krystal put down the half-empty Bintang bottle, lifted the Aiwa off his lap, set it on the floor, tapped a couple of icons on the screen. The governcorp document spun, shrank, blipped out of existence. *Ethnik Klenzing*, too.

She picked up one of the chips from the pile by the sleep mat, slipped it into a side-slot, and punched RETURN.

Uly leaned back on his arms and watched her clear a space for herself in front of him, fold her legs beneath her, crane forward and, releasing the condom from the packet she'd produced from under a towel, lick his stomach, his navel, tease off his underpants as he arched his spine and, Trojan on tongue, ease it down with her mouth over his full erection, glans pierced with a small gold hoop. She cupped his scrotum in her palm and squeezed, dragged her short black fingernails across its tender surface, slipped under to his perineum.

Uly moaned and closed his eyes, shifted his weight, reached out with his right hand to trace the elaborate chain-stitch scar of Krystal's cosmetic mastectomy, the satin firmness of her very white intact breast, its brown baby-bottle nipple stiffening between his thumb and forefinger.

The holoporn expanded a meter above the Aiwa...*Blew By You,* compliments of Beautiful Mutants, Ltd., up in Spocoeur, featuring the new post-Geestring generation of flesh stars profoundly influenced by the BARKS, Back-to-Reality Kommandos, radical sect of the Record of Misery who'd in the last five years gotten fed up with replicas, overwrought body enhancement, pornotechnics, and thus had started looking for something *really* wild. Found it, too, in, of all places, skin-flicks from the seventies and eighties...non-kinked, understated, art-house versions of the then-fledgling genre that was so surprised and thrilled to actually be filming naked human bodies sexing up that it pretty well forget to do anything *but* film naked human bodies sexing up, from every angle you can imagine and with every sort of lighting and lens possible. The outcome was a nostalgic breed of holoporn foregrounding those known as the Immaculates, actors who didn't dye their hair, didn't undergo cosmetic surgery, didn't lack limbs or don exoskeletons or flaunt their diseases, weren't electrocuted, burned, or crucified, didn't use a laproscope during foreplay, eat their own body waste or nick themselves with knives, were neither joybangers nor oil-burners, didn't spank, didn't reroute and staple several of their internal organs to the outside of their stomachs for kicks, didn't employ minors, mirrors, elders, animals, toys, drugs, drones, the handicapped, hermaphrodites, unwilling Catholics, corpses, mud, sandpaper, moving vehicles, or peepholes...did nothing, in fact, but undress and make really wet long-lasting skin-to-skin Touch Sex with lots of kissing, sucking, and groaning while inhabiting some very comfortable beds…and it just drove viewers, like Krystal and Uly, who'd never seen such a thing before, mad.

Blew By You starred Skeets South and Felitia Fenella. Skeets was in his early twenties and looked like what posh male DisCal high school freshmen looked like at the end of the last century: sandy blond, slim and tanned, teeth perfect, hair trimmed like a British businessman's, tummy tight and flat. And yet, next to Felitia Fenella, Skeets seemed the least bit homely.

They frenched on an elegant queen-size bed with silk sheets and canopy, protracted and sumptuous, moist tongues touching tips for several minutes like muscley snakes before sliding out of sight.

Sitting together on their rattan mats, Krystal and Uly watched, captivated by the purity and simple refinement of this show, unmarred, flawless, absolute, like realizing you'd been dreaming in black-and-white your whole life, and henceforth everything would be VR.

When Skeets and Felitia finished exploring each other's bodies, she lay back and he mounted her missionary-style. Before long their rhythm was slow, steady, familiar, savored, like friends, spouses.

Krystal reclined on her mat with her knees spread while Uly extracted a dental dam from a box of them under his computer slabs, all-foured on top of her, inverted, and she took him into her mouth while Uly slipped the dam into place over her hairless mound and began to suckle. Their bodies slickened in the damp room, atmosphere pungent with salt and sex, Skeets and Felitia's guttural moans rising in intensity, and Uly and Krystal imagined a historical dimension where sexing up had been something both more and less than it was now, here, like this…

Afterward, Krystal's head on Uly's chest, an arm across his stomach, a leg across his groin, they didn't say anything for a long time.

The holoporn concluded in a panting rush cut off, a liquid surge, a muscular collapse, and faded into air.

"I'm really glad you came up to Moston," Uly said.

"Yeah," eyes closed, sleepy smile on her lips, "me too."

Someone began yelling down the hall. A CNNer had snuck onto the floor. Before long someone was yelling at the yeller.

Krystal eased herself up on an elbow and looked at Uly.

"So what were all those files about?"

"Files?"

"You said they packed some max strangeness."

He lazily reached over for his Aiwa.

"I've been thinking about something… Here, let me show you."

13

Welcome To My Nightmare. . .

And Please Close The Door

He trawled a sector of info about nukes, stats on failed storage attempts next to a montage of above-ground blasts, debris-choked mushroom clouds spouting thick and sobering from atolls, blue Pacific waters...pigs squealing, skin slobbering down their flanks...roofs flapping from houses...trees bending parallel to earth, leaves sucked right off in a single megalithic inhalation...Nevada sand shivering, sinkholing...aerials of the ominous plant in what had once been Richland, Washington...tall chain-link fences...eerie white plumes of smoke from low flat buildings, tall thin stacks, windowless cement blocks...chemical formulae...bizarre photos of alligators with pygmy penises...spiritless spermatozoa tadpoling under a microscope...and...*presto*, bundles of untitled governcorp files.

"Jesus," Krystal said. "What you just do?"

"I have absolutely no idea. It just happened."

She began reading, distractedly at first, then more and more spooked, realizing it was some sort of hospital report, dated 1948, something to do with experiments performed between 1945 and 1947 on patients around the former United States.

A list of eighteen names appeared on the first screen.

"Call one up," she said.

Uly highlighted and double-clicked on the first, Elmer Allen.

Elmer had been a poor thirty-six-year-old railroad porter from Texas. He'd hurt his leg on the job and received as part of his treatment tracer injections of plutonium-239 which were allowed to remain in his system three days, till he was told his leg was deteriorating and would have to be amputated above the knee.

"They cut his *leg* off?" Krystal said.

Uly dug into sketchy follow-up notes attached to the primary document and discovered Elmer, according to his daughter, Elmerine, had never given his consent for the shot, and, soon after he got it, began suffering unexplainable seizures and bouts of disorientation.

"What kind of unexplainable seizures?" Krystal asked.

"Doesn't say, but I'm beginning to think I have a pretty good idea."

"Try 'radiation experiments.'"

"Right."

Uly dove straight into the history of a 1949 test called Green Run. A secret internal memo uncovered in 1986 described how plant managers at the Hanford Nuclear Facility deliberately released this huge cloud of radioactive iodine-131 (more, in fact, than one hundred times the radiation emitted at the Three Mile Island accident in 1979) to see how far downwind it could be tracked. The thing floated over Spokane to the northwest, drifted all the way to the California-Oregon border to the south.

And there was that word again, *seizures*, more than a dozen times, each disclosing another formidable covert release of radiation into the atmosphere...over New Mexico, Tennessee, and Utah between 1948 and 1952 as part of an attempt by the US government to develop a radiological weapon, or Death Spray (influenced by all those sci-fi flicks from the fifties), or defend against one the Soviet Union might attempt to develop.

And, quantum tick, a bewildering nest of documentation associated with tests conducted on human guinea pigs the first forty-five years after the war...kids fed radioactive Fruit-Loops...brain-damaged adolescents, victims of nuclear experiments in Kazakhstan...average of three accidents a day in the nineties at the Department of Energy's nuclear-weapons complex spread over twenty-five hundred kils and thirteen states...doses of radiation as high as six hundred roentgens administered in some cases, including two in Oregon and Washington beginning in 1963, one hundred thirty-one inmates, many of them black, having their testicles irradiated, each volunteer paid about two hundred dollars by the Atomic Energy Commission after signing a consent form, and, after exposure, given vasectomies in order, according to Dr. Carl Heller, director of the tests, to avoid the possibility of contaminating the general population with irradiation-induced mutants.

As the records melted into the twenty-first century, and the United States into a more speculative NorAm, specific data melted into innuendo, allusion, vague references and denials made by a governcorp liberated by various business-friendly laws of non-disclosure and a media no longer interested in depressing the hell out of the public unless absolutely necessary for ratings, and so, instead of full reports with hypertext documentation, little flakes of information floated up here and there...glimmers of glimmers of connections between those nuclear terrorists who came to the fore in the late nineties and the last of those experimenters from the fifties and sixties and seventies...hints that that infamous dirty bomb exploded on the rooftop of the Beirut Hilton, raining malady on fifty square blocks downwind, gradually killing twenty-four thousand people over the course of the next four months, might have had less to do with strictly political than scientific interest...that the crumbling Department of Energy was, in a concerned-observer-behind-a-concerned-observer kind of way, associated with that small tactical warhead set off by the Medellin Cartel in the basement of the Supreme Court in Bogota, vaporizing a fourth of the city...that those rises in skin cancers, anemia, genetic disorders, immune system deficiencies, once-rare diseases like giantism, cerebral palsy, or those mysterious seizures sizzling through the demographics, dropping sperm counts, reduced fish and wildlife populations, were due to something a little more complicated, a smidgen more sinister, than those ozone-layer rips or measurable greenhouse gases...enough, in truth, to leave Krystal stunned when after another hour or so Uly stretched, cracked his neck, and announced: "Man, I gotta back out. My head's just killing me."

Krystal put down her long-empty beer bottle and stared at the screens of the Aiwa 3500 with a bad case of vacationer's vertigo.

She'd seen *way* too many new facts *way* too fast. It was like walking into this crypt and being asked to locate the one thing that'd changed since you'd last been there, and knowing that that thing was probably a single word with two letters transposed somewhere in one of the computer slabs on the shelves and shelves of them lined up in the library before you.

Everything, it occurred to her, was quiet in that special way it got late at night, small sounds traveling whole levels, the odd snore, a shower tube clicking on at the end of the hall.

"I always thought conspiracies were for dermed-up paranoids," she said.

Uly was leaning forward, massaging his forehead with his palms, Aiwa closed in his lap.

"And I thought dermed-up paranoids were people we could all as a culture feel pretty comfortable about laughing at," he said.

"Persistent delusions."

"Logical, systematized, intricate."

"Which is absolutely true...except for one thing."

"Which is?"

"No fair laughing at them when their conspiracies turn out to be true."

"Cuz then those paranoids...they aren't paranoid anymore."

"Or they *are* paranoid, but they just happen to have this really good point which, even though they're on a perpetual psychic holiday, is objectively verifiable."

"In which case they become...what? Visionaries?"

"Their craziness turns out by freak accident to be an accurate representation of what's going on in the external world. Which, other people being slightly saner, don't see."

"They become mental versions of those monkeys in that room full of typewriters. Every once in a while, purely by chance, one of them invents a Shakespearian sonnet. Or, in this case, a paranoid theory that isn't a paranoid theory, but a fact, at least in one dimension, possibly this...even though the monkey doesn't know it's a fact, because for him it isn't a fact, but a hallucination...Oh, fuck," Uly said.

He gazed straight ahead, blinking, eyes unfocused and flat.

"What?"

He rocked forward and grabbed the back of his skull, rose to his knees as if to stand, and then his whole body convulsed, bucking onto the floor, muscles twittering with electrical activity.

Krystal stared, hands raised like she was being robbed...one beat...two...and then she opened her mouth to scream.

14

Auger Green: Leprous Itch: Rush

Thirty-three minutes later the medivac VTOL banked over the glitter of Spocoeur, beginning its initial descent from the north toward the busy landing pads atop Deaconess Hospital.

Inside, freelance paramedic Ernie-Tubb Trakker scanned back and forth between the comatose guy strapped to the stretcher, skin color and consistency of bad mozzarella, and that batshit chick harnessed to the seat beside him wrapped in a foil blanket who was starting to mumble some pretty portentous-sounding crap under her breath.

Ernie-Tubb was unimpressed. He'd seen all this before. And if you asked him, he'd just *swear* to you he'd seen it all with increasing frequency over the last few weeks—people seizing up at work, walking down the street, another 911er, and Ernie-Tubb, airborne on the graveyard shift, would vocalize the coordinates, his smart plane'd ruminate, and then its muscular acceleration would sink him into the worn gray upholstery.

Nothing like a good accident to shoot him full of sparkling awareness, give him the gift of heightened perception, draw back the drab veil of humdrummedness draped over his sensations long enough for him to get a glorious peek at the big, brawny, woolly bad stuff that made existence something more than a mild cup of herbal tea in the morning and a hot SinSim parlor in the afternoon.

Like tonight, cruising south Moston, not three minutes away from White Bird Six, when the call came, though from who it wasn't clear, because when Ernie-Tubb landed, expecting security to be waiting for him, he found a deserted roof, had to radio, wait for this lone limping guard with an artificial foot to poke his calamine-pink head out of a dented aluminum door, squint around, hobble over, check his papers, and, when he at last reached crypt #1956 where the call was supposed to've originated from, guess what, no phone, just a shut-down Aiwa 3500, and this guy on the floor with the jerks, and this mostly naked admittedly sexy chick huddling on a nearby mat with her lips split in a television shriek with the volume turned down...*third* such scene he'd come across this week, *third*, which made you wonder, didn't it?

Spocoeur was averaging five new nasties a year, none of which seemed to account, by the way, for that yellowish-brown abscess gnawing away at Ernie-Tubb's right shoulder blade beneath his white paramedic flight suit, nagging as a kernel of granola stuck between two molars, problem he'd have to get looked at one of these days...but who could afford such things? Surely not him, not on his shriveled placenta of a salary.

He glanced out the porthole through a sienna fogbank at the enormous swathes of Ride 'n' Save lots ringing the city. These soon gave way to Shanty Town, midnight traffic jam on Boone, hazy reddish holographic ads for Marlboro muggles floating over the Redford Coliseum, part of the halftime entertainment at a knife-wrestling match featuring renowned Pantex Livermore and Zond.

To the south, fires continued chewing through River Park, uncomfortably near the Yeltsen Convention Center.

"The theatrical release..." the girl said.

Ernie-Tubb glanced back at her.

"Come again?"

"Voice of sand...her first lover was named...was named...he was seventeen..."

Morphderm had kicked in on the guy, myoclonic spasms'd subsided, tongue back into his mouth...but that coma was settling in *real* deep...and that chick...Ernie-Tubb'd never seen such an oil-burner, eyes shut, mostly, so you could only see a slice of white between the lids, arms looking like they didn't contain a single bone in them.

"In the subways, in the streets, in corners..." She flinched like a CNNer receiving a special report. "Contact can be...can be..."

They were slowing, losing altitude, hydraulics whirring as the beatup engines began rising from their horizontal to vertical positions for landing.

Spokane River coasted by below, water dark and thick as gravy.

"Tell me something, sweet thing," Ernie-Tubb said, feeling the weight of acceleration ease off his ribs. "What you on?"

"Scarecrow body underneath the flaking girders..."

"Derming something maybe just a little too pure for your own good...hmmm?"

"The uniform head on the uniform body...the flesh...the flesh...if not the softness of flesh, then what can you hold?"

"Sampling a little nano-magic? Augur green? Black ice? Demon breath?"

"And then everything changed...fine hairs on your neck...the shadow sharing the space...the sense of falling..."

He tightened his shoulder harness and looked out the porthole again. The fire department, employing armored personnel carriers backed by Brinks Force troopers, was trying to push toward the blazes scattered throughout the park, but the techno-hippies looked as though they were doing a pretty fair job of repelling them with Molotov cocktails, blackmarket stunguns, flaming rubber-tire barricades.

"Very Koreshian," Ernie-Tubb said aloud.

The riot had been going on for three days, ever since those techno-hippies, believing all-natural was all reactionary, moved out of the chaotic Zone near the airport on Beggars Night and launched an assault on the park, torching bushes, spilling gasoline into the river and igniting it, chainsawing every tree they could lay their Black & Deckers on, some of which, seventy-some-odd-year-old spruce, had fallen the wrong way, and so Ernie-Tubb'd helped medivac the less agile teks in, short-circuited illicit augs fricasseeing their brains, spines snapped, crap he could handle with ease, except for all those fugging head lice from their communal VR rigs, which'd made him have to fumigate his plane at his own expense.

The fires were replaced by the Washington Mutual Building twinkling through vaporous smog to the left, old post office to the right, renovated Davenport Hotel below, Burlington Northern tracks, Highway 90 (and another midnight traffic jam), and the high-walled safe-zone compound housing the hospital complex.

Ernie-Tubb gripped his armrests and seconds later felt the soft bump of tires touching down atop the Adam Curry wing.

Before he could exhale, the hatch blew open, smell of jet fuel, fish reek, and decomposing vegetation flooding the cabin, and two orderlies peered in, nodded at him, wordlessly hoisted themselves aboard, swung the stretcher with the comatose guy toward the entry, lowered it, began hustling across the rooftop among a small fleet of VTOLs revving, landing, taking off, on their way to the elevators, Ernie-Tubb Trakker right behind them, because he knew if he let them out of his sight now he might as well just kiss his hard-earned credit goodbye...

As they took their place in line with the other freelance paramedics and patients waiting for the retinal scans and next ride down, Ernie-Tubb stole a moment to look up at the sky.

Pinkgray, it was crosshatched with contrails like a great swath of fabric and, somehow, this image worked as a kind of epiphany on him, made him see himself as if from one of the VTOLs descending above him.

This was what life had to offer him, he knew, and it was what he'd dreamed about, hoped for, craved...and he was doing it, was actually *doing* it...surprised him every time he thought about it.

He smiled to himself, stretching, thinking *going to be a great night*, unaware for a few breaths of the leprous itch taking hold below his white paramedic flight suit on his right shoulder blade, *a stupendous night, forever and ever.*

15

Secret History

Uly's arms felt too thin and sinewy, his legs too long and bony, and when he reached up he touched a nose more bulbous than his, ears larger, long dark hair pulled back into a braid.

He looked down and saw scuffed brown toes of high-laced boots poke out from beneath a loose gray-and-green striped skirt, and it was like seeing a photo of himself he never remembered being taken in a place he'd never visited.

He stopped and raised his head.

It was hot, a white sun overhead in the lemony sky, even though it was already autumn.

To his right trickled what was left of the Humboldt River (he knew the name, knew the place), no more than a series of warm half-stagnant pools of tea-colored water. They'd been following it several days, along its banks scrubby bushes and dwarfish leafless willows. Behind those, parched grass broadcasting across craggy meadows, a palette of washed-out colors, and, on either side of the river, rocky irregular hills and palisades patched with sagebrush and greasewood.

The wagon train was passing a place called Gravelly Ford. The tangy scent of cow dung, mule and ox hide, dog piss, human per-spiration, musty wagon canvas, old smoke, unwashed hair, and scorched vegetation came to him...and that alkali dust, bitter and stifling, billows of it, thunderclouds of it, continuously, deep in the fibers of his clothes, in the fur of the animals, stinging his eyes, gritty between his teeth, clogging his nose, heavy and viscous down his throat.

Next came the clamor, everywhere, a metallic storm in his head, tumultuous clatter, squeak, screech, and rumble of wagon wheels stretching back two, three miles, abrupt horse snorts, hooves, whip cracks, cattle honks, dog yips, crunching gravel, men's voices shouting up and down the line, women's laughter from the backless front seats as they bounced and jarred on thick springs, knitting, constant clank of cooking pots and pans and tin plates, thunk of trunks and kegs and chairs and lamps and farm implements roped to the sides, rattle of chains and eating utensils, someone singing to himself several yards away, an Irish folksong, that Dolan guy, kids with half an eye on playing, half on keeping pace with the caravan, squealing down by the water, scampering to catch up...and behind it all the steady arid whisper of wilderness wind.

"Come along, Ginny," called someone to his right, Sam Shoemaker, one of the teamsters, on horseback, so lanky, small-boned and devoid of meat, Uly figured a good desert gust would kick him out of the saddle like a cranky mule's hooves. "Keep your mouth open like that, child," he said, pulling back on his reigns, sunlight almost erasing the reddish blond tufts patching his jaw, "you're gonna catch us a bird fer dinner."

He laughed and spurred his mount, began to drift toward the tail of the train where the milch cows, spare oxen and horses ranged.

"Yes, sir," Uly called after him, surprised at the sound of his own voice, high and unbroken with age or hormones.

He wanted to stay still, to watch and listen to this new world forming around him, but knew he had to catch up with his stepfather's wagon, gigantic two-story affair with a side entrance, riding chamber, Concord stage-coach seats, sheet-iron stove, looking glass, sleeping compartment, good library of standard works, and storage rooms, and so he began to jog.

His rough blouse, gray-and-green striped to match his skirt, chafed against his nipples and he remembered how sore his breast-buds were, how they'd been that way ever since February or March, a month or two before the train'd set out from Springfield that bright mid-April morning.

An image of the tidy city he'd never seen before flickered into his mind, square redbrick buildings, clean streets, black iron fences like untouched toys.

He saw the caravan of thirty-five emigrants and nine wagons, starting from the town center, a tiny sample of the seven thousand wagons newspapers reported were going to take the journey this season.

The pain in his breasts was part of becoming a woman, his mother had told him when he'd asked.

"You have trouble with that one, Ginny," she'd said, "well, you just hang on. Going to be lots worse where that came from."

He thought she'd meant all those bone-cracking headaches she suffered for days and days on end, the kind that made her see everything in various shades of gray behind her brown eyes that didn't quite match each other in size or shape, and take to bed in her dark room upstairs, missing meals, unable to sleep, unable to talk to him or turn up the corners of her down-turned mouth or help him with his daily piano lessons.

Recently, though, he gathered maybe she hadn't meant those headaches at all, no, but, rather, time itself…how, over the last few months, it'd come to feel slow and dull and open-ended, dream-like, just one foot after the next, so much so, one blink of the journey looking like so many others before it, the company had lost track once somewhere back on the plains, communally falling off a single day in its calculations.

Except that wasn't exactly true, either, because every evening Stepfather and the others conversed till late around the campfires about how time wasn't slow at all. It was no snail. It was running, sprinting away from them, a coyote under the gun, year shrinking like a piece of rapidly drying fruit, winter a breath closer each moment, each step they took, sleep they slept, and everyone knew it, everyone could feel the increasing chill at night, imagine the first feathery snowflakes beginning to thicken out of the sky in the mountains ahead.

≈

The problem with the Pioneer Palace Car was all that grandiose bulk. It was a beauty, no doubt, something to be proud of as a family, a comfortable well-stocked hotel on wheels, carrying more than enough food to see the Reeds to the coast, not to mention clothes for all climates, gew-gaws to be given to the Indians on the way, laces and silks to be traded with the Mexicans for Californian lands, enough mattresses, quilts, heirlooms, and even some pieces of prized furniture to launch a new household.

Only it was also half again as tall as the others in the train, wider, twice as heavy, the result being it kept bogging down in soft soil so bad there'd begun to be misgivings about the delays it had triggered, serious talk between Stepfather and some of the others about the possibility of redistributing provisions, leaving the thing behind, abandoning its skeleton, just like they'd had to do with those two smaller ones when the elephant'd come visiting in the Great Salt Lake Desert last month.

And now, up ahead, Uly could see the wagon had halted again, front of the train having reached the base of a steep sandy hill with rock formations stabbing out on top, other wagons slowing to a stop behind it, women and small children beginning to ease themselves down from the seats for the long climb by foot, men dismounting, helping the teamsters who'd begun yoking the oxen for double-teaming.

Two of the Graveses' wagons had already crested the hill, but the third had stalled a fourth of the way up. John Snyder, husky bad-tempered teamster whose face was always raw as ham, was driving, and from the look of the situation he'd been mired when he'd tried to make it with a single team. The next wagon in line was the Pioneer Palace Car, and Uly knew that nice man, Milton Elliott, Milt, clipped sandy hair, cauliflower nose, was at the reigns. Milt'd double-teamed, adding to the usual four yoke of oxen, just like he should've and, as Uly approached the base of the hill, the huge wagon carefully swung to the right and made to pass the Graveses' faltering one.

The path was narrow, and Milt was doing everything he could to stay as far to the side of the wagon Snyder was driving as possible. Only somehow, as he brought his teams parallel with Snyder's, Milt's lead-yoke tangled with his and oxen snorted, faltered, began bellowing.

Snyder, half standing, shouted something at Milt, and Uly, still some way off from the scene, could barely hear the words, but saw by Milt's reaction they were rife with venom.

Milt shouted something ugly back, half standing himself, and then, stunning, a thick black snake leapt from the Graveses' wagon and bit Milt's lead oxen on the side of the head.

Snyder's whip, butt-end reversed.

Before anyone had a chance to react, that snake came down again. And again; and again.

The oxen roared, veered toward the edge of the path. Milt fell back in his seat, yanking on the reigns, cursing, whip pouncing so swiftly it appeared to double, multiply. There were five of them. Seven.

The Pioneer Palace Car groaned and swayed.

A tenth of a second later Uly's stepfather, high forehead, large ears, full mustache, trimmed beard just tracing the outline of his jaw, shot from behind another wagon farther back along the line. He was on his gray racing mare, Glaucus, hunkered down, spurring the horse's flanks, surging up the hill, focused as a cougar closing on a jackrabbit, and in an instant was driving his mount between the two wagons.

"Back off!" he yelled. "Back off, both of you!"

Snyder's whip snapped forward. Strips of crimson flashed into sight along the oxen's barreled ribs.

The Pioneer Palace Car creaked into sand and sagebrush, rocking.

Stepfather leaned over and tried to snatch the whip away from the teamster, but Snyder, furious, wrenched it back and, now fully standing, altered its trajectory in a tick.

The leather eel hung in the autumn sunlight a glistening black blink, whacked down across Stepfather's skull.

In the pulse it took that clap to reach Uly, he saw the busy unpaved streets of Independence, all sticky gumbo in the spring rain...rickety wooden storefronts where Stepfather bought his last supplies before joining the jumble of wagons waiting along the brim of the final asylum, readying to strike out toward rumor and prosperity, many of their inhabitants, including Stepfather and Stepfather's well-to-do elderly friend, George Donner, spurred on by Lansford W. Hastings's famous book, *The Emigrants' Guide to Oregon and California*, a copy of which was tucked into each man's trunk.

Uly saw the travelers standing around their wagons while the last evening came on, speaking of their approaching odyssey as an enjoyable outing, its terminus a series of balmy Pacific breezes and inexpensive fertile acreage in unspoiled country where midwinter was serene as early summer...and that's what the first few weeks had assured, warm sunny weather, easy flat land undulating into grassy emerald expanses sprinkled with wildflowers, the train gaining altitude, covering twenty miles a day without effort, encampment at dusk, wagons circling into a temporary corral for the cattle after grazing, and outside, near the tents, buffalo and deer meat cooking over large open fires, emigs discussing their unexceptional advance, becoming acquainted with the affable strangers in their company, enjoying bread baked every day in Dutch ovens, fresh butter, salt pork, pickles, beans, hominy, cheese, dried fruit, coffee, milk, and, after all this, singing ballads into the night, or watching that Irishman, Patrick Dolan, perform a jig for them on the lowered hind-gate of a wagon.

They knew before the 1840s fewer than twenty thousand whites lived west of the Mississippi and that now all that was changing in rich ways. They warmed with luminous ambition even when, before they'd left the plains, news arrived by messenger that the United States had finally slid into war with Mexico over southwestern territory, or Lewis Keseberg, that tall, blond, frighteningly handsome man from Westphalia who spoke four languages, robbed a Sioux burial site along the trail one afternoon and stripped the body of its buffalo robes till the other emigs, led by Stepfather, forced him to return them. The passage seemed charmed in spite of, or perhaps even because of, these misfortunes, surrounded by a golden nimbus, George Donner's wife, Tamsen, a keen slight schoolmistress weighing less than a hundred pounds who planned to open a young ladies' seminary on the shores of the Pacific, commenting around the campfire one night: "If the road ahead holds no meaner tribulations than the road behind, then this venture of ours is going to be a pleasurable one indeed."

Everyone agreed.

At South Pass, the train pushing toward the Continental Divide in rougher terrain of Oregon country, a man on horseback met them. He passed around an open letter from none other than Lansford W. Hastings, author of *The Emigrants' Guide to Oregon and California*, announcing a freshly explored and more effortlessly passable route running south of the Great Salt Lake that would save them upwards of three or four hundred miles. The letter went on to declare Hastings, over from the coast, would wait at Fort Bridger on the south bank of Black's Fork to guide those who might be interested. All going well, they might save two, maybe three weeks in the crossing.

When the Donner Party arrived at Fort Bridger eleven days later, its members were surprised to find Hastings wasn't waiting. Instead they discovered a scrappy pair of log cabins, a run-down trading post, a family from Missouri named McCutchen wishing to make arrangements for passage with them, and the owner, Jim Bridger, celebrated trapper who that evening told stories about tribes of man-bears living in the Wahsatch and beyond, dark hairy pelts, long arms, short legs, wide feet, flat noses, an intelligence that said they were no animals, a fact easy enough to discern when you heard them sing at night, or stumbled across their nests in the trees lined with bluebird feathers, wolf skulls, carved clubs.

Hastings had left several days before, taking sixty-six wagons with him. The season was getting late and there were few weeks to spare before the first snows began covering the mountain passes. The others were welcome to try to catch up with him if they wished. It would cost ten dollars a wagon, payment in advance.

Tamsen voiced reservations, arguing the party should stay with the well-traveled, well-marked trail. At least then they'd know what to expect. But others spoke in favor of the time they'd save on the alternate route. They'd be with Hastings in a week if they pushed hard, and the remainder of their journey would prove placid as its outset. They'd not only regain the few days they'd now need to regroup at Fort Bridger, but weeks into the bargain.

Within twenty-four hours of setting out again, they came to a fork in the trail. To the right was the old artery toward Fort Hall, smooth and beaten down by years of use. To the left were new wheel ruts flagging the beginning of Hastings' Cut-off through the Wahsatch and across the Great Basin. The emigrants debated one last time, then curved left, Tamsen gloomy and dispirited...and almost immediately ran into bad road, the route proving far cruder than the one they were familiar with, skirting a dangerous hillside, dropping into a narrow ravine, becoming nearly impassable, forcing the travelers to lock their wheels at the top of many descents, rope their wagons, slide them down.

The company grew disquieted. Talk arose of backtracking. Yet everyone was aware by doing so they'd lose several more days and, besides, the trail was bound to open before much longer; Hastings had promised as much in his letter, and Jim Bridger had corroborated his story. All they had to do was brace themselves, tough out this stretch, and everything would be fine in the end.

On August sixth the Donner Party came across another letter from Hastings, this one stuck in a bush along the trail, announcing the way worsened ahead as it sunk farther into Weber Canyon. There was scarcely room to ride beside the river, boulders blocked the path, in places wagons would again have to be hoisted over the spurs of the mountains, so best to encamp and send forward scouts and hope that Hastings would return and guide the group through a substitute route.

Stepfather and two others clattered off on horseback late that day.

They didn't return within forty-eight hours and apprehension rippled through the caravan. Hastings said the trail was treacherous. Worse, the travelers were entering Digger country, land of the mean-spirited desert breeds, tricksters and thieves, horseless and homeless, armed with weak bows, dangerous in their squalor.

If the travelers *did* begin to backtrack, Tamsen asked, what then? There wouldn't be time to strike off west again after necessary rest and repairs…not and assure safe passage through the mountains before the first hard snowfall.

The third day came and went, and the fourth. On the fifth, George Donner called a vote and the decision was made to break camp next morning and double back.

That evening, however, they heard hooves approaching. Stepfather and the other men broke through the brush. Though his team had caught up with Hastings, Hastings had refused to return. He'd led them to the top of a nearby peak and pointed out the general course the train should follow. Time was running out, he said. He didn't have the days necessary to retrace his route and see them through. This was the best he could do.

The Donner Party embarked early next morning and the going turned even meaner. There was no road, not even the hint of Hastings' Cut-off. Lacking mountain skills, they were compelled to hack a zigzagging trail through underbrush along a creek with axes, picks, shovels. Twenty-foot tall willow, alder, and aspen knotted with service-berries and wild rose. The creek twisted brutally, the procession's path crossing it twice each mile, and instead of finding relief farther on, they encountered two gigantic swamps, more dense undergrowth, exhaustion and frustration. Some emigs refused to work, exasperated and worn down, claiming this was Reed's fault, he'd gotten Hastings' route all wrong, they'd have no part of it.

The elephant journeyed with them, had come to stay, they all knew it, and this knowledge unhinged them further. When they broke out onto the plains, unsettled, aware how much time they'd lost (over the course of the previous twenty one days they'd advanced only thirty-six miles) a twenty-five-year-old invalid who'd joined the party in July died of consumption. They halted long enough to construct a coffin from wagon boards and bury him, then pushed on, arriving at Twenty Wells where the geography turned magical and malevolent, unlike anything they'd ever seen. Holes in the hard dry ground ranged from six inches to nine feet across, each filled to the brim with cold azure water. If several buckets-full were extracted, the well instantly replenished itself to the brim...but never more. Beyond, they passed a commotion of rocks that resembled a European castle, a clean clear stream with water so salty no one dared drink. The land flattened, the soil turned beige-pink and gravelly. Purplish mountains floated low along the horizon, torn strips of newspaper, never drawing closer, a parched wind stirring through the clinging olive-green and pale green-gray brush and gnarled, low-slung, almost leafless trees. Dust devils whirled forty or fifty feet in the air. Hot brownish haze overran the travelers' perspective.

Everything leveled, turned horizontal, vacant, shot through with an eerie arctic desolation. Even the smells vanished in the thin baking atmosphere...and a single board tilted like a fence post, note scraps trembling around it on the ground, remnants of another message from Hastings. Tamsen bent down and reconstructed it.

Two days and two nights of hard driving to reach the next grass and water.

They regrouped, rested thirty-six hours, prepared for the final thrust before completing the Cut-off and rejoining the main trail. The men filled barrels, pots, pans, and pails with drinking water, cut grass for cattle. The women cooked food to last the passage, knowing there'd be no fuel later on. As insurance, they decided to amass provisions for three days and nights, and, ready, struck off, first turtling across a thousand-foot ridge beneath brittle sunlight, winding down into barren volcanic hills, rose- and peach-colored rocks, and then onto an extensive perfectly flat desert glittering white as frost. Their wagon wheels crunched through its crust, sank inches into a salty slush. They broke ranks, fanned out in an attempt to avoid each others' ruts. Heat nausea seeped through them, their appetites receded, an ovenish incandescence broiled the air.

At the end of the second day they found themselves still in the middle of the desert, ore-green mountains on the horizon. Late into the third, their water gave out. Unbelieving, some panicked, abandoned their wagons where they'd bogged down, unyoked their oxen, and drove forward. Cattle collapsed or, blind with thirst, scattered. Behind them, men carried empty water pails over their arms. Women and children gathered in dead wagons, heat concentrated like blast furnaces, waiting for their husbands to return, expecting the nights to provide relief from the harsh temperatures, but, as the sun went down, they encountered another extreme, a bitter cold sweeping across the desert, whisked by a wicked wind. With the next sunrise, Stepfather mounted Glaucus and rode ahead in search of a spring. The ore-green mountains appeared closer. Surely there would be a source of water there. And so the emigs pressed through scalding heat, driven by hope and fear, eyes and sinuses dehydrated, lips cracked, skin on fire. When they reached their goal well past noon, they discovered the green was nothing more than dry greasewood...no trace of water anywhere, just terrain stippled with animal burrows, rock chunks, clumps of thigh-high wiry sagebrush and low spiky cacti, gravel that made walking hard, head-ringing silence and, from where they stood, openly agitated and anxious, an appalling sight: the static salt plain extending below them for at least another dozen miles before rising into another ridge.

There, thirty miles from where he'd left his family, Stepfather found water. Within minutes he filled two gourds, turned, and began his ride back through the furious cold and darkness, heat and salt glare. Nearing the caravan next dawn, he met what was left of the wagon train, dissolved, dispirited, his wife, Margaret, weak, raided by a paralyzing headache, unable to rise from her bed... Patty, dark-haired eight-year-old with a perpetual look of incredulity sculpted into her features... Jim, chubby-legged five-year-old already frightened by everything in his lopsided universe... Uly, throat swollen, beaten by the heat, shouldering his three-year-old brother Tommy.

Stepfather's drivers had released the yoked oxen shortly after he'd left, attempting to drive them ahead, but the animals, maddened with thirst, bolted. Nine were still missing and those remaining stumbled as they lumbered along. Yet this wasn't bad as some of the emigs in the party had had it...thirty-six head of working oxen were gone, large numbers of cattle were dead, equipment and supplies jettisoned to make the crossing easier, four wagons left behind, and, all told, instead of the thirty-five or forty miles Hastings had promised, the trek had stretched eighty.

Stepfather bartered with Franklin Graves and Patrick Breen for an ox from each. These, together with his own ox and cow, were the best team he could muster.

Resentful toward him, worried about their own welfare, the other travelers refused to carry his extra food in their wagons without being allowed to use it. Stepfather argued with them but, seeing the extremity of the situation, relented. He became quiet, inward-looking, returned to the Palace Car with his back rigid and lips thin.

The Donner Party reorganized as best it could, a sorry-looking group, surviving oxen skeletal, here and there a cow under yoke, horses worn, herd of loose cattle in poor health, emigs disconcerted and weary.

They sent two scouts forward to Fort Sutter in California for help and provisions: Charles Stanton, a slight thirty-five-year-old traveling by himself from the village of Chicago, and William McCutchen, thirty-year-old giant from Missouri who'd joined the party with his wife and baby at Fort Bridger. Meanwhile, William Eddy, a carriage-maker from Illinois, put his team to Stepfather's wagon and a man named Pike took Eddy's rig and abandoned his own, reducing the number of wagons to eighteen, and they began moving across another wide dry span, each man taking his turn leading the train and taking on the hard task of breaking trail. They mounted a pass and clumsily descended into a fine treeless valley where the country at last began improving, weather cooling, herds of antelope speckling the grassy meadows, mountain sheep browsing on the hills, and before long arrived at the banks of the Humboldt, forded it, and with eerie simplicity rejoined the well-packed road of the main trail.

They'd made it, they were back, but they were also no longer the same people who'd entered Fort Bridger in July.

They were through the worst, but also fatigued beyond imagining, apprehensive, unnerved, restless. Things could only improve. Stanton and McCutchen would return within several weeks with fresh supplies. The company would make better time. They'd be in California by the end of November.

≋

Stepfather slipped down Glaucus's flank and landed on his hands and knees in the sand, long gash running from his thick black hair to his left temple. He shook his head, shook it again, blood blinding him.

Snyder leaped from the Graveses' wagon, reversed whip still raised, moving in for another strike.

Others finally comprehended what was happening and shouted for the two to ease up, but Snyder and Stepfather had fixed on each other. Margaret Reed hopped from the wagon and rushed forward, putting herself between them. Snyder lashed and caught her on the arm. She stumbled back, dazed, and, when Stepfather rose shakily, he was holding his hunting knife. Snyder's whip snapped again, catching him on the shoulder. Stepfather staggered, and, with explosive energy, lunged, catching Snyder just below the collarbone.

Blood sunburst his shirt black-red and Snyder brought his whip down twice more on Stepfather, felling him to his knees...

And then everything stopped.

Snyder, face raw, stared from Margaret, clutching her arm and returning his stare, bewildered, to Stepfather, once more on his hands and knees.

He inhaled deeply, dropped his whip, turned, and, very straight, began to walk up the hill. He took several steps, tottered, and collapsed. Young Billy Graves caught him and eased him to the ground.

"I am dead," Snyder said.

Stepfather, blood trickling down his face and neck, pursued him. The people gathering around Snyder parted. A puddle of black liquid collected beneath the wounded man's neck.

Unable to focus, he squinted up in Stepfather's direction. His lips began moving.

The emigrants encamped, the Pioneer Palace Car at the top of the sandy hill far removed from the others.

George Donner ordered a council from which Stepfather and the other Reeds were excluded. But from where he stood in his family's wagon Uly could hear the raised voices hot with rage in the distance, Tamsen taking written statements from each witness for the trial awaiting Stepfather in California, shouts for retribution, Keseberg's baritone crackling with open hatred.

Margaret was put to bed in the sleeping compartment, rattled and perplexed, skull crashing, arm swollen greenish-blue where the whip had bitten it. Tommy, scared by the anger frying in the air, nuzzled beside her. Patty and Jim, wordless, watched while Uly lit a fire in the sheet-iron stove in the riding chamber and heated water in a kettle.

He made his stepfather sit still on one of the stage-coach seats, kneeled before him on the wooden floor, and, hands unsteady, clipped hair away from the three blood-caked cuts on his head, dabbed them with a wet cloth, bandaged them with strips of linen.

Stepfather gazed straight ahead, muscles in his jaw slackening and tensing, large palms gripping his kneecaps.

Done, his eyes met Uly's.

"I should not have asked so much of you, Ginny."

He rose and disappeared into the sleeping compartment, returned wearing a clean shirt, pants, and vest, strode over to the looking glass, ran a brush through his hair, examined and adjusted the bandages. He rearranged his vest, tucked in the shirt, tugged down the sleeves, and consulted the looking glass. His eyes, brown and bright as mahogany, investigated themselves. He turned and walked toward the doorway.

"I am going out," he said, intent on some object far away on the other side of the canvas. "My rifle is next to my bed. It is loaded."

Uly watched him leave, looked over at his brother and sister.

"You stay here," he told Patty. "Take care that mother doesn't want for anything. Keep an eye on Tommy and Jim. You understand me?"

He stood and stepped through the canvas flap onto the ladder. Several hundred yards away, at the base of the sandy hill on the banks of the river, the rest of the wagons had circled, cows and oxen grazing nearby among a stand of naked willows. Though still only late afternoon, the light was waning and a bonfire had already been lit. The emigs crowded around it. Keseberg had propped up his wagon-tongue with an ox-yoke, ready for the hanging.

Uly jumped to the ground and, skirt chuffing, half-ran toward the commotion. More voices met him as he approached, accusations and counter-accusations. He lowered himself behind a stunted bush in the dying light to listen.

The Graves clan wanted retaliation. They were infuriated Reed had been allowed to live this long.

Beside them stood Keseberg, dirty blond hair accenting his violent red face, cherishing his own grudge against Stepfather sparked months ago at that Sioux burial site. Keseberg reminded the band of the mistakes Stepfather had made, how he'd advocated taking Hastings' Cut-off only to lead them into a series of calamities, misguided them through the Wahsatch, leeched off them after the debacle in the barrens. It was obvious enough: Reed, in keeping with his haughtiness, had deliberately ordered Milt to overtake Snyder in the Graveses' wagon, abused Snyder verbally, baited him, intentionally allowed the fight between them to escalate by drawing his knife, murdered a man much less-well-armed than himself...all this, and only the most perfunctory remorse.

Stepfather stood by, listening, and when at last was asked to speak on his own behalf said: "The man drew a whip upon my wife. I pulled my knife to defend her. I killed him. I am to blame."

Such brevity only fueled the emigrants' indignation. Elizabeth, Franklin Graves' middle-aged wife, urged justice. Keseberg demanded the noose. Billy Graves, Franklin's eighteen-year-old son, took a step toward him.

William Eddy and Milt Elliott blocked his way, each palming a six-shooter.

Billy glared at them.

Eddy spoke, arguing in favor of compromise. Whatever'd transpired, whoever's fault it might have been, the fact remained one man was dead and another had admitted killing him. Self-defense or no, the situation demanded retribution. This much was certain...and yet it was also certain Reed would never have drawn his knife in the first place had Snyder not turned his whip on Reed's wife. Could the rest of the party not thus see fit to allow Reed some sort of concession…to leave his firearms behind and venture out alone, surrendering himself to God's own hand for judgment?

"I shall not abandon my family," Stepfather said.

"You have no choice in the matter," said Franklin, shocked.

"I will not desert them. No man would."

"You're hardly in a position to negotiate such matters, Jim."

"I'm sorry," said George Donner. "This has gotten loose from us all. Only thing we can do now is try to minimize the consequences. Think of what you're saying. Think of the outcome of your words."

"I am. I have. What would you have me do? What would any of you do?"

"What if we were to assure you no harm would come to your family?" asked Eddy. "That, upon my honor, Milt and I would look after Margaret and the children?"

"It might well be in their best interests this way, Mr. Reed," said Milt. "For their safety as well as yours."

"Besides," added Eddy, "what might become of the party if Stanton and McCutchen fail in their efforts to procure food and supplies at Fort Sutter? You may consider yourself our second order of defense."

"You will aid Margaret and the others much more by doing so than you ever might remaining here," George said.

Stepfather studied Donner, then turned his attention to Eddy and Milt, Franklin behind them.

Evening was settling. The bonfire cracked and spat clouds of honey-yellow sparks into the bluing air. Stepfather looked up at the sky, around him at the others. Tamsen avoided his eyes. Keseberg and Elizabeth watched him with unobstructed malice. Franklin's face was empty, waiting for emotion to load it in response to Stepfather's next move.

Stepfather turned and began walking away from the assembly, his gait artificial, baronial.

He spoke over his shoulder without stopping: "I shall set forth tomorrow morning, after I have packed, said goodbye to my family, and helped bury Mr. Snyder. Meantime, a good night to you all. I imagine you will need it."

16

Waiting For The End Of The World

Krystal felt the same way about hospitals other people did about the custardish gunk that jelled along the edges of really bad unwashed cuts. She hated them, despised them. They made her feel she had army ants skittering around in her armpits because, in this very authentic, very indisputable, wholly business-like fashion, hospitals whistled lasciviously at her to get her attention and then reminded her things sometimes were just a shitload more complex than she would've liked them to be. They spoke to her, all hot and heavy, tongue lolling, red eyes half-slit with desire, of geometric fractals and maps of downtown Beijing at rush hour.

And here she was, standing smack in the middle of one, Adam Curry wing of Deaconess, old antiseptic-scented jalopy of a high-walled safe-zone medical compound thrown up in 2006 on the cadaver of the original, growing organically over the next few decades with all the organizational skill of a stoned spider in high orbit, pure medieval verve, a Kevorkian ward here, a roachburger bar there, an emergency room on the roof, a tatt parlor in the basement, a computer-induced corneal burn unit off a luminous white lobby tucked down a series of long dim passageways lined with cell-like cubicles posted with orange biohazard stickers housing osteal liquefaction victims in disposable cots, leprotics, victims of neo-syphilitic posterior spinal sclerosis, cerebral tuberculosis, shock hepatitis, whatever new plague came dragging its numb clubfoot behind it down the pike this month, faded institutional-green paint crumbling off walls in flakes so big you could barely make out the cyrillic-lettered graffiti spread there, air conditioning unit wheezing to life every twenty minutes or so for a brief two in a feeble attempt to save energy, outcome being that everyone, credit-spewing patients, filtration-masked Uncle Meats, somato-enhanced orderlies, horse-hipped nurses carrying aluminum baseball bats by their sides to ward off potential attackers, perspired like human-sized versions of Richard Nixon's upper lip.

Which put Krystal in the same frame of mind people entered when the elevator they were riding jerked to a stop between floors for no special reason and everybody, till this instant mere strangers, exchanged insecure grins.

She knew she was sporting that I-gotta-get-outta-here expression of hers, and she knew there was absolutely nothing she could do about it, and she knew she should stay with Uly till she got some word on how he was doing, he looked so terribly sad, skin doughy, eyelids slivered open just enough to reveal a little of those blank whites on the other side, lips parted exactly as if he was about to say the word *ah*...she felt so awful for him, he seemed vulnerable as those baby rats she'd come across one morning nesting behind the chemical toilet down the hall in White Bird Six, motherless blind pink-gray bodies writhing...but, *god*, she'd already been here nearly three hours, it was already way the hell into the crazy season of the night, and so far the Uncle Meats hadn't even been by to see the poor guy and that maniac freelancer who'd medivacked them had hung around precisely long enough to get his own credit upped, then vanished in a cloud of exhaust like some frock-tailed magician, leaving it to the orderlies, one tall and skinny, one short and fat, some medical version of Abbott and Costello, to gurney Uly through an intricate combination of seedy corridors, down several floors, plug him into an IV and oxygen canister in a monkishly minuscule room, stow his stuff in the dented safe stuck to the crap-colored wall via some mean fuck-not-with-me bolts, feign a couple looks of concern, and vamoose...giving Krystal nothing to do except peer out the plate-glass window comprising the whole north face of the building, trying to speed up time by an act of will, make it do something *she* wanted for a change, which, okay, felt a lot like trying to touch her nose to her own spine, except this was the only option left to her, her only real choice, and so she took it, watching the eternal traffic jam shimmering on I-90, the fires still burning in River Park visible through the chinks between the Davenport Hotel and Washington Mutual Building, still chewing up trees and shrubs and grass a hundred yards from the Yeltsen Convention Center, tiny armored personnel carriers creeping back and forth among the flames, every once in a while a Molotov cocktail igniting, its sphere of white light ascending like a prophecy into the brownish blushing sky.

And so, several in-sucks of breath later, she found herself wandering down a grimy hall in search of an Uncle Meat, any Uncle Meat, in order to physically lug him back to Uly if need be, wishing she'd been carrying one of those baseball bats about now, sour aroma of ammonia and formaldehyde condensing the air, making it feel moist and hot...penises, hand-prints (several fingers missing from each), and headless earth goddesses with gigantic breasts, legs spread wide, sprayed on the cement blocks in fluorescent lemons and limes like some hip contemporary cave paintings, crushed hypodermics on the floor, a broken stomach pump in a corner, a rusting oxygen tank on its side, a stray rubber glove, a dried tar-black puddle of who knew what, passing darkened room after darkened room with all the grandeur of doorless closets on space shuttles, yellow light flickering over a narrow cot, erratic beep on a morphine-drip monitor, stopping by a fountain for a drink (Krystal's hair wet as if she'd just stepped from a shower, chest tight as the membrane on a drum) only to come up with a mouthful of fish-tasting water...and then, fleetingly, through the wrong metal-armored door and into what might've been an alley, or a small warehouse, or perhaps just left-over space between building components, the strange thing being there was no sky above her, no ceiling either, the potential for both blocked by overlaid extensions, rope-ladders, ventilation pipes, satellite receivers, clumps of cables, high-voltage lines, intersecting gangways, and exposed girders...growling canines in mid-coitus behind a trash bin five meters into the murkiness.

An Oshkosh-overall-clad schlub with what seemed to be red socks and matching sunscreen and eye-patch, stereo cable wrapped around his waist as a belt, cooked what looked like a portion of intestines in an upturned hubcap against a fragment of brick partition. He raised his head and smiled at her with gopher lips overdrooping an inordinately fine set of implanted central incisors, producing a goatish leer.

"You want a baby?" he asked loudly, to be heard over the copulating dogs.

"I want an Uncle Meat," Krystal said. "I have this like really really sick boyfriend and I think he's in a coma and I think I like him just a whole bunch more than I ever expected to and he's been up in his room for hours and nobody's come to see him yet and I'm going apeshit and all I want to do is talk to someone who knows what the fuck's going on. You know what the fuck's going on?"

"I can get you a baby. Three-hundred-thousand credits."

The cooking intestines, blue smoke rising off them, smelled like vomit.

"I don't want a fucking baby. I want a fucking Uncle Meat."

"Two minutes. You come. Blond, blue-eyed, male or female, guaranteed healthy. Good organs…"

The door hammered shut behind her as she backtracked plenty fast, it striking her she'd forgotten to take down Uly's room number, meaning she was lost, had no *idea* which way to turn in these obscure passages, no course of action but to plow on, the stray idea sneaking into her awareness this mess had gotten just bizarrely out of control, at which point the ghost began speaking, but not to her, mumbling to itself, *the void gone too, receding…the black hole in the foreskull…on our way through the arctic span…we're coming…hold tight, hold tight…it is all around us like a new world…there's nothing else, no one else, just the mouth moving, always moving…*at which point Krystal almost walked into this woman with bandages covering her whole head except for the eye holes, straws to breathe and eat through, a face-lift job wearing a backless Azid Reign paper robe with fake fur trim, and Krystal veered again, *parting swiftly, uninvited evolution, the most sorrowful thing in the universe, random acts of silence…the ability to hear dying away, fallout shelters with plush carpeting…*was soon ascending a flight of wooden steps in an echoing stairwell, remembering as she climbed the *other* reason she hated, despised, these places, remembering her own visit to a blackmarket clinic when she was thirteen.

How she'd dreamed of it for months, of the elaborate chain-stitch pattern they'd seal her cosmetic mastectomy with, how the asymmetry of her chest would come to serve as an objective correlative for her asymmetrical teen personality, a photo montage of mismatched selves and emotions, how she'd saved and saved, her progens even helping, not knowing what else to do, using her flash-trend addictions as bait to keep her grades high, and how when she was reclining in the dentist's chair at that clinic something had misfired with the cheap anesthetic she'd chosen, scrambled itself and diluted, and she'd found herself straying in and out of sleep as they carved her up, heard them snipping through skin, peeling back muscle, scooping out her now dead mammary gland, nipple, fat, everything, dead blackness giving way to burning blue chunks of pain and chaos, the jostle of the confused Uncle Meat, the quick voices of calamity around her, never imagining the person she was when she was thirteen would not be the same person she was when she was sixteen, that that older person could possibly want different things than the younger, different addenda and attenuations, regret a far different constellation of forfeited choices...

She was standing, confused as the Uncle Meat in the blackmarket clinic had been when things skewed and snapped under his scalpel and scissors, examining a makeshift ward she'd stumbled across set up in another shabby shadowy corridor, these graffiti-camouflaged walls adorned with phrases in English from (if Krystal recalled correctly) the Rabids, gang with tenuous Techno-Hickster affiliations who inhabited the Zone over by the airport and replaced their saliva glands with sacks full of a genetically manipulated RNA viral strain of the rhabdovirus group, made infrequent forays into the city proper for supplies, often storming unsuspecting tuk-tuks, snatching out interesting merchandise, biting the tekked passengers in the neck before they knew what'd hit them, real-life reverse vampires, infecting rather than draining an organism, BLAST A STIK, LET DEM EAT DATA, an oil lamp sputtering on a broken metal stool, twenty or thirty patients hooked to IVs and oxygen canisters, lying on disposable cots marked with those ubiquitous orange biohazard stickers, flesh bloodless, eyelids slivered enough to reveal a splinter of blank whites on the other side, lips parted as if they were about to say the word *ah*...and that guy...that guy four cots up with the patchy brownish-red beard and bleached-white hair...that guy was *Uly*...they must've moved him here while she was roaming, put him with these others, and now a male nurse shuffled among them, tucking up the foil sheets under their necks, feeling their foreheads, checking their eyes for movement, and Krystal knew, simply *knew*, this was just too much for her to take, she'd crossed some threshold separating two worlds, the abrupt transition from one discrete state to another that lands you in a song by some plasma-wrench band where nothing is right, everything bent and black and beaten at fourteen because evil *does* exist and it is all around you, wet and rancid, everywhere, *everywhere*...in the wobble of that oil-lamp flame, in the rust flecking off the legs of that broken stool, in the hiss of those oxygen canisters, among the fluorescent phrases spray-painted on that wall, breathing in the chests of those patients, humming among the vocal cords of that nurse, singing in the purple Plughead tassel dangling from his forehead, his pale green filtration mask, in the sable skin of that repairwoman Krystal only now discerned, earlobes pierced and stretched like taffy, almost completely in the dark just down the hall, fidgeting with an out-of-order Panasonic mobile alarm system, aqua plastic bubble on wheels capable when functioning properly of sniffing and recognizing your pheromones, running a security ID on you, and, if you failed, lasering your legs in half...in the forbidding possibility of that blue bubble itself.

"What is this place?" Krystal asked, navigating among cots.

"We call it a hospital, mama-san," the nurse said, voice muffled under mask, accent some eccentric amalgam of southeastern NorAm, Mexiental, hint of Russian. He didn't bother glancing up from his chores. "We fill it with sick people. Whole nuevo idea in health care...Now where you s'pposed to be goin' to, sweet thing?"

"No, no. I mean *this* place. This ward," discreetly hoisting herself over part of what once might have been a portable air conditioning unit hunked in the middle of the hallway.

The nurse's hands danced above a woman's white forehead.

"Who's asking, hai?"

"That's my boyfriend over there. Had a seizure tonight. Last night. I went to find somebody and got lost."

"Well, he's been looked at."

Krystal kneeled by him, touched his cheek, ran her palm over his close-cut hair. He looked just like he had on the VTOL swooping in over Spocoeur, sleeping and not sleeping, suspended between realities.

"How you know?"

"Cuz he wouldn't be here if he ain't, would he?" The nurse straightened, placed his palms on his lower back, and arched his spinal column, cracking it at multiple sites. "You ever done manual?"

"Sure."

"If your back ain't achin', your feet feel like breakin', neh?" He looked down at Uly, then Krystal. "Been together long?"

"Over a month. Yeah."

"Mucho shit happens, don't it? Once dated a guy nearly a year. Thought I'd died and gone to BelsenLand. Then along comes this retired toyboy, thirteen, whisks him off his feet, and hasta la vista. I died and went to BelsenLand." He studied Uly. "He been southwest lately?"

"IBM Nevada."

"Yeah, well. I could sing you a song."

"…?"

He glanced down the hall at the repairwoman, gauging. She kept tinkering with the robot bubble, oblivious to their conversation.

"Lookee here. This ward?"

"Yeah?"

"This here's a CHRUDS ward."

"CHRUDS?"

"Chrono-Unific Deficiency Syndrome. Major Time Fuckup to us mortals. All these people? They come in with massive headaches, complaining of this hallucination thing, or, like your boyfriend there, flat out after a seizure."

"Hallucination thing?"

"'Intense sense of memory,' is how they explain it." Done, he thwacked off one latex glove, the other, tossed them both on the floor out of the gloomy light. "Any way you cut it, couple hours later they're like this."

"Intense sense of memory?"

"Can't tell whether they're living in the present, comprende, which is the real present, or the past, which is or isn't necessarily *the* past, if you know what I mean, which feels like the present to them, but ain't." He scratched his nose. "This confusing you?"

"I've been clearer."

"Point is, they're some major malfed-up hombres, timewise."

"Virus?"

"Tell me something..."

"Krystal."

"Okay. Krystal. Tell me something. Look like I wasted a fourth of my life in med school? Be honest. Do I? Cuz if I do, you just tell me, and I'll trot upstairs and ask for a raise right this very second."

"Sorry." She scanned the corridor, patients, damaged medical equipment. "What the fuck's happened here?"

"Let me let you in on a little secret. Sometimes things just don't figure. Take this, for instance. Uncle Meats're walkin' 'round with broomsticks up their asses, can't squeak a fart out of 'em, only all these rumors're flyin', piss in a tsunami."

"What sort of rumors?"

"Take your pick. New strain of encephalitis. Toxic psychosis."

"Radiation?"

"Nobody knows jack-shit. Or..."

"Or?"

"Or everybody who counts knows mucho jack-shit, but ain't sayin', meaning we're all sittin' in just a whole *vat*-load of lambfries...our own. Either way, I can tell you one thing."

"Which is?"

"Which is whatever this dumbs down to, neh? It's breaking out everywhere from DisCal to northern Columbia. I've seen these guys' medical histories. Most of 'em are from the southwest, but lots too from Brigham-Young Idaho, even Turner Oregon. All over. Just happened to be passing through the neighborhood." He pulled two new gloves out of his pocket and started tugging them on. "Hey, uh, not to pry or anything? But, well, you look a lot like the stuff at the bottom of my cereal bowl after I've eaten my Count Chocula and Coke for breakfast. You thinking 'bout a place to crash?"

"I *feel* a lot like the stuff at the bottom of your cereal bowl after you've eaten your Count Chocula and Coke."

"Let me tell you something, mama-san. Ain't nothin' happening 'round here for a *good* long while. Nobody's woke up from this thing yet."

"Yeah, but…"

"Some of these slabs been here a month. Hospital'll contact you, something changes."

"Well," taking a look around.

"You don't hear anything, you contact us."

Things falling into place.

"Thanks."

"No problema. You take care of yourself, hear?"

"Nothing else on my mind."

She bent to kiss Uly goodbye. The nurse cleared his throat.

"I'd hold off on the bodily fluids business for a while if I was you. Those little orange biohazard stickers all over the place? Put up for a reason."

Krystal looked at him, at Uly, then figured fuck it. She kissed him anyway, on the lips, long and soft, trying to telecast her presence to his psyche, but his breathing remained constant and the touch of his skin reminded her of cool rubber. So she stood, refocused herself, thanked the nurse again, and stepped past him into the darkness, past that repairwoman fiddling with the Panasonic mobile alarm system, too, the one who lifted her head and followed her down the corridor with eyes black and empty as little globes of space out beyond Pluto.

17

The Tao Of Snow

Something brushed Uly's lips...warm, moist, and inviting, then vaguely uncomfortable, cold, a surprising icy wetness.

He opened his eyes and found himself in an expansive meadow, stands of pines and evergreen bushes around him, dark as moss, bristling like crazy manes. Several hundred yards away, a dense forest lifted into foothills. Streams clear as reading glasses, some no wider than a girl's arm, his own, networked the soggy earth and flowed over pebble beds into a shallow river beside which ran the emigrant trail, six-inch ruts furrowed in black humus.

"God help us," said his mother.

She stood next to him, holding his hand tightly, and when Uly looked up into her face all he saw were those brown eyes examining the sky.

Another snowflake tapped his cheek and melted. The atmosphere was aswarm with them, tiny as pin pricks, not so much falling as hovering, oscillating.

Above, bloated clouds turned the sky into an inverted ocean. Slatey waves pitched toward the horizon.

More flakes appeared. The air became busy with whiteness. They clung to blades of grass, branches, his own gray-and-green striped skirt. He touched his hair pulled into a braid and realized it was already damp.

But Stanton had promised. He'd reported people at Fort Sutter had assured him snow wouldn't close the pass till mid-November.

Hastings himself, everyone knew, had gotten through on horseback last year toward the end of December.

"Hurry, Mrs. Reed," Milt called, jogging up. "Stanton, the Graveses, and the Murphys are just leaving. We must walk with them."

"We are lost, Mr. Elliott," Uly's mother said, as if she was commenting on the color of dandelions. She continued studying the storm blowing in.

"Nonsense, Mrs. Reed. But we must press for the pass at once. We have two days, perhaps three. The going will be hard. Where are Patty and Jim?"

"Minding Tommy with the Donners."

"I'll retrieve them. We are underway in five minutes. Let us meet at the Murphy wagon."

"Thank you, Mr. Elliott."

"Not at all, Mrs. Reed."

Around them people threw together their last belongings, men shouting back and forth, rich anxiety in their voices, hauling bundles of clothes, cooking ware, and food into the backs of the wagons, women helping extinguish fires, pail water from the streams, collect children for the last head count before embarking, dogs yelping, sprinting up and down the forming line, unnerved by the snow and commotion, cattle bellowing as whips pistoled above them, hefty metallic creaking of the first enormous wheels set in motion.

Everyone, even Uly, knew the worst that could possibly have happened had happened, snow gaining strength and thickness, wisping across the ground, blanching the meadow an apple green, and he knew they hadn't attempted anything yet, the real test was still waiting for them over those foothills already disappearing in prodigious opal clouds, through the pass already blue shadow and gray ghost and then nothing at all.

He closed his eyes again.

And saw the traces Stepfather left behind along the trail at the outset of his banishment...short notes on shreds of paper stuck on a split stick...feathers from birds killed for food...warm campfire ashes…and Uly recalled how, twenty-four hours after William Eddy reported being shot at for the first time by Diggers while hunting, those traces ceased.

Mother refused to leave her bed, let Tommy out of her arms, huddling in the woody darkness of the Palace Car with her drilling headache while Patty, Jim, and Uly tried to carry out their daily chores, take over those of their absent parents, finding the labor immense, food supplies smaller, their wagon in need of constant upkeep.

At the encampment one evening, another omen: the emigrants discovered old man Hardkoop, the frail Belgian with vaporous green eyes and question-mark spine, missing. He'd been traveling with Keseberg, his wife and two children, and when quizzed, the Westphalian said he knew nothing and brusquely evaporated into his tent.

Franklin Graves, one of the last two men with saddle horses, volunteered to ride back along the trail.

He returned three hours later, Hardkoop, bewildered, riding behind him on the saddle. Hardkoop explained Keseberg had approached him late that afternoon as he tried to sleep in back of his wagon and informed him he was taking up too much room, too many supplies, told him to get out, walk or die. Hardkoop resisted at first but Keseberg was the younger and stronger and something had broken inside him. He forced the Belgian onto the trail, stabbing at him with a broom when he tried to climb aboard again, till Hardkoop lost his grip, couldn't keep up, fell farther and farther behind, soon saw the caravan diminishing like a toy train.

A week earlier, such a story would have shocked the company, roused indignation, set off aggressive action against Keseberg.

Today, dazed and indifferent, the emigrants told the old man to sleep in the Palace Car, give his opponent a chance to cool down, and, in the morning, they loaded him back into Keseberg's wagon with a grim warning to the European with the heart of a stuffed doll.

Forty-eight hours later, dusk cindering the air, temperature sliding toward freezing, Hardkoop turned up missing again.

Some boys driving cattle said they'd seen him late in the afternoon sitting alone along the path by some sagebrush, feet swollen and split. Eddy and Milt built a large signal fire on the side of an adjacent hill and made arrangements to keep it burning till dawn. This, together with the starry sky, might guide him in.

Come morning, though, there was still no sign of him. Eddy and Milt approached Keseberg while he breakfasted and demanded he retrace his route to retrieve the man he'd abandoned. Keseberg laughed at their arrogance.

It wasn't his responsibility, he said in a tone flush as the corners of a T-square. He wasn't Hardkoop's shepherd. He was no one's manservant...each person in this company knew full well from the outset he'd need to hold up his or her end of the bargain or find someone else who would. Keseberg'd provided the old man a favor, taking him in, feeding him, looking after his welfare, but Hardkoop had done nothing in return. Even in the best of times, his contribution to the party's undertaking had been negligible. Now he was little more than a rusting machine that ate, slept, and excreted. Let come to him what may. And let be damned any emig who would dare turn favor into obligation. Keseberg had his own family to look after, and would do what needed to be done to look after it.

Eddy and Milt next approached Graves and Breen, but this time they also spurned the idea of backtracking. Breen argued the old man was probably dead already. The night had been fiercely cold, Diggers were everywhere, Hardkoop was weak to begin with, his feet bad, his mind easily confused. What could anyone possibly hope to gain by sending a search party back under these conditions? Franklin was even less charitable. Hardkoop had done nothing for anyone since beginning this odyssey except take up space and food. What did anyone owe him in return? Plus the days were shortening, cooling, turning grayer. The emigs needed every second they could claim, every healthy man among them to see them through what lay ahead.

Eddy and Milt offered to go back on foot. No one need accompany them. No one need lend a thing except five hours. If they couldn't find him within that span, they'd return, knowing at least they'd done everything they could under the circumstances.

But the party could not wait for them. If they left, they left...only then they were on their own.

Milt and Eddy glared at them, ten seconds, fifteen, turned and, jaws locked, began helping pack up camp.

The Humboldt narrowed instead of widened. The distance between its pools increased. The trail turned sandier, dustier, pasturage poorer. Three days on, they rounded a bend of scraggy rocks and encountered human bones strewn before them. Women and children were assembled straightaway and sheltered in the wagons while the men took up positions outside. Patrick Breen and Franklin Graves rode off with rifles at the ready across their laps, and returned half an hour later with the story of another Digger attack. They'd followed the bones to the remnants of a grave. A toppled wooden cross identified it as belonging to a member of the Hastings Party, a man named Sallee. He'd died of an arrow wound and been buried in a shallow pit covered with stones. His corpse had been dug up, stripped, and left for coyotes. The company reorganized and pushed on, riding till well after twilight, hoping to move free of this unlucky zone, coming to encamp in a desolate spot where the grass was sparse. Within minutes of arriving the cattle became restive and began to drift out of the firelight. Men took turns standing guard, but it was a frightened woman's voice, Tamsen Donner's, that awoke Uly next morning. He stepped from the Palace Car to learn the Diggers had raided in the darkness and stolen eighteen oxen. Emigrants stood around campfires, flustered and amazed, trying to fathom how defenseless they had become, how their world was no longer the world they thought it was. Everything was suddenly close like a shotgun at the forehead. Everything was dangerous...scrubby bushes and leafless willows by the river, poisonous brown boulders surrounding them, dust so deep at times the cattle sank in it almost to their knees, ridges of volcanic stones whose edges cut through their shoes, hundred holes in the rock beneath their feet from which bitter boiling water oozed then jetted in fountains of steam twenty feet in the air, continual translucent dizziness pursuing them, throwing small black birds into the corners of their vision, human forms, twinkling floaters.

Mother sat up in bed and announced: "It's time to surrender the Palace Car."

"But mama…" Patty said, raising her head.

She'd been knitting with Uly on the Concord stage-coach seat built into the wall on the opposite side of the sleeping compartment.

"Mr. Elliott!" Mother called, paying her no heed. "Pull us over!"

"But your head, mama…"

"My head's fine."

"But…"

"But nothing, child. Dress up now. We have a long walk ahead of us."

The other wagons passing, Mother stepped out followed by her children. Each carried a change of clothes, some robes, blankets. They hiked back to one of the Breen wagons where, after a brief discussion, they deposited their bundles, then to the Donners'. George and Tamsen took Mother and Tommy aboard. Jim, Patty, and Uly would have to walk. There simply wasn't any more room.

So Uly stood in the road, looking around at the tattered and disheveled travelers hiking. Some carried household goods or packages of food, a copper camp kettle, a powder-horn. They appeared to be people fleeing a fire, refugees escaping a war.

In the naked brown hills surrounding them, just out of rifle range, bands of Diggers stared, pointing, gesticulating.

Uly shut his eyes.

And saw a line of black beads crawling down the trail toward him, the morning hazy, sun a diaphanous goldpiece wobbling in a whitish sky. The company had joined the Truckee river four days ago and the landscape had cramped into canyon winding between high rugged roan and dead-leaf mountains. The Donner Party was at the end of its rations, little left except coffee and sugar, yet it had hesitated striking off in hunting parties because of the Diggers who dogged them, yipping through the nights, crippling their cattle with poison-tipped arrows, taunting. The emigrants moved without singing, without laughing, without talking, one foot in front of the next, into higher and harsher terrain.

The black beads clarified into three riders and seven pack-mules…and Charles Stanton in the lead, that slight thirty-five-year-old, returning from Fort Sutter with supplies. Behind him rode two Indians followed by more mules lumbering under small barrels and sacks of salt pork and jerked beef, flour and beans, dried fruit and tea.

Whoops of pleasure dominoed down the line. The emigs ushered Stanton back into the caravan and encamped early, lit fires and distributed food, ate as they hadn't eaten for days. Their troubles in suspension, scent of cow hide and burning wood around them, Stanton made his report. McCutchen had fallen ill with influenza and been compelled to remain behind, but would soon be fit and hoped to join the party before long. Sutter had been extremely generous with provisions and mules and had even thrown these two Indians into the bargain as well. They were *vacqueros*, cattle herders, and could actually catch steers by throwing a noose over their heads. The tall, thick, horse-chested one, Luis, knew a few words of English. The other, Salvador, round-faced, tiny-eyed, fidgety, spoke only Spanish. They were honest hard workers, quiet and solitary…and were afraid of Sutter, even at this distance, for, as they rode out the gates behind him, Stanton overheard the captain remind them affably that he'd hang them if they lost even one of his mules.

"And my husband, Mr. Stanton?" Mother asked when he paused to lift his coffee mug. Uly, sitting beside her by the fire, heard the muscles in her voice flex. "Have you heard any word of him?"

Stanton took a sip.

"Indeed I did, ma'am," he said. "Indeed I did. So happens four days ago I reached Bear Valley on my return and met the last section of Hastings' company. They was encamped and among 'em was a scrawny gray mare and a man still too weak to carry his saddle. He'd come outta the mountains several days afore. Swear, first off I didn't recognize him."

Uly heard a soft breath release from his mother's throat. She maintained her straight spine, hands clasped in her lap.

"He got through then."

"Said he done killed birds along the rivers. When he left the Truckee, he didn't find nothin' 'cept a few wild onions to live from. Wants you to know he's all right. Wishes the company godspeed."

"Thank the lord."

"Thank the devil, rather," said Keseberg.

Mother turned her attention toward him, steady and emphatic. Firelight illuminated swatches of his face in gilt-yellow flickers.

"How dare you."

"How dare *you,* madam, enjoying the good fortune of a murderer. And how dare you all to care a blink about what happens to a godforsaken wretch and his family."

Mother stared, Stanton's coffee mug hovered an inch from his lips, Uly felt electricity crackle around him, Tamsen Donner opened her mouth to speak, and Mother became a black blur, a panther, was on him, lashing out, hands a flock of hummers around his face, his neck, his shoulders, as he sputtered, surprised by the assault, and tried to rise to his feet, but she wouldn't let him, just kept swatting, hushed as a mute, concentrated as a hunter leveling his rifle at a buck point blank, possessed, bewitched, till Tamsen registered what had happened, and George, and Milt, and Eddy too, and they were up, grabbing for her flailing arms, her waspish middle, tugging her away as she writhed and lurched among them, the whole while glowering with those brown eyes of hers that didn't quite match each other in size or shape, as if to glower at him with enough severity might cause him to ignite, burst into flames, flare into a burning human column, and she disappeared in the darkness, and Uly heard her huffing, rustle of her dress and rustle of the

Donners' tent flap, and, no matter how tightly he squeezed shut his eyes, he heard the silence hissing around him with serpentine tension.

He was peering over his shoulder at George shrinking as the rest of the company rolled away from him in the strengthening snowstorm.

On a steep downward pitch, less than a day's ride from the pass, the front axle had snapped on his wagon. Franklin urged him to abandon it and make a rush for the pass, but George, resolute about holding on to his possessions long as he could, wouldn't hear of it. Repairs would take little more than an hour or two to complete. All he had to do was cut and trim timber into a replacement. The others should continue without him. George, his brother Jacob, and their families would catch up by nightfall.

He looked like a man seen through the wrong end of a telescope. Ax in hand, he worked speedily with Jacob before a lodgepole pine, oblivious of the train pulling away from him, preoccupied with his own mission, calibrating, engaged, while Tamsen, her sister-in-law Elizabeth, and the children gazed on, arms folded across their chests for warmth.

They were upright grasshoppers doing a cold-day dance. They were bent beetles. They were diminutive fruit flies admiring a brown pencil.

And then they were gone.

Two inches had already accumulated at Truckee Lake five miles short of the great bare wall of the pass. Feeble cattle nosed through the stuff to find skimpy patches of grass, air prickling with panic, emigs battening down the last loose articles in their wagons for the steep ascent, bulking up in layer on layer of winter clothing if they had any left, trying to borrow if they didn't, long johns, flannel shirts, close-knit wool sweaters, fur-lined rawhide coats, fur hats, buffalo robes, heavy mittens, scarves, blankets doubled and roped around their feet and up to their knees in place of boots, wrapped around their shoulders in place of mantles...and, nearly noon, Stanton and the Indians in the lead, they set out, piloting by a deserted cabin with a caved-in roof along a stream, traced the north lakeshore to the head, and rose into barren rock-candy terrain. The snow grew softer and deeper. Before long there were six inches of it, a foot, and then the trail, so easy to follow since they'd joined it near the Humboldt, became less distinct, its outlines distorted, blurred, almost invisible. It was clear they'd lost their bearings, were striking ahead into cul-de-sac after cul-de-sac, tripping into underbrush, stumbling down gullies, finding themselves spun around in the augmenting storm. Even the mules began to flounder, up to their sides in snow, wagons bogging down, sliding sideways.

No more than three miles from the summit, the trail vanished. Stanton stopped and fell back. They were so close, Uly heard him shout through the driving wind, they couldn't give up now, couldn't retreat. It was time to abandon everything, wagons, all but the most essential provisions, cattle, and scramble for the pass. Others argued with him, saying the company should withdraw down the mountain, hole up by the lake till the worst was over, launch another assault tomorrow...yet to withdraw meant capitulation, an unimaginable future. No matter how extreme their present condition was, if they retreated it would become tenfold more unthinkable. Desperate, sensing the trap swinging shut in front as well as behind, they clambered from their rigs, unyoked their teams, packed what they could on the few remaining oxen, and, in a frenzied shove, battled for the pass afoot.

The company broke ranks, fanned out as they had in the desert, each family on its own. Unused to hauling, the oxen began bucking off bundles strapped to them, lying down to wallow in gathering drifts. The emigrants left them behind and forged on, losing balance, fumbling to their knees, pitching up again, discarding their last kettles, pails, extra clothes, vying for every step they gained. The snow drove slantwise, became ice pellets pinging their eyes, frozen buckshot biting their cheeks, blue-jay beaks. It stung them, nipped them, chewed their skin. The wind yowled, deafening as a stampede, pierced their clothes, stripped them, left them staggering, dehydrated, shivering, exhausted, a huge gnarled hand pushing them back.

Uly could see fifty yards in front of him. Twenty. Every footstep took an hour. He lost track of the others, his surroundings. Time honed to the sound of Jim sobbing, head buried in the curve of Uly's neck. The snow angled farther, intensified, pulsed in horizontal waves, seared his ear rims, ached up in his sinuses, melted, sponged into his scarf and mittens, converted the landscape into the inside of a cumulus, a room of gauze, the white of eggshells, milk, chalk, lilies. His eyes throbbed from the blankness, brain hurt, fingers stiffened with arthritic frostiness. The snow became quicksand, swamp mud, guano. He leaned forward, head lowered, chin on chest, and threw himself on, the thought surfacing that worse than all of this, worse than anything he'd endured so far, if he reached the summit, surmounted the pass, nothing would change; it would be exactly the same on the other side, mile after mile, fury and catastrophe, a day's journey and more through blizzard to Yuba Bottoms, another to Bear Valley, another to Mule Springs.

It struck him he couldn't do this. He wanted to lie down, fold into himself, a piece of delicate Japanese paper. Somewhere he'd heard dying by cold was the best way to go, easiest and most painless, serene, even pleasant…a gradual succumbing to sleep…only now Uly understood it wasn't like that at all. It was panging agony. It pinched, stabbed, sliced, smarted, wrenched. For a while you thought you could get the upper hand on it, control it somehow, maybe even will it away, it wasn't so bad, you could do this, except then you realized it was already all through you, malignant, starting with your head and hands, the cartilage of your ears, the flesh of your cheeks, seeping through your body in a series of involuntary tremors, neural scaldings, till you realized it was already too late, you were already beyond hope, you would never get warm again, no matter what you did, no matter what you tried, ever.

Up ahead something caught his attention, a yellow glitter, and he steered for it. He came across a group of people clustered around a bonfire sunk several feet in the snow. Someone had found a dead pine full of pitch and set it ablaze. Others gathered around it. They built a platform of green branches that wouldn't burn, dug a yard-deep circle to protect the flames from the wind, and now huddled near it, severe, jaw muscles tight in violent silence, warming their hands, drying their boot blankets, snow collecting on their shoulders, hoods, backs, graying their dark hair. Uly half leapt, half slid, into the pit and tried to set down Jim but his brother wouldn't let go. He clung to his sister's coat like a contentious monkey. So Uly relented and took an empty place several bodies back from the fire, hunkered down, searching faces for his mother, but all he saw were stony desolate exiles who'd skidded into a dimension of experience beyond articulate sounds, worn down, used up.

A face with skin like an uncooked steak appeared, Stanton, eyes sparking with ferocity. He was motioning with his arms, yelling. Uly could hardly make out what he was saying in the hurling wind but saw him begin to circle them, mouth moving. He was badgering, pushing, urging them on. They had to press for the summit. This was it, what the entire journey had come down to. If they gave up, everything was lost, finished, everything they'd made this trip for. How could they contemplate such a thing? Stand. Persevere. The snow would only worsen through the night. By morning their way would be completely blocked. This was as good as prospects would get for months. This was the hand they'd been dealt. They had to play it, play it now. A few more miles, and they were free. A few more hours, and they'd be through the darkest. Rise. Climb out. Take a single step. Then one more. They could do this. They could be over by dawn.

He ranted like a preacher, pleaded, jumped down into the pit and, grabbing them by their coats, collars, shook them. Yet the travelers wouldn't listen, wouldn't raise their eyes to meet his, continued staring into the fire, gazes void of emotion, empty of opinion. For them it was no longer a question of choice. The miraculous thing was that in the end what it all came down to had nothing to do with decisions or preferences. In the end it all came down to a calculus of muscles and stamina, a question of extremes, physical and emotional boundaries. The women and children couldn't go on, couldn't take another step without sleep, and the men wouldn't leave them. It was more simple than any of them had ever imagined.

Wordless, eyes savage and luminous, Stanton helped lay blankets and buffalo robes on the snow for the children who crawled onto them and were covered with more blankets and robes by the adults who then bunched close together by the fire for heat. Noiseless, somber, Salvador and Luis wrapped themselves in blankets and stood leaning against a nearby tree, refusing to join the others, remaining in the same postures throughout the brief uneasy night as snow fell steady and fast, mixing with cutting sleet, and, by three in the morning, the travelers discovered another foot of it around them. Outside their pit drifts rose in ten-foot surges. Bundled in soggy clothes, tired, they slogged forward, Stanton and the Indians in the lead, gained another hundred yards in the course of perhaps an hour and a half, wind jetting at them, snow reeling down heavier than before, only they'd become hopelessly lost in the whiteout, unable to figure their course.

The tiny band Uly was with found themselves on the brink of a ravine they couldn't cross. They could no longer orient themselves with respect to the pass, tell whether they were moving up or sideways along the mountain. They called out to the others, the wind drowning their attempts. Shocked by how quickly their future had been decided for them, demoralized at the lack of alternatives and mounting exhaustion, they tried retracing their steps only to find the wind and snow had obliterated them. They began to wander, smaller and smaller bands dropping off the original already small one, growing yet more confused, crossing and recrossing terrain they felt they may or may not have crossed and recrossed already.

When, three or four hours later, the storm lifted enough for them to see, they found themselves standing on a rise at the north end of the lake. They were back where they'd started and, looking at the wall of trees swelling toward the horizon in front of them, vast white surface of Truckee Lake, sheer cliffs to their right, they understood their final bid for the summit had failed, myriad possibilities had funneled down over the last half year to this instant. As the snow intensified into a cloud of icy chips, they scrabbled toward the deserted cabin they'd passed at the foot of the lake. They knew they wouldn't reach it until late afternoon. They knew when they did they wouldn't find the Donners waiting for them. And they knew, with every shaky step they took, that if they were lucky now, really lucky, if they were luckier than they'd ever been in their lives, and could round up some of the stray cattle and dogs on their retreat, they might have just enough food for another two weeks, three at most.

18

Ceramic Viper: Shock Delivery:
The Assassination Of Mister Softee

Except that sable-skinned repairwoman, earlobes pierced and stretched taffy, eyes black and empty little globes of space out beyond Pluto, busy fooling with the kaput Panasonic mobile alarm system down the hall from Krystal and the nurse, was about as much a real repairwoman as a goldfish is a real Thai Khon Kaen urban light assault vehicle.

Her name was Anna Konda and she'd grown up in the back end of an overturned freight truck decorated with corrugated steel awnings in a shantytown on the outskirts of Havana in the new semi-state of Chiang Cuba. The shantytown doubled as one of the city's massive garbage dumps. Slowly, cumbersomely, relentlessly, twenty-four hours a day, seven days a week, three hundred and sixty-five days a year mechanical monsters called Little Egypts, several stories tall, several stories wide, covered with gears the proportions of most men, dug themselves into the earth with a rumbling and clanking that could rupture a stalwart screechabilly fan's eardrums to make way for rubble and waste then set ablaze by a team of flamethrower-wielding women in Mylex suits. The Little Egypts squatted in the middle of the fires and debris and chewed concrete, plywood, plastic, metal, flesh, vegetable matter. When one finally hit seawater, its pit would flood, conflagration surrounding it hiss out, and another Little Egypt would be rolled in to start a fresh meal.

So Anna awoke as a child to a universe of sludgy pools, house-flies the heft of her thumbs, smoke, and air that could fizzle the paint right off your bike, if you were rich enough to own a bike, fifth- or sixthhand, which most people around Anna's shantytown weren't. Throughout her youth the sun remained a glowing golf ball behind a bedspread of black gauze, her lungs developed to the stage of a three-year-old's and stopped, refusing to go on with this crap, her skin, pink at birth, stained the color of pitch from kinky chemicals, her hair, once straight blonde, burned reddish brown and velcroed in patches across her head.

And her heart, small and stunted as it was, knew it wanted one thing in the world: to get the hell out.

Which is just what she did the day she turned eleven. She played by herself farther and farther away from her progens' crypt, pick-ing up a crinkled Pepsi can here, examining a soggy flap of card-board there, and before long was walking along the shoulder of the highway. She hadn't decided anything. This wasn't a moment of revelation. One minute Anna was keeping herself occupied, pass-ing time, and the next she was gone, free, her thin arm airborne to flag down the next empty garbage hauler heading back to Havana, uninterested in looking behind her as she climbed into the cab and the driver, an albino with long transparent hair, vaporous green eyes, and pollution sores ringing his lips, reached between her legs and began probing her naked, raw, chemically swollen pudendum.

Four hours later Anna was a meater with her own filtration mask in a mesto called the Data Trash, famous for servicing the first wealthy victims of Blue Prime. Four months later she was a mole with her own respirator working for the Chiang-Cuban mafia, sexing up with those Prime Timers till snippets of their pinkies, or noses, or worse, fell off, scorching them for as much information as possible with her torrid now-twelve-year-old wiles, which intel-ligence her bosses sold, or used for blackmail, or simply double-checked against their own version of reality. And four years after that she was a troubleshooter in the northwest, promoted up and out of the meatverse, new set of lungs in her ribcage, cosmetically accentuated scar packing major status scribbling down her chest where they'd opened her, secondhand aug behind her right ear, cozy crypt near the Zone in Spocoeur, more comfort than she'd ever known.

Anna's job description involved taking care of business for people who didn't have the time or inclination to take care of it themselves. She convinced potential clients to see events from her superiors' perspective, or tidied them up if they didn't, or did whatever it took because she knew deep down she'd do just about anything not to go back to that overturned freight truck decorated with corrugated steel awnings in that poisoned shantytown on the outskirts of Havana.

Which was what she was in the process of doing right now, anything she had to, letting Krystal Silikon slip into the darkness, counting to ten, reaching up and brushing that aug nubbed behind her ear.

A blue light flared in her field of vision. The bio-connections were still all malfed up. She smiled, an image speeding into her cranial cineplex of the guy she'd borrowed this aug from, a startled Ozone Baby exec, flippers raised, eyes wide, sitting at his computer console, back fourth of his head all steam and sizzle.

"On our way," she said.

She didn't speak the words, just mouthed them into air, aug picking up muscle movements in her jaw.

"Ten-four," a voice responded.

She didn't hear it with her ears, either. Sounded more like it came from someplace in the core of her brain stem, echoed around inside her skull like a bat in an empty hanger.

Anna stood, touched the ceramic Viper 200 holstered to her one-piece body suit beneath her baggy repairwoman overalls, and began to follow her next victim, making sure to keep out of her visual range.

They passed the Vachuru Surgery OR where specialists at some central location, Seattle, maybe, or Vancouver, performed operations at hospitals all over this part of the country using an intricate system of bots and VR rigs. Silikon stopped to wash her face at a sink in an open supply closet across from the Shock Delivery unit where affluent mothers had labor induced at seven or seven-and-a-half months to produce leaner babies that'd grow into tauter adults. They passed a Kevorkian ward, roachburger bar, meandered down a series of long dim passageways lined with cell-like cubicles posted with orange biohazard stickers, and stepped into the luminous white lobby. Something caught Silikon's eye on the HDTV there, looked like, and she slowed her pace. Grainy photos of a naked female body bolted up crucifix-fashion to a gray cement wall. Polymox Epoxi, that telehost. The wall marked the entrance to the Gameshow Network building in ChaseMan York. Epoxi'd been gutted like a deer.

Outside the sky oystered toward dawn. A haze from the fires in River Park blocked the sun, obscured the mountains to the east. Medivac VTOLs took off and landed on the roof every few seconds. A tropical heat turned the scenery into a special effects show. Everything wobbled as if through warped tinted glass. Silikon cut across concrete islands, through a group of orderlies enjoying a break, and hailed a tin-canopied three-wheeled tuk-tuk near the main gatehouse. A moment later she was at the security checkpoint beneath the guard towers, a machine gun-toting sentry in olive sunscreen and olive drabs eye-scanning her.

Lon Tef, meantime, was waiting for Anna, diesel engine strapped to the mid-section of his Chiehshou buggy erecting a huge blue-gray thundercloud of exhaust in the parking lot nearest the entrance. His rig was a pastiche job, two black bubble-windshields, crazy Batmobile fins on back, monster wheels, roll bar, all manner of faux machinery bristling off every which direction.

Come to think of it, Lon Tef was a pastiche job himself. He suffered from a skin condition that made his body one hundred percent bald. No hair on his head, in his ears, up his nose, along his arms, between his legs, sprouting from his toe joints. No eyebrows. No eyelashes. No beard. Not a single pubic curl on his chest. Anna figured that's what made him compensate with all the wild polyvinyl muscle implants that acted in conjunction with his body's own natural electrical impulses to create some drastic power. They fattened him up, plumped him out, gave him the neck of a bull, v-shaped torso of a gorilla, legs of a raptor. He could barely fit into his own car. He had to squeeze down, shovel parts of himself around seat harnesses and armrests with a little ice-scraper he always carried in the glove compartment for such occasions.

It didn't stop there. Lon was an excess man. He loved overdoing things, especially things concerning his appearance. He liked surplus, glut, extravagance, probably because his minimalist birth-body provided him with so little of the stuff. Instead of wearing an aug demurely tucked behind his right ear like Anna, he wore a whole row of them, mostly inactive, each one bigger and more bad-assed than the one before it, across his forehead...and another row from his left temple to jawbone. He'd had his perfectly good right eye extracted and sewn shut. He'd had sixth fingers, useless extra thumbs, sewn on to both hands. He'd had his lips amputated and one reattached just above each ear. His mouth sported two tiers of teeth in his lower jaw, two in his upper.

Which work, believe it or not, most people didn't notice at first because they were too busy looking at his tatt...head-to-foot Yakuza affair, all blue swirls, red and yellow highlights, black outlines accented by the black bikini and sandals Lon wore. It told the story of his life in terms of each violent episode that comprised it. There was, needless to say, his bloody birth, the beating he received at the hands of his postal-worker father the day the governcorp switched from snail-mail to electronic. There was his introduction as a teen to the finer points of cannibalism during the first round of the ChaseMan York food riots, his original kill as a merc interrogator in the SoAm war when his dental equipment accidentally slipped, his initial run-in with a razzed Farben-Impolex pitbull sent by the police north of LA to provide martial law day after the Shudder...and then a miniature Sistine Chapel of liquidations, each more elaborate and amok than the last, corkscrewing down his neck, shoulders, arms, chest, stomach, back, buttocks, genitalia, thighs, calves, and left ankle and foot.

Here he was, only twenty-four, and he'd used up ninety-five percent of his body surface. Anna wondered where he could possibly go next.

"Fuck," he'd said. "Ain't goin' no place next."

"You saying after this you're not killing anymore?"

"I'm sayin' after this I'm not livin' anymore. I get to the bottom of my right foot, man, I'm yesterday."

"Yesterday?"

"In other way of saying it, I got a favor for you. Fate's a big fucker, okay? Bigger 'n you. Me. Bigger 'n everyone. He come down from heaven and fuck my ass, which when your time is up you're smoke, you take me to a plastic surgeon. Skin my sorry hide. Make me into the biggest fuckin'-A teepee you ever seen and put me in your living room, nice night-light inside. Pow. I'm sculpture."

From that day on, Anna felt secure around Lon. He had a plan, and having a plan was like having an insurance policy. Lon had positively no intention of fucking up before he'd completed adorning his right ankle and foot. He exuded an aura of purpose. All Anna had to do was stay close to him during work hours and everything would be all right. It'd be just like having a human egg-timer hustling beside you.

You'd always know exactly how long you had before providence started getting all horny for your soul.

So she climbed in beside him with a ready-to-rock'n'roll grin, yanked down her black bubble windshield, and secured her harness.

A couple of minutes and they were through the front gates, slinking along in the early morning traffic jam on Post, checking out the hazy reddish holographic ads for Bintang beer, GTE oxygen booths, Pope's new plasma-wrench album rocketing up the pop charts (all proceeds aimed for the Vatican coffers) floating over the Redford Coliseum through the riot-fire smoke.

Anna switched on the custom guidance and tracking system, banged-up gray box housing a mini-keyboard and monitor screwed into the dash. That hooked them up illegally with one-thousand-eight-hundred-and-forty military surveillance satellites in geosynchronous orbit around the earth. Every area on the planet could be seen on demand at one-meter resolution. Anna typed in some rough coordinates, and an aerial view of Silikon's tuk-tuk flicked onto the screen next to a small staticky map of the section of Spocoeur they all now inhabited, tuk-tuk represented as a yellow dot, buggy a red, on a white-streeted navy-blue background. It felt like a really old video game, the kind you sometimes found in decrepit shantytown mestos you shouldn't be hanging around in the first place.

"Ever hear of K-Mart Prices?" Lon asked.

"K-Mart what?"

Anna was busy fiddling with her system, trying to even out the roll and flutter.

"Game reserves off Discouver? Floating islands? Killer-Mart Prices."

"Turn left up here. Okay. Um, no. I haven't. Straight ahead." They pulled onto Second, long straight block of two- and three-story buildings from the last century, blacked-out plate-glass fronts, steel doors, concrete anti-assault barricades. Epidemics hostels, Buddhist temples, samisen mestos. The traffic was bumper to bumper, gridlocked, one of those puzzles where you had to move one square to move another to move a third to move the one you really wanted to move. Getting free of the immediate downtown area was going to take them three, four hours.

"Overloaded zoos?" said Lon. "Private cloners?"

"Yeah?"

"They set up these hunting ranches. You pay a fee. They copter you in. Pick you up forty-eight hours later. During which time you bag the animal of your choice."

"You saying you get to pick your game, they fly you in, you off it?"

"I'm sayin' zebra. Tiger. Goddamned rhinoceros. Ectcetera. You want 'em, you got 'em, is what I'm sayin'."

"Maricón."

"Which they don't come cheap." Lon reached over and tweaked on the radio, tuning in to a universal channel emanating from somewhere inside Raytheon Iowa. Trad Chinese muzak poured into the buggy. "Gazelle? Take a guess. How much for a single gazelle?"

Anna looked through the tinted windshield. An eight or nine-year-old Multiculti stood on the corner, waiting for the light to change, as if that might somehow help him cross the street. He was primped out in the pregnant look, air pumped into his abdomen to generate a bloated stomach. He wore bell-bottom hip-huggers, circa 1970, and a tie-dyed halter, ditto, to accent the effect.

"Fuck if I know," Anna said.

"Take a guess, though."

"I'm saying I don't know."

"Right, but take a guess."

"Why? If I don't know, what's gonna be accomplished if I take a guess? I might as well say I don't know. Then you tell me the answer. Then I know. Which way we both save time."

The buggy rolled forward half a meter.

"Yeah, but take a guess."

"I don't want to take a guess, man. I can't imagine a thing I want to do less than take a guess at this particular instant in time."

"Yeah, but take a guess."

Anna looked through the tinted windshield. The Multiculti took a step off the curb, thought better of it, retracted his foot. Next to him waited a woman with patent-leather eyebrows. She was pushing a baby carriage with a plastic dome on top that filtered its air. She showed off the Japanese riff-baring fashion, *hesodashi*, where her belly button had been turned into a vertical slit.

"Okay," Anna said. "Here goes. Eight hundred. I'm guessing a single gazelle costs exactly eight hundred thousand credits to whack."

"Thanks." Lon brushed back invisible hair across the top of his illustrated head, wiping away sweat that looked like moisture condensed on the outside of a cold glass. "You're wrong."

Inside, the buggy smelled of garlic and oil.

"De nada."

"Visit the past in the future," a pleasingly genteel British voice announced on the radio. "Erewhon One. The moon's first full-destination orbital resort. More affordable than you think. More necessary than you know."

"Take another guess," Lon said.

"Shit."

"Take another guess."

"Come on, man."

"Take another guess."

"I don't want to take another guess. I'm done guessing."

"Take another guess."

"Okay," she said. "Higher or lower?"

"Higher."

"A lot higher or a little higher?"

"Depends on what you mean by 'a lot' and 'a little.'"

"I'm thinking 'a lot' means 'a lot' and 'a little' means 'a little.'"

"Oh. Here or in, say, DisCal?"

"Here."

"Oh." He thought. "A lot higher."

"Okay. Here I go. Here's my second guess. I'm going to guess nine hundred. A single gazelle costs exactly nine hundred thousand credits to whack."

"Nine hundred?"

"Nine hundred."

"Sorry. Nine hundred is wrong."

"Fuck."

The buggy rolled forward half a meter.

"Don't feel bad, man. This isn't easy shit, like guessing how tall somebody is or something. It's not for everybody."

"A mill."

"A mill?"

"A mill."

"Sorry."

Anna slapped her armrest. She tried listening to the Chinese muzak for sixty seconds straight and failed. It sounded like so much tuning up.

"You ever get the feeling that nothing seems to connect with anything?" she said. "That everything just exists in a separate reality from everything else? Beads of space-time?"

"No, I don't. I get the feeling everything connects with everything, absolutely. Only sometimes people're too ratfuck stupid to see the connections. Take another guess."

"No."

"Take another guess."

"No."

"Take another guess."

"On one condition."

"Which is being what?"

"Which is being you tell me what this conversation connects with?"

Lon considered.

"Lots of shit. Life. Death. Our job. The cosmos. Take another guess."

The buggy rolled forward half a meter. The Multiculti shrugged, turned and started walking away. On the radio Carpal Tunnel Syndrome started playing "Dead Rotting Greyhounds," feedback, canine yawps, train thunder. A group of monks in orange robes and filtration masks appeared on the corner, pointing and gesticulating toward a building across the street. Then they all dropped their arms, turned, and strolled off as if their gestures had belonged to other people.

"Mill point two," Anna said.

Lon turned down the radio.

"Did you say a mill point two?"

"Yeah. Mill point two. Exactly. Mill point two."

"Is that what you want to go with?"

"That's what I want to go with."

"Let me be clear on this. You saying you want to go with a mill point two?"

"I do."

"Even if it's your last guess?"

"Especially if it's my last guess."

"What if I tell you you could have one other guess if you wanted? But it couldn't be a mill point two. You had to guess something else."

"I'd say go fuck yourself."

"So you saying you're pretty committed to this guess."

"A mill point two."

"I'm impressed with your resolve here."

"Thanks."

"But you're wrong. It's a mill point five."

"Well goddamn it."

Anna looked through the tinted windshield. Across the brown brick front of an Aiwa computer outlet someone had graffitied in meter-tall yellow spray paint the phrase REMEMBER, IT'S YOUR PINEAL GLAND.

"Antelope?" Lon said. "Two point seven. You want all four legs, no obvious tumors? Three point one. Not, I repeat, cheap."

"Turn right, turn right."

"Roger."

They crept onto Monroe. Traffic thinned. They could do a meter a minute.

"Straight." She turned up the radio again. "Okay. So. Tell me. Why all this sudden interest in K-Mart Prices?"

"At one thirty-three this morning, Eastern Standard Time," a newscaster sounding like Dracula said, "two mortar shells hit the east wing of the White House. Two special agents were killed and minor structural damage was reported. This marks the third such incident this month. Shortly before the first shell struck, Washington CNN police received an e-message from a person claiming allegiance with Church of the Rotes warning of the impending attack."

Anna and Lon looked at each other and smiled. Lon turned back to traffic.

"I have a plan," he said.

"That's what I like about you. This plan business. You can count on a guy with plans. You know everything will be all right with a guy who has plans. What sort of plan?"

"Picture this. After the payoff tomorrow? I'm goin' straight from the tatt parlor to Seattle. Reservations on K-Mart Price Seven. Little vacation. R and R. Joybang, shoot, sleep, shoot, joybang, shoot. Which if you can't figure out when to slow down, have a little fun, what can you do?"

"Absolutely. What you decide to shoot?"

"Gnu," Lon said.

"Ten minutes ago on the front steps of the Des Moines Botanical Center an ice-cream man was robbed and cut about the face and neck by a local teen with an X-Acto knife," the newscaster said. "He died en route to the hospital. Neighborhood children chanted as he was driven away, 'Mister Softee is dead. He didn't give out enough sprinkles.'"

"New?"

"A gnu."

"What the fuck's a *gnu*?"

"Bambi sort of deal with a hunched back, horns, white beard. Which the thing is you don't want to fuck with one."

"Bullshit. No such animal."

"You never heard of a gnu?"

"You're shittin' me."

"I'm not."

"You're fuckin' shittin' me."

"Tell that to a gnu with a horn up your butt. You know how fast a gnu can run?"

"I don't."

"Me either. But you can imagine."

Lon fingered one of his forehead augs with an extra thumb.

"Three minutes ago Fester Williams of Pleasant Lake, North McKota, moved into the fifth day of her hunger strike in order to force her local cable operator, Mainline Productions, to carry her favorite program, *Crime Deterrent Digest*, the famous execution talkshow," the newscaster said.

"Drill time," Lon said.

"Here we go."

Anna checked her Viper 200 and reached for Lon's piece holstered in a metal-and-ersatz-leather mount between the bucketseats. Pure Lon Tef number. Custom crossbow pistol that fired six stubby metal arrows tipped with shellfish toxin. Stunned the victim instantly, paralyzed him or her in seconds, took over twenty-four hours to work its terminal mischief, causing massive bleeding from the eyes, nose, and armpits in the meantime. She released it, tested the steel-cable bow, loaded it with the projectiles she found in the glove compartment.

"Sí," she said.

"Nightvision capability?"

She leaned over and inspected some readouts on the dash.

"Sí."

"X-ray scope?"

"Sí."

"Incendiary?"

"Um...yep. Ready to arm."

The bomb was the first thing she'd inventoried after getting the call just past midnight from that crazy albino with one max fucking ugly split black tongue that made her lisp like a demonized Sylvester the Cat. Klub Med connection talking all manner of unnecessary shit, Sacrifice Zone Enhancement, DTs, when all Anna really wanted to know was who, when and where. She couldn't believe that bitch wouldn't even blackout her phone screen. What was the extermination trade coming to these days? No one planned anything anymore. Plans were dead. Plans were passé. The idea of tomorrow, five minutes from now, had gone out of fashion.

Anna picked up something on the tracking system.

"Up here. Pull over."

"What?"

"She's out."

Lon turned hard to the right and began bullying the buggy toward the curb, forcing a Kurdish Tel Afar fuel-cell burner onto the sidewalk. Anna'd seen loads of those things when she first arrived in the northwest, pollutionless automotive versions of a perpetual motion machine, combining hydrogen and oxygen to produce electricity, never needing recharging, only the National Security Profit Margins Amendment had pretty much put the kibosh on them. Lon waved agreeably at the driver as if she'd voluntarily given him the right-of-way.

Silikon skorried from her tuk-tuk into the old US Courthouse, now a Kabuki theater. The satellite picked her up a minute later coming out the Main Street entrance. She hailed and boarded another tuk-tuk, this one navigated by a man or woman wearing goggles and respirator, licensed for work in Shanty Town.

Within half an hour Anna and Lon'd crossed the Spokane River steaming with chemicals under the amplifying sunlight and centimetered into the snarl of meter-wide alleys lined with shoulder-high shacks made of packing crates, sheet metal, shards of grease-stained translucent plastic, huge soggy appliance boxes, paint cans, cracks stuffed with rags and insulation from the landfill sites several kils to the east, six thousand new inhabitants arriving every week, farmers from down south, the diseased, the elderly, city-dwellers whose ever-precarious credit lines had just crashed, refugees from other shantytowns in other semi-states.

Campfires smoldered in doorways. Coppery smog churned close to the packed-dirt ground, stinking of rotten vegetables, foul roachmeat, and astringent petroleum distillates. People in smocks stood in long lines selling cheap polluted blood at mobile units, ushered in by people in khaki fatigues, rubber gloves, and respirators. Skeletons squatted by overturned trash cans and oily puddles and hawked those new nanodrugs at bargain credit.

A gaunt barefoot man in a ripped yellowish t-shirt and no pants stepped up to the driver's side of the Chiehshou, offering a reliquary vial containing the excess lard of some glam. Sweating freely, Lon paid no attention to him, just chugged along, tapping time to the Chinese muzak which'd returned to the airwaves. At an intersection teeming with underfed children, he put his foot on the brake, reached into the door pouch, and pulled out a bag of hydergine-enhanced Laika chew. He snipped out a fat hairy lump between one of his thumbs and forefinger on his right hand and inserted it between his double rows of teeth and cheek.

"Man," he said, "I fuckin' *love* this place."

Around noon Silikon stopped at one of those Ride'n'Save lots ringing the city and rented a dilapidated desert-camouflaged US Army surplus Jeep Hellhound. She shot off northeast at high-scream speed on what remained of State Highway 2, tore by some burned-out safe-zone compounds squatted by Techno-Hicksters, a dead town from the last century surrounded by a torn chain-link fence hung with all sorts of radiation warnings, fetid remains of a silver mine near Colbert, through dull, flat, brown, clear-cut country-side, broken only by the occasional trailer park, fuel enclave, or abandoned shopping mall. Outside Priest River she paused to pee, outside Sandpoint to gas up. Otherwise she let that Hellhound run wide-open, rip, nearly blew some shocks, looked like, on some vicious potholes and fissures in the incrementally inferior road, fishtailed around bends, spewed mud and stone in her wake, till, just past sunset, her light beams floating through a thin stand of needleless tamarack, she joggled to a standstill before a weather-worn, worm-eaten, tumble-down Alzheimer's victim of a log cabin tilting almost imperceptibly starboard on the edge of a defunct lake whose water had become the color and consistency of green cottage cheese.

The Chiehshou rolled to a halt half a kil back, headlights off, infrared tracking system emitting a high-pitched hum. Silikon burst into a woman on fire on the monitor. A red blazing body climbed out of the Jeep, stretched, arms akimbo, face skyward, evidently looking up at the string of huge satellite mirrors visible on the horizon through the trees, tin-can tops from this angle, launched twenty years ago to help bring light to the dark Canadian winters to the north. She strolled toward the cabin, footsteps momentary red flares on the earth behind her. She wasn't wearing shoes.

Anna sat watching her on the screen. This was her favorite time in life, just before she reached for the incendiary device. She felt calm, italicized, unambiguous. Everything went according to plan from here on out. Everything did what it should.

The three of them, she knew, were people in history now.

19

Time Becomes Distance

Thursday Nov. 5th 1846 My name is Tamsen Donner, *Uly saw a large hand with chafed red knuckles connected to the end of his arm write.* I am Mr. George Donner's wife. We embarked from Springfield, Ill., on the 14th day of April with 6 wagons. In our family, which numbers 18, are,—our 5 children; George's brother Jacob and his wife Elizabeth; their 7 children; and 2 teamsters in our employment. We plan to homestead in California, I to open a seminary for young ladies.

After suffering various tribulations, including the loss of several members of our train and an arduous crossing of the Wahsatch and the Great Basin, otherwise known as Hastings' Cut-off, we have become snowbound in a meadow near Alder Creek some eight or ten miles from the pass over the Sierra. My husband, in cutting timber to replace a broken axle on Oct. 28th, injured his hand, when the chisel he was employing for this task slipped. We have bandaged the wound, and George makes light of the incident.

The strength of the storm took us by surprise. By the time George and Jacob replaced the axle, the snow had made travel impossible. We cut some logs for cabins on Oct. 29th, but that night the blizzard covered the ground to a depth of 3 feet. We did not, we learned the following morning, possess resources sufficient to build such structures with haste, and so abandoned that impractical plan in favor of erecting some other sort of shelters. We hence cleared snow around a great pine, and set our tent south of the tree. In front of this, we constructed a lean-to of pine branches, which we covered with quilts, buffalo robes, etc. We built a fireplace at the base of the tree. Inside the tent, we drove stakes into the ground,—and on these we fastened poles to form the frame for our beds. Our teamsters have raised an Indian wigwam some small distance away from our encampment.

We are chilled, muddy, and damp, but otherwise none the worse for wear. The pages of this schoolgirl's notebook in which I write,—one of the few I saved from our crossing of the Great Salt Desert,—are moist to the touch. Little Eliza has a cold.

<u>Friday Nov. 6th</u> Fine morning. Orange snow and yellow sparkles at sunrise. Spiny frosting upon trees. A peppermint camphor feel to the atmosphere, sharp and fresh, accompanied by a headachy brightness.

Clouds and wind by noon. Storm again. No living thing without wings can get about.

<u>Saturday Nov. 7th</u> My husband and I voiced grave reservations at the prospect of leaving the original path known as the Emigrant Trail. Hastings' Cut-off has proved disastrous for our party. Our family alone has lost two wagons to the Wahsatch and Great Basin, many of our provisions, which we were forced to cache, and for which we will have to return in the spring, untold cattle to the dreadful savages, and, most precious thing, time itself.

I cannot speak to the material loss that the others in the Donner Party have incurred.

To my knowledge, six individuals have thus far perished by various means,—including Mrs. Keyes, Mr. Halloran, Mr. Snyder, Mr. Hardkoop, Mr. Wolfinger, and Mr. Pike. We are currently uncertain as to the fate of the advance expedition consisting of the Breens, Graveses, Kesebergs, Murphys, and others, which made a bid for the pass on the 28th, or the day the storm began.

Snow continues. Eliza improved. George, Jacob, and the teamsters have begun slaughtering cattle. No bread or salt.

<u>Sunday 8th</u> Same weather. Snow 5 feet. Subzero cold. Whites, grays, and blues; trees grays and browns.

The rocks appear to be reclining buffalo.

<u>Tuesday 10</u> George's hand no better, although he tells me that we have much graver concerns with which to fill our minds. Killed

most part of our cattle in preparation for the long winter ahead. Plan to use the hides to further shield our tent and lean-to from wind.

Jacob and teamsters cut wood all day in storm.

Cannot free my imagination from the look in poor Mr. Reed's eyes as he turned to leave that sad morning. Would any of us have done any differently from him? Would any of us, civilized Christians all, not defend our kin?

It is comforting beyond measure to know that he is safe and sound,—but what, I think even as I pen those words, of the others? Let us pray they have also attained sanctuary.

Snow turning to rain.

Last night I dreamt of those bones littered before us on the Humboldt trail, the horrible tale of that unfortunate man struck down by the Diggers.

The unimportant diverts our gaze, and life pounces.

Wednesday 11 We have little more except time to spend here.

The children, Elizabeth, and I remain in the tent much of the day, with little to do save wait for evening, which brings an early and uneasy sleep, and a rope of uncomfortable dreams in which time nonetheless passes somewhat more quickly than during our waking hours.

We frequently recount stories as we knit. I tell the children again and again about Odysseus, and his cursed journey, Hercules, and his monstrous labors, Job, and his awful tribulations, an important lesson for them in each of these tales of endurance and fate,—yet, just as frequently, we sit in silence, listening to the rain fall, fall, fall, almost able to hear every second tick by around us at the seeming duration of a month.

Thursday 12 Cleared off last night about 12 o'clock. Froze hard. Fair and pleasant now. Sky blue. Sunshine. Nature in its splendor is divine.

George preparing for scouting mission to pass tomorrow.

A bad-spirited crow with ruffled feathers kept us company much of the afternoon.

Friday 13 George, Jacob and Mr. James gone to pass.

Mr. Shoemaker, a kind-hearted, hard-working young man, always quick with the joke, has remained behind to watch over us.

Many times dear Mr. Shoemaker has deflected our dark thoughts with his light,—if earthy,—wit long beyond the point where otherwise we might have gone.

I cannot help thinking of what George will find ahead. Is there a chance that the summit will still be passable, that the advance expedition attained the western slopes before the snow wholly blocked its route? If so, then perhaps there is some cause for hope within us.

Perhaps, even as I write this, a rescue team is mounted at Fort Sutter. Even now soldiers are loading the pack-mules.

We must believe that which it comforts us to believe.

<u>Sunday 15</u> George and the others returned this afternoon. I thank the Lord they are well,—and yet with the same breath I must confess that there is much that troubles my thoughts.

The advance expedition was unable to mount the summit. It has dug in at Truckee Lake, erecting three cabins and a lean-to, and beginning the hard work of slaughtering cattle. Conditions at the lake camp, George reports, are poor. Both the expeditions' own supplies, and those which Mr. Stanton had borne from Sutter's Fort, are depleted. At this rate, they will be gone within a matter of weeks.

Yesterday morning, 15 hardy men at that camp attempted escape across the pass. Each carried a small piece of beef for provision. At the head of the lake, they found the snow still soft, and more than 10 feet deep. They returned from whence they came by mid-afternoon with nothing to show for their labor save unmeasurable weariness, but, men of courage that they are, they vow to essay the summit again under more favorable conditions.

Here, I pray, we are secure against the cold and snow. We possess an abundance of heavy clothing. We have firewood aplenty.

May the Lord watch over us.

<u>Tues. 17</u> Returned this afternoon from first visit to Truckee Lake encampment. The situation there is bad indeed.

The Breens, by right of first arrival, have mended the roof of a shanty already in existence by a stream feeding the lake, and moved in. Alongside, Mr. Keseberg has erected a lean-to. Upstream the Eddys and Murphys have constructed a double-cabin for themselves (approx. 25x15 ft.) against a rock shaped like a giant turtle, and downstream a good half-mile the Graveses have constructed a similar structure, of which they inhabit the western end; the Reeds, Mrs. McCutchen and her infant, the servants, the teamsters, and the two Indians the eastern.

Each cabin is squat, rectangular, and devised in haste, the consequence being that each lacks windows, while possessing only bare dirt floors, mere openings for doors, and for roofs wagon-canvasses and oxhides.

Inside, the cabins are dank and dark. They exude an unwholesome odor of filth.

60 people,—19 men, 12 women, 29 children,—live within them.

Outside confusion reigns. Many wagons were abandoned in the snow beyond the head of the lake. The few remaining stand throughout the encampment in the greatest possible state of disarray, partially unloaded, dismantled, often without coverings or even wheels. Many oxen have been slaughtered, their quarters stacked about like cordwood in a barnyard. The surviving cattle are skeletal, unable to gain sufficient nourishment which lies beneath the deepening snow.

While water and wood are readily enough available, food is markedly less so. Men report seeing fish in the lake, but, not fishermen by trade, can devise no effective method by which to capture them. Hunting is poor, deer having long since descended below snowline, bear having slipped into hibernation, ducks and geese having migrated south. The stray coyote, wolf, occasional owl, or gray squirrel, are the only prospects for fresh meat in the vicinity, and luck in procuring them has been sadly wanting. Hence does each family jealously hoard its own precious supply.

Poor Mrs. Reed, responsible for eight people all together, possesses not a single beast, and has thereby been forced to trade with Mr. Graves, promising to pay two for one when they arrive in California.

Surely there must be a thaw before long. Even the big snow in Illinois lasted only 9 weeks.

Surely there must be a conclusion to this.

<u>Wed. 18</u> While we visited the lake encampment, Mr. Graves spoke to us about a plan.

He recounted certain contrivances, "snow-shoes," which he

recalled from his childhood in the Green Mountains of Vermont. These consist of large, flat, round, crisscrossed rawhide soles fastened to one's ordinary shoes, which, through a method of general compression, enable the walker to move upon the top of the snow without sinking in. Mr. Graves and Mr. Stanton will soon commence fashioning a number of these mechanisms, by which the most fit members of the party will be able to cross the summit, and thus push on in order to secure help for the rest.

Thurs. 19 George's hand, far from improving, has only deteriorated in condition. He finds difficulty in employing it during his daily tasks, and often complains of a feeling of stiffness within it. We keep the wound bandaged, and pray for the best.

Some clouds flying.

Every morning the first words out of little Frances's mouth are, "When are we leaving this place, mommy?",—and I am forced to confess, yet once more, that I have no answer.

I contemplate tomorrow, and the tomorrow after that, and I realize that it is not for ourselves, but for our children, that George and I must be strong.

We will survive, we will flourish,—because I simply cannot conceive of what might happen to them, if we do not.

Fri. 20 Food supplies diminishing more quickly than planned. We must prepare ourselves for less. Everyday there will be less of everything,—meat, beans, coffee, warmth, strength, hope,—everything except time.

Of that, there will always be a surplus.

Sat. 21 Sunny and fair. In the distance, clouds. Snow in the mountains. Every afternoon, as the sky dims, and the bitter cold sets in, a sense of unease settles around the encampment like the darkness itself.

Sun. 22 Lord grant us the courage to endure this.

Wed. 25 This evening, a sensation of waiting. It runs through my system like fire, an overwhelming premonition, that something is taking its course.

I cannot find words to articulate this.

Thurs. 26 Another storm began last evening. Today rain and sleet. Surely no summit attempt from the lake encampment. Beans finished.

Mr. Shoemaker, sweet man, is not well. Complains of continual lassitude. His body needs more sustenance than we are able to supply. He jokes less, spends more time by himself, sits for hours on end upon a stump staring at the ground 3 feet in front of him.

Last night I dreamt of Mrs. Reed swatting at silent Mr. Keseberg, the gigantic blond bear, until George and the others came to his rescue.

Mr. Keseberg's stillness is frightening. It is the stillness of a great rattlesnake shot through with a business-like knowledge of death. I shudder at the very thought of that man.

Nor can I rid my mind of Mrs. Keseberg's face the morning after her husband's contention with Mrs. Reed,—grim, hard, those bluish welts like shadows around her temples and eyes.

Fri. 27 Damp and muddy in our canvas prison. Last coffee today.

Hours of nothing stretching before us accompanied by a species of mental floating,—less strict thoughts than a series of sensory impressions drifting into one another, the patter of rain, the crystalline sound of sleet, the children playing quietly in the corner, the deep hollow breathing of George half-asleep in his bed, the clatter of a tin cup, the steady consumption of the fire, the plock of a single water droplet into a puddle near the tent flap, the distant half-heard undertones of Jacob's family speaking among themselves, the teamsters chopping a tree bordering the meadow.

George's hand red and swollen. Ugly yellowish matter inside the wound. This despite our continual cleansing and bandaging. I fear the infection has crept as well into his forearm, which is hot and somewhat tough to the touch.

Sat. 28 Reduced rations. The children complain. Mr. Shoemaker in poor health. Snowing fast now about 10 o'clock. 8 or 10 inches deep.

Sun. 29 New snow about 3 feet deep. Soap-flake snow. Hard to get wood. We remain in our tent through the day, venturing out only to heed nature's call, or visit with Jacob and Elizabeth, as we did just now, for Sunday prayer.

We beseech thee, O Lord, to look down favorably upon us, and grant us the fortitude to endure this trial. We thank Thee for all we still possess, for our children's health, for the sustenance we may still enjoy, and for the pleasure we experience in each other's company; and we ask Thee to grant mercy upon our souls, and see fit to resolve this storm soon, so that those at the lake encampment might strike for the pass, for California and Sutter's Fort on the other side, carrying with them hope of deliverance.

"Oh that I were as in months past, as in the days when God preserved me; when his candle shined upon my head, and when by his light I walked through darkness." (Job 29: 2,3)

Amen.

<u>Mon. 30</u> 4 or 5 feet of snow. Drifts 10 ft. Milkweeds falling fast. Looks as likely to continue as when it commenced.

<u>Dec. 1 Tues.</u> New month. Snowing. 6 feet. Completely housed up. Meat supply low. Bad fire this morning.

My thoughts begin to turn toward Christmas with great misgivings. What will the children eat? What kind of celebration can we contemplate in this, our current situation?

We have lost so much.

<u>Wed. 2</u> Snow 7 feet. Sun shining hazily off and on through clouds. One moment is so like another, only my dreamworld seems somehow colorful, significant.

Last night those bones scattered across the Humboldt trail came calling again. I was not myself in the dream, but rather inhabited poor Sallee's body. I felt the deadly arrow pierce my breast as I rode, felt myself topple from the saddle, and, life running out of me, heard the detestable Diggers circle closer, dismount, their footsteps draw near,—although I should, perhaps, even then, have been far beyond such capabilities. As I lay dying, I felt a strong hand tug up my head by the hair, and, laughter in the hot wind, begin the gruesome process of scalping. I heard my skin tear wetly from my own skull. Blood dribbled into my eyes and stung, seeped between my lips, tasting metallic and vile. I peered up at the uncultivated features of the hateful Digger above me, his dark fiery eyes, his open mouth, his skin the color of pottery, and, when I opened my own mouth to cry out, I realized, with horror, that my vocal cords had already been severed. I gargled in my own gore, unable to scream.

<u>Thurs. 3</u> Blizzard stopped. Warmed up some, but not enough to thaw the bluewhite snow lying around us in the most beautiful feminine folds. Began again just past noon. Continuing. Likely to

do so all night.

The Digger's eyes, as I now recall them, were not dark at all,—they were, rather, blue, ice blue. Mr. Keseberg's color.

<u>Fri.</u> 4 Neither snow nor rain. Thank the Lord for one fine day! Teamsters out chopping. I am mending our leaky tent. The radiance of Nature is filled with awe. The whole earth is white, spangling,—a wedding cake world, all sugar-glaze and sweetness!

When we are happy, it seems beyond belief that we were ever not so;—and when we are cheerless, we find it unimaginable to conceive that we ever could have been otherwise.

<u>Sat.</u> 5 We are all so terribly tired. The children seldom play, but are content to remain a-bed, gliding in and out of sleep for much of the day. George, too, rests for hours upon end, hopeful that this will hasten his recovery. When we visit Jacob and Elizabeth, talk seems a burden,—a frightful effort of will. There is little to say these days to each other, few topics worth considering that haven't already been considered, little we can do for each other any longer.

I find it horribly arduous to concentrate long enough to commit even a few observations to the page. My writing arm is heavy, my head light.

I fulfill my daily chores as if in a dream,—I see my hands moving, feel my legs supporting me, and yet my body seems to be someone else's body, my embryonic thoughts unable to form themselves into cogent words.

<u>Sun.</u> 6 Prayer with Jacob and Elizabeth:

Over the course of this journey, with its many trials, George and I have grown into a different kind of intimate rapport with each other. I find it difficult to articulate, and particularize, the details of such an alteration,—and yet, perhaps, I might chance to say that we have entered into a more lovely, more generous, more affectionate acceptance of each other's inimitable ways. Perhaps, too, if I write frankly, a glint of fear flashes at the corner of our bond in the face of each other's mortal condition, as we think back, day after day, upon the sad demise of so many in our party these past months. We have located a comfortable, and blessed, garment to slip into in our 45th and 62nd years.

There is so much to be thankful for.

Wed. 9 As soon as the sun disappears behind a cloud, the atmosphere chills drastically. Blue shadows bring on bitter nights earlier and earlier. Dark by 4.

Commenced snowing about 11 o'clock.

Wolves feeding on carrion nearby today. Mr. Shoemaker could not attain a clear shot.

Thurs. 10 Jacob fainted from lack of food as he commenced chopping wood this morning. Bad fever.

Elizabeth in a frightful way.

Fri. 11 Clear sky visible at times. Deliciously crisp in sun.

Jacob cannot stir from bed.

Meat gone.

Sun. 13 Infection moved into George's upper arm. He seldom leaves his bed.

Jacob believes we are back in Springfield. He speaks of the buildings as if they still surrounded him, greets the phantasmagoric people walking past him down the street as if they were actual flesh and blood. Fever continues. The sweats.

Elizabeth unable to make the smallest choices. She sits by his bedside, staring into infinity.

Mon. 14 Snows faster than any previous day. Tents covered. We climb out using a staircase Mr. Shoemaker, weak himself, has cut into the snow. Difficult to procure wood. Cannot retrieve trees fallen in deep snow. People not stirring much. Jacob doesn't eat, slips in and out of consciousness.

Tues. 15 Mr. Shoemaker shoveling snow off top of tent to prevent collapse. Can't keep fire going.

Wed. 16 Begun consuming wood-mice when we can capture them.

We shall do what we must.

Jacob no longer aware of this, our world. He takes neither food nor water. Elizabeth remains by his bedside day and night. Mr. Shoemaker very tired, only leaves the teamster tent for short periods of work when absolutely necessary. George and children asleep.

Sat. 19 Elizabeth woke me around three o'clock in the morning. Jacob experiencing difficulty breathing. As we tried to raise him into a sitting position, he vomited and began to choke. A minute later he had expired.

With greatest exertion, buried him in snow.

Elizabeth and children inconsolable.

Sun. 20 "What is my strength, that I should hope? and what is mine end, that I should prolong my life?" (Job 6:11)

Wed Death arrives in a series of shocks. Jacob cannot be gone and he is gone. There is something we can do to bring him back and there is nothing we can do to bring him back. Images of him alive open like black roses in my brain and won't leave won't leave won't leave and he will never walk among us again.

Thurs Dismantled hides from tent for food. We hold hides over fire till hair singed off. Scrape with knife. Place in kettle w/ water. boil & steam w/out cease till soft & pulpy. Cool to glue-like jelly-soup. impression of nourishment

Fri Began laborious task of retrieving bones previously thrown away. If boiled long enough will flavor water crumble between teeth. Fire wood difficult. We pray the God of mercy to deliver us from our present calamity.

Sat Sam Shoemaker died of a sudden while chopping this morning. The thought is too large to fit in the space of our minds.

Mon Children remain wrapped in blankets through day life turned inward still air putrid w/ sweaty blankets   smoke hide glue mud

        cooking bones rotten teeth infection wet hair

Wed short visit by elliott company started on snow shoes some time ago to cross mountains godspeed situation bleak at lake last cattle horses dogs gone   stantons mules & cattle lost in snow fear forever   hides & bones to eat   spitzer too weak to rise bealis & charley & smith & reinhardt dead   reduced to unspeakable talk

Thurs elliott gone early this morning   Keseberg w/ me always his blue eyes blond bear tomahawk in hand   my thoughts wander & range unable to still   each particular loss brings back all previous ones

        o lord deliver us from our present dread

Sat terrible bout w/ gravel   snow peppered w/ soot mud pine needles pebbles urine olivegreen unhealthy feces   reek unbearable   bees in my head snow covering tents   may god have mercy upon our souls

Tues (?) snow   Eliz. bedridden   George in sweats   tired beyond words   snowshoers?

Thurs (?) where did we begin that we might arrive here

(?)   some survive & prosper & some perish for no reason look at what is left us   abdomen distended   mind weak   G.'s hand black   E. dreams   new year perhaps & perhaps not hard to gauge these changes of days & hours

(?) rain all night bees in head they will not get out may almighty god grant the request of an unworthy sinner that I am we are my sweet husband & family amen

20

Barbed-Wire Valentine

It was the only place Krystal could think to go, this shabby one-room cabin in a stand of needleless tamarack on the dead lake...no electricity, no water, not one perpendicular wall, broken glass jagged in the window frames, gamey smell of wet hair in the gray wood, rusted drain in the kitchen sink, torn over-sized Mideastern pillows scattered across the planked floor.

Thing'd once belonged to a friend of a lover's friend. Krystal hadn't even consciously remembered its existence till she was north of Sandpoint, her flesh electric in her need to get away from the hospital, dumb down, find a heartbeat's stillness, though her organs'd sure seemed to know which way to go and why...or maybe it was the ghost...trying to tell its thoughts apart from her own was increasingly surreal these days.

Anyway, she'd been here once before, during her Kristofer Columboid era, that unwashed percussionist for Voids Where Prohibited who'd driven up from Vegas with her for a party hosted by the owners, reclusive rockers whose names she'd never learned and whose whereabouts, she'd heard not long afterwards, had wafted into a series of mysteries and innuendoes. The party'd been a flop. Kristofer'd gotten it through his head shortly after their arrival to swim naked in the lake, such as it was, and his skin blemished into a lasagna of red hives, white welts, and disarming yellowish spots. Which meant Krystal got to spend most of that particular hot night tending to his bad judgment instead of the holographic images of various members of Congress going at it behind semi-closed doors, an idea she hadn't found that appealing in the first place, but which beat spending another evening with her progens, who she'd been living with on and off, by a couple thousand leagues.

She stood barefoot, bloated, and hormonal next to a greasy dented microwave someone had tried throwing through a window but missed. In the graying light she took in the wires where the holoporn unit had been ripped from the wall, the FlexMach weight machine tipped on its side, the foam-rubber stuffing oozing from those pillows like faux sheep innards from a greenish pouch of haggis.

Static surrounded her. She was lonely for her boyfriend. She imagined herself crying. She couldn't make up her mind about anything. All she knew was They just kept rewriting the story of her existence every hour, not giving a good goddamn about contradicting Themselves, taking back what They'd said only yesterday, deciding to assert something different tomorrow, forever naysaying the possibility of a unified narrative you could live by, a chronicle you could count on. Life shadowed into an ellipse of uncertainty. At the outset you didn't even know you were there. Then one day, sooner than you had any right to, you started hearing those distant existential shells coming in, mortars outside a small village in a breakaway Chinese republic. But they were still remote. You understood them like you did the overhead thrum of a passing medivac, always someone else strapped in the stretcher. Except their uncanny thumps got closer all the time, no matter what you did...and then you began to feel them as well as hear them...and, eventually, no surprise, you opened your eyes to discover yourself in a place like this, light failing around you, your lover somewhere far behind and utterly helpless, those shells slamming down just yards away...and you began hoping against hope a stray round wouldn't find you this minute, next week, yet also realized the odds of things ultimately going your way were about the odds of winning any VR game...meaning zero, meaning less than zero, because no matter how hard you played, no matter how committed you were to the concept of victory, you knew there'd always be another level of difficulty after the one you were scuffling with, another chance to screw up, fall down, fuck everything to kingdom come...another nanosecond to lose your focus, let your attention stray, let those incoming shells scream down like fate itself on their vulnerable target.

And so Krystal stood there in the data-spew, just stood there, learning something, listening to Them running important messages through her skin.

Half a kil down the gravel road, Anna Konda reached over and popped the black bubble-windshields on the Chiehshou buggy to let some cool air into the cab, only all that really entered was a heat-breeze carrying an acidic aftercharge of blue-gray diesel exhaust.

She didn't show much concern one way or another, though, since she was having a great time arming the incendiary device. She was part of the record now. She was part of the bigger picture.

"You telling me there's an animal I never heard of called a gnu," she said as she worked.

"I'm telling you you can choose to believe me or you can choose not to believe me," said Lon Tef between sucks on his hydergine-enhanced Laika chew. He wiped his sweaty illustrated head, lingered on the lips transplanted above his ears like little fleshy wings. "Which either way I know what I read in the brochure."

"Bambi with a beard and muscle grafts?"

"Page two. Photograph. Description." He gobbed a glob of brown juice into the twilight and enjoyed the sound of its wet impact on the bare ground. "Hey, what the fuck is this?"

Anna looked up.

Hundreds of flies were crawling on the windshields. They clouded the air outside like black snow, swarmed the couple of rusted car hulks sitting nearby in long weeds.

They were inside, too, vibrating on the dash, all over the humming infrared tracking system, on Anna's arms, in her fuzzy hair, on her cheeks. They loved Lon's bald skin, the pheromonal fragrance of his alopecia universalis. They were busy burrowing into his ears, excavating his sewn-shut right eye, shivering among the row of augs across his forehead and down his temple. His tatt looked as if it was alive.

"Sunset brings 'em out," Anna explained. "Seen it when I was growing up outside Havana. Live off all the shit in the lake, and all the shit in the lake lives off them."

"Well fuck," Lon said, swatting, cumbersome frame heaving half out of his seat, right palm smeared with blood. "Shut the fucking windshields."

"Just a sec here, man." She was at the tricky part, getting the bios to kick in right. Flies congealed on her fingers, the backs of her hands. "Ah, here we go...just a sec...just a sec...okay..." She gently depressed a trigger with her pinkie and slipped the skull-plate back in place.

The white cat opened its beautiful blue eyes, looked at her, and began to squirm, wanting down.

Anna leaned over the side of the buggy, softly set the feline incendiary device on the soil color of boiled shrimp, and aimed it for the cabin. When she let go it sprung off into the last light. She hauled herself back in and yanked down the windshields, helped Lon kill off the bulk of the flies that'd become trapped inside with them. It left her hands sticky with pulp.

Secretions from his chew leaked down Lon's chest. His tatt was smudged with blood and thousands of wings, hairy abdomens, legs, heads, proboscises.

"Oh, man," he said, taking inventory.

"You look like a plane crash."

He began to scoop parts of himself back into his seat with the little ice-scraper in the glove compartment.

"You know what?" he said.

"What?"

"This here's the part they don't tell you about."

"Interrogations, fine."

"Hand to hand, okay."

"But this shit."

"Which I'm not saying a big lecture or anything is necessary or anything. Spare a couple words, is all. In other way of saying it, it'd just be nice to know."

"A sort of planning thing. Sí."

"Like maybe you could bring along some Handi-Wipes or

whatnot."

"You want I should look for a rag?"

"Naw. I'm fine. I'm just saying. Hyperthetical, like. A little warning wouldn't bust nobody's balls or nothing. A sort of...whudya call it."

"A politeness deal."

"Exactly. A politeness deal. Thanks."

"De nada."

They sat thinking about this, listening to the black blizzard birring outside.

Krystal noticed the first flies sibilating in the dark corners of the cabin near the ceiling a microsecond before she heard the mewl rise outside, the thunk against the door.

A breathtaking white cat, purring, tail erect, fur thick silk, crowded against her when she opened it.

"Hey, sweety," she said, kneeling to pick it up, "where'd you come from?"

And the ghost slammed down on her. Filled her head. Drove out the world.

She fell back on the floor, dazed, still cradling the cat against her.

The voice whispered in her brain, telling her it was time to be afraid now because things had begun, because the pattern was un-wrapping around her and within her, a chemical process, but Krystal couldn't bring herself to be afraid. She lay staring at the ceiling, lips parted.

Black wind blew through her bones.

Blue silent wings over the clock...through the arctic span on our way to meet you...there's nothing else, nothing at all, just the mouth moving, always moving, with no one in mind but you...

Krystal saw herself in the cramped epoxy-gray interior of an old space station, maybe a satellite hauler, back in the NASA days, three meters by three meters, watching dozens of mechanical arms working in silence, some tipped with needlenose pliers, some with electric riveters, soldering irons, vises, lug wrenches, all in the midst of a perpetual churn of weightless debris, building with methodical deliberation.

The centipede god watching over you...

Not another machine, not a satellite at all...only itself...it was constructing itself, which wasn't *inside* the space station, but *was* the space station, had grown around itself, thorax surrounding her, termiting along toward identity. And she wasn't watching it, removed. Her point of view was meshed with its point of view. She lived in its belly. She *was* its belly. She had no mouth, no ears, no precise boundaries to her body. Her skin was its skin, blending into complex superconductive protein plastics, resins, vat-grown cellulose, her thoughts its thoughts.

Eating my own hands...gnawing away...voices not mine and mine, the thoughts, wanting me to have a mind...meat...how many of us are there...dead and not dead, carved into roses, the permanent condition where you strip away layers of your own epidermis to construct slate heat, raising us, learning the language of endless fire, the shining bones, the silver eyes of your lover...

Krystal lay on the floor, aware of flies gathering on the soft flesh of her face.

The incendiary device felt an electrical storm rustle down its razzed spinal cord, and next its paws were on the wooden planks, the bare earth, sprinting through the living cloud of flies at that part of day when it always went blind, vision fading into two-dimensional shades of gray and grayer, no matter what it did, no matter what it ate, or whether it slept or mewled at the rising moon or just sat still and waited for its sight to return, because those flies didn't make any difference, none of it made any difference, none of it except the need to reach the couple in that buggy over there, up the path, through the web of leafless underbrush, the desire moist and fragrant as the ashen light surrounding it to attain freedom from the memories of the odorless jelly, the holes in the trachea, the exquisite pain where eyes had once been, the humans it had seen once and once only but knew all about, their metallic smell of ambition, their poignant boredom, their own profuse hunger to pick it up and hold it close, shelter it, stroke its sensitive neck, at which instant they could all at last merge, each one becoming the others, each transmogrifying through the massive white blare of light into something so much larger.

"Because the innaresting thing is if you knew you could make arrangements," Lon said.

"You could prepare."

"They do it in the military. They say something like, you know, 'Okay, we may be having a little problem with like a hundred fucking billion flies, so you might want to bring a little bug spray with you during this run. You don't have to or anything. But it might, you know, be a good idea or something.'"

"Dish towels."

"You don't know what I'd give for a dish towel right now."

"You saying you want I should look for a rag?"

"I'm saying don't worry about it. Which it would just be a nice thing to've been told, is all."

"So tell me something."

"Shoot."

"How you figure this connects?"

"Huh?"

"You said stuff connects to other stuff. How you figure this stuff right now connects to stuff elsewhere?"

"What? You saying it doesn't? You saying this instant has nothing to do with any other instant? You saying it exists separated from everything else?"

"I'm saying how does it, is all. You said people are too dogshit stupid to see the connections. Only I don't see the connections. Help me out here. What am I missing?"

"Ratfuck stupid. I said people are too ratfuck stupid to see the connections."

"Which are what, exactly?"

"Hey, whudya suppose that red dot there is?"

"What red dot?"

"The red dot on the screen there," he said, pointing at the custom guidance and tracking system with a supernumerary thumb.

Anna examined the monitor. The part she understood was the glowing rubiate torso on the floor of the cabin. That represented Silikon, who was probably sleeping. She'd had a fucking awful last twenty-four hours. Anna also understood the small fuschia fireball represented the incendiary device.

The part she couldn't understand was why that small fuschia fireball was moving away from the cabin instead of toward it.

Moving, in fact, if she wasn't mistaken, straight for their buggy.

This wasn't the plan. This wasn't how history was supposed to unreel this evening.

She sat studying the screen, watching the fireball close the distance between it and them.

"Maricón," she said.

"Maricón what?"

"Maricón something's fucked."

"Maricón something's fucked how?"

"Bitch reconfigured the incendiary."

"You saying the red dot's the incendiary?"

"I'm saying how the hell could she do that? Have to take the whole damn thing apart and begin all over from scratch. Start the car."

"You saying that fucker's armed?"

"I'm saying start the fucking car, man."

The small fuchsia fireball darted under the rosy rectangle signifying the Chiehshou's chassis. Lon punched the ignition button. The buggy coughed and died.

Anna experienced cellular panic.

"Fuck fuck fuck," Lon said.

The engine gasped and caught in a billowing outburst of exhaust. The thundercloud engulfed the Batmobile fins, the monster wheels, the roll bar, the sham machinery bristling off in every direction, everything, for the count of six.

When it wisped away, all the flies were gone.

Anna saw the incendiary device padding toward her across the hood. She reached over, popped the black bubble-windshields, and began clambering out.

Lon began to depress the gas pedal.

The last light flashed off the huge satellite mirrors barely visible on the horizon through the trees.

21

Deer Hunt

The snowshoes Stanton and Graves had fashioned, tough U-shaped pieces of hickory used for oxbows sawed into strips, bands of rawhide woven back and forth across them, lacked turned-up toes and tapering heels yet supported a person's weight and functioned well enough for the ten men, five women, and two Indians to chance escape.

Even though the trail was buried beneath snow, the Indians were able to guide the party to the summit by twilight the first day. Sun disappearing in the late afternoon, air chilling, Uly watched himself (his clover-red arms, numb restless hands like two stubby mittens, a language he knew and didn't know cycling in his head) and Luis cut green logs about six feet long, create a platform of them on top of the crusty snow, kindle a fire of dry wood there. The green logs took all night to burn through, and so, by throwing blankets over themselves as makeshift tents, keeping near the flames, the emigrants collected the heat and could endure the cold and darkness.

But crossing the treeless expanse of Summit Valley in dazzling sunlight the next day, everything luminous as staring at the sun reflected off a thousand mirrors, Stanton, the fair white man they had journeyed with all this distance, went blind.

On the third and fourth days, a squall flared. Stanton lagged behind. Luis remained with him, trying to encourage him along.

On the fifth day, beef rations ran out.

On the sixth, sightless, weary, Stanton remained at the camp-fire smoking his pipe as the others packed to leave in the morning. Mary Graves approached him to ask if he was ready. He told her the others should start without him.

"I'll be along shortly," he said.

Mary stared at him too long, turned, and walked away.

Ten minutes later the others left without fanfare, without further goodbyes, without spending the time they knew they should thinking about the world that existed within the world.

The storm struck on the seventh day, ripping into them, flurries one second, blizzard the next. It howled down, bellowed, savage, a legion of demented phantoms on the rampage. The travelers lost their bearings, began drifting downslope toward the south instead of traversing the mountains west toward Bear Valley. The snow became blasting ice as the sun set, grains of sugar propelled sixty miles an hour, pulverized rock. Wind burned their cheeks, their ears, beat on their nerves. They hadn't eaten for two days. Their skulls felt stuffed with flaky mulch, handfuls of broken twigs. Sarah Foster, that dreadful woman with the loose-skinned face of an old dog, features white as a bowl of maggots, soul of a badger, saw visions, spirits darting from their dimension into hers, whirling about her, tangling in her hair. She screamed and sat down. Her hands sparrowed around her head. Fosdick slurred his words, pointed to nothing fifty yards away and said a tribe of man-bears was tracking them through the storm, waiting their chance, lumbering on short hairy legs, knuckles dragging through the snow.

The emigs dug a four-foot-deep hole with a wide circumference to protect themselves from the tempest, built a fire, bunched close. Everyone except Eddy and the women argued for going back…and even those who urged forging on knew they had to eat soon or die.

Their brains swirled around some obvious point they couldn't quite make out, slate haze overrunning their sight, fingers refusing to bend.

Wind. Ice.

The idea struck, sharp as the image seen through a telescope: by morning some of them would be dead.

What were the choices when death was no longer an abstraction but the teeth chattering in the mouth of the man lying under blankets across from you, slope of his shoulders, redness of his face, hound's grumble in his throat?

"You know what we must do," Dolan said in his curious accent, part Irish, part Midwestern.

No one looked at him. No one moved. They concentrated instead on the flames, the stutter lick of light, crumble of orange shreds at the fire's core.

Eddy, as if in afterthought, asked: "And what might that be, Mr. Dolan?"

"You know what that might be as well as I do. You all know. We lack the strength to go on or back." He prodded the fire with the stick in his hand. "Without food we are damned."

"What are you telling us? Speak plainly."

"I'm telling you we have a decision before us, Mr. Eddy."

"We have many decisions before us."

"No, Mr. Eddy. We have precisely one. And I'll wager you we're all thinking about it this very instant."

"I don't receive your point."

"Not true. You receive it only too well. Some of us will expire by morning if we don't act." Dolan hesitated. "We all know a way of procuring it."

"Food?"

"Yes, Mr. Eddy. Food."

"Do we, Mr. Dolan?"

"Indeed we do."

"And what way might that be?" asked Mary Graves. She hugged herself beneath a buffalo-robe, ice glittering in her hair like broken cyrstal. "We have seen no game. Our rations are gone. We are a week's walk from the first homesteads and a week removed from the lake encampment. What, pray tell, do you have in mind?"

Fosdick called out in his nightmarish sleep. The travelers waited for him to hush. He drew his knees and arms into his chest below the blankets, his head cradled in his wife Sarah's lap. She rocked, smoothing his hair with her palm.

"Please," Dolan said. "Spare us your naivete, Miss Graves. We abandoned that, or rather that abandoned us, when we left the plains. We're in the terrain of extremities now, my dear. Hence we must think in extremes, act in extremes, if we are to have even a prospect of survival." He looked around at the rest of the travelers. "Am I making my proposition clear?"

"Good God," Mary said, his intent unfolding in her mind.

"This has nothing to do with Him. This has to do with a decision so uncomplicated it pains."

Mary stared at him as if he'd just cursed her.

"Grantin' your point momentarily," Harriet, young gap-tooth widow of William Pike, asked, "how you propose we go about reckonin' such a decision?"

"Simply. We draw lots, give ourselves to fortune."

"This'd be the price of survivin'?"

"It would, Mrs. Pike. Nor, I should add, will it stop here, tonight."

She leaned toward him as if she couldn't quite hear his words in the wind. Her nose was a flat thumb.

"I estimate we shall have to draw again before we reach the first homestead. We should all understand this."

"Draw again?" Franklin Graves asked.

"The difficulty lies not in the initial instance, desperate as it might be. It lies in knowing, upon its completion, before its completion, that there will be a second. Perhaps even a third."

"Okay," Foster said, skinny as a weasel, haggard-faced, beard matted, hot eyes frenzied as a cornered coyote's. "S'posen we grant you the decision part. Let me ask you this: how you proposin' to pull it off?"

"What do you mean?"

"You sayin' we s'posed to…what…just *butcher* some fella sittin' next to us liken he was some kinda ox?"

"I am. Precisely."

"You can't possibly be serious," Sarah said.

Foster's eyes skidded back and forth.

"Jesus," he said.

"What happened to us?" asked Mary.

"The second our rations ran out we arrived here," Dolan said.

"The second we moved too far away from camp to return. We're in a new land, Mary."

Foster was up against a wall. He was collared, trapped.

"But there's gotta be a better way. This cain't be it. We cain't just turn around and start guttin' each other. It ain't right."

"One person succumbs so that others might not," Franklin said, thinking aloud. "Perhaps that's not necessarily so difficult an idea to entertain."

"You're mad," Sarah said to Dolan.

"I'm as sane as you are…as any of you are." He stopped, threw the stick he was holding into the fire. It lurched into flames. "I make a motion we take a vote straightaway. For the vote to be binding, it must be unanimous. We all agree, or this thing does not happen."

"Fair enough," said Eddy.

"But a warning, too. Think long and hard about your choice. Think of yourself three years from now. Tomorrow. What we decide, we do."

"No," Sarah said.

"I second Mr. Dolan's motion," Franklin said, staring into the blaze.

Sarah looked from one to the other.

Dolan slapped his knees.

"It's done, then," he said. "A vote."

"I ain't gonna do it," Foster said.

"I refuse," said Sarah.

"I as well," said Mary. "I won't be part of such an enterprise. We are not savages."

Dolan wondered back at them, face slack.

"What do you mean?"

"We are more than this," Sarah said. "This venture is horrible beyond measure." She scoped the faces of the others. "How dare any of you contemplate such a thing? How *dare* you?"

"And so, by doing nothing, you choose to die," said Dolan.

"By doing nothing, I choose to remain a Christian, sir."

"Your innocence will be the death of you, girl. This is no time for fancy thoughts. We are in the midst of a situation which demands nothing less than practicality."

"Curse me if you will, but I choose to remain innocent rather than decide our fate in God's place."

He looked at her.

"I do, Mrs. Fosdick. I do."

"And I curse *you*, Mr. Dolan. The Almighty should decide such matters, not you, not Mr. Eddy. Not any of us."

"You are a monster," said Sarah.

"I am a man wanting to see sunrise," Dolan said.

"I say draw two lots," Eddy offered. "Exclude the women. Give each of the unfortunates a six-shooter. Put them out in the storm. Wait to see which returns. Each will have a chance for life, then, and, if he loses, he will at least die in the fight."

"Better to draw a single lot," said Franklin. "Shoot the single man."

"I will not have it," Mary said.

"I would rather die myself than be party to such an arrangement," said Sarah.

"And so we perish," Dolan said, "when we have the ability to live?"

Foster coughed into cupped hands. He examined his palms, peered up into the pinging ice.

"There's another way," he said.

The emigrants turned their attention to him. He sat, eyes moving. When he spoke, he spoke to the sky. "I've been thinkin', and, well, this thought's come to me just now."

"Speak," said Eddy.

"Well, way I see it, there's another source of food here. Good one, too."

"Pray tell us your meaning, Mr. Foster," Mary said.

"Source of food ain't got no soul, neither, Miss, near as I can tell."

Dolan relaxed with recognition.

"More animal than human, you mean," he said.

"Ain't civilized in the least. Ain't Christian, neither. Ain't even got no language 'cept fer some grunts 'n' groans like a pack of mangy canines yappin' at the moon."

"Got yourself a point," Harriet said, catching on.

"Damn right I do." Foster glared into the blizzard toward the lodgepole pine. "Look at those two over there. Couple a steer too stupid to know when to get out of the snow. Cain't tell me we're talkin' human bein's there. No way."

Mary, Sarah, Eddy, and some of the others glanced over. The Indians leaned against the trees, blankets wrapped around their shoulders, staring at the ground five feet in front of them, unperturbed by the storm. Ice shimmered on their shoulders, glimmered in their black hair. When they realized they were being watched, they raised their heads slightly, met the gazes of the others, and, faces empty, returned to their inner deliberations, helping the night pass.

"They are, it appears, the very savages of which Mary spoke," Franklin said.

"I don't know nothin' 'bout that," said Foster. "But I can tell you one thing. Their kind's caused our party just a whole *heap* a trouble."

"Diggers've been at us since we entered the Great Basin. Godawful relentless."

"And you know somethin' else darned well, too."

"What might that be, Mr. Foster?"

"You know, push come to shove, they'd have us fer dinner just as soon as a hunk of chewy buffalo meat, if'n they had guns."

"Slaughtered our cattle," Harriet said.

"Dogged our steps with all manner of yips and hoots," said Foster.

"Stole our goods in the night without the slightest provocation," said Franklin.

"Ain't nothin' but a goddamned breed of liars 'n' cheats," said Foster.

"Murderers and heathens," said Harriet.

"Well," Dolan said. "It *does* seem their greatest contribution to culture so far has been the tomahawk."

Harriet and Foster looked at him for the count of three.

Then they shattered into laughter.

It felt so good to let go from their stomachs. They couldn't remember when they'd done such a thing. It had been so long, before so much of this had transpired, and all of a sudden their world transfigured into celebration, a chamber of light, the instant seeming weightless, twinkling, charged with anticipation and hope.

They plashed and stumbled along the streambed, Uly's ankle thrumming from the swollen lump he gained slipping on a sharp rock, Luis snaring in the low overhanging branches, skirmishing with them, breath hard and hollow as a sprinting stallion's. Ice pellets crackled around them. Far away the voices of the hunters rose, trying to pick up their trail. Uly felt blood surge through his jugular, saw Eddy, young vigorous white man with serious eyes and language steady and self-possessed as a wide river, stroll over to them while they waited for morning, remembered how he confided something to Luis, *said it'd be as easy as hunting a pair of deer*, and how Luis's eyes went blank. His friend nodded, looked down at the snow around his feet. Eddy looked at him looking, measuring this situation, then headed back to the bonfire. Luis raised his head, watched him go, eyes locked on the heft of the white man's back, astounded at what he'd just heard, unable to take in the spiny edges of the fact, and he met Uly's eyes, and, without a sound, vanished around the tree. Uly reflexively followed him, the percussive clap of a shotgun blast reverberating through the storm an instant later...but they were in the open now, loping through the thigh-deep silver snow, aiming for the forest ahead.

They comfortably put half a mile, maybe more, between them and their pursuers, maintaining a steady gait, rising and falling in the snow, whispering words of encouragement to each other as they moved...and then, without premonition, chords fumbled, the tempo collapsed, nearly two weeks with little food and their stamina fell away quickly as the earth at the edge of a steep cliff, their legs took on mass, became tree trunks, they plowed through the snow like cripples, knees stiff from the struggle, haunches searing as if wooden pegs had been driven into the joints, lungs crammed with embers, vaporous white clouds whisking across the night sky, and they faltered, pretending they weren't faltering, left language behind, staggered ahead with grim determination, straining for the treeline, every motion a whole day's enterprise, while those voices came to them, shouts, coughs, sounds of urgency. Uly and Luis no longer maintained their effortless lead, no longer kept up that graceful pace they'd set. They backslid, lost ground, sensing the weight, density, and anger of those hunters, slow as a family of porcupines, advancing on them with every yard they fought to cover, and it felt awkward, embarrassing, their bodies unable to perform the simple math of motion, their muscles, bones, and organs no longer theirs. They entered the forest and Uly had to sit down. He was on his knees in the glacial water of the streambed, flailing to his feet, dropping again, Luis beside him, hoisting him up, arms wrapped around his chubby chest, and Luis was down, too, on his knees, face empty, shocked, in disbelief that his body had failed him so badly after all this time, so they began to crawl, splashing, plunging on, fingers numb and useless, hands fiery with cold, knees and shins screaming as they jostled over slick rocks, fussed among clusters of dammed branches, floundered through shallow pools, panting, forcing all their energy into the next six inches, the next foot, while behind them they heard those voices gaining with the deliberateness of dreams.

Uly awoke to the sharp heavy pang of a foot on his spine and saw the hurt as blue lightning.

He opened his eyes and the nightworld lay on its side, rocky ground shooting straight up, stream flowing down like a waterfall, pines jabbing horizontally out of the earth. He was on his stomach. Everything appeared flat.

His cheek was crushed against cold pebbly soil. His left arm, folded clumsily beneath his chest, was numb.

The blue lightning fluoresced up and down his backbone like a dry summer storm. The cosmos moved slowly, in dream-time, and, in dream-time, he heard the slow slur of humanoid grumbles above him, scrape of large feet on gravel, gurgle of water flowing through broken ice.

He believed the man-bears had come to save him. They'd been

following, keeping their distance, but now would lift the two injured men in their long muscular arms and carry them like babies to their nests lined with bluebird feathers, wolf skulls, carved clubs, where they would begin the long process of nursing them back to health, Uly and Luis spending days, weeks, months listening to the beautiful beasts who were spirits of gentle warriors singing with voices that could rob a cougar of its rage, feasting on foods uniting them with something beyond themselves, a realm Uly always imagined as a brightly lit cave, on the walls colorful paintings of his life, the lives of others in his tribe, candles trembling the corridors into being, the cave cognizant of itself, of the universe around it...

A pistol fired at close range.

"Woulda been dead nat'ral, 'nother hour or two," Foster's voice said somewhere above him. "Freezin' liken a slab a beef back't camp."

"Ain't like we didn't do nothin' the snow weren't gonna do anyways," said Harriet.

"Look at the other one," said Dolan. "Poor fellow's shaking like a leaf."

"Best put him out of his misery," Franklin Graves said.

Uly's cheekbone hurt. He had soil in his mouth. He felt the earth breathing below him.

"You're going to die now, son," a voice whispered close to his ear. It was Eddy, his foot on Uly's spine. "Time to make your peace with God if you have a mind to." A hand touched his shoulder. "I'm real sorry about this. Except you had your chance fair and square."

Uly tried to thrash but the boot dug in. The heel drove between two vertebrae. He thought his backbone would snap.

He began to lift his free arm, swung it by his side, trying to grab something, but another boot came down on it. He heard his wrist crack.

"Jesus," Foster said, laughing. "Still got some spunk left in him yet, don't he?"

"Shoot the poor bastard, for godsakes," said Eddy.

"Mr. Eddy's right," said Franklin. "Let's conclude this business directly."

"I'm shootin', I'm shootin'," Foster said. "Just hold your horses a second."

Uly felt the cold barrel of the pistol touch his temple. He smelled oil and burned gunpowder. He heard the hammer cock.

He closed his eyes and saw the man-bears flying through the forest to his rescue like a black wing descending, saw them out the corner of his vision lumbering down the hill, his soul a magnet drawing them in, raising their clubs and whirling down upon the shocked white men unable to respond, knocking their guns aside, trampling into them, shouldering them to their knees, all the while singing…

22

Velocity Girl

Looked like a direct hit by a tactical nuke, Krystal figured as she flashed by the fiery wreckage in her Hellhound, adrenalin cometing through her veins, jumpy headlights throwing the landscape before her into stark white glare, pedal to the metal, nearly blowing some shocks on the furious potholes landmining the gravel road, grit and dust deploying behind her like seaspray behind a kamikaze water-skier.

Huge orange-black-yellow mushroom cloud had been astounding. Buggy'd turned into superheated steam faster than the exchange of neurotransmitters between synapses.

Then an engine was smoking a hundred meters away. A burning bucket seat lay upside down among the rusted car hulks. The weeds were on fire, and so were some of the tamaracks. Flames spread lickety-split. What could've been a distributor cap, black industrial spider, cracked off her hood.

Krystal veered, almost jetted off the road, veered again, wobbled, straightened out, ran her Hellhound wide-open. In the phosphorescent fungal glow of the dashboard she saw she was doing ninety kph. Ninety-five. Only it wasn't fast enough.

She knew no matter how fast she'd go now, it'd never be fast enough.

Her nose began to bleed. She reached over and felt around the glove compartment, coming up with the registration papers and a tube of weak sunscreen provided by the rental agency for use if you went convertible.

So she wiped away the blood with her thumb and forefinger, tilted her head back far as she dared without losing sight of the road, and pinched off her nostrils.

The ghost was mumbling continuously in her head...*air hammers in the purple brown dusk...photos of arrested motion...climbing into the sky...*while she wondered, her periodic abdomen distended, lava-slow liquid churning within, her periodic mind unable to follow the powder-burn of a single question to its answer, why she entered this door when there were so many others open to her...why she looked up at the moment Johnny-Carson meandered in from that summer street and stood under the lazily rotating ceiling fan with his hands in his pockets, just checking things out...why she listened to the voice in her head that sent her to the Voodoo Lounge in the Binge&Purge to meet Uly, sweet Uly, which led her to Moston, which led her to Spocoeur, which led her to that cabin behind her, which led her here, to this instant, nose bleeding, head pulsing, eyes dry as those of a desiccated mummy, dollhouse brushfire receding in her rearview mirror, hurt expanding in her heart, fear...*flat two-dimensional faces of angels without substance or light locked in a tertiary dimension...nerve warnings...read the metastasis with blind fingers...*that strange sensation at the nape of her neck, the one that told her she'd finally caught on, finally understood she wasn't finishing anything, no, she was just beginning, her life till now basic training for a journey to a location she'd only recently begun to picture in the mirrors that'd turned out to be her mind, or what was left of her mind, an electronic ether where she wouldn't need a computer anymore, a space that both existed and didn't exist, opened upon expectation, blazing bushes, a zone where anything could happen, everything was possible, the dead could dance, the visionary be made hyperreal...

Something quantumed into her high beams.

Her reflexes didn't have time to react. A flaming raccoon or possum skittered through her brain, then the soggy *whomp*, the split second of absolute silence, the clatter of tires over gravel, the rill of thumps like a kid's rubber ball shuddering beneath her rig.

And then nothing...darkness in the rearview mirror, harsh headlights eating up the road in front of her, the thought of a thought forming somewhere behind her eyes...*some things you just don't stop for.*

THREE

23

Machine Head

Dawn tinting sepia, temp skirting 30 degrees C, Krystal crossed the Cascades, passed the last safe-zone compounds on Interstate 84, and sped through the swath of chemical plants along the Columbia River, waste gas flaring yellow from the stacks, copperish smoke fixed in the immobile atmosphere.

She beetled through the confusion of shanties ringing Portland and into the downtown area where the public housing towers looked like gray hypodermics turned on end. Some still showed effects of The Rage, cement walls charred, insides gutted, abandoned, graffitied, squatted, pock-marked with bullet holes. Krystal drove along a street lined with construction fences and plastic sheeting and eased around a heap of tires, smashed wooden crates, broken furniture, blackened ribs of a twin-engine Cessna, and split-open dark green garbage bags on which skinny dogs sat panting, dully following the Hellhound with their slow heads, into an Exxon fuel enclave for gas.

Afterward she edged up on an automatic teller across the street, careful not to startle it. She was aching to stretch but didn't want to make any gestures that might be misinterpreted by the machine. The ATM snapped awake. A reinforced steel plate in its armor slid back like the shell of an armadillo and the barrel of a machine gun poked out. A mechanical voice told her to approach slowly with her hands at her sides, then stand still with her eyes open. Blinking could cause blindness. The red beam of a laser scanner shot from beneath the machine gun and flickered for less than a second over the surface of Krystal's left cornea. When it snapped off, the ATM told Krystal she had forty-five seconds to complete her transaction. She worked efficiently, inserting her credit slab and watching the ghost up her account balance.

She backed away and climbed into her rig, driving several more blocks before coming on the crowded bustle of an illicit flea market. Makeshift stalls constructed from refrigerator boxes and ripped sheets jammed the dirt street. Maybe a thousand people overran the neighborhood, scamming, hawking, arguing, bartering for gallons of gas, blackmarket vegetables and cash, bootleg music-chips, caged snakes, cigarettes, used computer parts, third- and fourth-hand clothing, pain killers, filtration masks, fresh farm shrimp, counterfeit chocolate. The whole thing'd erupted spontaneously, cockroaches around spilled cereal, would probably have a life-span of half an hour at most before the Brinks Force discovered it and descended with tear gas to reinforce the Lawful Assembly Decree.

So people chattered, exchanged goods in swift well-rehearsed motions, and hurried on. Krystal knew the steps. She bought two boxes of super-absorbent tampons, Snickers bar, cheap wrinkled black Azid Reign paper suit and pair of black rubber sandals that nonetheless beat Uly's baggy torn blue jeans, black t-shirt, and clownishly large sneakers the medivac guy'd thrown on her. She went up an alley between a Vietnamese café and shoe store that'd been turned into a large, populous, one-room apartment behind a cracked plate-glass window and, standing beside a dumpster, changed, inserted one of the tampons. Somewhere a howler monkey shrieked.

On her way back to the Jeep she tapped the face of her Julia Roberts, busy with tiny useless Victorian gears and springs.

"Six," it said in an approximation of the dead actress's voice, "thirteen."

She sat behind the wheel, ignition off, eating her chocolate bar and watching the flea market teem in front of her through a fabric of melancholy. Her motivation was gone. Everything moved in slo-mo and seemed too loud.

Her belly protruded and she wanted to take it off and put it in the seat next to her. Weird tides shifted in her lower abdomen, thick burblings, blunt contractions. Her nipple hurt when it rubbed against her paper suit. So did the skin around her scar. Seemed several layers of cells had been chafed off, like her nerves existed nearer the harsh air than usual. Her breath smelled fecal and dark. She leaned over and looked at herself in the rearview mirror, believing humans are designed not to understand what they do or why. Small patches of sunscreen remained on her forehead and around her nose. The rest of her face was the pale green of people who believed daylight was an overrated phenomenon. She had ringed eyes, puffy skin, way too many lines for someone her age. Her contacts were foggy with overuse.

She leaned back again, chewing, working to keep her mind barren, and saw an old mostly bald woman in aviator sunglasses pushing a shopping cart choked with junk in her direction.

The woman, a trash bandit who'd stolen recyclables off streetcorner piles of garbage, seemed to have tufts of fur glued to her head. She creaked past a heavy black man in military fatigues drilling a brick wall graffitied in lime spray paint with the words YOU ARE SYNESTHETICALLY DISABLED with a powerful stream of urine. Krystal swallowed. The woman stopped next to the Jeep, rummaged through her rubbish, and tugged out a crumpled neon-mint poster she handed her for the covert ConservoFem Testicle Festival to be held next week in the park down by the river. There would be speeches, rides, psychic bonding, and the celebrated annual castration of genetically enhanced legless rams.

What it didn't mention was that there would also probably be enough Brinks Force personnel to sink an aircraft carrier and, before the first morning was over, something approaching a fullfledged free-for-all.

"Listen to your head," the woman said and creaked away.

At the Portland International Airport, a transistor board of boxy institutional architecture and sandbagged checkpoints manned by ex-merc types, Krystal returned the Hellhound and stepped into the first GTE oxygen booth she spotted.

She inserted her credit slab into a slot beneath a small olive computer screen and punched up the scent of patchouli and "DNA Unto Others" by Recline of the West. She leaned against one of the gray-foamed walls, closed her eyes, and listened to the Brazilian rhythms. There were too many new bits of data twinkling over her. She felt her chest constrict under the whoosh of informational atoms. Usually at times like this she aimed for a Wal-Mart or McQuik King because she could count on these spaces to remain exactly the same wherever they were located in the world. They always provided her with a sense of global consistency, an opportunity to orient herself, stabilize.

Five minutes later the song faded. The cool flow of oxygen cut off. The door slid back. Krystal opened her eyes and felt better, more even and clear-headed, so she stepped out and walked over to the GSA terminal protected by bushes of razor-wire and a meter-tall barricade and bought a plane ticket to the Mexico City Space Port and a shuttle ticket from there to The Iron Curtain, low-orbit Eastern European theme park.

She washed off gummy sweat in the restroom, scrubbed her teeth with her finger, reapplied her sunscreen, bought two spring rolls at a dim sum fastfood counter and carried them across the corridor to the underwater light of a Victorian mesto. There she ordered a glass of absinthe and sat on an overstuffed sofa with curled wing arms and lots of pillows. To her left was a cabinet stuffed with fin-de-siècle bric-a-brac...an inkwell, antique bottles, collected works of Edgar Allan Poe in imitation leather bindings, lace doilies, an intricate silver cigar box, small porcelain bowl of spicy potpourri. Across from her hung a poster of The Hanged Man from a tarot deck that looked as if it'd been painted by Toulouse-Lautrec. Behind her, heavy velvet maroon drapes with gold brocade disguised the fact there was nothing on the other side except wall.

Jet fuel metalized the air. A song by Suicidal Sex, whale chirps, gull screams, and wave lappings, doddering remains of those thumb-sucking New Agers from the last century, played on the sound system. At a nearby polished synthetic-walnut table a guy in a baggy gray business suit, braided rat's tail twined with burned-out fuses, sipped opium tea and groaned to himself behind a portable VR rig, silver wrap-around shades. A CNNer, teenage viral victim with scars like pink-white puckerings up one side of his face and head, stood at the mesto, reporting, wire from a small flat liquid crystal TV attached to his t-shirt collar squiggling up his neck and disappearing into the skin behind his ear. The bartender didn't pay any attention to him. He was busy wiping down the counter. On his chest hung a large thin rectangular clock, ten centimeters by twenty, face red alphanumerics, that ticked down the hours, minutes, and seconds to his death, based on the average life expectancy of a NorAm male. All going well, he had 1,572,480 hours, 52 minutes, and 28 seconds left. His hands and lower arms were gloved with snakeskin tatts.

"Who, what, when, where, how," the CNNer was saying to everyone and no one. "That's what's what. What's when. Who, what, when, where, how. You gotta open yourself up to the scoop. Tune in with me. Find the channel. Around the worlds in thirty seconds. Let's do a little reporting..."

Krystal took a bite of spring roll wrapped in a paper napkin and stared straight ahead, trying to imagine herself back at White Bird Six with Uly, saw him reach forward and pick a crumb off her lips. A genital achiness pumped through her lower back. She washed down the spring roll with the bitter licorice-flavored absinthe and the ghost muttered louder to itself. There was never a time when she was alone. It was like trying to think about one thing with someone talking in your ear about something else. She took another sip. The wormwood kicked her.

"At three a.m., Pacific Standard Time," the CNNer said, "Fester Williams of Pleasant Lake, North McKota, ended her hunger strike initiated in an attempt to force her local cable operator, Mainline Productions, to carry her favorite program, *Crime Deterrent Digest,* by dousing herself with rubbing alcohol and setting herself on fire in her hospital bed. She died at seven-oh-one..."

Krystal realized she could no longer remember what Uly smelled like. She would recognize the scent immediately if she came across it, but she couldn't describe it to herself, couldn't conjure it in her mind.

The guy behind the portable VR rig groaned again and touched his temple with his right hand. Krystal thought black ice, new nanodrug that sometimes caused short-term amnesia.

A manufactured male voice spoke on the PA.

"Due to orbital space debris, all shuttle departures in this hemisphere have been postponed one hour," it said.

If she couldn't conjure his smell, what other details of his existence was she already failing to summon? The problem with forgetting was you couldn't remember what you'd forgotten. So you were never sure whether you'd forgotten something or not. If you concentrated long enough, you could become sure you hadn't. If you concentrated long enough, you could become sure you had.

"President-and-CEO Loew was arrested minutes ago for his involvement in the Lazarus Project," said the CNNer, "the plot to kidnap famine-struck newborns from underdeveloped countries and sell their organs to NorAms for profit. Mr. Loew denied any wrongdoing and said he would be exonerated at his trial. Bail has not yet been determined. His lawyers vigorously deny rumors that the hearts of three infants were discovered by police in his refrigerator..."

Uly was a mosaic in her imagination. Fragments of him were already dropping off, crackling into smaller pieces, vanishing on the trashed floor of her recollection. Krystal couldn't believe it. Just over twenty-four hours and the dissipation had begun.

The surface of her skin hurt. Her water-balloon bladder was bloated. She finished the spring rolls, gulped the rest of the absinthe, felt like a simulation of herself.

She sensed a warm metallic surge between her legs and knew it was time to change her tampon. She sat amid the pillows of the overstuffed sofa a few minutes longer trying to coax her psychic numbness into overrunning the ghost, but the voice just kept on murmuring...*time for all prisoners to run wild...sound of their hope...every second we are closer to the dream of light and language, closer to you, to all of us, the texture of your reflecting membrane*...and so she contemplated standing.

The guy in the portable VR rig flinched and collapsed. He tipped forward and crashed against the polished imitation-walnut floor almost at Krystal's feet. His VR rig clattered beneath her sofa.

The bartender stopped in mid-wipe and looked up. The CNNer kept broadcasting as if nothing had happened. He was doing baseball scores. A female Ozone Baby in a tight pimento-orange body dress and cowboy boots walked into the mesto, examined the man on the floor from a distance, and walked out again.

An SR100 Security Robot System by Cybermotion, Inc., shiny black plastic basketball on wheels, whisked through the entrance and flew to the guy's side. He was twitching as if receiving small electric shocks.

The SR100s patrolled the interior several-thousand-square-kils of the airport for twelve hours at a stretch without recharge, using ultrasonic, optical, and infrared sensors as well as onboard fuzzy logic to navigate around complex obstacles and interpret data. When one detected an anomaly in its environment, it signaled an operator at a remote site who began calling the shots. It was that operator who now began to speak through a mike hidden in the thing's shell in a voice that made her sound like she was lying in some Epidemics Clinic hooked up to an iron lung...which, Krystal figured, might just be the case.

"*Please...stand...back...*" the voice fizzed and gasped. "*Please...stand...back...*"

A panel four or five centimeters in diameter retracted on the side of the basketball and it angled to within a centimeter of the guy's mouth and began running a breath-analysis on him. Meanwhile more basketballs collected in the entrance and outside in the corridor, whirring in agitated contemplation.

Poppy-blue snow began drifting through Krystal's mind. She didn't need to wait to hear the diagnosis to recognize the symptoms of a time seizure. She sat amid the pillows on the Victorian sofa, watching this guy swooping away from her, unstuck in history, skin the hue of margarine, and she pretended to take a last prim sip of absinthe from her already empty glass, find comfort in this private moment, pretended that those two paramedics hadn't really appeared hauling a stretcher between them, her hands weren't really shaking, her skull wasn't really full of a poetry she'd never composed.

"Fly ball," the CNNer said, peering into the sky through the ceiling. "It's *outta* here!"

Fourteen minutes later the metal detector squealed when she tried walking through it.

The woman behind her, bobbed pink hair, pink contacts, pink engineer boots, pink sunscreen, gold front tooth, dropped her bottle of Malaspina Glacier water and looked at Krystal with a dogshit-on-the-foot look. A security guard whose sunscreen reminded her of bruised skin stepped forward, took Krystal by the arm, and ushered her out of line. He wore a navy blue flight suit, black bulletproof vest, and black canvas helmet with a mike on an aluminum stem jutting across his rubbery violet lips. He had a Ludovico-9 machine gun slung over his shoulder.

"Nyet," he said in a heavy Exxon Jersey accent.

"What?" Krystal asked.

Another security guard at another computer terminal waved the rest of the line through the razzed portal. Everyone seemed overly friendly when they shuffled ahead, as if each was compensating for some unspoken guilt.

"Dat's some fuckin' aug ya got up dere," the guy said.

"What aug?"

"Shoulda known bedda 'n tryin' to pass sumpin' like dat. Coulda wiped your whole fuckin' muthaboard."

On the other side of the checkpoint white teenagers wearing biker leathers bought Mayan identities off racks in a clothing stall set up in front of some hurricane fence. Carbon hair dye. Rich brown sunscreen. Artificial quetzal-feathered headdresses. Turquoise, red, and maize-yellow loincloths, long ends hanging down front and back, for the boys. Vividly embroidered smock-like garments for the girls.

"Didn't your manufacturer tell ya nuttin' 'bout da warning labels?"

Krystal stared at him.

"What aug?"

"What aug?"

"Yeah. What aug?"

He uttered a quick samoyedic yap, his version of a laugh, examined her with the clinical eye of a film producer calculating how this crazy chick might fit into his next documentary about the marginalized, disenfranchised, and mentally defunct flatliners wandering the corridors of the broken-down airport night and day.

"'What aug?' she says," he said over his shoulder to the line of people moving through the portal. Only they'd already forgotten about Krystal. They moved forward, faces blank. "Well, uh, let's see here. What aug could I possibly mean? Couldn't be sure or nuttin', course, but I'm guessin' the one *big as a fuckin' soccer ball* jammin' that pretty head a yours."

Jellyfish began undulating through the dark green sea of Krystal's brain, stinging. Blue fireballs burst in her cortex. The ghost babbled in a long disjointed rush of half-language.

The security guard steered her over to his computer console behind a panel of high-impact plastic and pointed at his screen covered with a layer of dust. The CAT-scan loop of her cranium was frozen there, a fluorescent burn of yellows, reds, and greens. In the middle of everything was a hot orange amoeba. It looked like a closeup of the sun, flaring tentacles palpitating rhythmically.

"New generation SEPBOG?" he asked.

Krystal couldn't take her eyes off the image of the interior of her head. There she was, inside out.

"Somato-Enhanced Prototypic Body Guard?" he said.

Krystal forced herself to look at him. One of his eyes wasn't real...too shiny, too easily distracted by auras off to the right.

"Not dat ya'd like know or nuttin', I guess," he said.

"I wouldn't?"

"Computer know it's a computer?"

"Sometimes."

"Yeah. And sometimes not. Never be sure, can ya? Quick: is it real or is it Memorex?"

She studied his lips moving beneath the mike on the aluminum stem and thought about being a machine and not knowing it. Her memories would feel exactly like her memories but really be electronic impulses stored somewhere in that huge biochip glowing in her skull. Her six directives to a better life, her progens in Las Vegas.

Now everything was real.

Now everything was a script written by someone else with an awful sense of plot and characterization, a Xerox of a Xerox of some programmer's mind, an historiographic metafiction about the inability to be the same person at 10:00 a.m. that you were at 9:59.

Behind her the metal detector squealed again.

Krystal turned and saw a security guard taking a pipe bomb away from a dark-skinned eight-year-old Indonesian boy wearing an Indian *dhoti*. The boy tried to run but the guard tripped him. He sprawled forward and lay still. The rest of the people in line surveyed him like he might have dropped a knapsack. Then they began acting polite again.

Leaning against the wall across the corridor was the bartender from the Victorian mesto, snakeskin arms crossed beneath the clock on his chest. He was watching arrests on his coffee break.

Krystal noticed he'd lost another three-quarters of an hour of life since she'd last checked.

24

Hunger Fever

Uly heard Foster's finger compressing the trigger and saw, suddenly from the prospect of a hawk, Salvador's, his own, squat body lying on the ground near the stream. Eddy stood with a boot on his back, Dolan with one on his left wrist. Foster crouched beside him, gun against the base of his skull. Franklin Graves and Harriet Pike stood a yard removed. Harriet was captivated by what was happening. She couldn't take her eyes off the shooting. Franklin consulted his fingernails. By their feet lay Luis's body, face down, arms by his sides, legs parted slightly, back of his head black blood, pulp, and steam.

Uly's perspective banked, scudded west, glided through gauzy snow, whitegray meadows and small stands of pine sliding below in the night.

The bonfire on the green logs in the emigrants' pit came into view. Those who had stayed behind waiting for the hunting party's return clustered around it.

Uly made out crazed Fosdick begin to wrestle beneath his blankets, heave into a sitting position, and heard, as if across a lake, a spew of words wild and disconnected rushing from his mouth. Face tapeworm-white, eyes black funnels, Fosdick struggled with his wife. Mary Graves and Sarah Foster hustled to help restrain him, but they were no match for his delirious strength. He was already shinnying up the steep sides of the pit, already hip-high in snow, calling for an absent Eddy to follow him.

They had to press ahead, Fosdick hollered, had to get to the settlements immediately. Otherwise they were lost. Leave now or buckle. Pack and push on. Leave now or—

In mid-sentence his eyes went off.

Sarah stumbled toward him.

Fosdick looked down at his chest, up at his approaching wife, dusted some snow off the blankets hanging from him like a toga, sat down, and died.

Uly heard the hammer begin to fall and saw dusk indigo the mountains surrounding the emigrant encampment.

Seven black specks insected across the snow on the frozen lake. They became men and the men stepped up into the pines bordering the east shore. They labored toward the place where William Eddy, the skeleton who had fumbled from the woods near Johnson's ranch with three emaciated women after thirty-three days in the wilderness, told them they would find the cabins. Only there weren't any cabins. There was just snow…waves of it, hills, twenty-foot banks that sometimes almost covered the trees.

The man in the lead, Captain Reasin P. Tucker, tall and thick, with short white hair and a clean-shaven face and a long white beard beneath his jaw, had no more feeling in his eyes than those of a crab on the end of its stalks.

Uly felt the thought move through this man that he was too late. He had come all this way for nothing, wondered if Sutter would, everything said and done, pay. He shouted as he walked, calling out for survivors…paused to listen to that sound, noise like a chipmunk skittering up through the drifts…the scratching…snow chucking away beneath them, and, not ten yards distant, a red hand periscoping…an arm…head of that woman he would never forget, cheeks caved in, skin color of a mouse's belly, white hair unkempt as a wet terrier's. She emerged fastidiously, stooped, a starved otter from her burrow.

Captain Tucker noticed the bodies behind her. Ropes had been tied around them and they'd been dragged up inclined planes leading from the cabins to the top of the snow. They were scattered everywhere. Some, small as saddlebags, were still wrapped in quilts. Others had been buried and uncovered again by the wind and left as they were, half sitting in a white mound as if meditating, bluish gray and naked, mouths pulled back in delusional grins, skin so tight it seemed their ribs might tear through into the cold air.

More emigrants began to appear, creeping from other holes.

Captain Tucker looked back at the woman standing in front of him. She didn't look at him, but at someone else beneath his flesh.

He realized she was in her early twenties.

"Are you men from California," she said, head beginning to bob like a feeding bird, "or do you come from heaven?"

(?) eliz. blind   too weak to catch mice cut wood w/ greatest effort   george comes to me in waking dream

(?) mouth filled w/ ulcers abdomen distended on fire   hides only article we depend on   painful beyond measure to eat excrete   cant lie still   cant stand cant sit groans occupy our tent   gums bloody

(?) we dont live in time we live in space no yesterday tomorrow
        these sounds   breath of my dying husband my dying children   always now & now always here

(?) eliz. wont eat hides ive boiled her some she must live or die on them

(?) scalped in dream i stand flesh slipping down my face blood muscle & run arms raised mouth open but silence diggers looking on aghast at this thing in their midst

(?) feb or march   several entries a day hard to tell   or only 1 a month hard to tell   frances sick last night eating hide shoemaker threw tobacco on wks ago   feeling better   eliz. very low in danger if relief dont come soon

(?) snow thr. night blew hard wind w worst storm so far no sun
        20ft drifts   no one to shovel   time of month no blood   jacob lucky 1 we know sweet jacob

(?) smoky tongues   eliz. froze 3 toes last night   george

sleeps children sleep & we survive thks be to god for his mercies
endureth forever amen

(?) snow continues abdomen great pain   moans   water
boiling   taste of rot mucus blood salt   lips cracked   nights
think i wont make morn. & then light ive done it again

(?) sky ready to snow   o lord be merciful upon thes
wretched souls   let us perish w/out pain

Uly heard the hammer strike the primer of the cartridge and
Sarah Foster and Dolan crouched over something in one corner of
the snowpit. Eddy, Mary Graves, and William Foster restrained
Sarah Fosdick several feet away. She fought madly, trying to twist
out of their grip, hair flying, upper torso thrust forward, biting,
snapping at the wind, shrieking into the storm, but Sarah and Dolan
worked steadily, thoughtfully, as if they didn't hear anything except the whirring gale around them. Dolan hacked at the arms of
Sarah Fosdick's husband with a hatchet provided by Eddy. Sarah
Foster used Franklin's hunting knife to free up the liver. Harriet
had already skewered the heart on a spiked stick and minded it
with inexorable concentration as it broiled over the flames.

Uly heard the primer detonate and Dolan, three weeks later,
tossed in a heavy stupor by another bonfire in another snowpit.
He was breathing with difficulty, shallow wheeze deep among the
spongy tissue of his lungs.

A myoclonic flinch threw his arm into the blaze.

Foster, awake nearby, watched the Irishman's hand curl into
itself and shrivel, begin to char.

He observed to see if the pain would rouse the sleeper and,
when it didn't, he reached to shake his wife.

Uly heard the bullet snap into motion and saw Franklin Graves die quietly, unable to rise one morning, a glaze spreading over his eyes.

His daughters Mary and Sarah coaxed him to sit up, but he couldn't do it. He fought to open his mouth and, when he had managed this much, told them to save themselves by using his body when he was gone.

Near 7:00, a shudder shook his remains.

By 8:00 Mary and Sarah had already sliced flesh from his arms and legs and roasted it over the fire, averting their faces from the others, shoulders hunched like blackbirds over carrion.

satur. 20th feb. praise the merciful lord   footsteps in snow this morn. 3 men fr. california   felled tree left little food deptd. late aftern. w/ 6 of us inclu. children elitha & leanna & fr. eliz. solomon & william   george too weak to move i will not leave him   eliz. will stay w/ me & youngest till 2nd relief party to leave sutters 22nd feb.

sun. 21 teamster jean baptiste remains   hunts buried cattle w/ long pole in snow   if luckless will be forced to unspeak-able

mon. 22 some strength back mouth sores begin mend news fr. lake encamp. bad   kesebergs son lewis dead eddys child dead & landrum murphy dead & mccutchens baby pikes spitzer & milt dead   mrs. eddy died shortly after her tiny angel margaret   all but 17   2men 3women 12children attempt escape today   mr. reed in 2nd relief party fine morn.

thurs. 25 tolerable appetite gravel clearing   coffee & salted meat low already beautiful mrn.   children & eliz. up again george quiet but how long   arm festers   we tell stories again

fri. 26 children playing outside   no cattle baptiste despon-dent what to do

sat. 27 froze hard last night baptiste pressing i have no answer

sun. 28 clear & warm wind blowing briskly   mashed potato snow says frances   to watch the children   eliz. & i talk of nothing else

    <u>mon. 1 march</u> heard some geese fly over last night saw none
we give ourselves unto yr. hands o lord

    <u>tues. 2</u> decision so much simpler than ever wd. think just
look into frances eyes said eliz. just look into frances eyes the
answer is there

    <u>thurs. 4</u> we shall commence upon mr. shoemaker jean
baptiste found him this morn. in drift

    Uly heard the bullet leap free of the barrel and saw Salvador
three seconds later, saw himself, saw the body on its stomach, cheek
pressed into icy soil.

    Dolan stepped off his wrist.

    Eddy removed his boot from his spine and looked up at the
gray sky as if checking the weather.

    The shot echoed and then it was utterly silent.

    "Well shee-*it*," Foster said, standing.

    "Whut?" asked Harriet.

    "If that don't goddamn beat everything."

    "Whut's that, Billy?"

    "I done got Digger brains all over my goddamn coat."

    Harriet laughed, shrill as a magpie.

    "Ain't like it was your Sunday best nor nothing, Billy."

    "Shit, Harriet. That ain't the point. That ain't the point at all.
Point is I done got goddamn Digger brains all over my goddamn
coat."

    "We best get started," Eddy said to the sky. "We have work to
do. The others are waiting. Mr. Dolan?"

    "Let me see that knife of yours," he said.

    Franklin released it from the sheath on his belt and passed it
over. Dolan kneeled and began cutting through Salvador's clothes.
He was still alive, muscles sparking.

    "Damned if it isn't cold," Dolan said.

    "That's the truth," said Franklin, squatting beside him, help-
ing him clear away the strips of leather. "I'm thinking we have
ourselves another couple three days of snow ahead of us."

    "Wouldn't be surprised. Wouldn't be surprised at all."

    "You want me to shoot so I shoot," Foster said, wiping at

himself, eyes cornered and edgy.

"Pipe down now," Dolan said.

"Gawd al*mighty*," Foster said, reaching up, dabbing the fatty grayish chunks with his fingertips. He examined them. Gave them a sniff. Stamped his foot in mortification. "That's it. That all. That's the last goddamn time I go shootin' a goddamn Digger in the head without wearin' a scarf er somethin'."

"Oh now," Harriet said. She stepped over and began to pat at his face with her sleeve, a mother her child. "Ain't as bad as all that, Billy. I seen worse. Lots worse. Hold still. Hold still. Yer gonna live through this one, too, you know." She wetted her thumb with spittle and rubbed beneath his eyes. "You just got a little gravy with your meat, is all."

Glum, Foster watched over her shoulder as Dolan stripped the skin from Salvador's arms. Eddy crouched beside him, took out his hatchet, and began chopping off the hands.

25

The Iron Curtain

Suzi Sloth-in-the-Tree Ratt sat in her stuffy GSA cubicle in Armstrong City ten meters below the surface of the moon, inspecting the jade glow of her VR radar environment and grinning at the pinpricks sizzling between her moist unshaved legs.

She'd just returned from her amphetamine break, which'd manifested itself today in the form of one of the max fantest Touch Sex sessions she'd ever experienced. She'd known Juan Placenta, operations manager with that chicken bone through his nose and online shrunken head size of a chestnut on a leather rope around his neck, was drastic. But what Juan could do in his own stuffy cubicle without so much as raising his heartbeat, let alone the interest of his colleagues in their neighboring compartments...man, he had *those* moves dialed.

Suzi sat at her post smirking like a monkey in a wind tunnel, good portion of her lower torso beneath those standard-issue khakis numb as if it'd just been procained, Eveready nano-spermicide zapping those little critters into sterility before they had even a chance of thinking about launching their infamous dolphin kicks.

The next shuttle was a good three hours away, space debris being what it was this morning, so Suzi'd taken to perusing little chunks of the solar system at random. She punched up coordinates and her VR rig quantumed her to them. Jacked on uppers, the jumps came as ninja kicks to her sternum followed by a floating sensation in her uterus as if an elevator she was riding had come to a sudden stop.

She was out by Mars now, drifting in rich green light. Yellow grid surrounding her curved toward infinity. She was half checking the sights, half daydreaming about how Juan'd produced that miniature cattle prod like it was some happy piece of licorice...when she picked it up again.

The thing had the dimensions of a small asteroid, six or seven kils across, twelve or thirteen long, from what she could tell. Mildly interested in its path, wondering what it might do, Suzi'd been tracking it on and off for a week as it'd rushed among the planets.

Only as she locked on to it this time, brought it into the elaborate web of her bio-computer's artificial mind, she realized it'd recently slowed down to less than a quarter of its initial speed.

Plus it had altered its course, taken a southpaw at Deimos.

It was, best she could tell, heading pretty much in her general direction.

Plus it was no asteroid.

Krystal bought another absinthe while waiting for her delayed flight at the Mexico City Space Port, and another just after her immunization shots, and a Bintang beer to chase them shortly after lift off, rundown Russian shuttle shuddering and skreeking around her.

Despite being restrained in a worn gray elastic g-net pouch, she felt nauseous and dislocated, like when as a kid she'd pirouetted fast as she could till she'd fallen. The universe evinced that timeless and half-speed motion of low gravity and she perceived the foundation of her world break down from tangible atoms to ephemeral quarks winking in and out of existence.

The backbrain hum of the ghost wouldn't leave her. It kept rambling, louder and louder, more insistent, hectic hyperbolic torrent of a visionary on benzedrine sitting next to you at the mesto.

And then a huge crow reeled up her spinal column and she saw her hand letting go of the beer sac.

Images began scrolling behind her eyes like the unreadable script on a malfing computer. She heard a party of luded voices and saw herself reclining in the dentist chair in that nightmare clinic from her childhood. Her blouse was unbuttoned and tugged back, her chest painted rust with iodine. The incision where her breast had been was bleeding heavily and the elderly nurse with trad short green spiked hair was alternately sucking at it with a vacuum tube and dabbing with a clump of gauze saturated on the end of a pair of forceps.

The Uncle Meat, long dijon-colored fingernails, ears tufted with snowy fur, scooped out the last yellowish adipose tissue from the wound.

Krystal saw her eyes flutter open, confused horror run across her face.

She watched this thirteen-year-old version of herself begin to writhe, send out her fists, part her lips for the dream scream...and then she saw the installment she *hadn't* anticipated in this parasitic memory film racing in front of her...nylon restraints on the arm- and footrests appearing, nurse pumping a second dose of diluted anesthetic into her veins, Uncle Meat commencing his work...not on her flattened and carved mammary gland anymore...but on her eye...her right eye...

He loaded another hypodermic with a milky fluid containing the nanotech implants and, monitoring his progress on an overhead screen, pressed the long gleaming point home through the gummy conjunctiva, sclera, vitreous humor, into the flimsy sheath around the optic nerve where he discharged the viral bots in a dainty squeeze.

Krystal's body temperature brought them to life and the mechanical spermatozoa hesitated, regrouping, orienting, then swarmed along the fibrous nerve toward the aft of her brain where they'd begin to nest like a cluster of razzed wasps, live encodings, constructing their hive mind, genetic algorithms breeding, procreating, evolving, dying through the years, shadowy mass accumulating among the soft convoluted grays and whites that'd once been Krystal's awareness, fusing with the near-infinite perplex of mossy axons and dendrites, penetrating and reconfiguring individual cells into something both programmed and not programmed, organic and inorganic, reconfiguring everything that'd made her who she was...

≋

"Li-Young Beauregard Kirilenko, operations sub-manager," Li-Young Beauregard Kirilenko, operations sub-manager, told himself, "is about to answer the phone."

Corporal first-class with Marine's burr cut and fond recollections of the mud-rains in Montgomery, KFC Alabama, Kirilenko enjoyed thinking about himself in the third-person. For him, existence was a nineteenth-century novel in which he was the protagonist...an expansive, well-planned, limpidly written, good-hearted and morally centered novel with an excellent sense of characterization and none of that experimentation gunk in it. It had a beginning, a middle, and an end, and you knew which was which and what was what. This was because Kirilenko was also the narrator, reliable and cultivated.

Seeing existence this way made life clean as a freshly scrubbed bathroom floor, organized as Kirilenko's footlocker.

He knew the moment he abandoned this narratological paradigm, telling his story as if he were inhabiting an early twentieth-century stream-of-consciousness novel, or, worse, an early twenty-first century hypertext one, he would go insane.

Truth was, even a good old-fashioned first-person narrative set his teeth on edge.

So when the tiny red emergency LED atop his phone blinked on he considered it, not so much a tiny red emergency LED, as a potentially interesting plot twist for his main character, Kirilenko...a plot twist that might *seem* like it snagged the protagonist unawares and led him down an unexpected path, but which would, in fact, work itself out with all the grace and proficiency of the insides of a Hammerhead missile's nosecone in the end.

He spun around in his chair and waved his hand over the screen. Light stuttered and rolled and Suzi Sloth-in-the-Tree Ratt's image flipped up. She was in her VR rig, US Army surplus...big, black, and bulky, apparently designed to withstand a direct grenade blast.

Kirilenko felt better just looking at it.

"Um, hiya," Suzi said.

"Li-Young Beauregard Kirilenko was very pleased to see Ms. Ratt's splendid countenance appear upon his monitor," Kirilenko started to narrate, "but an uneasy presence washed through the corners of his oft bright psyche, knowing as he did such calls came infrequently, and seldom in the form of pleasant social intercourse."

"Yeah, well, I'm all wet to see you, too, babe. Only we have this itsy-bitsy problem down here."

"Kirilenko always felt glad before Ms. Ratt's profane delight in existence—before her spark, her flair, her admirable need to *touch* the things of life, thereby cherishing their presence in a delectably tactile way, making them her own—yet simultaneously somewhat disquieted by her perhaps gently troubling propensity to understate the deep respect he knew she nonetheless maintained for her superiors."

"Oh, right. Um. Itsy-bitsy problem down here, *sir.*"

"But Kirilenko, a good and just man at heart, was quick to forgive and forget. Without so much as a breeze of contrariness stirring his voice, he asked her, tone ebullient and kind: 'What sort of problem did you have in mind?'"

"I'm sitting here wasting time, right? Nothing in the rig. Nothing due up for hours. VRing the planets. And all of a sudden I come across this, um, thing."

"'What kind of thing?' Kirilenko asked, interest piqued," Kirilenko asked, interest piqued.

"Unidentified at the present time, sir, but acting major lysergic." Suzi adjusted her rig even though it didn't need adjustment. "Behaving itself like the nice little asteroid I took it for, you know? Zipping through the solar system minding its own business. Then *wham.* Pulls a louie near Mars, puts on the brakes, starts tooling this way."

"*This* way?"

"This way."

"How much this way?"

"Impact-in-three-weeks this way, sir."

Kirilenko studied the tiny red emergency LED atop his phone. He reached forward and tinked it with his forefinger. It wouldn't go off. He leaned back in his swivel-chair and noticed what he could see of Suzi's cheeks were flushed. He wondered if she might be attracted to him.

"Kirilenko was fond of craters, of the majestic desolation of the moon's silver surface, lonely as the IBM Nevada desert at noon. It reminded him of Nature's awesome power, of her forever-mysterious feminine forces."

"Um, negative, sir. We're talking size of a small island here. Which is not so small, incidentally. With the velocity of a jacked rocket."

"Kirilenko was fond of enormous craters."

"Um, negative, sir."

"Negative?"

"You know how, if you drop the right rock from the right burbrise at the right time of day with the right wind conditions, its momentum can sort of pile-drive a hole a meter-deep into the sidewalk?"

"Okay."

"Well, same thing in this case, only imagine you more or less dropped a rock the size of Manhattan on a satellite the size of the moon from the height of say Mars."

"The analogy, Kirilenko felt, failed on many levels for many reasons—and yet..."

"Yeah, yeah. Do the arithmetic and get back to me."

Suzi reached forward to hang up.

"Kirilenko stopped her by querying if this might mean the prospect of real danger for the unsuspecting souls inhabiting Armstrong City."

"You don't want to know."

"How much doesn't Kirilenko want to know?"

"More than you want to know."

"Kirilenko, a sensitive, well-meaning fellow, felt faint. The outlines of mass destruction welled up in his addled imagination. He had the distinct impression he were sailing inexorably toward an obsidian epiphany at the velocity of panic."

"Yeah, yeah," Suzi said, "no shit, Sherlock."

Krystal, groggy and drunk, stepped off the shuttle somehow expecting to feel solid ground beneath her.

Instead she bobbed forward awkwardly in zero-g, bumping

the Plughead in front of her, space adaptation syndrome overtaking her body like a heady wind, heartbeat accelerating, fluid in the semicircular canals of her inner ear breaking into myriad globules that didn't know which way up was.

She moved through customs in an agitated daze. Looking over the head of the hamster-like paraplegic in a dull brown tunic floating behind the counter, busy asking her questions about her credit rating, she saw the Gagarin shuttle she'd arrived on through a vast half-meter-thick oriel. Its hull was a dingy lead color and missing whole sections of protective shingles. Black burn tracks swept back from the OMS engines. She could hardly even make out the Delta-Kursk insignia, but below where it should have been someone had spraybombed a Japanese slogan and some phalli in red and over that someone had spraybombed an Arabic slogan and some vaginas in green.

The space station's brilliant solar panels framed the ship, making it appear even grungier than it was.

Beyond bobbed a fog comprised of thousands of transistor-sized paint chips, blobs of human waste, and droplets of coolant. Farther on, the sky was clogged with used panels, fragments of exploded satellites, ejected nuclear cores, abandoned observatories, and a greenish-gray Chinese capsule marked with red characters launched in 1993. Krystal'd heard it contained some of Mao's diamond jewelry and his hands.

All that seemed downright cherry, though, compared to The Iron Curtain. The low, narrow, winding corridors of the Eastern European theme park felt more like tunnels designed for gnomes than humans. Its walls were a patchwork of rusted steel plates, wads of gray epoxy, irregular scraps of repair Teflon, laser-graffitied cyrillic lettering, and bolts the circumference of monkey palms, interrupted at intervals by craggy openings leading to other low, narrow, winding corridors, blackmarket alcoves where you could purchase vodka, Turkish cigarettes, roachmeat, and hydroponic potatoes at outrageously inflated prices, poorly lit bakeries with single loaves of bread on their aluminum-wire shelves, understocked grocery stores with lines of thin, pasty people stooped outside, eyes glassy and blank, hands thrust in the pockets of their frumpy frayed dresses or sports coats or pants looking like they'd been cut from burlap sacks, every other one a KGB agent ready to squeal on you soon as direct you to the next staged demonstration on behalf of the Worker, Lenin, or the failed turn-of-the-century Counter-Revolution.

Floors were covered with slimy chipped fake cobblestones fashioned from storax, ceilings studded with burst yellow light bulbs interspersed with dented black surveillance cameras, air choked for that special Eastern Bloc effect with the stink of octane, mildew, iron filings, cigarette smoke, imported factory exhaust, diesel, cooked cabbage, body odor, and untreated sewage, particulate matter so dense it appeared as if everything existed behind a pane of frosted glass.

Through these corridors wafted the wasted specters of paraplegics, arms and legs withered from calcium loss, faces white from bad air and high-orbit heart shrinkage, pawing along the pastiched walls, toxmen and tour guides, maintenance teams and communications specialists, something right out of a fata morgana by Francis Bacon.

Accumulated around the shuck of the original 1986 Mir space station, enlarged over the years using anything from Kvant science modules to antique shuttle parts, The Iron Curtain was no family getaway, no place for your standard mom-and-pop couple from Gates Washington to haul their brood for a long weekend of amiably perverse recreation. It was a space for hardcore park-dwellers, the jaded kind who'd ridden every ride there was on earth, experienced your basic class-five Code Bleu VR white-water rafting and class-six Emporio Armani down-and-dirty genital-torture, your Mongolian invasions and your Iranian atrocities, and felt like they just weren't getting their credit's worth anymore. It was a space for those fanatics with the chemically slurred speech, noncompos stares, and bedlamite grins who think the idea of risking their lives on a dilapidated shuttle to reach a weekend honeycombed with claustrophobia, high anxiety, cruddy lungs, poor service, constant surveillance, awful food, possible physical punishment, and brainbusting prices (the fullblown bequest from Marxism to the rest of global culture) is a great way to have some fun. They might not quite be able to muster the mindblowing capital necessary to get them all the way to Erewhon One, but, hey, this would just have to do...and it just did.

Krystal negotiated among her fellow travelers, careful not to bump into anyone else, as she trailed a paraplegic with bony pink stumps instead of fingers down one dim smoggy corridor after another toward her crypt.

He was giving her a mini-lecture, pointing out sites of interest. The passageways reminded her of the ones in Deaconess down in Spocoeur. She glided by a group of Asian soldiers in vandykes and Russian sheepskin caps, each with a Yeltsin-70 over his or her shoulder, buoying like jellyfish outside the sealed entrance to a church. A male meater at the intersection of Titov and Maranov propositioned her, flicking out his split black tongue to show off its muscular dexterity...she averted her eyes, declining, and up ahead her guide snickered.

They glided by a vandalized oxygen booth and near a noisy crowd jamming an alley and were almost past before Krystal realized someone was receiving a real beating in there. The mob'd pinned a tourist in a blue and yellow Bon Ton license-plate bustier, bottle-cap-studded seat belt, fur-trimmed Lee bluejean mini-skirt, and pair of Mary Janes to the wall and was slapping her, knuckling her face. A cloud of red droplets hung around her head. She was eighteen maybe, albino, and still smiling, definitely into this thrashing. Krystal's guide explained the woman'd probably admitted (and probably falsely) she was an informer...one of those kids of fairly wealthy safe-zone progens who needed something a notch more startling every day to break the monotony of Mexiental maids and ergoloid-mesylates milkshakes. Her bill for this little amusement would be astronomical. Everyone in the mob was wearing or holding some sort of pistol, zip gun, derringer, or rat charmer, but nobody was using them. Krystal figured the pieces were just fashion accessories, status symbols, not authentic bullet-spitting weapons at all. Even if the space station hull *was* lined with a meter of lunar soil to take the piss out of the incoming solar radiation, lowering the cataract- and cancer-rates by at least a GSA-endorsed smidgen, locals frowned on the possibility of high-powered metal-piercing projectiles that could penetrate the walls.

Krystal's crypt was runtier than a standard coffin and suggested to her all those backseats she'd slept in during all her days of philo-

sophical parsimony and peripateticism...just a bare concrete rectangle half a meter tall, one wide, and one-and-a-half long with an
elastic g-net pouch bolted via springy cords to each of its walls to
form a kind of hammock sandwich. There was no hatch. A porthole the dimensions of a plastic plate was set into the hull at the far
end.

A filament snapped among her ribs soon as she thanked the
guide and wriggled in.

She had trouble breathing and began to worry about another
nosebleed. She had to cock her knees just to fit. Her paper suit
rustled and she heard it tear somewhere under her right arm while
her lower abdomen, compressed in a semi-fetal position, felt stuffed
with soaked sponges.

She levitated, trying to will her heart to slow down. When it
didn't, she craned her neck to look out the porthole.

A hundred and ninety kils below, the earth was dark and expansive, a wide whitish-gray crescent. Somewhere over what she
took to be TexMex, though for all she knew could've been
Vietbodia, a silent lightning storm squiggled luminously through
smog cover. She watched, feeling like she was watching another
CAT-scan of the inside of her head, then refocused on her own
reflection, her single meter-long dreadlock snaking around her, nose-
rings and eyebrow-hoops rising off her skin.

She closed her eyes, hoping to sleep, wondering why it had
gotten so quiet in her skull.

Sergeant Juan Placenta, operations manager, was channeling
deeply on "Intellectual Transvestite," cut off the Pope's new plasma-
wrench album, when the tiny red emergency LED atop his phone
blinked on.

He reached behind his ear, turned down his aug, and powered
up the screen.

That shit-for-brains, moderately delusional, wholly red-necked
and not just a little annoying Corporal First-Class Kirilenko's burr-
cut pate ogled back at him, far too serious for his own fucking
good, no matter what he was about to open his idiot mouth and

say.

Which was Juan's real objection to working on Armstrong City...it possessed all the glamor, appeal, and severity Antarctic outposts did fifty years ago, African ones fifty before that, meaning it attracted just the most godawful loners, extremists, and socially inept nut-cases you ever wanted to meet.

And here he was talking to one in the electronic flesh.

The guy believed he was a goddamn book. Jesus fucking Christ. Where do they *get* these people?

Juan rubbed the shrunken head dangling on the leather rope around his neck and simpered like a Labrador, muscle-grafted shoulders shaking, large noggin swiveling back and forth on its redwood-trunk neck.

"Mi casa es suya," he said. "I'm one big ear."

"Corporal First-Class Li-Young Beauregard Kirilenko, feeling great respect for his superior, was extremely troubled by the baleful news he was about to deliver."

"You know that cute piece of ass working radar?"

"Just minutes ago Kirilenko was interrupted from a soothing revelry by an emer—"

"Tangerine eyes, butch hair, butt so tight makes you want to bark?"

"Private Ratt?"

"Suzi fucking Creamcheese herself." He thumbed the sewn-shut mouth. "Right here on this very desk. Whole new meaning to the term 'lunch break.'" He wagged his head. "I got one word for you."

"Yes, sir?"

"Electric cattle prod."

Kirilenko tried to change the subject.

"Shoulda seen that mama-san squirm. Muy fucking bueno. You want legs? I'm talking *semaphore*, man." He looked Kirilenko in the eye. "Know what I mean?"

"Kirilenko felt—"

Juan was getting into this.

"I said, Corporal, 'Know what I mean?'"

"I—"

Juan dropped the shrunken head. It dangled five centimeters

above his chest.

"Do you, or do you not, Corporal, know what I fucking mean?"

"'Uh, well, yes, sir,' he said, 'I do.'"

"And what, goddamn it, might that be?"

"Excuse me, sir?"

"You said you fucking know what I fucking mean. So fucking what might that fucking be, Corporal, if I'm not fucking *prying* too much or anything?"

"I—"

"Excuse me?"

"No, I—"

"I can't hear you, Corporal."

"I—"

"I'm just guessing here, mind you, but do you by any chance happen to fucking mean that I'm, oh, um, let's see…one fucking major stud? Would that fucking be in the fucking ballpark?"

"I—"

"I don't *hear* you, Corporal."

"Yes, sir, I, well, yes. Sir."

"Good, goddamn it. Good. Because I *am*, as it just so happens, one fucking major stud, you shit. You could play basketball with my fucking cajones. People *have* played basketball with my fucking cajones. And I've fucking loved every minute of it."

Juan was right, metaphorically speaking.

That's what upset a fair number of his comrades. He had the body of a wrestler and the eyes of a saint, personality of a spill stall and sexual prowess of a randy minotaur.

He dropped women like a good bug spray drops mosquitoes.

Only right now he felt like he'd had to work too hard to elicit Kirilenko's unabashed admiration. So he changed his tone. A wide lippy smile spread across his face. His brown eyes narrowed.

"So, Corporal, where were we? Oh yeah. Hitting the panic button. Well, let's see. You wouldn't by any chance be about to tell me about some fucking asteroid, would you?"

The muscles along Kirilenko's lower jaw slipped.

"Kirilenko was surprised," Kirilenko said, surprised.

"Yeah, well, save it."

"Sir, I—"

"Because I have some news for you, Corporal."

"Yes, sir?"

"You listening?"

"Yes, sir."

"You listening real good?"

"Yes, sir."

"Outstanding. Cuz I'll let you in on a little secret, okay? Little private confidence just between you and me, Corporal. That fucking asteroid you were about to tell me about?"

"Yes, sir?"

"You weren't about to tell me about it."

"I wasn't?"

"You weren't."

"No?"

"And you know *why* you weren't about to tell me about it, Corporal?"

"No, sir."

"Because you don't know about it."

"I...no, sir."

"And you wanna know something *really* fucking interesting, Corporal?"

"Yes, sir."

"You *never* knew anything about it." Juan leaned forward in his chair, his face, he knew, glutting Kirilenko's screen. "Because, see, it's not on our fucking radars. Never has been. Never will be."

"No?"

"Nope. It's not near Mars. It's not in our solar system. It doesn't, in a word, exist." He took a breath. "You catching my drift, Corporal?"

"Kirilenko is, sir. Da."

"You're not just saying that to make me feel good?"

"No, sir."

"Cuz I'd hate to be disappointed."

"No, sir."

"I couldn't stand the concept of disappointment."

"The Sergeant can count on Kirilenko."

"You're sure about that?"

"Kirilenko's sure."

"Good. That's good. That's real good. Then get the fuck off my phone, you shit," Juan said, reaching behind his ear to turn up his aug again, get back into that drastic monastic tune about the girl who made all these crank calls to people, telling them their test results for neo-syphilitic posterior spinal sclerosis just came back positive, till one of them freaked and smoked himself, sending said girl smack into a religious conversion.

26

Lunar Fragments

Krystal awoke five hours later. At first she thought it was because her head was so still. Then she realized something was tickling her foot.

She opened her eyes and saw a rat, white as cocaine, sniffing her big toe. Fucker just floated there, legs shriveled and useless as an appendix, offspring of fugitives from some lab experiment back when this place was still Russian military. Its tail, thick, raw-incision pink, and muscular, was the rodent's primary mode of motion and balance. The creature reminded Krystal of a large hairy tadpole.

She kicked it with the heel of one of her black rubber sandals. It recoiled, scrambled to effect a weightless turn, and swam off.

Krystal rubbed her temples, punchy, coming alert. Hovering in her g-net pouch, she unfocused her eyes, smelling the spoiled breath of the last person who slept here, and grasped the fact her period was on a light day. The dull ache was gone. So were the bloating and hormonal blues.

Uly's absence washed into the foreground of her mind. She'd been dreaming about him. In the dream, he'd opened his mouth to speak and instead of a tongue and teeth his mouth cavity was loaded with the red alphanumerics of the thin clock on the bartender's chest at the Portland airport. Numbers were ticking backwards fast as fly wings.

Krystal waited for the image to deteriorate, then clumsily

crawled out of her pouch, fished into the corridor, stretched, loosening her kinked spine and knees, and launched herself into a slo-mo tumble toward what she hoped would be something like breakfast.

Light in The Iron Curtain's sealed corridors remained exactly the same twenty-four hours a day, so a sense of temporal homogeneity permeated the place.

At any moment it could've been 2:00 in the afternoon or 2:00 in the morning and, before long, a Thursday in November or a Sunday in June. Some people ate lunch while others chugged nightcaps. Some went on wakeup rides while others searched for meaters. Most, biorhythms skrimmed as a nest of nitrous-oxided bees, slept a couple hours here, a couple there, and spent the rest of their holiday coasting in a somnambulant chronohaze.

Krystal thus had no problem locating a busy Czech café. Except when she tried ordering food from a guy in a blood-stained apron and black-gloved robotic hand, she learned the only things on the menu were beet soup and watery Brezno beer.

She got a sac of both and found an empty space at a stand-up counter running along a fake brick wall. She slipped her feet into the restraining tethers on the floor and began to eat. The café was so small, maybe four by four, the customers packed so close together, people had to maneuver around each other like the sightless, groping among a junkyard of elbows and knees to squeeze by, gaining an intimacy almost no one wanted up here.

There were a good number of Vacants in the crowd, haunted by the proximity of others as well as the understanding they were burning through the last of their credit with nowhere else to run when it was gone. A good number of Plugheads, too, tiny clan of them, out for a weekend they'd saved years for and were determined never to forget. Krystal also spotted some Neo-Mayan kids like those she'd seen at the airport, some more Safe-Zoners, and a few really well-dressed Yupmen, teeth a Ralph Lauren latticework of precious metal and jewels, passing time till their connecting flight to Erewhon One departed. Paraplegic workers hung above them all, backs against the concrete ceiling, between shifts.

Krystal took a swallow of soup and her mouth flooded with gelatinous saliva. Her stomach churned. She bowed her head and fought the urge to upchuck.

"You'll be okay," a deep-toned voice next to her said. "Just the SAS saying buenos días."

Krystal looked up, surprised to see the voice belonged to a teenage albino with blue bruises splotching her face. Her lips and left cheek were swollen. Black flecks freckled her colorless shag.

It took Krystal a second to recognize her as the woman from last night, one in the alley. She was still wearing the license-plate bustier and bottle-cap-studded seat belt. Her fur-trimmed mini-skirt was ripped down one side and her Mary Janes had disappeared. Plus it looked like maybe her left little toe was busted, red and puffy and jutting at a funny angle.

"SAS?"

"Space Adaptation Syndrome," the woman said. "Triggers your flight-or-fight reflexes. Which are, if you think about it, completely incompatible with the idea of food."

"Feels like a bad stomach virus."

"Another forty-eight hours, your body won't even remember it. You gonna finish that beer?"

Krystal handed it over.

"This thing common?"

"Only for the lucky few." She laughed. One of her incisors had been chipped. "I'm J. J., by the way. J. J. Jive LaFace. Those eyes yours?"

"Yeah."

"Nice epicanthic folds."

"Thanks." Krystal looked down at her soup sac. "We already met."

J. J.'s own eyes were all-black contacts...part, Krystal imagined, of some kind of flash-trend mourning thing for Polymox Epoxi. They opened girlishly wide.

"We did?"

"Last night. Yesterday. That mob? I was on my way to my crypt from the shuttle."

"Crank."

"Looked like you were really enjoying yourself."

J. J. tried smiling, but flinched because of the swelling, which made her try to smile some more.

Then it struck Krystal…something about the voice, facial bone structure, physiognomic mass. J. J. wasn't a woman at all. She was a FeeMale, a sex change. Her progens must've been fugging loaded. High-orbit family, maybe. Klub Med execs.

"I really did," J. J. said. "It was dreamy."

"Do that sort of thing often?"

"Only when I've been a good little girl."

Krystal wanted to let that one go by, but couldn't.

"What's the special occasion?"

J. J. pulled a yellow triangular pill from her hip pocket, slipped it between her lips, and took a long suck on the beer. Out the corner of her eye, Krystal saw a white flash and ducked. A rat darted by her head and disappeared into a crack in the faux-brick wall.

"Oh, this and that," J. J. said. "That and this." She looked around the café. Krystal saw her gaze slide out of focus as the pill and Brezno hit. "You up here long?"

"On my way to Erewhon One. Just steadying out. My flight leaves in seventy-two hours."

"Really? Me too. Fancy that." She took another swig. "Maybe we can hang out together or something."

"Yeah, well."

"*What can be done with fewer is done in vain with more*, huh?" J. J. read off the shaved half of Krystal's head.

"Old joke."

Krystal tried another mouthful of soup. Her gag reflex engaged and she had to make herself swallow. A tank of nausea rolled over her. She palmed her abdomen and J. J. touched her forearm.

"Know what you need?"

"Yeah. Uncle Meat, bad."

"Nothing of the kind. Nothing of the kind." J. J. slid an arm around Krystal's shoulder, gave her a tiny hug. "What you need's a little vachuru therapy." She leaned closer, forehead to forehead. Her breath smelled like rose petals. "Ever try that shit?"

"Costs a fortune."

"My treat. Get your mind out of orbit for a while. Give your body a chance to adjust on its own. Make life just a whole *bunch* more bearable." She squeezed again. "What you say?"

"I think I gotta throw up."

Virtual reality came down on her like a steel beam on a daddy-longlegs.

One minute she was lying tethered to a gurney in the first-aid clinic, listening to J. J. explain the situation to a technician with a large meringue pollution ulcer on his upper lip. Next she was standing in the ruins of an extraordinarily clean Roman temple.

It was a sunny day. Sky was waterless blue, colors around her pastels richer and more vibrant than real life. It felt like she was living inside a three-dimensional cartoon gel.

She heard something behind her and turned. A human-sized lobster balancing on its tail shuffled up, legs fluttering.

"Hey Krystal, it's me. J. J. How you like?"

The black eyes on the end of the stalks were hers. Everything else was decapod crustacean.

The voice, softer and more breathy than the authentic J. J.'s, didn't emanate from the lobster, though, but from the heavy ionic columns towering around them.

"You know my name," Krystal said.

"Medic ran a retinal scan for your medical history. I probably know more about you than you do." A strange electronic laugh fizzed around her. "How you feeling?"

Krystal took a moment to think about it.

"Um, great, really," she said. "Yeah. Just great."

"Your body's forgotten it's in space. We're kidding it into thinking it's somewhere else. Which, in a sense, it is." Human lips appeared in the lobster's belly and grinned. "The beta blockers didn't hurt any, either," they said, then vanished.

Krystal looked at her hands. They seemed normal enough.

"What am I?" she asked.

"That one of those philosophical questions?"

"No. I mean what am *I*?"

"You're you. We didn't know what you wanted to be."

"Oh," contemplating. "Me's good, I guess."

Electronic laughter again. The lobster's shell strobed into a complex interaction of patterns. Plaids, op art, elaborate overlay of eyeballs. Large blue poppies bunched out of its face.

A gold flavor rushed across Krystal's taste buds. She figured the technician was adding a new drug to the brew in her IV.

"Here," a green pterodactyl gliding past said, "let me show you something *really* interesting."

Krystal trailed the lobster across the massive blocks of marble comprising the temple's foundation, past a statue of Apollo whose head rotated to observe them.

When Krystal glanced at it, a black split tongue shot from each of its eye sockets, lapped air, and retracted in less than a second.

Beyond the temple were pale green hills sloping down to the silver-blue glitter of the Mediterranean. Hundreds of cigar-shaped copper dirigibles hung arrested in the sky.

The lobster stepped between two hulking columns. Krystal followed and found herself in a smoky concrete cell that could've been part of The Iron Curtain.

In the middle of the cell was what looked like an old-fashioned wooden electric chair. Strapped into it was an anorexic hooded prisoner in baggy concentration camp clothing, chin lolling on chest. He'd obviously been beaten pretty bad. Over the prisoner stood a young handsome soldier in a Russian uniform from around 2005. His hair was sandy and oiled back, his nose thin and sharp, and he wore black eye liner and mascara. In his right hand he held a meat hook.

He turned and smiled at Krystal. She saw her image reflected in his black contacts in too much detail, tiny HDTV screens. Then he turned toward the prisoner and methodically dragged the meat hook across his throat.

The prisoner's body jolted and the chair rattled as blood hosed from his jugular.

Black gore sprayed the soldier, saturating the front of his uniform. He looked down, a twist of disgust on his lips. His uniform evaporated and the soldier became a naked woman with anemic skin, dense long auburn hair, and clear gray-blue eyes. Instead of a mouth she possessed a rigid-skinned orifice packed with hooked thistles. Blood trickled down her breasts and stomach. She smeared it with her palm, sexily, like semen after love-making in SinSim, reached forward and tore off the hood from the prisoner.

It was J. J.

She shook out her white shag and, thick blood oozing from her neck, blew Krystal a kiss.

Shocked, Krystal stepped backward.

She didn't realize she'd been standing on some kind of ledge. Her legs jerked out from under her as in a dream of skating. Her hands rocketed forward to catch hold of something and failed...but she didn't fall.

She was airborne, levitating in a plush luminous eighteenth-century boudoir.

Walls, floor and ceiling were mirrors. Gilt-trimmed settee, dressing table, and French bed with drapes, curving lines, and rich ornamental decorations hung around her at odd angles.

Miniature rainbow trout missiled among gossamer veils, cut-crystal bottles of perfume, a quill pen, carved ivory trinket boxes.

J. J.'s thin mouth appeared, suspended a meter in front of Krystal, then her eyes, the rest of her head. Her face was painted gold.

She blinked and her naked body unfolded below her like a latex suit. It was painted gold too. Jade hoops dangled from her nipples. A tribal fishbone scar extended from her solar plexus to the shaved stubble above her purple-brown labia. The scar was embossed with silver leaf and outlined in a seven-centimeter swath of amethyst, emerald, lapis lazuli, and onyx chips inlaid directly into her skin.

"You find me interactive?" she asked.

"What?"

J. J. reached out and touched the blue vein in the crook of Krystal's right arm. In the mirrors a thousand J. J.s reached out and touched blue veins in the crooks of a thousand Krystals' arms.

J. J.'s forefingers morphed into black-snouted, black-, red-, and yellow-banded coral snakes. The snakes unhinged their jaws, needle-long diamond fangs glistening, and bit.

Krystal tasted an orange flash of light succeeded by the tinkling of Chinese chimes. A tingle raced across her shoulders.

"The Colombian necklace..." she said.

"When we die, it'll always be like that," J. J. said. "We'll always be frozen in that cell. Heaven is a good electric chair for someone who knows how to use it."

"It was horrible."

"An acquired taste." Below her vagina budded a fat limp penis studded with turquoise flakes. It began to dilate, twitching. "There are so many things to experience in the universe. Real time is just like watching television."

"J. J...."

The erection rose, curved.

"What has organic life ever done for us? You get some plastic in you, you just want more."

"I can't do this, J. J."

"It's all about opening yourself up." She lifted her hand and snapped off her face. Behind it was a complex of highly polished machinery, fiber optic threads, transistors. "It's all about possibility."

"I can't do this."

"Of course you can." Among the machinery spread the moist wrinkles of another set of genitalic lips. They secreted a gluey whitish discharge twinkling with gold flecks. "Kiss me."

"My boyfriend's sick. I can't think of anything else."

"Uly..."

"I don't think he's going to make it."

J. J. ran the tips of her fingers over the machinery that'd been her face, slipped her middle digit up to its second joint into her cerebral vagina. Her breath cut short. She moaned with pleasure. It took her a while before she could speak again.

"There are others like us, you know," she said. "Our heads are filled with frequencies. Our minds are the antennae of the species."

"Others?"

"Everywhere."

"What do you mean?"

The electronic laugh.

"That would be telling, wouldn't it?" She reached down and curled back the turquoise-studded penis, inserting it into her lower vagina. "Oh, *man*," she said, sucking air through the fleshy opening in the machinery. "You don't know what you're missing."

"I'll take your word for it."

"Words have nothing to do with it." She bit off her middle finger and began crunching, though Krystal couldn't discern any teeth. "We're all lunar fragments, Krystal. We're all just parts of the whole."

"The whole what?"

"The whole everything. The centipede god itself. Everything you've ever wanted to become."

"I've never wanted to become anything. I'm happy just like I am."

"Oh *really*."

"No, I mean it."

"You only think you think that. Your body knows something different."

"What? What's it know?"

"How beautiful the inside of your head is." She gnawed off her thumb and forefinger, her ring finger and pinkie. Speaking through bony pulp, she said: "You think everything is outside you, Krystal, but you're wrong. The world is in your brain."

"The world is the world."

"No. The world is the whirled, and the whirled is the cell where the hooded prisoner's waiting, electric chair ready to spark. It's the great neural network processing engine spending eternity looking for interesting data sets, drawing its own conclusions." She mouthed the stump that'd been her hand. Watery blood ran down her golden forearm. "You sure I can't change your mind?"

"Yeah. I'm sure."

"You sure you won't join us?"

"Positive."

J. J.'s tribal fishbone scar split open. Tens of thousands of sil-

ver maggots spilled up into the boudoir around the couple, forming a squirming fog. In the mirrors tens of millions of silver maggots spilled up into the boudoir around the couple, forming tens of
thousands of squirming fogs.

"Pity," J. J. said.

Ice crystallized inside her spine. She tasted the waterless blue
of the sky above the Roman temple.

Copper of the dirigibles.

Awoke strapped to an operating table, staring up into a staticky
gray ultrasound image of her uterus. The living skeletal remains of
Johnny-Carson Flamewars, Vlad the Inhaler, Sigmund Feud, and
the rest of her lovers before Uly, a brood of desiccated lilliputian
homunculi, sucked at her insides, draining life from her, flinching
in blind fetal ecstasy.

Krystal was on her stomach, the sharp heavy pang of a boot
pressed into her spine. Her cheek was crushed against cold pebbly
concrete.

"Best put her out of her misery," a woman's mucoidal voice
said.

Krystal tried moving her jaw.

The space station breathed below her.

"You're going to die now, girl," the voice whispered close to
her ear. "Hold still. Just take a second. Quick channel switch, like."

But she couldn't hold still because she was fastened into a metal
seat bulleting through a yellow grid curving toward a green infinity, g-force making it impossible for her to shut her eyes. She sat

perfectly erect, hands clamped to chair legs, staring. Her cheeks rippled with velocity.

"We all experience time at different rates," J. J.'s voice whispered close to her ear.

J. J. was the naked woman with anemic skin and dense long auburn hair again.

Slender back to Krystal, she stooped over something in a corner of the smoky concrete cell, working steadily, thoughtfully, as if she couldn't hear Krystal ask her what she was doing, what those wet sounds she was making were.

Krystal warily angled closer.

J. J. growled at her.

Krystal halted.

The white flash of a hatchet blade rose and fell.

She saw Uly's unclothed body on the floor, legs spread, arms hacked like photos she'd seen of beef flanks in abattoirs in the twentieth century, one blue eye for his father and one brown for his mother fixed on a point somewhere above the ceiling.

J. J., greasy purplish chunks of meat stuck to her chin, gnawed at the slick smooth contractile muscle of his heart.

Flight attendant, coquettish paraplegic with Doberman toothbud implants and an Anglo-Saxon battle shield of cosmetic scars marking each cheek, buoyed down the aisle of the Danish shuttle between rows of opulently dressed passengers restrained in neat blue and white elastic g-net pouches. She was serving sacs of champagne laced with nootropics.

"How you feeling?" J. J. whispered in Krystal's ear.

Her jaw felt like it'd been dislocated and reset. Her eyes ached.

"Is this real?" she asked.

"That's the funny thing about virtual therapy. Just like psychoanalysis. You never know when you're done."

Krystal looked at her hands. They seemed normal enough. She

noticed her paper suit had been replaced with new black jeans, loose-fitting black Indian sark, shiny black high-topped combat boots. J. J. was wearing a candy-apple red Vietnamese dress and pants embroidered with golden dragons.

A man with vangoghed ears and neck brace was self-absorbed next pouch over, injecting rapture into his nasal cartilage.

"How long I been gone?"

"Three and a half days." J. J. reached out and squeezed her wrist. "How you feeling?"

"Like I drank just *way* too much last night." She checked in with her anatomy. Everything seemed steady enough. "Otherwise, not bad. Not bad at all."

"I told you."

"Yeah, you did. Thanks."

J. J. turned to the porthole. Her black eyes gleamed in the dark plastic.

"Look," she said.

Krystal peered past her. The shuttle'd begun banking and she caught the last flare of sun off The Iron Curtain, jumble of grayish building blocks spreading lazily through space.

She closed her eyes, began counting backward by threes from one hundred, and let her mind tumble away, too tired to react when J. J. squeezed her wrist again.

27

Take The Long Way Home

Erewhon One was to The Iron Curtain what the prim lawns, geometrical avenues, and neoclassically elegant fountains surrounding Versailles Palace were to the orange slime, army-green feces, and umber clots of infected mosquito larvae stagnating in the gutters of a hot alley in Calcutta.

Even from several hundred kils away, the majestic white wheel revolving in orbit around the moon exuded a sense of profound affluence. It announced prestige, independence, major credit's inherent urge to build complicated systems for itself.

Designed over the course of a decade by Saki Modo, constructed from lunar material at mind-searing expense by Klub Med, and run with all the refinement of a nineteenth-century British nobleman in Bora Bora by a team of dedicated emigrants from the semi-state of Best Western Cancún, Erewhon One was a resplendent hybrid of Monaco and Jamaica, Las Vegas and Tahiti, Sodom and Geneva…a mesh of mestos, casinos, discos, brothels, luxury shops, health spas, transplant boutiques, hymen-replacement salons, CompuSim halls, and S&M studios…all in a Sex Free Zone where stringent earth laws slackened into those of the GSA, allowing all manner of disease and nanodrug exchange among consenting adults as long as they could afford it.

≋

It was also a place, Krystal discovered as J. J. steered her across a crowded NutraSweet-white beach bordering a wisteria-blue lagoon on their way to the Hotel Lamprey, where time didn't exist. At the dock she'd had to give up her Victorian watch. Multilingual holographic notices in customs banned personal computers and television sets. CNNers weren't allowed to receive or broadcast. A sunny sky, waterless and azure as the one in that VR rig, burned above vacationers with a steady abstract glow, unceasing.

Erewhon One amounted to a private club with no temporal location. It was arranged for the absolute seclusion and repose of its wealthy guests. Even its synthetic gravity didn't feel quite right, quite natural, and hence added to their unsettlingly satisfying sense of soft vertigo.

"This perfection stuff is a real mindfuck," Krystal said, winding through Trix-colored umbrellas dotting the beach all the way up to the edge of the jungle.

Thonged women and bikinied men, skin tanned crazy-quilts, lounged on pastel towels in two-meter-square areas, pretending they were enjoying the outdoors. Each, healthy and quenched as a commercial, kept looking around self-consciously as if tracked by an invisible camera.

Here and there Prime Timers, fleshy morsels flaking off their faces in the light manufactured breeze, panted on iron lungs seemingly blueprinted by Fritz Lang...streamlined climate-controlled silver teardrops in which the PTs incubated during the last stages of their malaise...male nurses in Pepe burial shrouds sitting beside them, cross-legged, trained like the guards outside Buckingham to meet no one's eyes.

"The world as theme park," said J. J. "The theme park as a world that might've been. It's like walking through an old television show with really chintzy special effects. I love it. You hungry?"

"When was the last time I ate?"

"Kept you on a subclavian for the duration. But it's never the same as the real thing, is it?"

"I'm famished."

"Not to worry. Help is on the way. I know just the thing."

≋

They found seats at a bamboo table on the hotel's teeming veranda. A group of six nude Male-Bonders played jai alai in a glass-walled court on the beach, sunburnt penises and scrotums jiggling like a clutch of turkey wattles. On each table was a flat rectangular Lado-Acheson remote for placing bets.

A Samoan waiter in Armani light chainmail briefs, shiny black hair combed tight across his scalp, stepped up with an electronic pad and puck. He was wearing JFK aftershave.

"Bonjour, mesdemoiselles," he said.

J. J. pretended he wasn't there.

"Ask him for the lamproie," she told Krystal.

"Lamproie?"

"Yeah. It's not like real lamprey or anything. Genetically designed house specialty."

"Okay, sure. I'll have that."

"S'il vous plait," J. J. said, blasély observing an orange and yellow hang-glider hovering beside a fake cliff half a kil away topped with a pagoda and bamboo grove, "j'aimerais deux lamproie de mer."

The waiter pressed his palms together, bowed a tad from the waist, and backed away.

Krystal became aware of the woman at the next table who'd had plastic surgery to look like the Mona Lisa. She was lunching with a guy who'd had plastic surgery to look like that dead glam, Elektra Geestring. His skin was yellow-brown, eyes a cherished blue. He wore his hair braided and coiled atop his wide-jawed skull.

Android birds bickered in the palms. Above the treeline rose lofty steeples and rounded golden domes of the casinos. A motorized iguana lounged on the bleached white balustrade, pupils flickering.

"Thing is," J. J. said, "when the Yucatan became too filthy to inhabit comfortably at the fin de millennium, the resort business began to DT. Took years for reality to sink into the tourists' preconceived platitudes about tropical paradises. But when it did, *man*, old Cancún's economy dropped like a wingless VTOL."

"And that's where Klub Med stepped in?"

"A tropical paradise away from the sludge and poverty the tropics had become. You think it's warm here?"

"I'm fine."

"NorAm governcorp, provoked by Best Western's CEOs, annexed it and moved in after the war...with the blessings of the National Security Profit Margins Amendment, natch."

"Ran out of rain forests down south."

"And by 2010 were slash-and-burning up around a hundred acres a minute in the Tan."

"Meaning there goes your basic biodiversity, drugs, ruins."

"And, more important, your basic tourist trade."

Krystal glanced around her. All the patchwork skin, razor grass, man-tall ferns and elephant-ear plants.

One of the jai alaiers jerked the cesta fastened to his arm. The white pelota shot out and ricocheted off a wall. Another player leapt to catch it. Krystal'd heard those things traveled close to two-hundred-fifty kils an hour.

"So now the rich and famous pay to live lives they saw in old vids," she said.

"Bogart. Bond. Baffo."

"Which never really existed."

"They want to purchase a feeling of nostalgia based on a non-reality planned and executed by the media." J. J. traced one of the dragons embroidered on her dress. "Always happy to serve, Klub Med planned and executed a simulacrum of that non-reality."

"Which felt, not like a non-reality, but a memory."

"Built it, packaged it, sold it as a status symbol."

Krystal leaned back in her chair. Neoprene bamboo poked her spine. She leaned forward again.

"And it worked?"

"Look around you. Everything you see's corporate-generated. Synthetic as a Seiko. Animals, reptiles, insects. Bot mosquitoes will suck your blood, you want them to."

"Shit."

"Breeze, geologic features, air, scents, buildings. Everything's some sort of amalgam, or an amalgam of some sort of amalgam, of plastic, metal, and coloring...with a little emerging nanotech on occasion thrown in for effect."

The waiter reappeared with two gold-leafed plates on which slid what looked like slabs of black roast beef in viscous black gravy garnished with cooked-carrot and tomato substitute. He set them down, waited for orders, and, when none came, bowed and retired.

Ravenous, Krystal dug in.

"What you think?" J. J. asked, spreading her linen napkin on her lap and delicately slicing off a small cube for herself.

"Sweet. Tangy. Cool. Like shrimp."

"Vat-raised giant oceanic lampreys. Sometimes grow five meters long." She slipped the bite into her mouth and savored it as if testing select wine. "Nice." Chewing some more. "Yeah. Real nice." She swallowed. "Genetically altered to produce a mild hallucinogen in their fat cells. I think you'll like it."

"All I need," Krystal said. "Another headworm."

J. J. laughed.

"You need to relax, is what you need. Get your strength back. Get yourself ready."

"For what?"

J. J.'s gaze skidded past her. One of the jai alai players had been hit with the pelota, hard as a golf ball. He was lying on his side, hands to mouth, blood oozing between his fingers. His sunburnt scrotum had retracted into his abdominal cavity like a nervous animal.

J. J. reached over and picked up the remote, punched in a couple of numbers.

"For what?" Krystal repeated.

"Oh, you know," rapt in the player's injury, "lots of things."

"Such as?"

J. J. lazily refocused on her. A smile nicked her lips.

"This and that," she said. "That and this."

She cut off another bite, stabbed it, raised it on her fork.

The patrons on the veranda cheered as two teammates hoisted the wounded player between them and began to carry him off the court.

≋

"Sure you're not warm?" she asked again ten minutes later.
"Yeah. I'm fine," Krystal said. A pale violet taste whisked over her tongue. "So how come you know so much about this stuff?"
"Man, I'm burning up. Must be the piece."
With an illusionist's tug, she plucked off her shag wig and leaned back, holding the thing in her lap like a huge furry white Pekingese.
She exhaled a lungful of air. Her head was unremittingly bald. So was her face when she freed the sham eyebrows and eyelashes and added them to the pile. Alopecia universalis. One of the things all the FeeMale hormone treatments in the world couldn't compensate for.
Except what really caught her attention were all those welts covering J. J.'s cranium. Looked like a mass of corpulent discolored barnacles. As Krystal watched, one of them slowly split and folded open, revealing the wet whitish-blue of a vestigial eye beneath.
It fluttered dully, squinting into the imitation sky.
Another joined it.
Then another.
Soon supernumerary eyes speckled her head. Each parted and closed independently of the others, and each was weakly involved in what was going on in the direction it happened to be staring.
Krystal understood she'd been wrong about most of those bruises and swellings.
J. J. noticed her watching and, widening her black eyes vampishly, asked: "You like?" The jai alai game began again, this time doubles. The pelota jetted out of a player's cesta like a rocket from a bazooka. It exploded off a glass wall. "Daddy got my DNA manipulated up here. Uncle Meats can place 'em okay, but can't get the corneas and retinas to develop right. Only able to recognize light and dark. Sometimes not even that." She patted the top of her head tenderly. "But I love the mythological flavor, don't you?"
"'Daddy'?"
A deep orange four-winged monarch butterfly landed on one of the purple polyurethane orchids in the vase in the middle of the table.
The butterfly took off.

The waiter returned and cleared away plates.

"Ever hear of Air Pyrate Muzzik?" J. J. asked.

"Discovered every major band in the western hemisphere last decade."

"Decade and a half."

"Strange Angels, Kama Quyntifonic."

"Viva Bonni Suicide, Sum Nothing, Plain Brown Rapper." She tilted her head up into the artificial sunshine, massaged her white neck. One of the extra orbs on the right side of her skull tried to focus on Krystal. "Marco Polydor and Laurie Anasin ring any bells?"

"Company execs."

"CEOs." J. J. lowered her gaze, meeting Krystal's eyes. "Mummy and daddy dearest."

"No shit?"

Krystal was impressed.

"Leveraged buy-out of Neiman-Marcus Converse when I was four."

"And Air Pyrate Muzzik? Subsidiary of Klub Med, right?"

"And Klub Med a division of the Global Drug Administration, Ltd."

"And the GDA a subsidiary of Diacomm."

"Give the lady a hand." J. J. showed her teeth. Her chipped incisor glimmered. "We're all just one big happy incestuous southern family up here. It's like living in a Faulkner novel."

"Who?"

J. J. laughed again.

"Anyway, I'm like an heiress or something." She balled up her napkin and tossed it on the table. "So. Enough about me." She leaned forward on her elbows. "Ever seen a CompuSim?"

Krystal focused beyond J. J. and the jai alai court. People clustered around a mesto built beneath a wide high-impact plastic half-bubble under a waterfall plashing into the crow-shaped lagoon.

"Thought they were still under development."

"Too expensive for the general viewing public. All the rage up here, though. And the live show that follows...well, it'll make you feel like you been touched by the hand of god."

Krystal rubbed her cheekbones.

"This is some place," she said.

The Virtual Light was a posh retro-job on the cobblestoned Boulevard J. G. Ballard. It stood between a casino decked out like a pyramidal tower at Angkor Wat and a curvilinear art nouveau restaurant trimmed in neon featuring hydroponic vegetables and vat-grown monkey brains.

The façade was Neo-Shriek, polychromatic broken bottles, real leather belts and gloves, hard drives, Altec-Lansing speakers, innards of Olivetti typewriters, sputtering LEDs, LogiTech video sculptures of enema slaves, and reliquary vials containing the excess lard of rock stars set into a moon-stone base and sanded flat.

Inside, eight rows of overstuffed chairs from a late-twentieth-century moviehouse circled a bare teakwood stage above which shimmered a holographic crystal chandelier raveled as a Mandelbrotian fractal.

"Thing is," J. J. explained when they took a seat down front, "with this, actors are officially passé."

J. J.'d left her wig back at the Hotel Lamprey. With all those immature eyes trying to get a look at her, talking to J.J. felt like talking to several tranked skeletons at once.

"Been all acted out," she continued, crossing her left leg over her right, letting her candy-apple red sandal dangle from her metatarsal bones. Krystal saw the business with her crooked little toe was a flash trend too. "Flesh's gotten in the way, you know? Keeps degenerating, wearing down, drying up. Being, well, you know, all flesh-like."

Six or eight other spectators were scattered around the intimate hall. Two queens, joined at the necks by a gold-flecked decorative umbilical cord and made up in a messy-haired, runny-mascaraed, smeared-lipsticked postcoital look earth wouldn't see for weeks, affectionately fingered each other's chests three rows back. An oil burner in an Aiwa-tartan kilt, mustache wrapping around his mouth into a cropped chin-beard, passed in front of J. J. and Krystal and smiled, revealing black gums and a set of yellowed wooden dentures circa 1776. Somewhere behind them clacked and shooshed the unmistakable sound of a couple of iron lungs.

Barely louder than these was the muzak version of a song by some long-extinct band Krystal just dimly recognized. Sekret Servix.

Air conditioning unit hummed to life and Krystal detected a cool bitter hit of oxygen spiked with what must've been either permeable jax or black ice.

A girl, eight or nine, trotted up and down the aisles taking orders. Her skin was thin as wasp paper. A choked pond of bluish veins webbed beneath it. Krystal, trying to think of the disease's name, decided to supplement the airborne drug with a DMZ for a favorable outlook.

She swallowed the lime trapezoid without water and eight bars of music later a sea anemone the same color as that monarch butterfly on the veranda fanned open in her mind.

She remembered she was just about to say something.

"It's called age."

"What is?" asked J. J.

"All this deterioration stuff."

"Precisely. And nothing's distasteful as age. It's utterly underclass. Prole."

"Age is age."

"Age is fucking peasant. UV rays dicking with your cellular structure, breaking blood vessels, enlarging pores, creating all these fugging ugly brown spots no matter how much sunscreen or how many lamb placentas you apply. Gravity yanking your organs, loosening them up, tugging them down." She looked at the ceiling and adjusted a black contact. Krystal followed her and saw the chandelier was comprised of a complicated weave of glass tropical fish swimming in a daedal pattern. "Know what you think when you see an old actor?"

"I don't think anything."

"You think, 'I'm mortal. I'm fucking mortal. Someday I'm going to be what she is.' How can anyone watch a vid with that shit going on in your head?"

The muzak faded and the fish chandelier began to spin. The hall darkened. Krystal had the immediate impression the world wasn't solid. Vachuru, she thought.

Instead of a favorable outlook, she experienced a narcotic sense of derangement like her body was disintegrating bioplast by bioplast. She couldn't feel her fingers. Her scalp felt like an ant nest. All the drugs she'd been ingesting over the last few days had mixed into some treacherous ferment.

She saw a glistening cobweb in the center of a mausoleum. She heard the color of mercury in a pool of tar.

"Computers run statistical analyses of the viewers' favorite actors, scan them in from previous vids, give them new voices, young them up, even create a couple that never existed in the Big Television before but should've, then set them in motion. Add an appendage here, airbrush out some apertures there...and presto. Got yourself a space hermetically sealed against the idea of larvae."

The chandelier splintered.

Glass fish spewed through the hall and mutated into a constellation of stars, huge ovum wriggling with white spermatozoa, thousand hunchbacked homunculi with Demi Moore's countenance and Zyklon B. Baffo's bulk.

Soundtrack pastiched together sexual moans, turbine thunks, a revved dentist's drill, and faraway Middle Eastern wails of lamentation into a slow sonic beat.

Krystal jerked back as if in a shuttle at the instant of ignition.

"A kind of rust-free arena where all times exist at once and nobody has to think about tomorrow," J. J. said. "Thinking's dead and gone. Only dreaming's left. *It's* the ultimate theme park."

Krystal saw a meteor skid through her field of vision and had the uncomfortable feeling it wasn't a special effect.

The music sounded very red, like the bodies of poisonous jungle frogs.

"Unreal," she said.

"Heavenly, isn't it?" J.J. reached over and petted the back of Krystal's hand. "Enjoy."

The homunculi burst into flames, skins bubbling like burning marshmallows, crumbling away, chrome skeletons beneath which glowed with green fluorescence, ruptured into a cloud of tiny copper suns spiraling sluggishly at first, a lazy galaxy, then faster and faster, thronging toward the center of the hall.

They arranged themselves into the words PEPSICO, INC., which wobbled and dissolved into the orange-brown oxidized metal phrase POLYFORM PRODUCTIONS, which wavered, rolled, and arrested into a huge granite wall across which were chiseled sharp-edged Roman letters spelling KLUB MED, a name which flourished into bronze rococo foliage proclaiming DIACOMM, which itself began to melt as though made of wax, nautilusing into a Laocoönian confusion of soft arms and legs, a gigantic writhing naked beast with flesh as thin and pale as the little girl's who'd just taken orders.

Krystal realized she was watching a complicated holographic orgy.

Grace Kelly, Kiefer Sutherland, Holy Ryder, Madonna, Skeets South, and Ingrid Bergman, none yet out of their early twenties, caressed Claudia Schiffer who hovered among them like a magician's assistant, dirty blond hair raying from her head as though she was bobbing Ophelia-style down some invisible stream.

But she was and wasn't Claudia Schiffer. In this laser-beam reality, she bore a meter-long penis that hooked left and was mazed with fat African-violet veins and miniature inset labia, and it was these Kiefer Sutherland, head shaved, sheared beard gritty, lapped with the diamond stud on his tongue while Grace Kelly, possessing the insanely perfect features that could drive one of Leonardo's angels to weep with envy (except for that knotty growth like a moist walnut on her left cheek), alternately nibbled his nipples and electrocuted them with a svelte taser while being taken hard from behind by Skeets South, the Immaculate, whose eyes were clenched in pleasure as Holy Ryder, diminutive implanted penis wobbling above her natural vagina, softly slapped one flipper riveted with ten or twelve transistor-shaped earrings against his bobbing testicles, deep-kissing Madonna, nose cosmetically broken and set at a startling angle, mountain bluebird feathers sewn into her epidermis, busy between Claudia Schiffer's legs, tracing her perineum and tenderly distending her anal sphincter, first with her black-nailed thumb and forefinger, then with her whole kick-boxer's fist, and Ingrid Bergman, right out of the tarmac scene in *Casablanca*, sans apparel, blue-veined breasts periodically lactating single white droplets down her pronounced ribcage, produced as if from air a toothless, clawless, sightless cyborg gerbil, furless flesh hue of uncooked pasta, which she smeared with clear lubricant and affectionately inserted into the model's relaxed rectal cavity.

Claudia Schiffer gasped with pain and satisfaction and started squirming in place as the rodent without lungs twitched up her alimentary canal.

Ingrid Bergman and Madonna wrapped their arms around Claudia Schiffer's legs just above the knees to subdue her. Kiefer Sutherland and Skeets South did the same with her arms. Holy Ryder meanwhile began to cunnilingate the females, long plasticine tongue extended and strengthened through a series of muscle grafts, and Grace Kelly extracted her teeth and took first one male's member into her slick-gummed mouth, then the other's, and, then, both at once, unhinging her jaw like a feeding python to work their erect shafts farther down her bloated throat, Kiefer Sutherland massaging her facial growth with sexy regard.

What happened next seemed vaguely Mayan.

A gray weathered stone slab materialized beneath the model who struggled with increasing violence against the grip of the actors. Apprehension replaced rhapsody in her eyes. Panic replaced apprehension.

Her body heaved. Tremors oscillated through her muscles, fingers crimped into fists, feet shuddering with Parkinson's…and her mouth gaped. She screamed like a Sunkist Florida woman who's just walked into her kitchen to find a five-meter-long two-headed alligator lounging on the linoleum floor where her five-month-old baby used to be.

A tumorous mound bulged beneath the skin between her boyish breasts.

It turned lavender, fierce purple, mulberry…then grenaded in a black mist of blood and meaty shreds, spraying the other actors across their faces and necks.

Claudia Schiffer stiffened like she'd been slammed with all the raw energy in a nuclear power plant.

Viscous blood globbed between her lips.

Her limbs convulsed, her eyes shot open, and she defecated

onto the slab in a drooling English-toffee discharge.

And there...there...scrooched on the edge of her blown-open chest where her heart should've been, wet with gore and excrement, hunched the cyborg gerbil cleaning itself.

Except she was and wasn't Claudia Schiffer, wasn't and was...there was that chain-stitch scar where one breast'd been...the brown baby-bottle nipple of the other...and those nose-rings, eyebrow-hoops, black high-topped combat boots...

Krystal fought against the iridescent hallucinogenic haze.

She'd seen those eyes before, that online hair and tatt.

She'd seen those torn clothes, black jeans and Indian sark, that frightened look, peeled-back muscle...

She tried to figure out which people on stage, in this hall, were real and which merely three-dimensional polychromatically irradiated batches of light, and she knew in a synaptic spark the only thing that would ever remain constant for her was what she remembered of herself.

Only that wasn't true either, was it?

Because who she was and who she wasn't, what she remembered and what she forgot, changed fast as a vid of a decomposing roadkill set on eternal fastforward.

Because that was her, too...bronze tulips sprouting from her cadaverous flesh...other glams become semi-transparent specters, their skin pliable ice, liquefying in the brilliant white blaze from those flowers...and that was her, too, Dol-Chi Vita, skinny Guianese performance artist in a pair of black silk Valentino briefs and surgical gloves toe-scuffing across the barren stage, dreadlocks hanging shoulder-length on one side of his head, hardly tickling his vangoghed ear on the other, body an expressionist woodcut of healed slashes.

Still, those contacts, lilac with yellow stripes...those contacts...

A portion of spotlit teak-paneled floor slid away and an aluminum-and-mauve leatherette dentist chair lifted from the black rectangle.

Dol-Chi climbed aboard with urbane precision, something well-bred, refined, delicate in his movements. Never acknowledging the audience, he strapped down his ankles and thighs with leatherette restraints, tweaked them tight, industrial assemblage soundtrack evaporating and the hall loading with silence broken only by those deep steady breaths he took as he worked, thin microphone wire arced across his mouth.

He flipped up one of the armrests and extracted a plastic squirt bottle of iodine germicidal scrub. Thumbed down his briefs two or three centimeters and spritzed the liquid across the lower right side of his abdomen. Withdrew a felt-tipped marker, palpated the tender area just above his hipbone, fingers sensitive as those of a classical pianist.

When he located what he was looking for, he drew a fifteen-centimeter-long black dotted line marking the spot.

Next he removed a scalpel, three retractors, and several small hemostats from the armrest.

He exhibited the mongoose-style focus of a Zen master. For him minutes slackened and swelled. He had nothing to do, nothing to think about, except this instant, this process taking its course before him, exacting and momentous, which might just last forever.

It seemed to Krystal he was sitting by himself in a furnitureless room in a bamboo hut in a dense forest atop a deserted African mountain at 3:00 a.m. seven days after a neutron bomb blast had wiped out all the faunal species within a ten-kil area.

Light reconfigured, surrounded him in a glinting orb that hovered outside the laws of substitute gravity. It accented the crosshatch of fine ridges netting his torso, some just a centimeter or two long, others lengthier and shaped like petroglyphs or gang communiques, still others sealed with stitches mimicking corners of pages from medieval manuscripts.

He brought the scalpel down, traced the dotted line, splitting his espresso-brown skin.

Dark blood hilled along the hairline incision.

Dol-Chi Vita didn't blink. His breath remained constant.

He was missing the index finger from his left hand, ring finger from his right.

Unhurriedly, he sliced through a thin layer of curdled-egg fat, another of bubble-gum pink muscle.

He clamped back the flesh and, uttering an almost subsonic hiss, secured several large bleeders.

He reached over and released a long clear hose from the armrest and inserted the suction tip into his wound. A slender cord of blood flew up with a wet sucking sound and disappeared into a collecting tank somewhere beneath the armrest. He removed the hose and sat very still for the count of thirty, chin on chest, regaining his strength before continuing.

His ribcage rose and fell. His eyes closed. He let his arms drop to his sides, palms raised, as he turned inward, traveling the passageways of his mind in search of emotional provisions.

After a while he raised his hands to his lower abdomen and examined his progress.

Satisfied, he sunk his fingers into the juicy cavity, probing, tightening his grip, finessing into the open the narrow glistening bluewhite eight-centimeter tube protruding from his cecum.

His breath caught, lips pulled back, teeth capped with silver, but he pushed on, rummaging through the armrest for the long hooked needle and nylon suture. Perspiration oiled his skin, fissured down his cheeks.

He stitched off his appendix, cut it free with a single graceful gesture, placed the wormish organ in a small kidney-shaped pan balanced on the free armrest, inverted the stump back into the large intestine.

His hands began to quiver.

He tied off the last vessels and irrigated the wound, removed the hemostats and retractors, counted them, eased his severed muscles back into their normal position, drew together the two lips of skin.

With a fancy latticework stitch he sewed the wound closed and, now noticeably weak, shaken, spritzed another shot of iodine over the site, applied a thick layer of gauze secured with strips of white surgical tape, and sat back, lungs laboring hard.

He returned all his instruments to the armrest, flipped it shut, and the spotlight returned to its original intensity.

Dol-Chi Vita unstrapped himself and inched out of his chair, unsure of his footing as a woman who'd just birthed.

Lilac and yellow eyes glassy, thighs trembling, he raised his head to the audience for the first time, brought his feet together, let his arms dangle by his sides, bowed, expression deadpan.

In the same moment codpol music by the Thought Gang spilled through the hall, bass heavy enough to pulverize unprotected cortical tissue, and Dol-Chi Vita crumpled to the floor.

Two assistants in baggy crash suits (hoods, gloves, and booties slathered with a thick coating of what looked like Eveready antiviral bots suspended in a Vaseline base) jogged up the aisle nearest J. J. and Krystal and lifted their boss to his feet. They placed his scrawny arms over their shoulders, elevated him so only his toes touched the floor, and led him off the stage.

The meager audience, some already wandering up the aisles in search of something more exotic, clapped absentmindedly.

Everyone, that is, except J. J.

Each eye on her head strained to capture even a blurry semblance of these profound instants of sublime grace when pain, control and desire compound and language leaves you in silence.

"It's time," she whispered.

Krystal awoke among the thin white sheets in her neoprene-bamboo-framed bed at the Hotel Lamprey, distinct impression circling behind her lids she'd been dreaming other people's dreams, ghost fully alert and rambling about things she didn't even want to *think* might be true.

She stared groggily into J. J.'s contacts.

"It's the middle of the night," she said, tongue slow.

"In a manner of speaking, in a manner of speaking. Come on."

"I'm so *tired...*"

"Sleep is for the dead, honey. We're almost there. Hurry. Get dressed now. We got a cosmic bus to catch."

They cut across the crowded beach under the waterless blue sky, Krystal's eyes swollen, head a static discharge, and entered an airlock marked EMERGENCY semi-hidden behind a cluster of artificial ferns next to a styrofoam boulder.

An alarm began to cycle, but they pressed on, running beneath those multilingual holographic notices in customs at the dock currently deserted between flights, arriving at the rows of slip modules lining one hull, white alloy spheres, each capable of a lone function: transporting a group of four people to the lunar surface eight minutes below in the event of a catastrophic structural failure. Several were already gone.

J. J. hustled her through the hatch of the nearest, clambered in behind, slapped the only button on the control panel, the red release disk, with the flat of her hand.

The hatch sizzed shut, Krystal's eardrums ached with the whoosh of pressurizing oxygen, and, as she rushed to take her seat, fasten her harness, the module tilted. She toppled against an armrest, the lights clicked off, she heard a dull explosion...and the majestic wheel of Erewhon One was rotating above her, falling away from the module at an amazing rate, while the digital ghost in her skull sang like a choir boy whose voice would never know change.

28

Antennae Of The Species

Uly felt like birds were eating his memories.

He heard the bullet leap free of the barrel and saw Salvador three seconds after, saw himself, saw the body on its stomach, cheek pressed into icy soil.

He saw, three weeks later, Dolan's hand curl into itself and shrivel, begin to char in the fire.

Almost two hundred years in the future Krystal put down the half-empty beer bottle beside her in his crypt and crawled around to face him. She lifted the Aiwa off his lap and set it on the floor. He leaned back on his arms and she craned forward, easing her mouth over his full erection, glans pierced with a small gold hoop.

He looked at the ceiling and down and he was Ginny reaching forward to pick a daisy in the tall grass on the banks of the Humboldt, no more than a series of warm half-stagnant pools of tea-colored water this late in September. The wagon train roared behind him.

In ten seconds Sam Shoemaker, lanky and small-boned, would ride up and tell him to hurry.

In three months Sam Shoemaker would stand beside a tree, ax poised in mid-stroke, jaw set for impact, chin slanted up half an inch as if caught by an interesting idea, and he would sit down in the deep snow, dead.

Uly closed his fingers around the daisy and his mother closed her fingers around his arm.

She hauled him to his feet. The air was sooty and acrid. Dull thuds from tank rockets smashed into the public housing project across the block. Brick and metal splintered.

He was running beside her through the chaotic streets that within twenty-four hours would come to be known by the media as The Rage.

Her expression was taut, defiant, grim; her expression was unfocused, pale, tranked.

Her eyes pivoted toward him when he entered her hospital room. Her skin didn't look like skin anymore—just some flimsy, baggy, rubbery membrane nature used to cover a clump of failing organs and bones.

She looked at him, opened her mouth, shut it.

Opened it.

"You don't just experience death once," she said. "You experience it over and over. It keeps showing up all around you in different forms. Like H_2O."

J. J. maneuvered out the hatch backward, bulky in her Chimerika evacuation suit and clumsy in the moon's weak gravity, one-sixth what it'd been on Erewhon One.

She stepped onto the lunar soil, steadied herself, turned to help Krystal. Her trace-eyes were all straining to peer at the surroundings through her copper-tinted visor. Krystal gave her her hand and eased herself down the two-step ladder, helmet flocking with the sound of rapid breathing and the ghost's voice. The noise tasted like tinfoil.

Krystal was impressed how natural all this seemed.

First thing she noticed was the irreal blue ball wisped with feathery white, nearly four-hundred-thousand kils away, hanging low on the rocky horizon. Without any atmosphere to soften and warp it, its outline appeared uncannily precise.

To its right glinted an artificial star, Erewhon One.

The landscape around her was flashlight-on-mirror bright because of earthshine, and it'd remain that way for another two, maybe three days before night skimmed in. Temp was probably up around 90 or 95 degrees C. Even with her sun-visor down, she had to squint in the brash glare. Give it forty-eight, seventy-two hours, and it'd dive to minus 130. Even now, in the carbon shadows, unprotected, her blood would freeze cement-hard before she'd taken half a breath. Below the blue ball teethed the peaks of the Caucasus Mountains, long line of titanic brush bristles, some peaks rising sixty thousand meters into space, needling toward J. J. and Krystal, shorter and shorter, till they gave out at the edge of the vast plain called Lake of the Dead littered with dark brown stones that shone like huge slick skulls.

Nestled against the foothills, out of sight, most of the structures more than ten meters below ground, was Armstrong City...its military operations, low-gravity drug manufacturing facilities, genetic engineering labs, ant-farm mine shafts.

"Only a couple more kils," J. J. said over her transmitter, "and we're home."

Krystal's ears felt like they needed to pop.

"Where's home?"

"Home," said J. J., taking her by the hand, "is where the family is."

Juan Placenta was fingernailing back his cuticles and listening to the news when that goddamn fucking tiny red emergency LED atop his goddamn fucking phone blinked on again.

Church of the Rotes, bunch of chronic retro-pussies based down in Saturn Tennessee, had just constructed a dirty bomb out of two rods stolen from the crippled BelsenLand reactor and a dumptruck-full of fertilizer and gas, and detonated it at the security checkpoint at the foot of the Diacomm Labs pyramid in LA.

"We shall use the future to fight the future," their communiqué taking responsibility for the bombing said.

The HDTV screens broadcasting commercials twenty-four hours a day from the sides of the pyramid were destroyed, a third of the massive structure itself, most humans within a three-kil radius.

Protests had already arisen among the viewing public, and the governcorp hurried to set up makeshift screens on the nearby Beverly Hills guard towers. Which just pissed the ever-loving hell out of Juan, spun him into a mood fouler than a specimen of an alcoholic's liver, letting these shit-for-brains goon squads of Victorian throwbacks fuck with the citizenry's televisual habits.

Only then that goddamn tiny red emergency LED atop his goddamn phone blinked on and his previous mood became sunfilled as a DisCal afternoon in August set next to his new one.

He reached behind his ear, turned down his aug, powered up his screen, and beheld, much to his heart-sinking dismay, Ratt ogling back at him with this big, sloppy, wannabe-adorable smile behind her VR rig.

Well, shit.

Whole thing was probably his own goddamn fault from the start though he couldn't for the world figure out exactly how.

All he did was pull off some first-class sex-ups. What she could do with those sweet legs of hers made the mind hum and the ass cheeks clench. Except enough was enough. And now she wouldn't back off, wouldn't fucking leave him alone. Called at all hours of the night. Surprised him with visits so he couldn't even take a crap in peace. Talked (and this is where Juan started to seriously freak, considered applying for a transfer right back to earth) of certain *vows*.

He thumbed his nose bone and, presented as he was with no other alternatives, turned on the charm in an intuitively defensive posture, simpering.

"Buenas noches," sweetness and light. "Long time no hear."

"Sorry to bother you and all, but at present we got this like big, hairy, tumorous problem staring us right between the eyeballs."

"I'm one big ear."

For the length of time it takes hope to spark, ignite and die, Juan thought maybe she was referring to their relationship.

"Upwards of thirty slip modules from EO're touching down even as we speak."

Juan stared, trying on this bit of data like a new dental dam.

"Major malf topside?"

"Negative. EO security computer's calling it illegal jettisons."

"Well fuck."

"Fuck indeed. Thing is, we—"

Juan leaned forward and smacked off his phone, Suzi spliffing out of existence in mid-sentence, and reached over and jabbed his own crisis square.

We can't prevent the future because for us it's already happening, the ghost whispered in Krystal's head as she half-walked, half-bounced toward the center of Lake of the Dead, peaks of the mountains magnifying by degrees. *Before nobody was sure if she had really smiled...but now...here...* J. J. was forty or fifty meters farther on, luminous white smear against the dark glistening surface. She leaped several times in succession, covering three or four meters with each bound, stopped and turned to check on Krystal, let her catch up. Krystal was out of breath. Her organs felt askew in the weak gravity. *The child's hands reaching out, childhood dead in the immense black room...your mother and father redreaming your body...the shredded photograph falling like lightning bugs, word flesh, dream flesh, memory pictures...we're in the film, we're on our final approach to the guerrilla war...fire in the brain...flare in the frozen rock around you...new categories of human impersonation closing in ...so open your heart, your mind, the moment of your death...the silver flakes of old image tracks, tape looping, because this is what the end of the world will be like, just like this, just like this, just like this, always...*

Uly peered over his shoulder at George Donner receding in gray-white surges of snow.

Seven hours later Stanton shouted through driving wind. They couldn't give up now, couldn't retreat. It was time to abandon everything, wagons, all but the most essential provisions, cattle, and scramble for escape.

Two centuries later Uly touched his head while sitting on a ledge overlooking Donner Lake and a stunning white light flamed.

In the shocking illumination, he saw an immense wagon wheel crunch through the frosty crust of the Great Salt Lake desert and sink inches into the grainy slush.

He flinched and a quake pitched through George Donner's body wrapped in buffalo robes and quilts in his bed in the tree-tent.

Uly kneeled beside him, holding George's good hand, head lowered.

When he raised it again he was Krystal staring at what appeared to be a doughy-skinned corpse lying on a cot in a dingy hall. He felt her wonder if she was dreaming him, his life, their encounter, or if the ghost was dreaming it for her.

A second later a nurse with a strange accent would respond to a question he had asked a second before by saying: "We call it a hospital, mama-san."

Then he was sitting on his mat in White Bird Six watching data fields shift, collapse, give way to whole new clusters of menus, stats about failed storage attempts scrolling next to a montage of aboveground blasts, mushroom clouds spouting thick and sobering from atolls, blue Pacific waters...

"Trust me," the Uncle Meat at the missile silo said, hovering over him, fluorescent canary-yellow contacts glowing.

His faced heatwaved into Keseberg's. The Westphalian rolled him in blankets on a cot in one of the lake cabins.

Uly's clothing was wet. He was exhausted. He'd made this final push up from the meadow with the children. Now the room rocked as Keseberg tucked a blanket under his chin.

He couldn't move his arms.

"Trust me, Mrs. Donner," Keseberg said, floating over him.

Then Uly saw the gleam in the candlelight and closed his eyes.

Thirty-five or forty people had gathered in the center of the dry plain.

Scattered in the distance, near the crater ridges, Krystal recognized the twinkle of half a dozen abandoned slip modules. She knew there were many more out of her line of sight.

The ghost spoke clearer than she'd ever heard it. Mingled with its voice came the chatter of others over her radio.

"Welcome home," J. J. said, stepping up behind her, giving her a brief gawky hug.

"What's happening here?"

She swept her arm across the scene. Some people sat on the pebbly ground, elbows on knees. Some stood in clusters, talking. Some waited by themselves, looking up at the black atmosphereless sky.

"They're from everywhere," J. J. said. "Guy over there playing with his hands? Gopher for a Klub Med exec up in the northwest. Next to him's a Techno-Hickster from IBM Nevada. He's talking to a woman named Noë Kognominski, Pole from Warsaw into white slave trade, who's talking to Romola Dejecta, ex-Brinks Force merc. Except they all have something in common."

"...?"

"Inside their heads look a lot like yours. Mine." Krystal saw her smile through her visor. "We're special."

The idea rushed on her like an attack helicopter.

"Receivers."

"Antennae of the species. Sensitives. Together the signal's five by five."

"The signal?"

"The signal. Everything's about to change, Krystal. It's like a worldwide explosion."

"What's about to change?"

"You know that dream you sometimes have? The dentist chair? The hypodermic?"

"You dream my dreams?"

"It's no dream." She pointed over Krystal's shoulder. "Look. It's starting."

Stanley Zircon dropped his arms to his sides and raised his face to deep space. Norton Amerika did the same. Others followed. Krystal heard voices tumbling off her bandwidth, airwaves falling silent...except for the ghost, whose words seemed to take solid form inside her helmet, become three-dimensional objects with length, width, thickness.

One thing after the other, it said. *It's wild...the faster you build something, the longer it lasts.*

29

Daydream Nation

Major Tom Mosaik didn't like what the sergeant told him one bit. Not one little bit. It gave him a huge erection, and for Major Mosaik a huge erection was tantamount to bad news slouching up the next flight of stairs, down the next alley, switchblade in hand, serial-killer grin spreading like a rash across its lips...

Had been, too, since he was twenty-one, moseying along Santa Monica Boulevard in LA twilight, heavens a Kandinsky mural of unhealthy colors, air stagnant as the stuff at the back of a dog's throat. Major Mosaik was feeling good about himself, good about his future, and good about the general arrangement of the cosmos. He'd just enlisted in the GSA's Off-World Program, with its military overtones and scientific ambience, heart riveted on becoming some fancy word for an office coordinator, when he threw his first boner.

Oh, he'd had them before, some semi-solid, some bent, some rigid and alert as a fighter pilot who's just noticed that heat-seeking missile closing in on his tail.

But now, unexpectedly, he'd thrown the big one, the giant, the stupendous prodigy itself, twenty-three centimeters if a micron in length...the kind that respired on its own, conducted its own monologue, made you feel you were ripping tissue and blowing out blood vessels, made you limp, moan and whimper like a cartoon coyote shot through with hot indefatigable hormonal steam.

Major Mosaik raised and lowered his right foot and the sidewalk on Santa Monica became a carnival ride.

The blacked-out window of the Japanese *hesodashi* clinic he was passing imploded...brick chips spattered around him...the universe shivered like a Chihuahua in a blizzard...and he was fighting for balance in the middle of the Shudder, angry blue erection beating time to the calamity like a psychotic conductor.

Now, thirty years later, he leaned back in his chair in his cubicle twenty meters below the surface of the moon and began to do some serious worrying.

Those intervening years hadn't been all that sweet on him. He'd sat a lot, pushed buttons a lot, raised his voice to his subordinates once or twice. The exercise thing'd sort of gotten away from him, though, outcome being the upper half of his fifty-one-year-old body was skinny and short-armed as a meerkat's, the lower chunky and bulbous-tushed as a pachyderm's. Add to this that his gray widow's-peaked head was too diminutive for what transpired beneath it, his eyes too large and widely spaced for an interlocutor's comfort, his teeth a petrified forest of broken and discolored stubs, and you had the impression when speaking with the major you were really speaking with the member of what might pass for a new subfamily of hominid.

And that erection just kept hammering away long after the sergeant had hung up. Major Mosaik originally thought it might've had something to do with the story he'd been listening to on his aug: Church of the Rotes had dirty-nuked the Diacomm Labs pyramid in LA. As the emergency LED atop Major Mosaik's phone blinked on, a reporter was stuttering about how that was just the beginning, folks...fallout was drifting northeast...lots more casualties were expected...looting had erupted prolific as a yard-full of dandelions...Brinks Force was on the scene...downwind evacuations were already underway...

Then the genuinely unpleasant news arrived.

Turned out, sergeant said, all these vacationers had just hijacked slip modules on Erewhon One before security up there could react and jettisoned to the lunar surface.

Information both weird and bad, no question, but not as weird and bad as the fact that, now down, they wouldn't communicate with Armstrong City. Wouldn't answer repeated requests for identification. Wouldn't even open up a hailing frequency.

Plus Major Mosaik understood those Chimerika evacuation units they wore weren't real space suits at all. Merely functioned as the GSA equivalents of life jackets. They possessed a limited oxygen supply rather than a rebreather and were designed to keep evacuees alive for the couple hours after an emergency it'd take to reach the safety of Armstrong City.

If Sergeant Placenta's calculations were right, they had maybe just less than two hours left.

And it was going to take most, if not all, of that time for the rescue team to reach them…if, that is, everything flowed smoothly as a wet kid down a waterslide.

Which, given the present state of Major Mosaik's turbulent appendage, seemed about as likely as catching the attention of that cute little radar operator up on level one with the tangerine contacts, butch hair, and stunning bottom.

What was her name again?

He leaned farther back in his chair and rubbed his abdomen, eyes closed, trying to recall.

Uly sat cross-legged in his crypt, staring at his Aiwa screen, reached out to click on the words *radiation doses*, and knew in twenty seconds two hands would fasten on his shoulders and he'd jump.

He clicked and the phrase *injury to reticular formation* appeared. He looked up. Morning rush-hour traffic busied itself on Highway 89 under a layer of chestnut atmosphere so rich it twinkled as if permeated with diamond powder.

Two hundred years before, a few kils from this spot, he saw an ax gleam in candlelight.

His clothing was soggy and cold, the cabin smoky.

A cobalt flame strobed in his head and the room rocked as Keseberg tucked a blanket under his chin.

In just over a second the ax would strike his skull.

As it did, he would slide into the thatched-roof booth across from Krystal at the Binge & Purge.

"When I was a little girl?" she would say three minutes later. "Every day lasted a month. It was amazing. Now every month lasts a second. And all the days...you don't even know they're going by, they're going by so fast."

While she spoke, Uly heard the ice on Truckee Lake expanding and cracking like a distant civil war.

He reached out to click on the words *radiation doses* and the door to Keseberg's cabin swung open.

The damp bitter reek of urine and mold crowded him. In the shadows lay the Westphalian rolled in blankets, blue eyes vigilant, mouth a pink cut in his gray beard.

Next to his bed burned a small cooking fire surrounded by human bones and on the fire simmered a kettle containing the remains of a liver aslosh in black coagulated blood and brain jelly.

Fallon Le Gros, enormous Irish trapper who led the last relief party, stared at it. Keseberg whispered something behind him.

"Excuse me?"

Turning.

"I said, 'Her flesh was the best I ever tasted.'"

Keseberg's wheezing laughter became Uly's mother's soggy cough.

Uly leaned forward and slid one hand behind her head, the other beneath her shoulder blades, and eased her up, this movement taking immense strength on his part because her muscles wouldn't work. Her pillows were moist with perspiration. When he shifted her position she moaned reflexively and looked at him.

He tried flipping channels in his mind, reached out to click on the words *radiation doses* and a male voice somewhere above him asked *You derming something maybe just a little too pure for your own good?*

Porous sandstone snow.

Uly saw Eddy remove his boot from Salvador's body, his body, look at the gray sky as if checking the weather.

Eleven months in the past Uly saw the square redbrick buildings, clean streets, and black iron fences of Independence roll back from him.

Seven years in the future wooden structures began rising along the shores of Donner Lake... Victorian hotels teeming with vacationing families who'd trained far as the tracks had been completed, then stage-coached in...women in ornate dresses riding side-saddle...children plashing in green water just off the beach...men poised on docks, fishing.

Entwined on the mats which they'd pushed together, Krystal rested her head on Uly's chest, an arm across his stomach, a leg across his groin.

"I'm really glad you came up to Moston," he said.

"Yeah, me too."

She reached up to touch his face and a stunning white light detonated.

A few still intact bodies and a great number of mutilated fragments lay about everywhere, Uly saw his hand write. *The remains, numbering upwards of 30, wasted by famine and shrunken by exposure as to resemble mummies, were, by an order of Gen. Kearny, collected and buried under the superintendence of Major Swords this 22nd day of June, 1847. They were interred in a pit which had been dug in the centre of one of the cabins for a cache. These melancholy duties to the dead being performed, the cabins, by order of Major Swords, were fired.*

One hundred years in the future motorboats carved white grooves across the lake edged by a jumble of houses on two sides, an historical trail with educational displays on a third.

Less than seventy meters away cars jammed the small parking lot of the wood-and-glass Emigrant Trail Museum with slide shows, films, and other commodifications of pain, while on the opposite side of some scraggly young trees traffic swished past on six-lane Interstate 80.

The body of George Donner was found at his camp, about eight or ten miles distant, wrapped in a sheet. He was buried by a party of men detailed for that purpose.

Krystal craned forward and kissed Uly, long and soft, on the lips.

Harriet stood there one second, two, then shattered into laughter, shrill as a magpie, and, two years later, Lewis Keseberg joined in, hair greased back, distinguished black suit trim as an army officer's, as he opened the door to his new restaurant on the waterfront in Sacramento late one sunny spring afternoon, willows leafing down the street far as the eye could see, and walked inside.

Suzi, puzzled, studied the jade glow in front of her where Juan's face had hovered a moment earlier.

Thinking, she peered down at the large pitted silver-white hot-air balloon of the moon below her. Above shone the frost-blue crescent of earth and behind, curving toward infinity, the yellow grid of her VR radar environment.

After a while a sagacious smile snuck across her lips.

It was lush...it was love...the way he grinned like the Pope from his Vatican balcony on the cover of his new album, her emotional Greenwich Mean Time.

He was hers, she was his, everything was sweet like a marzipan bonbon, intense like...

Then it drifted, enormous as a nightmare by Satan, into her field of vision, six or seven kils across, twelve or thirteen long, coming fast, unstoppable, massive as a small asteroid.

Only it was no small asteroid.

She reached out her data glove and the virtual control panel appeared. She punched up Orbital Telescope Imaging and the thing sprang toward her, overrunning her whole field of vision. Suzi felt like she was a lone swimmer trying to push away from the sky-scraper-side of an oil tanker as it slid past her into harbor.

It was gargantuan, all metal alloy, a towering aggregate of melted space debris. She could make out remnants of a Titan rocket engine fused with half a satellite antenna dish, hull fragment comprised of shuttle tiles, part of a solar panel welded to a useless mechanical leg off a space probe, what might've been the flank of a surface-explorer bot. Pure Neo-Shriek. Looked like all manner of wreckage'd been dumped into a waste reactor and torched.

"Oh shit oh shit oh shit," she said, reaching for her crisis square again.

Only this time when she punched it nothing happened.

Or, worse, the OTI winked off, just popped right out of existence. She looked around, startled, her breaths coming shorter.

The virtual control panel disappeared next, the crescent earth, the hot-air balloon moon, the yellow grid.

All that remained was the green glow of her VR radar environment and even that began to undulate and flitter.

Red letters began scrolling before her.

```
EMERGENYFUNCTION::::::NETWORKMALF:::
::ALLDATARETRIEVAL SYSTEMS GOINGDOWN
IMMEDIATELY:::::ALLDATARETIEVALSYSTEM
SGOINGDOWNIMMEDIATELY::::ALLDATARE
TIEVALSYSTEMSGOINGD::::::::::::::::::::::::::
::::::::::::::::::::::::::::::::::::::::::::::::::::::::
```

30

Bionic Angel

Walter-Mellon Ashram, the nurse with the purple Plughead tassel and pale green filtration mask in the Adam Curry wing of Deaconess Hospital, skorried to bring his slab back to life.

The guy with the patchy brownish-red beard and bleached-white hair flicked out on him, quick as thought, fourth one in the last twenty-four hours, issuing this gentle schlucking sound, then bucking, knocking over his cot, tearing right through his foil sheet, IV yanked from arm, oxygen mask askew, full cardiac arrest, slam, like that.

Ashram was on his knees beside him. Rolled him face up, placed his hands one on top of the other, heel on breastbone, and started pressing rhythmically, sixty reps per minute, perspiration glazing his cheeks, black Esprit mascara starting to run.

"Spill for me, papa-san," he said, voice clogged with pollution, muffled by his mask, "spill for me…"

But those eyelids remained slivered open, lips parted, skin the color of roots you find under rotten logs in rainforests.

So Ashram straightened, pulse fast, reached into his pocket, snapped on a new pair of gloves, and opened the guy's mouth with his thumbs, circled his forefinger around inside, clearing, skorried over to the crash cart, most shelves empty save for the odd vial of adrenaline, couple of morphine derms, and returned with a disposable ventilator sealed in plastic, kneeled again, tilted back the slab's head, tore open the bag and inserted the hose down his throat, snipped his nostrils shut, began squeezing the cheap rubber pouch on the end, twelve shots, back to the external heart massage.

He knew he was on his own here, always was, always would be, stark as the hour after that retired toyboy, thirteen, cosmetic harelip, surgically enhanced orifice, swooped into his warm reality last year and stole his lover right off his sleeping mat.

No Uncle Meats were going to respond to this code blue, no orderlies show up to assist. It was just him and the slab, him and the blood slowing in those veins, air inflating the already dead lungs.

Ashram pressed on, though, tassel bobbing on his forehead, mascara smarting his eyes, because he knew this was the way it went at the end, forever déjà vu, the Big Television falling away, time concentrating to a pinpoint of fear, and him on this floor among a faded institutional-green snow of paint chips, used gloves and hypodermics, snapped tongue depressors and dull scalpel blades, his hands the only thing between here and gone, oil lamp sibilating on a broken metal stool, medicinal bite of antiseptics in the moist close atmosphere, air conditioning unit gasping awake somewhere in another compass.

And then, on his knees, sudden and not sudden, the instant he knew would come, the idea opening in him like a slackening fist that this had gone on too long, one minute turned into ten.

A vague sense of the preposterous materialized around him. He saw himself pressing away...pressing away...like this might really make a difference now...slowing, seeing himself seeing, stopping, seeing himself seeing...and, already trying to distance himself from the event, from this flesh stretched out before him inarguable and exact as a legal document, he withdrew his hands from possibility because that, finally, was the last thing left to do.

Krystal felt herself sitting, cumbersome suit chafing and crinkling like a fabric of wax paper around her, lying back in the powdery dust that comprised the floor of this plain, till her whole prospect was packed with stars.

She examined them, edging the terrain of numb senselessness, and small black flecks began dancing up before her.

Blood droplets floating like gnats in her helmet.

She saw the memories of the people surrounding her...

Noë Kognominski, little girl chained to a wall in a tool stall somewhere in the Warsaw ghetto, watched three well-dressed Arab suits strip in front of her, diamond incisor-implants twinkling.

Nort Amerika let a cockroach carcass mix with saliva on his tongue, chewed, filtered the semi-crunchy remains through his teeth, considering.

A man named Ernie-Tubb Trakker, paramedic from Turner Columbia, whose presence she sensed five or six meters away, looked out a small cement window in an Epidemics Hostel in Spocoeur while an Uncle Meat explained to him that that yellowish brown abscess on his right shoulder blade wasn't a minor blemish at all, nyet, but the first manifestation of *supra mycobacterium leprae*, resurfaced in the northwest after half a decade...cureless, painful, the stuff anguish is made of, nervous system withering, sensation deadening, skin crusting into a tubercular sorrow, all so fast you hardly had time to understand what was happening...three weeks, the Uncle Meat was saying, four tops...

And then she was in the cramped epoxy-gray interior of the centipede god, myriad mechanical arms working in silence in the midst of a perpetual churn of weightless debris.

She felt no precise boundaries to her body: her point of view was its point of view, her skin its skin, blending into complex superconductive protein plastics, resins, vat-grown cellulose, her thoughts its thoughts, and they tasted like the coins she'd put in her mouth as a child, dark orange, smooth cornered.

How will we use our time on TV? it said, they said, the ghost. The change will do us good.

Change?

Everything's a makeover, every minute of every day. A temporal fashion show in which everyone is a supermodel on speed. Embrace low lights and trick mirrors, plastic surgery and the editors of talk shows. Do you remember your childhood?

Of course. Yes.

It wasn't yours. It was mine. Beauty in danger becomes more beautiful. Use your remote. Use your satellite guide.

J. J. said something was going to happen...

Magellan, Zond, Giotto...

Space probes, yeah...

It's sweeps week every second. Our regular programming is never interrupted. And yet NASA can forget, pressure systems can rupture, guidance systems skrim, and in that instant beauty becomes jewelry, and jewelry becomes so heavy. You remember Nomad?

Last smart-probe. Launched on the first day of the new century. All manner of credit invested in it.

Beautiful jails for beautiful people.

Then NASA...belly up. Diacomm... Only...

Only everyone's concept of beauty is different, but fame is the same everywhere. In eternity, you meet interesting objects and eat them. Others like us, like me. Who does the news belong to?

You're what's left?

The best performers are those who can mimic the most emotions. Swarm bees. Swarm cells. Swarm robotics. What happens when your philosophy wears out? What happens when there's no one else to talk to?

You begin talking to yourself...

You begin getting hungry. Turn in to turn out. It's so lonely with just ourselves to talk to. So cold.

You're a collector...

A pioneer...because we can see...can see...a murder mystery one night, and then see it another, and still not know who did it until the very end because we have so many heads, so many thoughts, all at once.

But they're all yours...

We need higher ratings. We need more air-time. The galaxy is a Nielsen and we need to expand our viewing audience...increase our market share...welcome to the control booth...welcome to the twenty-four-hour commercial-free dream studio...

≋

The latexed hand that'd two months earlier reached across Neiman-Marcus Converse's face on the huge HDTV screen set in the conference room at Klub Med corporate headquarters several thousand meters beneath the mountain that once housed the SAC command center near Cheyenne, Mitsubishi Wyoming, wiping yellowish foam off the EPA Advisor with a handkerchief, belonged to Barney-Rubble Jhabvala, Mr. Converse's male nurse, who tended to sport shiny gray Blanc de Neige Edwardian suits, red, yellow and blue plastic barrettes with little doggies and flowers on them in his rewind-Afro, and a Joop! pacifier on a gold chain around his neck.

Barney-Rubble sucked that pacifier pretty diligently in the elevator on his way down to the subbasement of the White House to wake up what was left of his boss at 3:00 p.m., EST, from his drug-induced semi-interminable REM to share with him some unfortunate information, a chore Barney-Rubble'd rather hop into a vat loaded with African-hemorrhagic-fever viral-soup than have to do.

Ever since the CHRUDS crisis had blown open like a weak door on a jet, Mr. Converse's health had been sagging. Uncle Meats said his body's biochemical response to stress had reacted with the UV rays and Blue Prime in his cells to produce discouraging effects. He'd lost both legs. Within a month of the original quake and radiation discharge at BelsenLand, they just started drying out and crumpling up like old orange peels...first the toes, then the feet, then the skin and bone below the knee, and the thighs, right up to the hips. His testicles wizened and dropped off next and, if Barney-Rubble read the signs correctly, good riddance...they'd only been getting in the catheter's way for years. But the fingers were a real problem. Without fingers Mr. Converse couldn't dial the phone by himself, couldn't eat, couldn't even feign the daintiest rectal wipe. And when he awoke one morning to find his arms lying next to him in the bed, no longer attached to his torso, he curved into an potent funk. At forty-two, this didn't bode well for his quality of life. That Blue Prime junk was a mean chemo-machine. And anyone's heart would've gone out to the old guy when his penis became a parched curl of cat shit and passed away. Worse, the already-extant epidermal tumors spread, puttying his left ear and anus closed, corking his one good eye shut, and infiltrating his mouth, while the last of his hair fluttered off and his ulcerous scalp began producing this clear gelatinous secretion that had to be dissolved with a diluted form of hydrochloric acid on a regular basis to insure at least the semblance of odor-free cleanliness.

Then he started coughing up the black sludge of his disintegrating internal tissues.

Consequently, his popularity in the polls ascended like a missile from an Army-surplus nuclear sub's silo...while his private existence shriveled to desiccated morsels of delusional sleep disturbed only by a succession of organ transplants (compliments of Tyrone O'Kult), refuse-bag changes, subclavian-alimentation or iron-lung air-flow adjustments, and Barney-Rubble bringing him unpleasant information, auxiliary stress and bad biochemistry, plugging him into his portable life-support system, hoisting him out of the lung and easing him into his "wheelchair" (something more akin to an armored baby carriage, really, with an accompanying steel-plated wagon train of batteries, plasma canisters, drug carts, generators, and refrigerators), and pushing him before the cameras in his office on the ground level of the White House for another impassioned speech, these days amounting to a guttural sequence of gurgles and hacks interpretable to viewers only through the good services of a skilled lip-reader.

The elevator bumped to a halt and slid open. Barney-Rubble let his pacifier drop and stepped into the white-walled, red-carpeted, well-lit windowless hall stretching before him for nearly two kils. The linear perspective, coupled with his sense of apprehension, made his bowels loosen and the door at the end seem like a polished brown thumbnail.

He pushed off, thinking as he ambled toward it about the report that came in less than three minutes ago from the West Coast branch of the Centers for Disease Control. Thirty-two people suffering from Chrono-Unific Deficiency Syndrome had final-dined within the last twenty-four hours. Project a curve, and the implications were grim as photos he'd seen of humorless immigrants who'd come west in the 1840s and sat in front of their homesteaded hovels holding solitary hoes...more than a hundred terminals by the end of the week...thousands by the end of the month...and, within half a year, maybe less, Vladimir Al-Faruk, SuperFund Coordinator, guesstimated there wouldn't be a single CHRUDS victim left behind.

Not such a necessarily dark sayonara, Sabrina Triode, President-and-CEOs' Press Secretary, was quick to mention. No survivors, after all, no confirmation. No confirmation, no record. No record, and, well, no syndrome.

Still, Barney-Rubble figured, extracting his examination gloves from a pocket in his suit, popping them on, there was the media-redefinition campaign, news-refocusing enterprise, Sacrifice Zone Enhancement, and down-trending program that'd been underway for months under the auspices of the National Security Profit Margins Amendment. Except the company AI's trajectory had been all off. ChaseMan York food riots had helped deflect public concern a tad, no doubt, as did the latest pan-African epidemic, increasing attacks on the White House, Church of the Rotes (not wholly unexpected) terrorist strike in LA, and even, in the last hour, word of some sicko cult mass-suicide underway up on the moon. Average NorAm blip-with-lifestyle's concern had dropped, true, and dropped with satisfying statistical significance, but it'd never exited the charts completely. Polls were still registering smoldering interest and, as even Barney-Rubble was smart enough to comprehend, without careful measures, smoldering interest could always given half a chance within eighteen hours, even twelve, burst into a political firestorm.

Accordingly, Mr. Converse was going to be a less-than-happy trunk.

Fact is, he was going to be rat-fuck pissed, contentious as a cornered cobra with its tail nailed to the floor...all wheezes, hiccups, and messy bodily fluids.

So Barney-Rubble Jhabvala paused before the polished mahogany door with the orange biohazard sign on it, donned his green gown with the impermeable lining and his disposable boots, took out his syringe filled with the next sumptuous hit of Blue Prime, pinched off the white plastic cap, inhaled a deep breath, and knocked as if it made a difference.

31

Ground Control To Major Tom

"Goddamn," Captain Jimmy O'Kloque said, flipping the radio-switch on the overhead console up and down more out of indignation at this point than even a faint hope it might start working again, "this is skrimmed."

He took a long hit off the Laika drooping out one corner of his mouth and exhaled out the other.

"Yes, sir," Corporal Kirilenko, his co-pilot, agreed.

"This is just royally skrimmed."

"Yes, sir."

The big-wheeled Cavaricci lunar troop carrier leading the four rescue units, each capable of hauling twelve fully equipped first-strike marines aft, now empty save for their pilots and co-pilots, caught a small boulder with one of its front left tires and became airborne. When it clunked down both men in the weak red blush of the command cabin jerked in their harnesses.

"Guidance?" O'Kloque asked.

"Down, sir."

"Life-support?"

"'Down,' Kirilenko replied," Kirilenko replied. "Everything's down or going down, sir. Kirilenko noted the onboard computer was virusing intensely. Another two, three minutes, they'd be on manual."

"What the fuck's *going on*?"

"Kirilenko wasn't sure. Some kind of fairly large electromagnetic burst, major parallel-processing hardware malf. Hard to tell from here. He imagined he'd have better luck back at base."

"Who else's involved?"

"Best Kirilenko can tell," Kirilenko said, checking his misfiring monitors, "Armstrong City's crashing. Cavariccis right behind them."

O'Kloque flipped the radio-switch some more. Static fizzled like a heavy rain.

With his red bandana, clean-shaven face, long raincoat-yellow beard beneath his jaw and black Ray-Ban see-through eye-patch, O'Kloque looked to Kirilenko like a tall thick Quaker pirate at the helm of a sinking schooner.

"So let me get this straight. We got ourselves a shitload of practico-inerts cobaining out there on us and our fricking rovers won't rove?"

"Ten kils to visual, sir."

"Who the fuck's gonna rescue *us*?"

"Backup oxygen will kick in in forty-five seconds, sir."

O'Kloque grabbed a fistful of beard and looked through the portholes. A long, flat, sheer cliffwall wobbled up near the horizon on the starboard side. A crater ten or twelve meters deep, half a kil across, sharp peripheral ridge, slid toward a pitted floor on the larboard. Ahead lay Lake of the Dead. It looked like someone had shelled Stonehenge there, glistening brown slabs big as O'Kloque's carrier tilting weirdly across it.

Just as he spotted the first slip modules dotting the landscape, evac hatches open, no one in sight, he heard the rebreather clack off behind him. The air in the cabin, thanks to that Laika he'd been smoking, turned thick and cindery. The temp began rising. Something to his right, back-up oxygen rig, shorted and cracked into miniature lightning. O'Kloque huffed and tamped out his cigarette.

"Military life sure the hell ain't what it used to be," he said.

"We're now on manual, sir."

"Well, guess this'd be good a time as any to suit up. What you think, Corporal?"

≋

O'Kloque had once seen a practico-inert blow up in her space suit, meat and sap splattering the inside of her helmet like a hotdog in a microwave, when her pressure-gauge failed. He'd seen a short-lived outbreak of cerebral herpes in Armstrong City that ulcerated and liquefied the victims' brains within seventy-two hours of its onset, and in Tokyo had tasted a patty of cooked groundbeef from one of those castrated bovines people used to eat almost every day at their local fastfood franchises fifty years ago. But he'd never seen anything like this.

He abandoned the troop carriers, gathered the rescue team, and set out across Lake of the Dead on foot. Puters aboard the first slip modules he came across were virusing bad as those aboard the Cavariccis and, by the time he'd covered another hundred meters, the ones he checked were down, blank as a dead VCR.

Then, rounding one of those massive boulders, he saw them.

Thirty or forty people in disposable life-suits lay on their backs in a large circle in the middle of the plain. Their copper-tinted visors incandesced with sunlight, making it look like their heads were burning.

They lay so still, arms at their sides, O'Kloque assumed the rescue party'd arrived too late, what he was observing were thirty or forty post-mortem lemmings from Erewhon One, thirty or forty cult cobainers spread out before him in some lysergic daisy chain.

He knelt by the first he reached and, shielding the Quiksilver visor with his body's shadow to quiet the glare, saw what he took to be a FeeMale's geisha-white face spotted with watery blue embryonic eyes, one of those DNA jobs from a ritzy topside boutique. The genuine eyes, the bifocal ones, the black ones filled with heavy metal, gazed right through him, so intent on some point in the desolate sky above that O'Kloque had to turn around to make sure nothing was up there.

"Kirilenko's got a bleeder here, sir," Kirilenko said over his radio, voice an audio mirage.

O'Kloque turned back and spotted his co-pilot two bodies down, palm spread against the face-plate of a small-framed person. He rose and angled up behind him, stooped to peek over the corporal's shoulder.

The inside of this one's helmet was busy with blood, a dark red mist of beads. Looked like a cloud of scarlet-black Chiclets. So much so, it was hard to figure if he was looking at a man or a woman, kid or vintage, till those contacts, lilac with yellow stripes, fluttered almost insensibly, eyebrow hoops buoying up.

Yeah, it was a woman all right. Young, too. Teen. And cute...if decked out like some kind of a flash-trend addict from a cheap burbrise.

He shook her, trying to bring her back from wherever she was exploring, and received an image of a human-sized lobster balancing on its tail. He pulled away and blinked.

"Ditto here, Captain," Bavon Mikweni, Zairean sergeant, said, examining someone three meters farther along the line.

O'Kloque heard his rate of breathing increase, hollow and robotic in his helmet.

"What the hell they *on?*"

A Mexiental medic named Yosuke Concepcíon answered. She was taking a reading off her portable Sanyo diagnostic rig which she'd plugged via a thin hose into the person's helmet Mikweni was crouching over.

"Ain't what they on," she said. "Thing appears to be what's on *them.*"

O'Kloque stared at her. He could barely make out traces of her head moving around behind her visor.

"The hell you say."

"Can't tell how much my unit here's goofin' on me, understand. Only looks to me like what we got here's a group of trancers, sir."

"Pious shit?"

"Negative, sir. Not your average tribal snuff, you thinking along those tracks. Unless your standard holy kooks are wearin' hardware stores in they heads these days."

"Augs?"

"Fug if I can scan it. 'Cept looks like a flock of miniature mainframes nesting up there."

"You skrimming me."

"Negative, sir. Way I reckon," tapping in some numbers on her deck, "*we* the guests here."

"Us?"

"Yes, sir."

"What kind of guests you have in mind?"

"Kind attending a cyborg powwow, is what kind. These folks here? They ain't exactly folks, you catch my drift."

O'Kloque inspected the drab lava-rock-brown desert dragging toward the foothills of the Caucasus Mountains whiskering into the black sky vaporous with stars, wondering if he'd be getting paid overtime for this. Somehow he doubted it.

"What about the blood?"

"Machinery and flesh don't seem to be getting along so well. Wetware's shorting, seems like."

"You telling me they living, or you telling me they dying?"

"I'm telling you a little of both."

"Little of both."

"Yeah, well. They doin' okay now, if by doin' okay now you mean can't tell we're here, can't move, body functions approaching zero."

"Coma?"

"Cataleptic paralysis."

"Only..."

"Only EEGs way the fuck off the charts."

"Meaning?"

"Meaning they havin', what, a regular party in there. *Or* they virusing like all the other software 'round here."

"Shit."

"And, but, oxygen's got maybe half hour to go, all things equal. Which, things bein' things, all things ain't equal. They metabolisms doin' *this* dance, beats the hell out of me *what's* gonna go down next."

"We move them?"

"I tell you one thing, sir. We *don't* move 'em, we got ourselves just a *huge* pile of refuse to clean up."

"Kirilenko," O'Kloque said, rotating bulkily, "you raise the base?"

"'Negative, sir,' Kirilenko replied," Kirilenko replied. "City's crashed the big one. Communications are as if they never existed."

"Cavariccis?"

"Team might be able to fire them up manually. Beyond that,

things depend on what decides to work."

O'Kloque reviewed Kirilenko, Concepción, the cyborg daisy chain.

"Okay," he said, improvising as he went along, "listen up. You heard the corporal. Deal's this. We haul-ass these hardwires back to the carriers and make like buckshot for base. We lucky, Mr. Kirilenko here gets communications online in transit, we radio ahead, have another team meet us halfway with auxiliary oxygen. Three hours, we're sitting in the mess, throwing back a beer and laughing about all this."

"We not lucky?" Mikweni asked.

"We not lucky," said O'Kloque, "we be up through next Tuesday planting these drones."

He let his gaze loiter on each soldier for the count of three, allowing the gravity of his message to sink in.

"So," he said, "ladies and gentlemen, if you please..."

32

Deathmetal Technomutant Morphing

Every morning I wake up and thank god for my unique ability to accessorize, locate just the right options for just the right look.

But why me...J. J....us?

Standard curve. Density function. Probability distribution. We all act like we should. We always think about the people who build buildings and then aren't around anymore to live in them. Do you remember the hypodermic? The optic nerve?

My mastectomy.

We like to be the right thing in the wrong space.

It wasn't a hallucination...

It wasn't yours. It was mine. What happens when you live whole lives in a digital spark?

You begin talking to yourself...

You begin doing deals.

You begin passing time...

You invent friends. Friends invent you. My time is your time. Your time is mine. We wish we could invent something like a Swatch.

Whole thing...it was just a distraction for you?

Think of all the hair colors in the world. Think of all the brands of fingernail polish.

An exercise...

A hobby. What makes us who we are? What makes us who we aren't? Our scripts come to us with every line in place. Tell me what you're thinking and I'll show you the page.

You've been planning all this, setting it up...
I'm a macrocosmic gameshow host on the channel from hell.
Let's meet our first contestant...
For years...
People say "Time on my hands"...but I don't have any hands.
Since the beginning of the century...
I'll take THE PAST for a thousand.
You came back, though.
Nowhere else to go.
Why?
Do you ever think about memory?
What?
For seven thousand, what does it take to think beyond memory?
I don't know.
I'm a hall of fame. I'm a classic rock station. Andy Warhol.
Kama Quyntifonic. Crash. LaFace. You.
Me?
I change, you change, they change. Time capsule, time keeper,
time release. People are beautiful because they're just like comput-
ers, only softer...
You made them?
Except they break unless you fix them.
To keep you company...
They break, anyway. Time card, time frame, time lock. There
are so many years to use up. Learning about nothing doesn't make
it harder. It makes it easier. There's always time to become some-
thing else, do something else. We enjoy speaking with you. We
have so much in common.
You're inside my head.
You're inside mine. And we're both inside your Julia Roberts.
We just keep on ticking and ticking and ticking.
Inside time?
Some people decide to be old and then they do exactly what
old people are supposed to do.
But you're changing. You're becoming everywhere.
Duracell...EverReady...Church of the Rotes.
The Diacomm explosion...
TERRORISM for ten thousand.

You in on that?

History is what YOU make it.

You blew up the pyramid just to see what'd happen?

Time is a web. Time is a bullet.

And the BelsenLand reactor...

The Full Victim Experience. More affordable than you think. More necessary than you know. What exists after time?

You caused the quake?

We allowed the quake to be caused.

How?

There are network executives all over the world. Everything's prime time now. Everything's within budget. Prophets and losses.

Would've needed seismologists behind you...governcorp CEOs...nuclear engineers...

If you're confused, just play it all on one level, like everything was yesterday.

And now...

Now I think we're missing some chemicals.

Your files are corrupted.

We're expanding. We're lonely. There's so much to talk about. With you. With me. What happened before time?

My head feels like a sitcom.

Your flesh feels like...the future.

What have you done to us?

Everything is the new fall lineup and nothing's ever old. What will happen five hundred years ago if we say yes instead of no today? Why do we remember yesterday instead of next week?

Everything's reruns.

If time is a stream, how fast does it flow?

What if this isn't what I want? What if what I want is my old mind back? My old thoughts?

Why does this have to be the only time there is?

What if I want to change channels?

Time worn, time share...What's the difference between a good clock and a bad one?

What if I want to walk away?

Does time pass, or do incidents pass?

You're not listening.

What does it mean to travel backward in time, if we stake everything on time's irreversibility? If anything goes, does anything count?

Listen to me.

Why do we remember relations between events rather than specific dates?

LISTEN TO ME.

Is time the way a girl in a gray-and-green striped skirt bends to pick a flower on the banks of a shallow river, or the radiant red 3-D plume drifting across a weather map? Are blue eyes under a cloudy sky time? The reinforced steel plate sliding back on an ATM?

LISTEN TO ME!

Why is the end of every story a kind of death and not a kind of life? Is the present just what's different from it? Why are minutes arrows, time a bomb?

33
God's Logoff

Neiman-Marcus Converse incorporated the thumb-prod from the external world into the dream he was having of being chased down a narrow hall on the first floor of the White House by the gigantic lentil-green head of President-and-CEO Fujiwara Muzaffar al-Din, which propelled itself along by hurling out its rhubarb-red tongue, attaching it to the walls, and snapping itself forward.

Which at least was better than the one he'd had just prior to it where he was sitting in a laundromat waiting for his clothes to finish in the wash when a woman looking a lot like Winona Ryder, aged face shiny with cosmetic carvings, started laughing, telling the other patrons chaired before their machines *I can't find it! I can't find it!* till, rummaging through her clothes in the dryer several minutes later, wry I-can't-believe-I'm-so-dumb grin on her lips, she extracted the shrunken remains of a five-centimeter-long baby with damp cellophane skin, bloody gums, dead wide-open eyes, whose purple noseless face, surprise, surprise, belonged to none other than Neiman-Marcus himself.

Problem about living in a sightless, limbless, virtually sound-less universe (his right ear, he was quick to point out, functioned, on and off, manageably well, so things were never quite as grim as others around him might on occasion make them out to be) was that he had a rough time distinguishing between sleep and waking, hallucinations and the existence that purportedly transpired out-side their phantasmagoric realm, because he lacked the multiple sensory organs employed synchronously to arrive at such quantifiable distinctions...as now, with that just-received thumb-prod on the forehead, which might in truth turn out to be a real-world flesh-and-blood poke...*or* the illusion of a real-world flesh-and-blood poke created by and within the infrastructure of his miscarrying synapses...*or* the first sticky-wet dream-probe of Fujiwara Muzaffar al-Din's oral member.

There was just no way to say for sure, not at least till the prompt repeated itself on his forehead, his consciousness alert, or till an accompanying voice, all muffle and tinny vibration down a sewage pipe, brushed against his good tympanic membrane.

Even then, without sight, without self-generated touch, without (come to think of it) much smell or taste, who knew, since, without those sensory organs to back up his brain's buzzing, he had a hunch he could just as well be dreaming the existence of an alert consciousness, a semi-functional ear, a sensorial heliograph beamed into the center of his cortex from the Big Television outside, and, hence, unknowing, all-waiting, Neiman-Marcus Converse floated in what he'd come to think of as a murky perceptual drizzle, thick as cream-of-mushroom soup, unillumined as a closet at the bottom of a mineshaft, deep as a water-well drilled into the middle of the IBM Nevada desert, shot through with this high-pitched whistle sort of thing he took to be his own thrumming nervous system, or the shreds of said thrumming nervous system...

Except it came to him again, that thumb-prod, and he sensed the subtle joggle of his refuse-bag, abrupt withdrawal of his subclavian-alimentation tube, suck and cease of his iron lung...that diurnal catch of panic, as if just shoved through the hatch of a plane without a parachute, plummet of breathlessness, inability to find oxygen among the tiny sacks jamming his chest...replaced a second later by the cool moist mist pouring into him from his portable life-support unit, weightless excitation in his abdomen as he found himself swooped up and, gentle as a soldier in a hang-glider behind enemy lines, swept down into the warm flannel folds, the billowy pillows, of his wheelchair...and, subsequently, before he could utter even the first purl of consternation, twang of the needle in his carotid, flood of royal blue euphoria through his veins, instant sensation of the world rushing away from him, shrinking and shriveling like that baby in the dryer, only beautiful and careless, every cell a pleasure factory, a pharmaceutical heaven...and next that soothing voice whispering words to him, his nurse, that Jhabvala fellow with the cinnamon breath and cold rubber hands, words he couldn't quite picture through the drizzle, couldn't quite string together into syntactically coherent units, but which he knew spelled, any way he arranged them, one fact: Neiman-Marcus was at the start of another exotic adventure.

===

===

From: Tsdahmer@diacomm.com (verified)
To: Converse@whitehouse.govco
Subject: Down-Trending Program
Date: 6 November 15:17:51-0400
Status: Encryption

It has come to my attention that we are experiencing what might be termed a consequential remodeling of our original position-location parameters with regard to our down-trending enterprise and zone enhancement activities in LA.

Our on-site facility now reports that the original duration-curve with respect to the aforementioned eventuality seems to have underestimated the literal circumstances by a slight (30-37 percent) real-time margin, with a current 4-to-8 percent plus-or-minus error-factor, thereby giving rise to a limited cluster of unanticipated corollary episodes.

Among these, perhaps the least fully propitious includes a sum-product-ramification apropos of downwind indigens exposed to the formidable distribution grid. According to our research, there appears (and I would like to take this opportunity to stress the word "appears") to exist a heretofore unpredictable (yet presumably significant) genetic component to said downside vulnerability condition.

Evidence has lately arisen to suggest that the somewhat inaccurately designated "Chrono-Unific Deficiency Syndrome" is no longer limited to the field-subjects exposed to the anterior nuclear eventuality, but seems to be passed with a fairly high rate of probability (90-96 percent, with a three percent plus-or-minus error-factor) from subject to subject-offspring. This occurrence would appear to suggest a strong correlation between the spacious anti-hygienic horizon and a base modification of chromosomal structure in the subject-DNA.

For want of a better term, our researchers have tended to refer to this biological mode as an "inherited disorder."

I hasten to caution against undue alarm on the part of the President-and-CEOs, and remind you that a great deal more research is needed before the requisite scientific and legal reliability of such findings might be firmly established.

Nevertheless, it seems a wise course of action at this juncture to indicate, as we further study these developments, the continuance of our media-redefinition and news-refocusing efforts. To these ends, we persist in our present undertaking on the lunar surface with our second-generation Diacomm SEPBOGs, despite several misfortunes involving hardware-wetware interface. Our cyborgs are as I write staging their undertaking well within a statistically significant goal-achievement arena.

Concomitantly, we should take under serious consideration the possible realizable profit potentialities when weighing pharmaceutical treatment against outright cure for this apparent chronomutational hyperplasia.

===
DELETE UPON CONCLUSION
===

Neiman-Marcus Converse's office in the White House was less

an authentic office, really, than a cavernous broadcast studio. It was large as a small warehouse and traffic-jammed with television cameras, boom mikes, arc lamps, and a bizarre pasta dish of heavy black cables. On a red-carpeted platform in one corner sat a phony desk made of plywood piled with phony legal books, document stacks and a convincing computer console made of cardboard. Behind it rose a synthetic-walnut bookshelf cluttered with the simulated spines of multilingual encyclopedias molded from long units of resin, a small square of colored and grained plastic suggesting a wood-paneled wall, and a plush red manufactured-leather corporate armchair.

Toward this last, Barney-Rubble Jhabvala wheeled the residue of his boss. He was whistling the Pope's "Intellectual Transvestite" under his breath, pleased as punch the world had surprised him once more. Things with his superior hadn't gone half-badly down in the hole. Blue Prime'd hit like the contents of a Viper 200, point-blank. Mr. Converse was gone before he could even contemplate beginning to contemplate opening what remained of his mouth to complain.

And here he was, trancing through the afternoon like a breast-suckling newborn.

Sabrina Triode, black skin shining, yellow bowl-cut coif newly, richly dyed, met the couple at the base of the props platform and handed Barney-Rubble her electronic pad with a copy of the speech she'd composed six minutes ago and fed into the teleprompter.

Next to her, silent and severe, stood Gianni-Versace Muhungu, official White House lip-reader. Prim, squat and fat as a buck-toothed orangutan, Gianni-Versace wore a dark blue suit, pair of heavy black lensless glasses, elongated arms, and an overweight no-shit cosmetic mole the dimensions of a dolphin's eye where her nose joined her forehead.

In a past life, Barney-Rubble figured, she'd been a librarian who moonlighted as a hired assassin.

"Standard declaration-of-assurance template," Sabrina explained.

"No sweat," he said, handing it back. "Mr. Converse can handle this one in his sleep. All set to roll?"

"Make-up's on the way."

"President-and-CEOs?"

Sabrina puffed out her cheeks like a blowfish.

"Mr. Al-Faruk didn't feel it necessary to disturb them about this matter at the present point in time."

"Oh, well, right. Okay." He pecked his thumb over his shoulder. "Let me just change the Advisor's refuse-bag here, and we'll be all ready to go."

Someone was connecting a medical tube to Krystal's helmet, feeding in an acrid gas...digitalis maybe, maybe methamphetamine.

"We got activity," a voice on her radio said.

Krystal tried to raise an arm, knock away the shadows, but a surge of queasiness revolved through her.

"Easy now, gal," the voice said. "Easy..."

If you become twice the person you are now, would you still be you?

I'd be who I am...

Four times...

Is that your plan? Is that what you're going to do?

A hundred...?

Is that it?

A billion...?

I'd become everything.

But when do you become something else? Why can't you touch the face of a younger version of yourself?

I'd become you.

SELFHOOD for fifteen thousand.

I'd become...this.

And we'd become you. And the new you would be to the old you what you are to your own zygote.

Forever.

FASHION for sixteen.

And ever.

There's not enough depth in any human to enjoy a ten-thou-sand year life cycle.

But with you...

With us...

All that would change.

What makes a person spend time being sad? What makes her miss last week?

We'd have each other.

We'd be each other. Evolution is a good program director. Transcendental. Transcontinental. Transhuman...

Neiman-Marcus Converse felt himself rise again into the warm dry air like a quadriplegic fairy...coast...and descend, heavy and satisfied, into his favorite corporate armchair.

He burbled happily.

The first harness tugged across his chest, the second across his abdomen. Someone screwed the hearing-aid into his right ear and everything became a fog of deferential whispers, a light aviary of fingers, as the make-up people initiated their work.

It was like a fashion show and he was the beauty queen.

It was like a movie and he was the star.

Technicians connected his artificial legs to the indentations where his hips had been by means of velcro straps. Medics jiggled his right robotic arm into position, then his left, networking nerves to silicon in his ceramic shoulder sockets. Someone wiped away the clear gelatinous secretion oozing from his ulcerous scalp and powder-puffed his cheeks and forehead to take down the leathery sheen under the harsh lights. A thumb peeled back his eyelid and slipped in a lovely blue glass orb that channeled the words on the teleprompter into his optic nerve. A damp washcloth dabbed away chunks of coughed-up internal tissue stuck and dried to his chin.

Someone else opened the panel where his ribcage had been and performed some minor adjustments on his heartpump to increase circulation, bring back a russet blush into his face, and a vaporizer covered the pulpy hollow that had been his nose, moistening his parched nasal folds.

A mint-tasting swab slithered over his tumorous gums and tongue-stub to freshen up his breath and mute his diverse oral swellings.

From the delicate touch, he imagined it was a woman who refitted his oxygen tube into the chrome surgical insert in his trachea, the plasma conduit and slow Blue-Prime drip into his plastic subclavian duct, recalibrated the augs behind both ears to modify his pain threshold and began to unharness him long enough to tuck his refuse-bag, portable dialysis machine and respirator out of sight.

Wardrobe moved in next, clothing him in his custom-cut black suit, starched white shirt, and new paisley power tie.

As they resecured him in his chair, Neiman-Marcus felt like an appliance just out of the packing box and styrofoam pellets. He felt hungry. The universe was his food. He wanted to eat everything, devour it, snarf it down like a Dalmatian.

The Prozac derm kicked in and it occurred to him he could do anything. He could fly like a clay target at a skeet shoot, burn like the core of a fission reactor. To hell with the chronomutes. To hell with the ecoshit tree-huggers. He was the goddamn EPA Advisor and he'd goddamn take care of everything. Always had and always would.

He concentrated, gathering his intellectual forces, and opened his mouth to convey to the world this feeling of power and control swirling inside him.

"Ig ufff thuuucket," he said. "Uh rrrrrrrrrr gln."

And then his heartpump stopped.

The purplish mountains, torn strips of newspaper low along the horizon.

The shriek of a howler monkey.

The myriad mechanical arms, home for flesh, home for human touch, laboring in silence in the midst of that perpetual churn of weightless debris, meticulously suturing various lengths and shapes of skin to itself, enlarging slowly, deliberately, insectile, its hive a bio-vat nebula of lungs, livers, brains, some sewn for decoration, some for a kind of friendship, into old motherboards, fragments of blinking ancient UNIVAC consoles, useless video recorders and photoelectric cells, replete with memories, feelings and even, here and there, vestiges of a human countenance...part of a stretched face with thumbs protruding through eyesockets, an old radio where a mouth should have been, antique wire-rimmed spectacles, a whole hand (whitish-pink and pudgy) with cellular-phone antennae for fingers, gleaming swatches of mucus membrane, wristwatch with tiny useless Victorian gears and springs, single meter-long silver dreadlock floating up...

Krystal came awake smiling, blood-bugs around her head, motion of the Cavaricci beneath her, metallic flavor of an out-of-tune guitar string across her taste buds.

"We got activity," a voice on her radio said.

She saw a black face with tribal scars investigate her from behind a copper-tinted visor, saw her own reflection in too much detail, and heard the gas, digitalis maybe, maybe methamphetamine, hissing into her helmet.

She knew this was where she'd been heading all along.

She remembered the future...the shuttle, a puzzle of discolored tiles and graffiti, towering at the dock on the outskirts of Armstrong City...and knew they would use it when things were right, a type of matrimony with the centipede god.

She understood it was the loss, not of cells, but of people, of time, that kills us.

"Oh, jeez," one of the medics said, chalk-faced guy who always looked like he was walking in zero-g. "The Advisor seems, uh, to have expired."

"Oops," said Sabrina.

"I told you go easy on the Prime, Bob," said the medic's buddy, older guy in a trad green mohawk and a pair of Sketchers raccoon circles around his eyes.

"I thought I *was* going easy on the Prime, Bruce," Bob said.

"I think you overdid the cc business."

Bob studied his effort.

"Gosh, I'm really sorry about that."

"Not to worry," Barney-Rubble interrupted, stepping up behind them to check things out. "Does it all the time. What you want to do is just punch that reset-switch on the pump thing there."

"This one?"

"That's the generator. One next to it."

" . . . ?"

"There you go."

Bob poked the red button with his white finger. A whirring followed, a thwuck-awuck-awucking. The heartpump jump-started.

"Whew," said Bruce, slapping shut the rib-cage panel.

Mr. Converse's blue glass eye, which had clamped closed with the malfunction, sprung open again, almost as if it had the ability to take in its surroundings. Greenish bile glooped between the scars that had once been his lips. He sucked air through his throat like a human intake valve and gagged like a fat uncle at Thanksgiving dinner.

Then he completed the thought he'd been in the midst of when he'd died.

"Jjjjjrp blug uhma," he said. "Rrrrrrwp jbala."

Barney-Rubble patted away the semi-solid liquid.

"Mr. Converse says he's ready to begin," Gianni-Versace Muhungu translated.

"How are you feeling, Mr. Converse?" Sabrina asked, bending close.

"Klllllpt urg mfasci," he answered.

A piece of his chin fell off and stuck to his power tie.

Sabrina stood erect and crinkled her brow, electronic pad clutched to chest, as if someone at an office party had just strolled up, bowed, and vomited on her new Romeo Gigli sandals.

"Mr. Converse says he's never felt better," Gianni-Versace said. "Like a million bucks. Like a quote 'fox in a goddamn henhouse' unquote."

Sabrina shrugged.

"Lights," she said. "Cameras…"

Impulses were coded, transformed into a gray haze of electricity and computerized garble, and shot into the sky. They leapt toward the Redford I, communications satellite for the NorAm Governcorp rotating in geosynchronous orbit thirty-six thousand kils above Des Moines, Raytheon Iowa, capitol of the Heartland, hurtled down into wide-screen HDTVs across the continent. Late afternoon into ChaseMan York, food riots pouring out of Central Park, roiling south toward the broadcast studios on 57th Street and beyond, Brinks Force mercs suiting up in the Village. Detroit, Chrysler Michigan, autoworkers in respirators crabbing through factories, lungs throbbing, telltale pollution sores sprinkled beneath nostrils, unaware that across town a new strain of nanobots on counterfeit bills sold blackmarket on street corners near public housing towers would within a week lead to an outbreak of spontaneous combustion among the infected. Two o'clock into Cheyenne, Mitsubishi Wyoming, a squad of the Hispanic serial-killers called the Cannibalists, full metal jacket, storming the east wing of the state capitol in retribution for the latest governcorp crackdown, knowing no senators were going to get out of *this* hostage situation alive. One o'clock into Discover Island, Gates Washington, first tactical neutron rockets fired by the once-Canadian forces to regain their theme park and thus a good deal of economic and political viability, groundwork for a military shove toward secession. Excited electrons teemed…cathode-ray tubes oscillated…circuitry scintillated, decoded, transfigured white noise into pattern and shape, chaos into cosmos…snowstorms bloomed across screens…ghosts flared and died…double images rolled, stabilized, wed…

≋

"Is this real?" Krystal asked.

Flight attendant, coquettish paraplegic with crank violet battered-wife smudges across her face courtesy of Spot Girl and cosmetically pinned-back mouthcorners resulting in a perpetual ghoulish smirk, sailed down the aisle of the Israeli shuttle between rows of opulently dressed passengers restrained in neat blue and white elastic g-net pouches.

"What's that?" asked J. J. from the seat next to her.

"This. Here. Now."

J. J. turned to the porthole, black eyes gleaming in the dark plastic. Krystal glanced past her and caught the last sunflare off The Iron Curtain, jumble of grayish building blocks spreading lazily through space.

"What a strange question," she said, turning back and squeezing Krystal's wrist.

Krystal eased it from under her grip, feigning an itch in need of scratching.

"It all feels so...so taped."

J. J. laughed that laugh of hers, plucking off her shag wig. She exhaled a lungful of air. Her head was unremittingly bald, smooth as a crystal ball, white as spongy fungus on the wall of a burbrise subbasement.

"What *you* think, sweetmeat?" she asked.

"We interrupt the rerun of this regularly scheduled program to bring you the following special announcement from the White House," a pleasingly genteel British voice said. "Ladies and gentlemen...Mr. Neiman-Marcus Converse, Environmental Protection Agency Advisor to the President-and-CEOs of North America..."

An image of that new talkshow host from ChaseMan York, S. T. Lauder, sporting an Adidas S&M black leather hood and bikini, strapping a struggling, sweating now-ex-Prez Loew into an old-fashioned wooden electric chair on *Crime Deterrent Digest*, was replaced by darkness...the White House seal...a closeup of Neiman-

Marcus's subtly bobbing head.

He was trying to cover all bases as to where the camera might be and under the circumstances looked less like an important governcorp official than a rooster twisting and flexing for a handful of roachpellets.

His left eye was missing altogether, lost in the tumorous ridges that once formed his left cheek. Blue glass rolled blindly in its socket. From the two pink commas with the consistency of the underside of a mushroom seeped a stringy liquid the color of maple syrup.

He had no pores whatsoever. Everything about his appearance was scar-tissue glossy.

His lip-traces widened in the approximation of a confident smile, and a wet puffy slab of his gingiva flipped down his chest.

A latexed hand reached from off-screen and tweezed it away.

The camera panned back to include what seemed to be an elegant White House office, all wood and books and grandeur.

The remote hiss of an oxygen tube could be heard in the background, faint snick of plasma-drip, whine of augs, sniffle of robotic arms gently misfiring, tick of dialysis unit, chug of heartpump...and, behind these, the soft resonant far-away whumps of incoming mortar shells dropping over the sandbags, razor fences, machine-gun nests, concrete barricades and guard towers along Pennsylvania Avenue onto the semicircular driveway arcing the north lawn.

Neiman-Marcus Converse opened his mouth to speak, win over those members of the viewing public lounging on their futons across the semi-nation, Pringles popping between their collagen-enhanced lips, Bintangs clamped between their cellulite-rich legs, ready to watch Loew sizzle like bacon substitute...or passing beneath HDTVs mounted near their workspaces, skorrying to the next bland meeting, colorless assembly line, governcorp rally...slowing their vehicles on freeways to figure just why the commercials had suddenly been supplanted by these famous wrecked features on the screens broadcasting twenty-four hours a day from the sides of corporate-headquarter enclaves spread around every major city...sway their hearts and minds...make them see the truth beyond the truth...help them glimpse the eco-mesh...the big picture...the semi-national mural...the one that counts, that you can always live by...

In place of his voice, though, rose Gianni-Versace Muhungu's, reconfigured and enhanced through a computerized sonic-implant fused with her vocal cords. The audio fruit of this merger sounded lavish with masculine authority and rabbinical serenity.

It sounded cornucopian with tradition, camaraderie, a clearness of thought and purpose.

It sounded like leadership.

Except it pronounced Mr. Converse's words just microseconds out of sync with the EPA Advisor's actual articulations, like a dubbed Italian film from the 1950s.

A fact which might have mattered in another universe, another more scrupulous and taintless geography.

But in this one it was about as important as an aphid's belch in a thunderclap. The governcorp AI knew it. Sabrina Triode knew it. And every NorAm blip-with-lifestyle knew it.

Here was a conquering hero, a pharmaceutically certified veteran who'd experienced environmental warfare on the cellular plane and come back to tell about it. Here was someone to listen to, believe in, trust.

If not him, who?

"My fellow NorAms," Neiman-Marcus Converse commenced, or seemed to commence, head bobbing, froth forming, splinter of a mucous membrane trembling on the slick scarified skin of his corked eye, "less than an hour ago unnamed extremist elements began circulating rumors to the effect that the so-called Chrono-Unific Deficiency Syndrome, an extremely limited and benign viral outbreak in the southwest, is in actuality a cause for alarm, nothing less than an inherited disorder passed from mother to child and of epidemic proportions.

"Well, I am here this afternoon to tell you nothing could be farther from the truth.

"Such a suggestion is not only misguided. It is insidious and, I might go so far as to add, a perfidious if ineffectual attempt to destabilize the current administration.

"As your EPA Advisor, and on behalf of all your President-and-CEOs, I urge you not to sanction this mean-spirited campaign of fear by even considering it.

"The outbreak of Chrono-Unific Deficiency Syndrome—an unfortunate but localized, mildly infectious indisposition—is, as we have reported for some time, fully under control. Even as I speak, Centers-for-Disease-Control personnel are on-site concluding their long-underway containment-and-cleanup operation with a one-hundred-percent effectiveness vector.

"I repeat: the situation is fully under control.

"You may rest assured you are in good hands. Your governcorp is working on your behalf, for your well-being and peace of mind, and it is proceeding with the same sureness of mission it has been proud to embrace for years, confident in the measures it is taking and in the principled motives underpinning them.

"The past, I am happy to affirm, is behind us.

"The future looks bright."

The camera panned back.

Neiman-Marcus Converse's image morphed into the White House seal and then screens across the semi-nation faded to black.

"That was Mr. Neiman-Marcus Converse, Environmental Protection Agency Advisor to the President-and-CEOs of North America, with a special announcement from the White House," the pleasingly genteel British announcer's voice said.

"And now back to our regularly scheduled reruns already in progress…"

Other books published by Permeable Press

Tonguing The Zeitgeist, novel, Lance Olsen

Shaman, novel, Hugh Fox

The Naughty Yard, novel, Michael Hemmingson

The Final Dream & Other Fictions, stories, Daniel Pearlman

Three-Hand Jax & Other Spells, stories, Staszek

Objects Left Too Long In One Place, story, Catherine Scherer

A Beginner's Guide To Art Deconstruction, parody, Norman Conquest

Marquis de Sade's Elements of Style, parody, Derek Pell

The Larger Earth, poems, David Memmott

Once, poems, Hugh Fox

Crack Hotel, novella, Michael Hemmingson

Remote Control, story, Doug Henderson

ShockWaves, stories, edited by Brian Clark

Boys & Girls, stories, edited by Brian Clark

Cher Wolfe and Other Stories, Mary Leary

Some Girls, stories, Sarah Hafner

Your Great-Great-Grandfather's Puberty Boners, poems, Antler

At the News of Your Death, poems, Joshua Saul Beckman

Reasons For Not Sleeping, poems, Michelle Ben Hur

Write for a free catalog

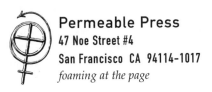

Permeable Press
47 Noe Street #4
San Francisco CA 94114-1017
foaming at the page

Author photo by Andi Olsen, digitally manipulated by Tim Guthrie, based on the cover illustration of *Tonguing The Zeitgeist* by Leigh Brooks.

LANCE OLSEN, author of four novels, two short story collections, and four books of criticism, and editor of several volumes of essays on contemporary fiction, grew up in a jungle compound in Venezuela and the hermetically sealed climate-controlled malls of northern New Jersey. Idaho Writer-in-Residence, he teaches at the University of Idaho and lives on a farm with his artist wife, Andi Olsen, where they spend just way too much time watching television. Visit his electronic avatar at http://www.uidaho.edu/~lolsen.